To Alain & Vicki
with much love

3/08

THE
PINOCCHIO
SYNDROME

THE PINOCCHIO SYNDROME

DAVID ZEMAN

DOUBLEDAY

New York London Toronto Sydney Auckland

PUBLISHED BY DOUBLEDAY
a division of Random House, Inc.
1745 Broadway, New York, New York 10019

DOUBLEDAY and the portrayal of an anchor with a dolphin are
registered trademarks of Random House, Inc.

Book design by Stephanie Huntwork

Library of Congress Cataloging-in-Publication Data
Zeman, David.
The Pinocchio syndrome : a novel / by David Zeman.
p. cm.
1. Viruses—Fiction. 2. Legislators—Fiction.
3. Women journalists—Fiction. I. Title.
PS3626.E44P66 2003
813' .6—dc21   2003046151

ISBN 0-385-50955-3

July 2003

First Edition

1   3   5   7   9   10   8   6   4   2

To Susan and to Karen

ACKNOWLEDGMENTS

I want to thank Ernst H. Huneck for invaluable technical advice generously given during the writing of this book.

My heartfelt thanks also to my agent, Deborah Schneider, for sympathy and support as well as a stellar performance in representing the book around the world.

Thanks to Steve Rubin for his belief in the story, and to Jason Kaufman for helping me through preparation of the final manuscript.

Finally, to Susan Lei, my love and my undying admiration.

Pinocchio looked at Candlewick. To his astonishment he saw that Candlewick's teeth had grown very large, and that his ears were growing longer.

Pinocchio looked at his own face in the mirror, and saw that his ears were growing longer too, as were his teeth. He looked down at his hands and saw that they were turning into hoofs. So were his feet.

Pinocchio cried out in terror. But his cry came out as the braying of a donkey.

—PINOCCHIO

PROLOGUE

May 15
Aboard the cruise ship Crescent Queen
Somewhere west of Crete

IT BEGINS with a fairy-tale prince and an open sea . . .

"Look at the way he moves."

"He's sexy."

"Look at the way his ass moves when he jumps."

"Don't you two ever think of anything else?"

The *Crescent Queen,* a charter cruise ship of American ownership staffed by an English crew, was sailing smoothly on a calm sea, her decks bathed in Mediterranean sunlight.

Three girls, all thirteen years old, were standing on the promenade deck, their eyes riveted to a volleyball game being played by eight boys their own age. The boys were sweating from their exertions, calling out encouragement to each other as they changed position and dove for the ball. The deep blue of the waves made a brilliant backdrop to the game.

The prettiest girl, Gaye, was also the shyest. She had a crush on the dark-haired boy who was now serving the volleyball. She lacked the confidence to approach him or even to smile when their eyes met, but she had made no secret of her feelings to her two friends.

Their names were Alexis and Shanda. Alexis was a tall girl with unruly auburn hair and a determination to wear as much makeup as she could get away with. Shanda, whose parents were both physicians, was the most aggressive of the three. Her mother, back home in Connecticut, had already endured many sleepless nights over Shanda, who seemed to be on a fast track leading to cigarettes, alcohol, and perhaps pregnancy.

The present cruise had been chartered by the National Talented and Gifted Scholarship Association, whose acronym was TAGS. The purpose of the Association was to encourage achievement by junior high school students around the country by sponsoring events that would reward the students for good grades and challenge them intellectually.

There were eight hundred students aboard, along with sixty-five teachers from around the country and a crew of sixty. The cruise was six weeks long, with extended stopovers in Australia, New Zealand, and Hawaii. En route the students were given intensive course work in language, science, and history. There was to be a competitive exam given on the way back to New York, the winners to be honored with scholarships and a guaranteed return cruise next year.

A less-than-publicized fact about intellectually gifted children is that they tend to be sexually precocious. This was particularly true of Shanda, whose career in junior high had already included some amorous adventures that she had managed with considerable difficulty to keep secret. Shanda had quickly gravitated to Alexis the day the *Crescent Queen* set sail from New York Harbor. The two had co-opted Gaye into their friendship because they envied her beauty and were beguiled by her sweet, gentle personality.

An only child, Gaye had been lively and rambunctious until the onset of puberty dropped a shroud of self-consciousness over her personality. For a while she was so withdrawn that her mother sent her to a child psychiatrist. Then it was discovered that her IQ was 164. Her moodiness was chalked up to her high intelligence and the routine identity crisis experienced by gifted children. It did not help that she was the only daughter of Kemper Symington, the United States secretary of defense, a highly visible architect of the current administration's foreign policy.

Like everyone else on board, the three girls had become aware of handsome Jeremy Asner, a tall, athletic boy from Riverside, California, who was the sole representative of his school district on this cruise. Jeremy was a junior high school all-American in soccer, and had dreams of a career in politics.

A well-spoken, polite boy whose gray eyes had a dreamy and somehow withdrawn quality, Jeremy had quickly become the most popular boy on the *Queen*. Shanda and Alexis had coveted him from afar for several weeks, but had made no romantic headway with him. Now they had decided their best bet was to set Jeremy up with Gaye, who exceeded them in physical beauty and seemed more Jeremy's type. If Gaye got to first base with Jeremy, the victory would be for all three.

The only problem was Gaye herself. She was too shy to approach Jeremy directly. Weeks of wheedling by her two willful friends had not moved her. Before long the cruise would be over and it would be too late.

Tonight, however, was the Week Five dance, to be held in the main ballroom. According to the rules set by the social committee, anyone could invite anyone. Girls were free to invite boys. Shanda and Alexis were giving their final push to Gaye.

"You've got to invite him," Shanda said. "I talked to his roommate. He doesn't have a date. He's even thinking of not going to the dance. He's just waiting for you, Gaye!"

"I don't know," Gaye temporized, looking across the deck at the boys, who were now changing sides. Under the bright sunlight, his dark hair tousled by the wind, Jeremy looked almost too handsome to be real. She felt unworthy to approach him. He looked like a prince out of a fairy tale.

If only I knew he liked me . . .

Sensing Gaye's thoughts, Shanda said, "Look, he thinks you're cute. His roommate told me. But he thinks you're standoffish. He's afraid to talk to you."

Gaye took this news with suspicion. "When did you talk to him?"

"Last night after dinner," Shanda said. "For God's sake, Gaye, can't you see this is your chance? You can ask him to the dance. That way he doesn't have to get up his guts to ask you. There's no risk. It's guaranteed!"

Gaye had only known Shanda for a few weeks, but she was familiar enough with her mannerisms to know when she was lying. This story didn't sound right.

"If he likes me, he can ask me," she responded.

"He can't, dummy!" Shanda exploded. "He's afraid of you. Don't you listen?"

Gaye still hung back.

Then something happened that forced the girls' hand. Jeremy left his friends and headed toward the academic area amidships. The game went on without him.

"I can't do it," Gaye said fearfully.

"If you can't, I will," Shanda said.

Still a bit out of breath, Jeremy called something over his shoulder to one of his friends. He was coming straight toward the girls.

Gaye knew she was trapped. Shanda, the aggressive one, would not hesitate to speak to him on Gaye's behalf. Jeremy was only a dozen feet from her now, not looking at her but coming straight toward her.

"Come on, dummy," Shanda hissed in her ear as she pushed her forward.

The push was rough. Gaye's slender young body was flung forward, right into the path of the approaching boy. She tried to catch her balance, but it was too late. She saw Jeremy's arms react as his eyes turned to her. In that last split second she thought, *Shanda was lying. He doesn't like me. He can't—*

The thought never completed itself. Before she could turn to dart a look of reproach at her friend, Gaye Symington ceased to exist.

Shanda and Alexis were sharing a grin of complicity when their bodies turned to vapor.

No one heard the blast or even saw the flash. The deuterium and tritium that fuse in a hydrogen bomb are heated within a few microseconds to a temperature of ten million degrees centigrade. The energy from the reaction heats the surrounding air to a temperature of 300,000 degrees after one hundredth of a millisecond.

There would be no wreckage for the searchers to find. The only proof that there had been a ship here, and a nuclear explosion, would be a digital blip on monitor screens in radar installations around the world.

Jeremy Asner's last thought before death canceled his brain was *She's prettier close up.*

BOOK ONE

THE PIED PIPER

The Piper was angry when the townspeople refused to pay him for getting rid of the rats. In revenge, he decided to kill all the children of the town. He lured them to the river with the song of his pipe. The children could not resist the song, any more than had the rats. They hurried to the river and flung themselves in, one by one. All were drowned.

Only one child survived—a deaf boy who could not hear the song of the pipe. He remained at home, and found out afterward that all his friends were gone.

—"THE PIED PIPER OF HAMELIN"

1

SIX MONTHS LATER

Liberty, Iowa
November 15
11:45 A.M.

SNOW FELL silently, like a sleep coming over the land.

The postman came around the corner, pulling his bag behind him. The wheels of his cart left moist black trails in the fresh snow on the sidewalk. A crumpled snowman, made from yesterday's storm, regarded the passing postman pathetically, its corncob pipe falling down its face.

It was the biggest snow on record for this time of year. School had been canceled yesterday. Today was Saturday, so the town's children could enjoy what was left of the accumulation with their sleds and flying saucers.

The postman wore his Saturday look, a bit more watchful than usual, as he started to cross the street. Saturdays were more dangerous for him than weekdays, and more interesting. Children were on the loose. With children came snowballs, pranks, and sometimes an unruly dog. He had to be on his toes.

But something stopped him in the middle of the street. He stood still in his tracks, his cart beside him, his eyes fixed on something beyond the houses and the trees and the snow-covered lawns. One hand was raised toward his chin, as though to stroke it thoughtfully. The other was at his side. His eyes blinked as a wind-blown snowflake plopped on the lashes. His mouth was closed, the jaws set rigidly.

No one would find him for ten minutes. As luck would have it, the children were all inside their houses, playing in their rooms, watching Saturday-morning television, or getting ready for lunch. Those mothers who were not out at work did not expect the mail until after noon, so no one came out to check a mailbox.

During those ten minutes the postman did not move a muscle. He was as rigid as the dying snowman who sagged under the new-fallen snow.

The mother was standing in her kitchen, watching the news station on TV as she talked to her sister on the phone.

"No," she said. "Just getting ready to give the kids lunch."

She paused, listening to something her sister was saying.

"No," she said with some anger. "I'm so fed up with husbands, I'm not going to move a muscle. They can get along without me. I've had it."

She craned her neck to glance into the playroom. Her maternal radar had alerted her to the fact that the little ones were up to something.

"Just a second," she said to her sister. Then she held the phone against her breast and shouted at her older child, the boy, "Stop doing that to her!"

There was a pause. The mother went to the door of the playroom and gave both children a hard look. "Lunch in five minutes," she said. "Don't leave this room until you clean up this mess."

They were five and seven. The little girl was quiet enough when left to her own devices, but the boy, Chase, was a terror. When he wasn't torturing his sister he was putting her up to some sort of mischief. It was impossible to leave them alone in a room for half an hour without a crisis resulting.

The mother went back to the kitchen, the cordless phone in her hand. On the TV screen was the face of Colin Goss, the controversial right-wing politician whose rise in the polls had alarmed many observers.

"God," she said, "there's that maniac Goss on the news."

"Turn it off," her sister advised.

"I wish I could turn *him* off," the mother said.

Both sisters hated Colin Goss, a perennial independent candidate for president who had lost three times in the general election. They considered him a pure demagogue, a menace to freedom and a potential Hitler. Their husbands, however, had been swept up in the recent groundswell of support for Goss. It was difficult to get through an evening without an argument on this subject.

"Gary watches all Goss's speeches on C-SPAN," the mother said. "He actually thinks the guy makes sense."

"So does Rich. I've heard him say it a thousand times. Colin Goss is strong, Colin Goss is the only man who has the guts to do what needs to be done. To me he's a madman. Also, he's icky."

"Creepy. You're right."

A lot of men admired Goss for his success in business and his strength and toughness. They viewed him as a dynamic leader who could "save the country." But when many women looked at Goss's face they saw a lecher, a dirty old man. There was something cruelly sensual about Goss that repelled them.

Colin Goss's main campaign issue was, and always had been, antiterrorism. A Nobel Prize–winning biochemist who had built his own pharmaceutical empire from nothing, Goss had gone on to become one of the richest conglomerators in the world. His influence was said to extend to every corner of government and the private sector. Over the years Goss had had runins with terrorists whose activities had affected his business dealings overseas. In the 1990s he emerged as the most eloquent, and certainly the most strident, antiterrorist in American politics.

Goss's views never caught on, primarily because terrorism had not yet hit Americans close to home, and also because his speeches bristled with thinly veiled racism, particularly against Arabs and other people of color. When Goss talked of "cleaning up" the Third World and the American underclass, many political observers cringed. Rhetoric like this had not been heard since the fascist movements of the 1930s.

But the World Trade Center attack changed the political climate. And with that attack still fresh in the public mind, the *Crescent Queen* disaster created a new political world.

"If it weren't for the *Crescent Queen*," the mother said, "no one would give Goss the time of day. But people are scared out of their wits."

"Well, it's no wonder," her sister said. "All those poor children vaporized out in the ocean. It's unbelievable."

Military and scientific observers had determined that the *Crescent Queen* was destroyed by a tactical nuclear weapon delivered by ballistic missile. No terrorist group had taken credit for the attack. The president had promised that those responsible would be brought swiftly to justice. "The *Crescent Queen* disaster must not only be solved," he said. "It must be *avenged*."

But in the six months since the attack, the combined efforts of the federal intelligence services had failed to identify the perpetrators. A state of fear unequaled since the Cuban missile crisis had set in among Americans.

A week after the attack a terrifying piece of video was sent to the major television networks and cable stations from an unknown source. It showed the *Crescent Queen* floating placidly in the Mediterranean, in such close focus that the name of the ship was visible on the bow. Then the nuclear explosion vaporized the vessel, and the camera pulled back to show the mushroom cloud rising majestically over the blue sea. The video had clearly been shot from a surface vessel at a safe distance from the blast.

"It gives you the creeps," said the sister. "Just waiting to see where the next one is going to drop. I can't sleep at night."

"Gary thinks the Muslims are behind the whole thing," said the mother. "He says the nuclear technology is being provided by Iraq or Libya or somebody, and the Muslim terrorists are pushing the button."

"Maybe he's right. But it doesn't make much difference, since we don't know what to do about it. I feel like a sitting duck. I'm scared for my kids."

"Do you know what Rich says? He says kill all the Muslims and everything will fall into place."

"Gary is exactly the same. He says nuke the Arabs and divide the oil resources among the developed countries, and our troubles will be over."

Many American men had similar opinions. It was hard to avoid unreasoning anger when they saw news video of Muslims marching in the streets of Middle Eastern capitals to celebrate the *Crescent Queen* disaster. Shaking fists and holding up signs that read DEATH TO AMERICA, the Muslims considered the attack a victory over the United States. Islamic terrorism was on the upswing, spreading throughout developing countries like a cancer. Governments in the Middle East, South Asia, and North Africa, intimidated by the Muslim groundswell, did not dare to refuse safe haven to the terrorists, even though this brought economic reprisals from America.

Meanwhile the continuing oil crisis, fostered by hostile Arab states, aggravated the recession that had begun just before the president's election. Unemployment was at its highest point in a generation.

Few Americans dared to remember the time, only a few years ago, when the worst problem the nation faced was what to do with the surplus. The old world was gone. A new one had taken its place, a world in which one held one's breath and waited for disaster to strike.

"You know," said the mother, "I believe Gary honestly thinks that's what Goss will do if he gets into office."

"You mean kill all the Muslims?"

"Yes. That, or something like that—crazy as it sounds."

"I don't know . . . It does sound insane, but I'm not sure I would completely put it past Goss. There's something about those eyes of his . . . You know, Hitler never actually said he was going to kill people, either."

"I can't believe we're actually saying *if he gets in,*" said the mother. "Ten years ago it would have been unthinkable."

"Yeah, but that was before the *Crescent Queen.* People want revenge. Men especially."

"The recession has a lot to do with it too. Being out of work for two years can do something to a man's mind. I know it's done something to Gary's mind. He never used to be this way."

The president's popularity was at an all-time low. There was talk in Congress to the effect that he should resign. A constitutional amendment would permit a special election in which the American people could choose a new leader. Colin Goss was a visible spearhead of this movement. In the new climate of fear and anger, Goss was viewed as a viable candidate for president. His standing in the polls had been increasing steadily as public confidence in the administration declined.

"Rich says if Goss runs for president he'll be the first one at the polls. He wants to vote for Goss that badly."

"I just pray it never happens."

The mother turned away from the TV. As she did so she saw the postman through the window, standing in the middle of the street. She frowned as she noticed his immobility. His shoulders and cap were now covered by a light layer of snow.

"Listen," she said to her sister, "I've got to go. There seems to be something wrong with Mr. Kennedy. I'll call you back, okay?"

She hung up the phone, quickly looked in on the children, and threw on her coat. She remembered at the front door to put on her boots. She made her way across the snow-covered lawn to the sidewalk, and then into the street.

An odd stillness hung over the block as she moved toward the silent mailman. There was not a car in sight, not a tire track the entire length of the street. Snowflakes swayed downward like pillows from the gray sky.

She was close enough now to see the snowflakes on the mailman's nose and eyelashes. His face was rigid. He reminded her of the Tin Man in *The Wizard of Oz,* who simply froze in one position when the rain caused him to rust.

"Mr. Kennedy?" she asked. "Are you all right?"

The postman's eyes were a pale blue. They gave no sign that he had heard her. Something about them was strange, but it would not be until much later, telling her story to the health authorities, that she would put it into words by saying that his eyes were as though hypnotized from within.

She called to him several more times, and dared to touch his sleeve. But he was like a statue, completely oblivious of her.

She saw a couple of neighbor children coming toward her.

"Stay back, children," she called. "Mr. Kennedy may be sick."

The children moved reluctantly away. The mother hurried inside, told Chase and Annie to stay in the playroom, and then called 911. The operator got the street wrong, and it was not until about twenty-five minutes later that a police car rolled to a stop alongside the immobile mailman. By now some more children had emerged from the surrounding houses and were gawking from their front lawns.

One of the policemen approached the mailman. He noticed a wet area on the man's cheek. Looking down, he saw the remnants of a snowball on the ground at the mailman's feet.

"Children, I want you all to go inside your houses now," he said, motioning to his partner, who herded the children away.

The policeman tried to help the mailman into the cruiser, but the mailman seemed to resist, clinging to the spot where he stood. His jaws were clenched tightly, and he had a look of empty, meaningless stubbornness on his face.

After another few minutes of indecisive parley, an ambulance was called. When it arrived two paramedics discussed the situation with the police and finally lifted the mailman onto their gurney and slid him into the back of the ambulance.

"All right, children," said one of the mothers who had ventured onto her frozen stoop. "It's all over now. Let's all get inside before we freeze our noses off."

The children, bored now that the police car and ambulance were gone, went back into their houses.

————

THE EMERGENCY room physician who examined Wayne Kennedy that afternoon found all his vital signs essentially normal. Heart rate, blood pressure, even reflexes were well within normal limits. But the patient could not speak or perform simple commands. ("Wayne, can you lift your little finger for me?") His eyes were seen to notice a flashlight beam as it was moved across his field of vision, but when asked to follow the light on command, he could not or would not obey.

By evening Kennedy had been moved to a semiprivate room adjacent to the intensive care ward. The doctors did not understand his condition, so they did not know what to expect. Emergency life support might become necessary if some unknown toxic or infectious agent was behind his illness. On the other hand, the silence and the stubborn immobility suggested a mental disturbance, and Kennedy would have to be watched for this as well.

By nine o'clock that night, most of the physicians and interns on duty had had a look at the patient, and none could offer a constructive thought.

The nurses were told to keep a close watch on him, and he was put to bed for the night.

In all this time Wayne Kennedy, a fifteen-year veteran of the postal service with a large family of his own, had not uttered a single sound.

2

Alexandria, Virginia
November 16
7 A.M.

KAREN EMBRY was dreaming.

The fringes of a troubled sleep procured by nearly half a bottle of bourbon made her dream intense and disturbing.

She was applying for a job in a very tall building. The elevator thrust her upward with such force that the wind was knocked out of her. She thought she was going to wet her pants.

The personnel director greeted her when the elevator opened. Looking down at herself, she noticed with a shock that she had nothing on below the waist. Just the suit jacket and foulard she had worn for the job application, the large purse and the red leather shoes.

She opened the purse, which seemed inordinately huge, to search for the missing skirt and underwear. The purse was completely empty.

I've got to get to the ladies' room. She saw the door marked "Ladies" and went through it. The personnel director smiled indulgently, as though to say, "Yes, go ahead, I'll wait for you." But at the last second he darted into the ladies' room behind her.

There was something magical about that entry, for when they got inside he was no longer a man, he was a little girl. Karen looked at herself in the mirror and saw that she, too, had regressed through time and was small again, as she had been back home in Boston. She was still naked below the waist. So was the other girl.

"Let's touch each other," the girl said. Karen thought she recognized her as a childhood friend, Elise perhaps. The girls stretched out their hands to fondle each other.

A tremor shook the building. *It's an earthquake.* The building tilted suddenly to one side. The doors to the toilet stalls swung open with a bang.

Karen tried to escape, but the little girl had hold of both her hands. The building was falling over with an enormous roar. Karen was tumbling through space, about to be buried by tons of concrete and steel.

Help! Help me!

With a scream in her throat, Karen woke up.

The alarm was ringing. She reached sleepily to turn it off, realizing with a smile that the roar of the crumbling building in her nightmare had actually been the buzz of the alarm clock.

The headache hit just as she was fumbling for the button. The empty glass beside the bed reminded her of how much bourbon it had taken to leave her in this shape. A throb in her bladder told her she had to pee. No wonder the dream had been about a bathroom, she thought.

With a groan she got out of the bed and stood up.

"Jesus," she said. The headache was much worse. She staggered to the bathroom, flung open the medicine cabinet, and found the Advil bottle. She shook three of the brown tablets into her trembling hand and filled the dirty water glass from the tap. She moved to the kitchen. Mercifully, the coffee-maker was full and ready to perk. She had remembered last night, despite the booze, to fill it.

She turned the machine on and padded back to the bedroom. The churning sound of the coffeemaker was like a fist squeezing repeatedly at her throat.

"Jesus Christ," she moaned. "Hurry."

It took seven long minutes for the coffee to perk. The Advil still had not taken effect when she brought her first cup back to the bed. With her eyes half closed she turned on the little bedroom TV.

Washington Today, one of the most-watched political talk shows, was on. Dan Everhardt, the vice president, was being assailed by two right-wing senators who challenged him to defend the administration's policy on terrorism.

"Just tell me how you can defend a policy that simply doesn't work," one of them demanded.

"The fact is that our policy on terrorism *does* work," Everhardt said. "In cooperation with other governments around the world we have prevented countless terrorist attacks over the years."

"Not as many as you could have prevented."

"That's not quite fair."

"Not the World Trade. Not the *Crescent Queen.*"

Karen smiled. Dan Everhardt was not a good debater. A quiet family man, a former defensive lineman at Rutgers, he projected honesty and integrity rather than glib eloquence. The president had chosen him as his running mate for precisely that reason.

Everhardt was very popular. He stood six feet five inches tall and was, in his ruddy way, quite handsome. Unfortunately, his slowness on the uptake was hurting him in this debate against two strident pro-Goss spokesmen.

"Those were terrible tragedies," he said. "But we learned valuable lessons from them. I—"

"Not the lessons we needed to learn," said one of the senators. "The World Trade should have taught us to destroy these fanatics *before* they attack us. The *Crescent Queen* tragedy took place precisely because we had not learned that lesson. Nine hundred innocent people slaughtered, most of them children. And we still don't know who is responsible. We sit here like sheep waiting for the slaughter. The next hydrogen bomb could land on New York or Washington. Don't you people in the White House have any conception of what we're up against?"

Unfortunately for the vice president, the show's director took this opportunity to cut to an image of the mushroom cloud rising above the blue Mediterranean where the *Crescent Queen* had been.

Even more unfortunately, the moderator now interrupted the proceedings to bring in Colin Goss himself, via split screen from his corporate headquarters in Atlanta.

"Mr. Goss, can you bring some perspective to the debate going on here?"

"Well, I hope I can." Goss leaned forward, his sharp gray eyes fixed on the camera. "I honor my distinguished colleagues, and I think they speak out of a sincere regard for our nation at this perilous time. However, I don't agree with Vice President Everhardt's logic. I don't think our policy on terrorism works. Let me put the analogy to the vice president in a different way. Suppose a farmer has a sheep ranch, and wolves are breaking through his fences and killing his sheep. He has consulted the best experts about the fences, and has learned that no fence can be built that will completely protect his sheep. He now has two choices. He can either close down his ranch, sell his sheep, and give up—or he can shoot the wolves that are killing his sheep."

He joined his hands in a gesture of resolve. "The American people seem to feel, as I do, that it is time to fight back against the mad dogs who are massacring our children."

Karen smiled. *Time to fight back.* That was one of Goss's favorite campaign slogans. *Mad dogs* was his code word for terrorists. "You can't negotiate with a mad dog," he liked to say.

Goss had leaned back, but his eyes still seemed to glare into the camera. Those eyes had made him a national figure, for they expressed a powerful will and great intelligence. But some observers said they were also the reason he had lost the three presidential elections in which he had run. There was something dangerous in Goss's look. Some saw it as strength, others as ruthlessness. He had the look of a leader, but perhaps of a bad man.

Dan Everhardt was caught off guard by Goss's analogy.

"For one thing," he said, "we have fought back. We fought back with great success in Afghanistan . . ."

"Our campaign in Afghanistan only provoked the terrorists," Goss retorted. "And did it prevent the *Crescent Queen* disaster? We knew for years that the terrorists were developing weapons of mass destruction. The handwriting was on the wall. Yet we did nothing, and look where it has gotten us." He smiled patronizingly. "In sports there is an old saying, 'The best defense is a good offense.' I wonder if the vice president and his administration have ever really understood this."

"There's something about your analogy I don't like," Everhardt said tentatively. "For one thing, in this civilized world we don't solve our problems by taking out guns and shooting people."

"On the contrary," said Goss. "We use force to defend ourselves when the adversary doesn't understand reason. Perhaps the vice president doesn't remember how we defeated Hitler and Saddam Hussein."

He leaned forward again, his eyes darkening. "But the situation is even simpler now. This is not a territorial struggle, as it was with Hitler or Saddam. These terrorists have only one aim. They want to kill Americans. They've said it over and over, they don't make any bones about it. To *kill Americans*. And our response has been to sit here waiting for them to attack. That response is worse than cowardice. It is insanity."

At this point Dan Everhardt made a crucial error.

"But how would we know who to attack?" he asked. "We don't know who was behind the *Crescent Queen*."

There was an audible intake of breath among those present. Everhardt had admitted his administration's weakness, both intelligence gathering and in retaliation.

Colin Goss's lips curled in disdain. "If we had the right leadership in Washington," he said, "we would know who to attack."

The silence that followed this remark was deeply embarrassing for Everhardt and those who supported the administration.

"Well, I . . ." Dan Everhardt stammered.

The moderator came to his rescue. "We have another special guest via satellite. The junior senator from Maryland, Michael Campbell, has accepted our invitation to join in this debate. Senator Campbell, how would you respond to Mr. Goss's analogy?"

Karen smiled again as she sipped at her coffee. The Goss camp must be pissed off to see Campbell come to Everhardt's rescue. Campbell was a good speaker and a good debater.

"I agree with Dan Everhardt," Campbell said. "I think Mr. Goss's analogy is faulty." The contrast between Campbell's handsome face and Goss's jowly middle-aged countenance was immediate. So was the contrast between Goss's angry gaze and the reflective, almost tender eyes of the young senator.

"I do agree," Campbell said, "that there are mad dogs in the world, but I think that our system of laws and of international covenants is an instrument designed precisely to fight those enemies. Let me put it this way: when a rancher's property is threatened by wolves he sits down with his fellow ranchers and they discuss together what must be done to control the wolf population and to protect their collective properties. By working together they solve the problem. No one rancher, by simply charging out onto the prairie with his rifle, can solve a problem that concerns everyone."

The force of this argument made itself felt. Campbell, despite his youth, had been able to articulate the mature, wider view that was needed to combat Colin Goss's bloodthirsty metaphor.

Colin Goss looked at Michael Campbell with well-concealed dislike.

"And what happens," Goss asked, "if the rancher and his friends can't agree on precisely what should be done to fight the wolves? What if the larger ranchers and the smaller ones don't see eye to eye on the matter? What if their negotiations drag on for months or years? How many sheep must be lost before something positive is done to stop the wolves?"

This was an undisguised allusion to the Bilateral Agreement of last year, which followed a summit conference that included Israel, the United States, and leaders of the major Arab nations. That agreement had promised a united front against terrorism. But the terms of the agreement were so vague that in its final form it was hopelessly watered down.

Nine hundred students and teachers aboard the *Crescent Queen* were bombed into vapor exactly six months after the signing of the Bilateral Agreement.

Dan Everhardt had no answer to this. Michael Campbell, though, seemed to have anticipated the question.

"Again I don't think the analogy is quite right," he said. "The purpose of collective cooperation among the ranchers is to use every appropriate method, including deadly force, to stop the wolves that are killing the sheep. I'm sure Mr. Goss remembers that it was a collective effort by a coalition of countries that forced Saddam Hussein to withdraw from Kuwait. The campaign in Afghanistan that defeated the Taliban was also an international effort."

"I agree with Senator Campbell," threw in Dan Everhardt. "We can't use vigilante tactics to fight terrorism. It's the civilized world we're trying to protect. We have to go about it in a civilized way."

"There's one more thing I'd like to say," Michael Campbell said. "Many of my ancestors were Irish. What happens if you are attacked by a terrorist group, and you fight fire with fire, bombing one of their schools for every one of your own schools that is bombed? Assassinating one of their leaders for every leader of your own who is assassinated? You get Northern Ireland. Is that what we want for our children and our children's children? There has to be a better way."

"Smart," Karen said aloud. Campbell was modest, he deferred to older and more established politicians. But he had a knack for putting the case in such a way that ordinary people could understand it.

In the last couple of months the administration had discovered Campbell as a powerful weapon against the strident Goss forces. Campbell was too young to be identified with the late-twentieth-century policies that had failed to control terrorism. He was handsome, well spoken, and—most important of all—a living embodiment of great physical courage. As a teenager he had developed a serious curvature of the spine that required a lengthy hospitalization. As part of his rehabilitation he took up competitive swimming and became an all-American at Harvard. A second operation became necessary in his junior year, and he came back from it to win two gold medals at the Olympics as a first-year law student at Columbia.

Campbell's political career had derived immediate momentum from his Olympic triumphs and the pain he had overcome. He won his Senate seat from Maryland in a landslide. He was admired by men for his courage and coveted by women for his handsome looks. Voters of both sexes admired his beautiful wife, whose face appeared every month on the cover of *Vogue* or *Cosmopolitan* or *Redbook*.

Karen yawned and took a bigger swallow of the sour-tasting coffee. She had to admit that Campbell was a handsome man. The body that had made him famous as an Olympic athlete was still hard and attractive. He had a clear, youthful complexion that went well with his crisp dark hair. The combination of his youth and his arguments for moderation was powerful.

On the split screen Colin Goss seemed aware of this. He was looking at Michael with a condescending smile. His personal dislike of Campbell was well known. He considered Campbell an ambitious punk, wet behind the ears where the issues were concerned, a matinee idol trying to make a career out of his looks and charm. Yet he realized that Campbell was now a dangerous enemy, politically speaking.

Mercifully Karen's three Advil were beginning to work. She got up, poured another cup of coffee, and headed for the shower. Leaving the coffee on top of the toilet where she could reach it, she stood for a long time under the steaming water. Then she soaped herself, washed her hair, and turned the water much colder for a final wake-up rinse.

She hung the towel on the rack and walked naked into the bedroom. As she was opening her underwear drawer to locate a pair of panties, something on the TV screen stopped her.

Washington Today had been interrupted for a special report. On the screen was a live image of a roadblock surrounded by empty Iowa farm fields, along with a reporter interviewing a worried-looking public health officer.

"We're still trying to assess the situation," the public health man said. "We know that there are victims in several communities in this part of the state, but we still don't know how many. We're evacuating them as we locate them."

The reporter asked, "Sir, can you comment on the rumors that the mystery illness leaves its victims frozen like statues in the position they were in when it struck?"

"I don't know that it's a 'mystery illness,' " the man replied. "We're still assessing it, as I said. It's true that the onset seems to be sudden, but I can't really say any more at the present time."

More questions were shouted at the official as the camera cut away to video, apparently of victims of the disease. A man was shown slumped behind the wheel of a semi trailer on a frozen interstate highway. A school bus was shown stopped at an odd angle in the middle of a rural intersection, the expressionless faces of children visible behind the windows. A helicopter shot showed a skating rink adjacent to a high school or middle school. Skaters lay in unlikely postures on the ice, some face down, others in a sort of fetal position.

Karen stood gazing at the screen, the panties still in her hand. Goose bumps started on her arms. She frowned.

"Mystery illness," she said aloud.

3

AN HOUR after the *Washington Today* broadcast, Vice President Dan Everhardt was in his EOB office, already laboring under a mountain of work.

It was a beautiful day outside. The Washington Monument thrust boldly into a sunny sky while the last of the fall colors daubed the trees along the Mall. A perfect Washington day, cool and crisp. The kind of day that D.C. natives dreamed about throughout the steam bath of summer.

This was football weather. It brought back pleasant memories of college games in which Dan had tested his strength against some of the toughest linemen alive.

Had he been looking out the window, he might have seen Karen Embry's little Honda pass by on 17th Street. Karen was on her way to the Library of Congress. She had some medical research to do, and not much time to do it in.

But Dan Everhardt was looking at the list of appointments on his computer screen. The list was long. It was going to be a tiring day.

The phone on Dan's desk rang. His secretary said the president was on the line. Hurriedly Dan sat down and pushed line two.

"Mr. President. Glad to hear from you."

"Danny, how are you?"

"Fine, Mr. President."

"I'm just calling to congratulate you on your performance on *Washington Today*. We all liked what we heard." The president's voice had its usual composite tone, at once caressing and demanding. He was a man who knew how to get what he wanted from political men without browbeating them.

"Thank you, Mr. President. I'm glad Mike Campbell was there," Dan replied. "In all honesty, I'm not a genius at thinking on my feet. That sheep ranch bit of Goss's had me thrown. But Mike jumped in and bailed me out."

"Michael is a good boy," the president said. "He's bright, and he has the right instincts. I told him how much we appreciate his help. He says he'll go anywhere for us."

"I'm glad," Dan Everhardt said. "We might need him. Have you seen the polls today, Mr. President?"

"Let me worry about the polls, Danny."

The president's reassurance was sincerely meant, but the fact remained that in the latest opinion polls the public's approval of the administration was at an all-time low. Nearly fifty percent of registered voters told pollsters that if a special election for president were held today they would cast their votes for Colin Goss.

"Frankly, Mr. President, I'm worried that I didn't do a good enough job," Dan said. "If it hadn't been for Mike I would have looked like an idiot."

"You did fine, Danny. The choice before the people is clear. At the moment they're expressing their worries about the future by flirting with Goss. But they'll never take that into a voting booth. All we have to do is sit tight and keep doing our job."

"I hope you're right, Mr. President."

They said good-bye, and Dan Everhardt let out the sigh of relief that had been trapped in his lungs throughout the conversation. Had he heard a hint of impatience in the president's reassurances? The thought made sweat stand out on his palm as he replaced the receiver. No matter how ingratiating his manner, the president was still the president. His tolerance for malingerers was zero. Everyone knew that.

For a moment Dan sat thinking about Colin Goss. Not since McCarthy had an extremist of the Right worn so hateful a mantle. Dan Everhardt had done a senior thesis on Hitler at Rutgers. There were obvious parallels between Hitler's anti-Semitism in *Mein Kampf* and Goss's speeches about terrorism. The megalomania, the paranoia. The caricature of the opponent as a subhuman cancer cell eating away at the heart of the civilized world.

Obviously it appealed to something in the psyche of the voters. Since the *Crescent Queen* Americans were lining up by the thousands to hear Goss's speeches, and writing letters to the editor of their local paper to say that he was the man to "save the country."

To inflame the public further Goss had recently begun placing "public service" ads in major newspapers and magazines, stressing the theme that it was "Time to Fight Back" or "Time for a Change." Criticized by journalists and even advertisers for electioneering on behalf of himself at a painful time, Goss responded by placing some of the ads on television. It was not unusual these days to see commercials on cable and network stations featuring Goss, a fatherly expression on his face, talking about the "crisis" America faced and the need for Americans to "make the tough choices" at this critical time. Several of the ads showed Goss before a back-projection view of the *Crescent Queen* explosion.

Those who tried to keep the ads off the air were frustrated by Goss attorneys who cited their client's right to free speech. The advertising managers of the television networks were loath to say no to Goss's money, especially when the public seemed to be responding so positively to the ads.

This was going to be a tough battle, Dan Everhardt realized. Goss was throwing everything he had into the effort to force the president out of office. The political situation was meeting Goss halfway. People's fear of another nuclear attack, possibly on American soil, was greater every day. The status quo was a continual state of terror. More and more voters wanted a change at any price.

Dan was glad Michael Campbell was on board. Mike was hugely popular in his own right, and every word he said in the media got listened to.

Michael would probably run for president himself eventually. His natural ability, combined with his good looks and the huge profile brought by his Olympic victories, would make him a strong candidate for the White House. His wife's beauty didn't hurt, either. The only slight negative was their childlessness. But no doubt in the next few years that problem would be solved.

In the interim, Dan Everhardt was vice president of the United States. He had no presidential ambitions for himself. He was loyal to the president and determined to help him stay in office. In this tempestuous time the country needed a sane, wise leader more than ever.

Dan Everhardt looked at his watch. Twenty minutes remained before his conference call with the majority leader.

He stood up and stretched. His back gave him a twinge, a reminder of his football days. He also had a trick knee, the result of surgery on the anterior cruciate ligament. But mostly he felt tired. The stress he had been under recently was taking its toll.

He reached for the intercom.

"Janice?"

"Yes, sir?"

"I'm going to take a quick shower. Take messages for fifteen minutes, will you?"

"Certainly, sir. Did you want to return Senator Buerstin's call?"

"After I get out."

"Yes, sir."

Dan Everhardt noticed himself in the mirror as he moved toward the bathroom. His bulk was beginning to sag, he noticed with some displeasure. The heavy-plated lineman's armor was taking on the look of a middle-aged man's spare tire. He wished he could find more time for workouts. But these days so many things kept pressing in on him. One less martini at night would help too—but that was not an option either. His nerves were strung too tight. Things hadn't been going all that well with his wife. They hadn't really talked in a long time. As for lovemaking, that was a sore point.

He went into the bathroom and peeled off his clothes. He would put on a fresh shirt after his shower, as always. He sweated a lot.

He draped his jacket over the hanger that hung from the hook on the wall. He threw the shirt into the little hamper, then took off his pants and folded them. He turned on the shower, waited for the water to warm, and got in. A wave of sudden weakness stole through him. He worried briefly about his heart. He was over fifty now, and not in the best of shape.

He felt empty. He thought of Pam, lying in bed when he said good night to her last night. She had looked so lonely. He wanted to reach out to her. But so much water had run under the bridge. Like the water ceaselessly disappearing down this drain, even as it pounded down on him from above. All of life, slipping through our fingers, he thought. Nothing permanent.

He recalled the graduation speech he had given at Rutgers last year. He had had that thought at the time—"Nothing is permanent"—but he had not had the heart to express it to all those fresh-faced graduates. They would find it out in time. Why spoil their happy years by bringing it up now? Better to be gentle.

Depressed thoughts like these did not come naturally to Dan, who was an optimist by temperament. But just at this moment they seemed cogent and inescapable. The whole world was like a house of cards, ready to crumble at the slightest touch.

A house of cards . . . He was thinking of these words when a greater weakness came over him. The soap fell to the floor of the shower with a splat. He made to bend down toward it, but his arm didn't move.

Something was wrong. He had sensed it a moment ago, perhaps even earlier. But he had ignored it, decided it was nothing. And that was the opening it had come through—his own obliviousness.

His body seized up, frozen like an engine thrown into reverse at full throttle. The room was yellow, then red. A sound like screeching trumpets was in his ears. He didn't even try to reach for the walls. He sought only to get out the cry that would bring help. But his throat was locked tight, nothing would come out.

Pam. It was the last word in his mind, but it never came near his lips.

He sagged against the wall of the shower. That was where he would have remained, had it not been for the slippery soap under his feet. He fell to the tiled floor with a crash, his bulk forcing the shower door open. His head emerged from the cubicle, water dripping from his hair onto the floor. The bar of soap lay innocently on the drain.

His hands were clenched at his sides. His eyes were wide open. He looked as though he were preoccupied by something beyond this water-soaked room, something terribly urgent and transcendently important.

He tried to make himself move. It was impossible. He lay staring straight ahead, as he would be when they found him.

4

Hamilton, Virginia, on the Chesapeake Bay
November 16, 6 P.M.

JUDD CAMPBELL, having just finished watching his videotape of *Washington Today* for the third time, rewound the tape on his VCR and began the program all over again. He called out to his daughter, "Ingrid, get me a Guinness, will you?"

"Another one?" Ingrid, who watched her father's intake of alcohol and tobacco like a hawk, gave her usual protest.

"For Christ's sake, daughter, no sermons. Just get it!"

Judd used the remote to speed through the early exchanges between Dan Everhardt and his adversaries. He stopped when Michael's face came on the screen. Judd's eyes, a startling blue-green with touches of gold deep in the iris, focused on his younger son with a combination of great tenderness and stern judgment. Michael was the bearer of the Campbell name and of his father's torch.

Outside the window loomed the Chesapeake Bay, gray and choppy under a momentary cloud cover. One brave soul was out there on a sailboat. Judd did not look at him.

Behind him loomed the house, its sixteen rooms sprawling under high ceilings, the bedrooms placed along the upstairs front with spectacular views of the Bay. Judd had bought it as a "summer cottage" when he was based in Baltimore, and had fallen in love with the place and moved in permanently. His children loved the beach, and Judd himself was a dedicated sailor and fisherman. His wife had died here. He still kept her bedroom exactly as she had had it when she was alive.

His cardiologists would no longer allow him to sail a small boat alone, but he went out often on his yacht, the *Margery*, both to sail and to fish. He liked to conduct business meetings aboard the boat, and didn't care if the colleagues who attended got seasick. He felt more lucid on the water, more free of the fetters of dry land.

Judd Campbell was a self-made man, and liked people to know it. He came from an impoverished Scotch-Irish background and had made his mark on the business world as a textile manufacturer and importer before he was thirty. His patchwork empire of factories grew into a conglomerate that included everything from hotels to telephone companies. Though not a modern man by temperament, Judd saw the computer revolution coming in the 1980s and invested millions in the PC and software markets. By age fifty-five he was an institution in American business.

But he was hardly a household name. And now that age and chronic heart trouble had forced him to retire, he knew he never would be.

It was Susan who brought him the glass of dark ale. She and Michael were having dinner here tonight. Susan had arrived first, an hour ago, and was helping Ingrid in the kitchen. Michael was due before the meal was served.

"Ah, here's a face I can live with," said Judd. "Thanks, sweetie."

"Ingrid is still muttering about your ration." Susan smiled.

"Let her mutter. Come here, look at your husband." Judd gestured to the TV screen on which Michael's handsome face was shown.

"I've seen him before." Susan patted her father-in-law's shoulder. "Have to get back to work. How many times have you watched that thing?"

"Never mind." Judd went back to his TV as Susan left the room.

Judd Campbell did not try to disguise the special feeling he had for Michael. Even as a toddler Michael had shown a kind of energy and strength that his two older siblings lacked. Judd had taken the child to his heart, teaching him to excel in everything he did. When Michael was learning to swim, to ride a bike, to throw a ball and swing a bat, Judd had repeated familiar anthems in his little ear.

"Excellence without victory is like frosting without a cake."

"The man who finishes second is not a man. He is only a footnote."

And of course the legendary Vince Lombardi maxim. *Winning isn't everything. It's the only thing.* Judd took this as holy writ, and made sure his son heard it often.

When the boy was very small he did not seem to understand these injunctions. But as he grew older, their deeper effect made itself felt. He attained success in everything he did. Though slight of build he was a natural and graceful athlete, a student to whom high grades seemed to come naturally, a handsome young boy to whom popularity came without being sought.

When Michael became a national hero at the tender age of twenty-three for his courageous performance in the Olympics, Judd knew that the door of opportunity was open for the Campbells. Michael had all the equipment needed to make a mark on the world in a way his father had not. Michael had intelligence, ambition, guts, and—the one quality Judd lacked—charm.

For a dozen years Judd had supported his favorite son in his political career with money, contacts, and advice. They made a strong combination. Michael's political rise had been meteoric. Unlike Judd, though, Michael did not need to make the pursuit of success a grim crusade. He had no chip on his shoulder, like the one Judd had inherited from his impoverished immigrant childhood. Instead he had a talent for diplomacy that made him many friends among political men, including those who opposed his party and his views.

It was this talent that allowed him to take in his father's overbearing demands without being offended by them. He seemed to understand the vicarious commitment of Judd, a profoundly unsatisfied man, to Michael's own career. He went from achievement to achievement easily, almost tenderly, as though he wanted to give his father a gift he knew Judd needed with all his heart.

Michael was the only Campbell child to possess this instinctive ability to "handle" Judd. Stewart, his older brother, had attained a life of his own only at the price of leaving the family and cutting off all contact with his father. Temperamentally unsuited to the world of ambition that Judd lived for, Stewart had locked horns with Judd as a teenager. After his mother's death their conflict had escalated into open war. Stewart stayed away after college, paid his own way through graduate school, and got a doctorate in history. Today he was a professor at Johns Hopkins. Though he lived only forty miles from Judd, he had not visited in fifteen years.

Ingrid, less willful, had remained at home, renouncing a husband and children of her own in order to care for Judd in his waning years. She was Judd's emotional slave, though she affected the role of stern caregiver as she rationed his intake of alcohol and fought against his addiction to cigars. She also devoted herself to Michael and to Susan, whom she treated like an adored younger sister.

Judd had been ruthless as a businessman, walking over those who stood in his way and browbeating even his most loyal employees. His great downfall had been his tendency to do the same in his family. It had lost him Stewart's love, and had reduced Ingrid to a shadow of what she might have become. But somehow Michael had survived and even flourished under his father's stern aegis.

The only untoward incident in Michael's otherwise normal childhood was the spinal curvature that began to afflict him in his mid-teens, a severe scoliosis that threatened more than his youthful athletic career—it actually threatened his ability to lead a normal life.

But it was precisely this challenge that brought out the killer instinct in Michael, making him into an all-American swimmer and then an Olympic champion. As an additional silver lining, it was during his convalescence after the second surgery that he began courting Susan Bellinger, a heartbreakingly pretty Wellesley freshman who came from a broken home and was working her way through college as a model.

Susan helped him recover from the surgery and watched in wonder as he went back to swimming and slowly, relentlessly pushed himself back into Olympic form. She fell in love with Michael as a weak, pain-ridden young stranger about whom she knew next to nothing. Three years later she was married to him as a celebrity. And she herself, as his attractive young wife, soon became a celebrity too.

A brilliant law student, Michael became editor of the *Law Review* and joined a prestigious Baltimore law firm upon his graduation. He ran for the House of Representatives four years later, and was elected to the U.S. Senate before he reached the age of thirty. The leaders of his party quickly identified him as a rising star and even a potential standard bearer. Michael's future looked every bit as stellar as his past.

Judd Campbell got up from his chair and stood before the TV with the remote in his hand. Judd was tall, at least six three in his stockinged feet. His hair was thinning now, with only a few touches of the old russet among the gray. His emerging forehead, high and strong, made him look as vibrant as ever. Not a few friends and colleagues had remarked over the years on his resemblance to the actor Clint Eastwood. He was a handsome man. Chronic heart disease had done nothing to dim his sex appeal.

He froze the image of Michael long enough to call into the kitchen, "Susie, would you bring me a bowl of peanuts?" Susan appeared at the doorway. "What, Dad?"

"Peanuts," Judd repeated. "Unsalted peanuts, for an old man."

"Coming up." She moved away along the hall. Judd's smile lingered as he heard her light steps.

Judd loved Susan more than any woman except his late wife. When Michael had first brought her home to him—Michael still on crutches at that time, and Susan more a confidante than a love—Judd had taken to her immediately. Her delicacy reminded him of Margery. Under her sunny blond looks there was a ruminative, somewhat depressive streak that made him want to protect her. And also a sweet, maternal quality that made her an ideal nurse for Michael during the most painful times.

And there was her extraordinary beauty, hardly a thing to go unnoticed by a red-blooded man like Judd. He admired her looks, and he also cannily reflected that she would be an ideal mate for Michael in his political career.

The greatest tragedy to befall the Campbell family had come when Margery, Judd's doting wife of twenty-six years, committed suicide. No one had seen it coming. No one had thought Margery capable of such an act. Michael was seventeen at the time, Stewart twenty-four, Ingrid twenty-two.

The loss had been devastating. It was probably the real cause of the rift between Stewart and his father, though the pretext was Stewart's determination to follow an academic career. It also brought on Judd's first serious heart attack. And it was certainly the proximate cause of Ingrid's spinster-hood, for Ingrid began devoting herself to her father's needs after he became a widower.

Judd never got over the loss of Margery. It was not until Susan came along that he started to live again. True, he was living through Susan and Michael, and Michael's career. He sensed this obscurely, but buried the knowledge under his ambition for Michael and his tenderness toward Susan.

Susan went into the kitchen, where Ingrid had interrupted her work to watch a news report on the little TV that was kept on the counter.

"Ing?" Susan asked. "Where are Dad's peanuts?"

Ingrid didn't answer. Susan moved to her side and looked at the little screen. A reporter was shivering against the background of a frozen farm field while the graphic "Mystery Disease" was shown.

"The public health people say they're trying to get the situation under control," the reporter said. "That means hospitalizing all the victims, proba-bly under quarantine, and cordoning off the affected areas. None of the offi-cials would comment on what the disease is. Sources have told us it seems to be a genuine mystery."

"What's going on?" Susan asked.

"Some sort of epidemic." Ingrid turned to face Susan. "Probably the flu. The media are hyping it as usual. Where's Dad?"

"Watching his tape of Michael. He wants peanuts."

"No way. I'll handle this."

As Ingrid was moving toward the living room Susan heard the front door open. Her eyes lit up as she went to greet Michael. He gave her a long hug and kiss.

"Where's Dad?"

"Watching you on TV."

"Again? Doesn't he ever get enough?"

She watched him hang his coat in the closet. He had changed clothes at his office, and wore slacks and a light sweater. A breath of the outside air had come in with him, and his cheeks were cool against her lips.

"I talked to Stew today," he said.

"How is he?" Susan asked.

"Great," Michael said. "He sends you his love." He was hanging back, not moving toward his father's den, because he could not let Judd hear him mention the name of his older brother in the house.

"Did he see you on TV?" Susan asked.

Michael nodded.

"Was he favorably impressed?" she asked.

"If he wasn't, he probably wouldn't have told me."

As the oldest of the Campbell children Stewart commanded Michael's respect. Stewart was at the opposite end of the political spectrum from his father. If Judd was a stern judge of Michael's ambition, Stewart was the judge of his integrity. Stewart hated politicians but made an exception for Michael, whom he considered a huge cut above the rest in character and brains.

Susan and Michael exchanged a brief look. They were both sad that Stewart could not be here tonight. Even though Michael's career was a common link between Judd and Stewart, the rift between the two was too deep for Michael to bridge.

"Hey, Ing," Michael greeted his sister, hugging her around her broad shoulders.

"Hey to you, big shot." Ingrid smiled. "Nice work today."

As Susan watched, Michael went to the door of the den and looked in at his father. Judd had not heard Michael's arrival and was glued to the TV, watching his son's image. Michael went forward and, with an odd gentleness, put his arm around his father and kissed his cheek.

"Ah. Here you are." Relief joined with an almost painful devotion in the father's voice as he held Michael's arm. Strangely, Judd did not turn his eyes away from the TV. He remained focused on the abstract image of his son while holding Michael's hand to keep him from getting away. Susan dared to reflect that this schizoid intimacy was part and parcel of Judd's love for his son.

Michael glanced back at Susan with an understanding smile, as though to say, "You know what Dad is like." Nodding, Susan turned away.

In the kitchen Ingrid was whipping the potatoes. The news report on the situation in Iowa was over, eclipsed by a story about violence in the Middle East.

"Sweetie," Ingrid said to Susan, "would you finish this for me while I get the roast out?"

The phone rang. Since both women were busy Michael answered it. His face clouded as he listened to the caller.

"When did this happen?"

Susan turned to look at him. She knew that voice. It meant something serious.

"Where is he now?" Michael said into the phone.

Through the dining room Susan could see Judd, who was still absorbed in his videotape. Michael hung up the phone.

"What's the matter?" Susan asked.

"Danny Everhardt," Michael said. "He was taken sick late this morning. They took him to Walter Reed."

"Sick in what way?" Susan asked.

"Something strange," Michael said. "He can't move, can't talk. His secretary found him on the floor of the bathroom, half in and half out of the shower. He hasn't said a word since."

Susan looked at Michael. The TV still murmured in the kitchen. Outside the house a gull shrieked, once, and was gone over the waves.

5

Walter Reed Army Medical Center
Gaithersburg, Maryland
8 P.M.

DAN EVERHARDT was discovered by his secretary ten minutes after the onset of his illness. Alarmed by his failure to emerge from the still-running shower, she opened the door and saw him lying under the spattering water, his eyes still open.

Within the hour the vice president was taken to Walter Reed, where he was placed under observation in the intensive care unit. His vital signs were normal, but he continued to display symptoms of a massive disturbance of function whose precise characteristics were difficult to pin down.

The night of his admission his primary physician received a visit from a Secret Service agent named Joseph Kraig.

"Dr. Isaacson," Kraig said, shaking the physician's hand. "Thank you for making time to see me."

"We received a call from the White House asking us to cooperate with you in every way possible," the doctor said, not looking very happy about Kraig's presence. "It seemed only reasonable to go along."

The doctor studied Kraig, who was a deceptively ordinary-looking man in a dark suit. Kraig looked to be in his late thirties, prematurely gray at the temples, with shoulders and arms that bespoke good physical conditioning. He had quiet eyes whose neutral expression suggested a coiled inner force kept carefully hidden. Something about him was frightening; something else was reassuring. It was hard to tell the difference.

"What can you tell me about the vice president?" Kraig asked.

"Well," said the doctor, "it's very ambiguous. At first we suspected a stroke. There is a rather dramatic impairment of mental function. But the tests we've done so far—EKG and so forth—don't indicate any circulatory problem. I'm leaning toward the functional, but I'm far from sure."

"Functional?" Kraig asked.

"By that I mean a mental or emotional disturbance without a physical basis," the doctor said. "Of course, it's too soon to say."

"Could you show me?" Kraig asked.

"I'd rather not," the doctor said. "It wouldn't be appropriate for anyone outside the family . . ."

"Has the family seen him?" Kraig asked.

"Only his wife. She didn't think it would be good for the children to—"

Agent Kraig moved closer to the doctor and spoke in a low voice.

"I understand your concerns, Doctor. But it is important that I get a clear view of the situation right away. Would you like me to have the head of the Secret Service call you?"

The doctor sighed. "No, let's get it over with. Let me see if he's awake first."

The doctor left Kraig to wait in the corridor and disappeared into the hospital room. After a couple of minutes he emerged.

"Come on in."

Kraig followed the doctor into the room. Vice President Everhardt was propped up in the hospital bed, looking at the television screen on the ceiling. Not for the first time Kraig noticed the vice president's size. He had the bulk of a football player.

"Mr. Vice President, I'd like you to meet someone," Dr. Isaacson said. "This is Agent Kraig. He's with the Secret Service."

Everhardt looked at Kraig. There was something wrong with the expression in his eyes. Kraig could not put it into words, but the gaze didn't seem lucid. The eyes seemed elsewhere.

"That's Kraig with a 'K,' Mr. Vice President," Kraig said, moving forward to extend a hand.

Everhardt ignored the outstretched hand. He kept looking at Kraig for a few seconds, then looked back at the TV screen, on which an old Arnold Schwarzenegger movie was playing.

"You can call me Joe if you like," Kraig said. "Everybody does."

Everhardt gave no sign of having heard the remark.

"Mr. Vice President," said the doctor, "I'd like to show Agent Kraig a couple of the things we were trying to do before. If that's all right with you."

Everhardt looked at the TV in silence.

"Just to make sure there's no mistake," the doctor said, "is your full name Daniel James Everhardt?"

No response.

The doctor took one of Everhardt's hands. Everhardt looked down at his hand.

"Can you just give my hand one firm squeeze?" the doctor asked.

Everhardt stared at the clasped hands, but did not obey the command. At length he looked back up at the TV, leaving his hand in the doctor's.

"All right, Mr. Vice President. Can you just look from the TV to Agent Kraig, and then back at the TV?"

There was no response.

The doctor gave Kraig a significant look. Then he pushed the call button on the phone beside the bed. A moment later a nurse appeared.

"Yes, Doctor?" she asked.

Everhardt looked at the nurse. His hand remained in the doctor's.

"Nothing, Nurse. My mistake," said the doctor.

The nurse left the room.

"Mr. Vice President, can you look at me?" the doctor asked.

Everhardt, whose eyes had returned to the TV screen, did not react to the question.

The doctor escorted Kraig from the room.

"You saw the essentials," he said.

"He seems aware of his surroundings," Kraig said.

"He is. His reflexes are normal. He reacts to new sights, to sounds. But he can't do anything on command," the doctor said. "Nothing at all. He can look at the nurse when she walks in, but he can't do it if I tell him to look at her."

"Did he walk in here under his own power?" Kraig asked.

The doctor shook his head. "When they found him he was immobile. Rigid. He seemed to resist any attempt to move him."

"What about language?" Kraig asked.

"He hasn't said a single word since they brought him in. He can't repeat a word, or even a sound. He's groaned a couple of times, but he hasn't spoken. We don't know if he can speak."

Kraig was perplexed. "I'm not a doctor," he said, "but this seems very strange."

"It is very strange," the doctor said. "To have a paralysis of function this massive while all the vital signs are normal, and while he can obviously see and hear and react, is not something I've ever seen."

"What are you going to do?" Kraig asked.

"Keep him under observation. Run some more tests. Some more blood studies to look for infection or a metabolic disorder. Some more sophisticated neurological studies. An EEG and skull X ray to rule out an atypical seizure disorder or brain tumor. Maybe an MRI."

The doctor gave Kraig a look. "And, I think, a complete psychiatric workup with a thorough history."

"Why psychiatric?"

"Well, his condition has some features of catatonic schizophrenia or certain types of conversion disorders. We'll also have to rule out a factitious disorder."

"What's that?"

"The layman would call it faking," the doctor said. "I'd prefer to call it a kind of stress-related dysfunction. As you know, the vice president is under considerable stress at the moment. As is the president."

"You mean the calls for a special election?" Kraig asked.

"There could be a lot of ambivalence about a thing like that," the doctor said. "Especially in these troubled times."

"I see what you mean." Kraig knew that Dan Everhardt was a career legislator who probably would never have dreamed of running for high executive office if the president had not chosen him as his running mate five years ago. Now that the president was under attack, Dan Everhardt had to absorb the same blows from the media and from hostile forces in Congress.

"You're saying that he has a strong motive to be sick," Kraig offered. "Because it would get him off the hook politically."

"That's correct," the doctor said. "Not that it's a conscious decision on his part. The symptoms wouldn't be this convincing if it was."

There was a silence. The doctor started to say something, but stopped himself.

"Yes, Doctor?" Kraig asked.

"Did you hear about that strange epidemic out in Iowa?" the doctor asked.

"You mean the people who can't talk?"

"Yes. It's just a hunch on my part, but the vice president's symptoms remind me of the reports about those people. I think it would be worth checking out."

"I'll take care of it," Kraig said, making a note on a small spiral pad.

The doctor looked worried. "If this thing wasn't confined . . . If it was a communicable disease of some sort . . ."

"Yes?" Kraig raised an eyebrow.

"We wouldn't know how to combat it," the doctor said. "We wouldn't have a clue."

Kraig looked at him in silence.

"Of course, that's very unlikely," the doctor went on. "What happened in Iowa is probably some kind of mass hysteria."

"Probably?" Kraig asked.

"Probably," the physician concluded. "In any case, we'll work with what we have."

"Thank you for seeing me, Doctor."

"The hospital administrator tells me the media are waiting for a statement," the doctor said. "I waited to hear from you. From the government, I mean."

"I appreciate it. We can draft something together," Kraig said.

An hour later Joseph Kraig stood beside the hospital spokesman, an administrator named Dr. Cobb, as he faced a large group of reporters outside the main hospital entrance. Video cameras were running, the bright lights making Kraig squint.

"Dr. Cobb, how is the vice president?" The question came from several directions at once.

"The vice president is well," Dr. Cobb said. "We've been running a lot of tests today, and the patient is understandably tired. The tests will continue tomorrow."

"What is the current diagnosis, Doctor?" Again several voices shouted this at once.

"We're not prepared to make a definitive diagnosis until a full battery of tests has been run."

Every word so far, Kraig reflected, had been approved by the White House. This was no time for ad-libbing. Kraig's eyes scanned the mob of reporters and video men. They looked like jackals closing in for the kill. The microphones on their poles were like the proboscises of oversized insects who fed on the pain of humans.

"Doctor, is there any truth to the rumor that Vice President Everhardt's condition has baffled your physicians?"

The question was asked by a young female reporter with dark hair, a woman Kraig did not remember seeing before.

"No truth," Dr. Cobb said.

"Doctor, is it true that the vice president is mentally incapacitated?"

"Not true," Cobb answered with some irritation.

"Doctor, is there truth to the story that the vice president's illness is connected in some way to the epidemic in Iowa?"

The questions were coming from the same reporter, who outdid even her Washington peers in rapid-fire attack.

"Not at all," Cobb said.

To Kraig's surprise, the next question was addressed to him.

"Agent Kraig, are you concerned about protecting the health of other federal officials?"

Kraig narrowed his eyes at the reporter. Who was this hound, anyway?

"It's our job to protect the president and those who work alongside him," he said. "I don't see how the vice president's condition affects that."

"Does Vice President Everhardt's incapacitation make you worry about the safety of other government officials?"

"I wouldn't call it incapacitation," Kraig said.

"Have you interviewed the vice president yourself, Agent Kraig?"

"Yes, I have."

"And how did you find him?"

"I have nothing to add to what Dr. Cobb has told you."

"Agent Kraig, isn't it true that Vice President Everhardt hasn't said a single word since he became ill?" The reporter's dark eyes seemed to bore into Kraig.

Kraig frowned. He had had enough. "I repeat, I have nothing to add to what Dr. Cobb has told you."

Karen Embry nodded with a politeness tinged by lingering suspicion. She looked crisp and professional in her dark suit and blouse. Her hair had been brushed with care, and her makeup accentuated her delicate features. There were a lot of female reporters present, from the wire services and cable stations as well as the local media, but none was quite as attractive as Karen. It would have been hard for an observer to recognize in her the young woman who had dragged herself out of bed at seven o'clock this morning with a crushing hangover. But there was no such observer. Karen made sure that no outsider ever saw her without her professional armor on. And her beauty was part of that armor.

The news conference lasted another twenty minutes, all of them uncomfortable, as Dr. Cobb parried questions from dozens of reporters. Finally, citing the late hour, the doctor called a halt to the session.

Grateful to make his escape, Kraig left the hospital and drove back to his office.

———

SINCE THE attack on the Pentagon of September 11, 2001, many of the major federal agencies had been covertly moving around the city. The Secret Service was presently located in a nondescript office building a block away from HUD, in the shadow of Interstate 395. From the weedy parking lot full of unmarked vehicles no one would have guessed the place was a government facility. Only the name tags the agents and secretaries clipped on as they approached the entrance betrayed the true nature of the operation.

Most of the agents were out, but Kraig's boss, Ross Agnew, was in. It was Agnew who had gotten Kraig this assignment. They had known each other as trainees twelve years ago. Agnew, a graduate of the University of Virginia and a former FBI agent, was a natural-born administrator and a gifted politician. He was the temperamental opposite of Kraig, a field agent who liked solitude and distrusted authority. But they got along well.

"How is Everhardt?" Agnew asked.

"He didn't look good to me," Kraig said. "But I'm not a doctor."

"Not good in what way?"

Kraig shook his head. "A sort of paralysis," he said. "He can't talk, and he can't obey simple commands. So far they can't find anything wrong with him physically. If it's mental, it's bad mental."

"I take it he's not in any condition to go back to work," Agnew said.

"No way." Kraig shook his head.

Agnew thought for a moment.

"Well," he said, "I'll tell the White House. They're not going to like it. Deep concern at the top level. You know what I mean."

Kraig nodded. He cared little for politics. If it weren't for that maniac Colin Goss angling to get into the White House, Kraig would not have cared who occupied the place.

"Do you think the president will have to appoint another man?" Agnew asked.

"If Everhardt goes on this way, I'd say so," Kraig replied. "He's incapacitated."

"Who do you think it might be?"

"Search me." Kraig sat down.

He thought for a moment before saying, "Everhardt's doctor was wondering about the epidemic in Iowa. There are some symptoms in common."

"Really?" Agnew asked. "Which ones?"

"I'm not sure." Kraig frowned. "I don't know that much about Iowa."

There was a silence.

"Does the doctor think this might be something communicable?" Agnew asked.

"He doesn't know. He seemed worried by the prospect."

Kraig sat listening to the muted hum of the traffic on the expressway. He looked at the pictures on Agnew's walls, most of which showed sailboats or fishing boats on the Chesapeake Bay. Agnew was leaning back in his chair with one leg crossed over the other. His knee stuck up well above the desktop. He was immensely tall, six feet eight or nine, and had once had the misfortune of guarding Chris Webber for three quarters in the NCAA semifinals.

Then he asked, "Do you see this changing our drill about the president or the top executive people?"

Agnew raised an eyebrow. "Why would it change anything?"

"I had a reporter ask me that question at Walter Reed," Kraig said. "It was a strange question, but it had me thinking in the car. What if it were possible to incapacitate a public official intentionally, as a form of terror?"

"Hmm," Agnew mused. *The Ipcress File.* Is that what you're thinking of?"

"Yeah. If you can't kill a guy, or force him out through scandal, you mess up his mind somehow."

"Science fiction," Agnew mused. "But anything is possible."

There was a silence.

"Why don't you fly out there and see what you can learn?" Agnew asked.

"Iowa?"

"Yeah."

Kraig nodded. "Okay."

"But first go home and get a good night's sleep," Agnew said. "I have a feeling the next few weeks aren't going to be fun."

Kraig gave Agnew a long look. "Right," he said.

Kraig stood up and left the office.

6

KRAIG DIDN'T get home to his Virginia condominium until after eleven. He was looking forward to a shower and an evening of reading and music.

His profession forced him to read newspapers avidly and to be aware of current events and the trends behind them. He got so sick of the real world after a day of work that he couldn't bear to watch television at home. He listened to a lot of music—Coltrane and Miles Davis when he was younger, but increasingly Beethoven and Mozart—and read novels. He looked for stories as far removed as possible from this time and place. Mark Twain was a favorite. So were Balzac and Dumas. He liked to immerse himself in the longer Dostoyevsky novels, and sometimes even read Shakespeare.

He had weights in his basement, and always found time to do some bench pressing and curling. He ran in the mornings to keep his legs in shape. Since his divorce he found concentration and work easy, but sleep difficult. In some ways the loneliness of his profession suited him. In other ways he felt empty and rootless, adrift in a life that didn't really belong to him.

He e-mailed his daughter in Florida every day, and spoke to her on the phone once a week. She was ten now, and very busy with her own life. He spoke to his ex-wife as seldom as possible.

The apartment building loomed before him with its combined aura of home and of homelessness. Lights were on in all the units except his own. Sighing, he turned off the car.

There was a girl sitting on the steps. As he drew closer, carrying his brief-case, he recognized the aggressive young reporter from the foyer at Walter Reed.

"No comment," he said. "I'm off duty."

"My name is Karen Embry," she said, getting to her feet and holding out a hand. "I don't want a story."

Kraig stood looking at her without taking her hand. She was of medium height, maybe five five, but she seemed smaller because she was visibly underweight. The journalist's typical lean-and-hungry essence was evident in her, but there was something else as well, something downright under-nourished and, Kraig thought, sad. She had long dark hair, which she obvi-ously made the most of. Her complexion was fair, her eyes large and dark. She was very pretty, or would have been had she been anything but a re-porter.

These impressions kept him from sweeping by her into the condo with-out a word.

"If it isn't a story, what do you want?" he asked.

"Just a couple of minutes of conversation," she said.

He looked at his watch. "It's been a long day," he said.

"I work long hours," she said. "My sources tell me that Everhardt is really sick. That there's no way he'll be coming back."

Kraig shrugged. "I really couldn't say. I'm not a doctor, Miss—what did you say your name was?"

"Embry. Call me Karen." Now that his eyes were adjusting to the dim light Kraig saw that there was something unusual about her features. Some-thing European, perhaps—though there was no trace of an accent in her voice.

"How come I haven't met you before?" he asked.

"I moved down here from Boston fairly recently," she said. "I'm working freelance. I specialize in public health stories."

"That's nice," Kraig said.

There was a silence. The reporter knew Kraig wasn't going to give her anything she could use. But, like any good journalist, she wanted to establish him as a contact.

"I heard it was something about the decision-making process," she said.

"What?"

"Everhardt. Something to the effect that he can understand things—some things at least—but can't make decisions based on what he knows. So he can't act. He's paralyzed."

Kraig turned toward the parking lot, beyond which a sad vista of apartments and two-story office buildings blocked the horizon.

"No comment," he said.

"I heard the White House is really worried," she said. "Without Everhardt for the polls, they're not sure the president can hold off Colin Goss."

"I'm not a pollster," Kraig said.

She nodded. "A lot of people are concerned about the viability of the administration. The voters are terrified of another nuclear attack like the *Crescent Queen*. Goss has been pulling a lot of strings in Congress. If anything happens to make the president look weaker than he is already, there might be a resolution asking him to resign. This Everhardt thing certainly doesn't make him look stronger."

Kraig said nothing. He knew Colin Goss was putting pressure on the administration. Frankly, he thought it would be better for the country if Goss was in that hospital bed instead of Dan Everhardt. Goss was a true menace. In this sense, Kraig did have a political mind.

"That's not my department," he said.

There was a silence.

"I heard that some of the doctors think Everhardt's problem may be functional," she said.

"What do you mean by that?" Kraig asked.

"Mental. Emotional. Everhardt has been under a lot of stress recently. Maybe he cracked under the strain."

Kraig was looking at her face now. There was an odd concentration in her eyes, almost an animal concentration. He wondered for a split second whether she was on something, some sort of upper. But he rejected the idea. She was simply a newshound, ready to knock down any obstacle that stood between her and a story. Her kind didn't need uppers. The stories themselves were their drug.

"Everhardt is a good man," she said, "but he's not really cut out for the presidential wars. Consider the way Colin Goss had him buffaloed on *Washington Today*. Maybe the pressure was getting too great for him."

Kraig cut her off. "I don't have anything for you," he said.

"As I say, I don't want you to leak anything," she said. "I just want . . ."

Kraig gave her a dark smile. "What is it you want, Miss Embry?"

"Call me Karen. Please."

Kraig was not taken in by her friendliness.

"What is it you want?"

"I don't want to chase windmills," she said. "I would like to have a contact who can help me stay on the right track. I really don't want to print things that aren't true." She hesitated. "Call it a friend I want," she said. "And I can be a friend in return."

Kraig gave her a long look. A tough reporter, wise to every angle an evasive government would try to pull on her. Looking for a scoop, and willing to trade. Trade what?

Something told him not to blow her off completely.

"Then stop jumping to conclusions," he said, "and start looking for better sources."

"That's why I'm here." That intent look was still in her eyes.

"I have work to do," Kraig said, taking out his keys. "See you."

He went inside and closed the door. The ceiling light in his foyer sent dim rays into the empty apartment. He felt an urge to turn on all the lights in the place and fill it with music, as quickly as possible.

But after hanging up his coat he looked out the window to see if the girl was gone.

She was standing on his steps, looking at the closed front door. She had pretty shoulders under that long hair. She must be cold out there.

He felt an impulse, half sexual and half pure loneliness, to let her in and give her a drink. He hesitated for a long moment. Then he reached for the doorknob. At that instant she started down the steps to the parking lot. She moved quickly, all business, her car keys in her hand. Yet as she opened the car door she looked younger, almost girlish.

Sighing, Kraig turned back to the emptiness of home.

7

November 17

EIGHTEEN HOURS after she left Joseph Kraig's apartment Karen Embry stood in a hospital ward in Des Moines, Iowa, staring at a little girl.

The girl's arms were curled around a ragged teddy bear. Her fingers were frozen against the fur. The creases in her hospital gown remained exactly as they were when it was put on, for she had not moved since they brought her in. Her eyes were fixed on the ceiling of the ward, as though the answer to a long-pondered riddle would appear there at any minute.

The ward was crowded. There were no medical facilities in the affected part of the state capable of handling the victims. The majority had been taken by ambulance or National Guard transport to hospitals in Sioux City and Des Moines.

The epidemic that had spread through a dozen towns in five counties now seemed to have stopped. No new victims had been found since the initial outbreak. This fact came as a relief to the public health officials, but did little for the harried medical professionals who were struggling to deal with fifteen hundred gravely sick adults and children.

A cold front was sweeping across the Midwest and the Plains states, bringing wind chills below zero. Local inhabitants were wearing down jackets and parkas they had not expected to need for another month. Visitors, like Karen, found themselves underprotected against the intense cold.

The Centers for Disease Control in Atlanta had sent a team of specialists to investigate the epidemic. Unfortunately for them, there were no unaffected citizens to interview. Every man, woman, and child in each affected town had been struck down by the mystery illness.

Karen learned all this upon her arrival at the university hospital in Des Moines from the CDC official in charge, Mark Hernandez. Though Hernandez was not happy to see Karen, he had been instructed by his superiors that good relations with the press were crucial at this sensitive time.

He helped Karen put on anticontamination gear. "It's almost certainly unnecessary now," he said, "but we're still being careful." He took her to a quarantined ward lined with beds occupied by immobile, empty-eyed patients of all ages. Overworked nurses were busy feeding and caring for the patients.

It was a disturbing sight. Men, women, and children, still looking healthy and well fed, lying silent in their beds. They looked like film extras hired to play the role of the sick.

Karen was struck by the look in their eyes. They seemed to be hypnotized from within. It was a fixed stare, but not suggestive of dementia. There was something almost visionary about it.

When she remarked on this to Dr. Hernandez, the doctor shrugged. "It is strange. But so far we haven't been able to attach any significance to it."

"I'm puzzled by the symptoms," Karen said. "Shouldn't there be fever or chills or nausea, or something to indicate the internal disorder?"

"Off the record?" the doctor asked.

Karen nodded. "Of course."

"I'm puzzled myself." He shook his head. "The symptoms make no sense. All the vital signs are normal. The patients seem conscious, but their will seems to be paralyzed. Their power to act, even to feed themselves."

"Were any of them able to walk?" Karen asked.

The doctor shook his head. "Judging by where we found them, the illness stopped them in their tracks. If they were sitting, they just stayed there. If they were standing, they remained standing until weakness made them keel over. It's like being struck by lightning. They just froze."

Karen was thinking of Vice President Everhardt, lying helpless in a bed at Walter Reed. She wondered whether he looked like the patients here.

"What is your people's thinking on this?" she asked.

Hernandez shrugged unhappily. "Frankly, we don't know what to think. We're concentrating on life support, nutrition, and so forth. We've quarantined the communities involved. We're analyzing water and soil samples, even the air. It's possible that something got in there and affected the whole population. Whatever it was, it didn't affect anyone else. Each pocket of infection is completely encapsulated. People in the surrounding communities are healthy."

He looked at Karen. "But even if we find a vector, we still don't understand the symptoms. They're not like anything infectious I've ever seen or heard about. The body keeps functioning normally, but the patient is incapable of action."

"Have you heard about the vice president's illness?" Karen asked.

"Yes, I have. Why?"

"It presents some intriguing parallels to this one," Karen said. "Lack of voluntary motor capacity, inability to respond to commands, but apparently normal perception and vital signs."

"Really," the doctor said. "How did you know that?"

"I never reveal my sources," Karen smiled. "It was told to me off the record in Washington. You might want to talk to your people there, though Walter Reed is buttoned up tight."

"I'll think about it." The doctor shook his head slowly as he scanned the ranks of helpless victims. "If it's the same disorder, that could be a bad sign."

"For Everhardt?" Karen asked.

"For all of us." The doctor shook his head. "If a thing like this ever started to spread . . . and us without a clue as to how to treat it . . ."

As they were leaving the ward they passed the bed in which the little girl lay holding the teddy bear.

"How did that get here?" Karen asked.

"I think they found her at home," said Dr. Hernandez. "She was in her playroom. I suppose one of the paramedics brought it along to keep her company here."

Karen looked more closely at the child's eyes. Did she know where she was? From her glassy stare the reporter could not tell.

For the first time the tragedy around her struck Karen. What if this little girl never moved again, never spoke again?

Karen took her leave of Dr. Hernandez and went downstairs to the hospital cafeteria. Her stomach was rumbling, for she had eaten nothing since early this morning. Unfortunately smoking was not allowed in the hospital. She would have to wait for a cigarette until she was outside.

She put a tuna sandwich, a granola bar, a container of yogurt, and a bag of potato chips on a tray and filled a Styrofoam cup with black coffee.

As she was carrying the tray toward a window table a familiar voice sounded in her ear.

"Miss Embry. You get around, I see." It was Joseph Kraig, the Secret Service agent she had talked to last night. He was sitting alone at a table for four. He looked unhappy and somewhat more tired than the first time she saw him.

"So do you," Karen said. "May I join you?"

"Why not?" He pushed back a chair for her. She threw her coat over one of the unoccupied chairs and sat down.

"That doesn't look warm enough for you," Kraig said.

"I haven't been outside much," she said. "Have you?"

"Now that you mention it, no."

He watched her peel the top off her yogurt.

"You don't look as though you eat enough," he said.

She shrugged off the comment, sipping at her coffee with a look of distaste. "I hate hospitals," she said. "My grandmother was in a succession of them when she was dying. If I never see one of these cafeterias again, it will be too soon."

Kraig nodded. He had his own hospital memories. He did not care to revisit them.

Karen ate a few spoonfuls of yogurt, then sat back to study Kraig's face.

"What I really need is a cigarette," she said. "These hospitals are too strict about smoking."

Kraig nodded. "The world is tough on smokers nowadays."

"Did you ever smoke?" she asked him.

"In high school," he said. "I quit when I got to college."

Karen nodded, glancing at the thick wrists emerging from his suit jacket. His fingers were square, almost stubby. The backs of his hands were broad. She guessed he worked out, perhaps too much.

"How did you get into the federal agent business?" she asked.

He smiled, reflecting that it was indeed a business, like any other.

"I was young, I had just gotten married. I wasn't sure what I wanted to do with my life, and we needed money," he said. "A friend of mine was an FBI agent, and he told me about the salary and the benefits. From there, things just evolved."

"Are you still married?" she asked.

He shook his head. She recognized the slight curl of his lip as the outward disguise of a pain he didn't like to talk about. It was a look she had seen on her own face in the mirror.

He struck her as a straight arrow, but not as shallow. He looked like he had been around, made his share of mistakes. She liked that in him.

"How about you?" he asked. "How did you get into the reporting business?"

"I always wanted to be a reporter," she said. "Even in high school. It keeps you busy. You meet a lot of people."

"People who aren't necessarily glad to see you," Kraig added.

"That's right," she said, nodding. "But at least it gets you out of the house. I'm not that fond of my own company."

She took a bite of her tuna sandwich, grimaced, and drank a swallow of coffee. "Jesus," she said. It had been years since she tasted food this bad, even on an airplane.

Kraig smiled understandingly.

She switched to the granola bar and ate half of it before saying what was on her mind.

"It's the same thing, isn't it?" she asked.

"What?"

"The same disease," she said. "The same as Everhardt."

Kraig gave her a steady look.

"You don't listen, do you?" he said. "No comment."

"On background?" She smiled. "Off the record?"

He shook his head.

She was watching Kraig closely.

"All vital functions normal," she said. "But the patient can't act. Can't obey simple commands, can't talk, can't walk, can't feed himself. A paralysis of the function of action or decision."

Kraig said nothing.

"They're looking for a vector," Karen said. "But they don't really have a disease, so the vector may not help. There is no known disease that produces these symptoms."

Kraig asked, "How do you know?"

"I never reveal my sources." She shrugged. "Anyway, as it happens, I know a little something about this sort of thing. I did a double major in biochemistry and journalism in college. I've done a lot of reporting on diseases. This is definitely something new."

Kraig shrugged. "If you say so. I'm not a doctor."

She leaned forward, a hint of her clean-smelling cologne reaching Kraig, who smiled slightly.

"Out here there are hundreds of victims," she said. "Each area is covered completely. But in Washington there is only one victim. The vice president of the United States."

Kraig kept his poker face. But he knew she was right. If Everhardt had the same disease, dozens of others in Washington should have it by now. Something here didn't add up.

"Everhardt is a key to the president's popularity. He's big, he's down to earth, he's popular among men as well as women. It took the party a long time to come up with him as a running mate. Take him away, and the administration is a lot weaker with the voters. He won't be easy to replace."

Kraig was silent.

"And what about the president's political enemies?" she asked. "What about Colin Goss? How does he feel about this turn of events?"

Kraig shrugged. "Am I supposed to have a reaction to that?" he asked.

She crumpled the wrapper of the granola bar and threw it on the tray.

"Something isn't right," she said. "About Everhardt. And about this." She glanced around her at the deserted cafeteria.

Kraig said nothing.

"I'm going to find out," she said. "With you or without you. When the time comes, it may be you asking the questions."

"Maybe." Kraig nodded.

"I'm betting twelve years of journalism that you won't like the answers," she said.

Picking up her coat, she left the cafeteria. Her shoulders looked very small under her sweater. A tired young woman, no doubt an incurable workaholic, who did not bother to hide her unhappiness.

Kraig liked her. There was a tranquil hopelessness about her that struck a chord in him. She had given up on something a long time ago—love? belonging?—and the emptiness it left behind gave her sharp definition as a person. The reporters he had known were shallow people, slaves to their own ambition. Karen Embry was a human being, albeit a scarred one.

Kraig wondered what she looked like without those clothes on. What her cologne smelled like closer up, when one's lips were against her skin.

He hoped he would never see her again.

8

SUSAN CAMPBELL was the only child of a wayward New Hampshire beauty queen and a philandering Boston blue blood named Lee Bellinger. Their marriage had lasted seven years. Susan was six when her father abandoned her mother. A series of boyfriends had followed, along with a desperate search for money that led "Dede" Bellinger into brief forays into television, radio, advertising, and public relations, until her taste for alcohol and her notoriously poor driving ability got her killed in a one-car accident on the New Jersey Turnpike.

Susan was brought up by two straitlaced Bellinger aunts who sent her to the best private schools and offered her the combined wisdom of the Bible, the *Farmer's Almanac,* and Ralph Waldo Emerson as a guide for living. At fourteen she entered Rosemary Hall as a thoroughly confused young girl with braces, skinny legs, and a worried look.

Four years of private school in the company of privileged girls from the best families in the nation did little for her confidence. She was a shy freshman at Wellesley when a friend introduced her to Michael Campbell, a Harvard junior who was about to undergo a second serious spinal operation after his first one had failed. Michael was frightened; Susan took it upon herself to encourage him. It was in that gesture of giving that she became a woman.

By the time Susan caught her breath Michael had won two Olympic gold medals and was a national celebrity. He finished law school two years after the Olympics, and two years after that ran successfully for the Maryland state legislature. By now Susan was his wife, and she helped him campaign for the U.S. Senate. Her extraordinary blond beauty made her an attractive partner for him on the campaign trail. She had worked her way through college as a catalog model specializing in sportswear and lingerie, and for several years her scantily clad image was on every package of silk panties sold under the exclusive S/Z brand name. That image still haunted her, for the feature articles on her in women's magazines often included it.

Susan was too beautiful for a political wife, and too shy. Michael's campaign advisors did not quite know what to do with her.

Then something happened that changed Susan from a minor asset to a crucial weapon in Michael's political arsenal. She was invited to be a guest on *The Oprah Winfrey Show*. At Oprah Winfrey's request Susan brought along the photo album that documented her early years with Michael.

A small comedy of errors took place as Oprah's camera was zooming in on the photo album.

"Now, what does this show?" Oprah was asking.

"That's Michael holding the flowers he brought me after our first fight," Susan said.

"Fight?" Oprah looked at the camera. "What were you fighting about?"

"Sex." Susan blurted out the word before she could stop herself.

"Sex?" Oprah scented an opportunity.

"Yes. He thought I was too straitlaced about it." Susan stopped in midsentence. "Uh-oh. I guess I shouldn't have said that."

"Not at all," Oprah pursued. "Straitlaced in what way?"

"Making out in public. Things like that," Susan said.

"Oh, you mean you're more reserved than he is?" Oprah asked.

"Yes. I'm rather shy," Susan said. "It comes from my New England background, I guess."

"And Michael isn't?" Oprah asked.

Susan laughed. "No. Michael isn't shy."

"What sort of venue are we talking about?" Oprah asked.

"You mean for making out?"

"Making out. Yes." Oprah glanced at the audience.

"On the beach in the moonlight," Susan said. "That sort of thing."

"So he likes to take risks," Oprah prodded.

"Risks? Well, he's very romantic in general, but, yes, I suppose you could say he likes to take risks."

"How far do you think he would go?"

"You mean if he thought no one was watching?" Susan asked.

"Mmm—yes," Oprah agreed.

"Oh, the fifty-yard line at the Astrodome, maybe," Susan said. Her hand went to her mouth instantly, but it was too late. The audience was in hysterics.

"Oh, shit," Susan said, blushing.

And that was the final note, her embarrassed use of profanity. The audience's laughter was mingled with applause. Viewers had never seen a politician's wife speak with such spontaneous candor before.

The clip became famous. Not only did it show off Susan's unpredictable personality and her charm, but it also referred to her sex life with one of America's most desirable men, a man whose handsome body was known to women all over the world.

At first Michael's public relations men were horrified. The sight of Susan on the Oprah show with her profane comment bleeped out seemed a disaster of limitless proportions. But Michael's tracking polls went up instead of down in the weeks after the broadcast. As for Susan, she was now famous in her own right. She had become a major positive overnight.

At age thirty-two Susan found herself not only the wife of a U.S. senator and the darling of the press, but also a member of a complex and difficult family. Judd Campbell, whose willfulness had done permanent damage to his relationships with Michael's siblings, loved Susan and had co-opted her as a surrogate daughter. In more ways than one Susan felt exposed and off balance. But she had no choice. She had cast her lot with Michael, and she could not look back.

———

SUSAN AND Michael had both been busy in recent weeks, too busy to find time for lovemaking. Their first chance came the weekend after the onset of Dan Everhardt's sudden illness.

They met in the bedroom an hour after dinner. Both were eager. Their clothes came off quickly. Michael gasped when he felt his wife's naked body against his own.

"God, I want you," he said.

In no time, it seemed, the preliminary caresses were over and he was inside her. His embrace was gentle, though the heat rising in his loins made him groan. Her hands were on his shoulders, her legs wrapped around him.

Susan's eyes were closed. Michael's eyes were open. He was looking at her face, whose expression might have denoted pain as much as pleasure. She was very beautiful, he thought. Her breasts, still firm as those of a young girl, pressed against his chest. Her hips moved under him, her sex gripping him in its subtle feminine way, exciting him all the more.

Her hair covered the pillow like a splash of golden liquid. He moved faster. She slipped her hands down his rib cage and held him around his back. Her fingers touched the scar that ran down his spine.

He was very hard inside her, and very long. His strokes became slower, more deliberate. She felt him probing for the core of her, seeking to inflame her. The crisp, earthy smell of him grew more intense. Little moans sounded in her throat.

He kissed her, his tongue slipping into her mouth as his hands pulled her harder onto the straining shaft. She arched her back.

"Oh, Michael . . ."

His last thought was for her closed eyes, her fresh young cheeks. She was so beautiful, so innocent . . .

The paroxysm came so suddenly that he gasped. The flow was long and rhythmic. His loins trembled. His breath came haltingly. It was as though he were drowning.

He stayed inside her for a long time. His pleasure ebbed slowly, and when at last he had returned to himself he kissed her cheeks and her forehead. The complicated eyes were looking at him now, and she was smiling.

She drew him to her breast and held him there. He listened to the beating of her heart.

After a while he ran a finger through her hair.

"You're beautiful," he said.

She just smiled.

There was a silence. They lay looking at each other.

"I'm sorry," she said.

"You have nothing to be sorry for," he replied.

Another silence.

"I love you," he said.

"I love you too."

Susan lay back against the pillow and stared at the ceiling. "I'm not myself, Michael."

He nodded.

"It's this awful year," she said. "With Danny Everhardt sick, and all the things in the media . . . I've lost my balance."

"Sure. I understand." Michael remained on his side, looking at her. "Don't worry about it."

"Thanks."

There was a silence. Michael was looking at his wife and thinking about the fact that every time they made love there was an excuse.

Susan never had orgasms with him. Not anymore. Probably, he thought, the most important reason was the pressure on them to have children. It had made them both uneasy about their sexuality and even their relationship. Making love had become an endlessly reiterated attempt at something, rather than a simple sharing of affection and pleasure.

It was hard to sort it all out. He loved Susan more than ever. He delighted in everything about her. Her sweetness, her quirky humor, even her fearfulness. He had known before they got married that she was a bit on the neurotic side. He didn't mind that. It was part of her charm, even if it did make her somewhat more dependent on him.

But as time went on and they became famous, their childlessness had become more and more of an embarrassment. An ambitious political man needed a wife and children. A family.

Consultations with physicians had done nothing to clarify the issue. There was nothing wrong with either of them. Not that medical science could see.

But Michael was aware that the problem had existed even before the issue of childlessness came up. Susan's ability to experience sexual pleasure in his arms had lessened in direct proportion to the sacrifice of her own independent needs to be his wife, a political wife.

But perhaps it went further back still . . .

Michael often looked back on those early days, when he was a virtual invalid being nursed by Susan and his sister Ingrid. The intimacy between himself and Susan was born of the long, arduous convalescence from his second spinal operation. When they finally made love, weeks after his body cast was removed, their sex was not only a discovery of each other but a test of his return to health. She had wanted to make him feel strong and competent. They were both nervous that night.

She had been on top. Her bare knees rubbed against his ribs, her hands rested on his chest. As they grew hotter her hair fell over his face and she repeated his name, *Michael, Michael,* in a voice scalded by sex. The softness of her was amazing. He could feel how deeply she wanted him inside her, possessing her. His orgasm had made him forget all about his back.

Could she have been faking even then? It was possible. After all, she wanted above all to help him, to be useful to him. Perhaps that very loyalty had somehow poisoned her, made it impossible for her to take real sensual pleasure from his body.

There was also her painful childhood. Her father had been an unrepentant philanderer and had abandoned the family. Her mother never really recovered from the loss. Letting herself go sexually with a man might be a difficult issue for Susan.

Nowadays she seemed more tense after making love than before it. Of course she tried to hide it, using tender embraces and affection as her shield. But he knew her too well to be fooled.

Michael let these painful thoughts have their territory in his mind as he cradled Susan's delicate body in his arms.

"I spoke to Pam Everhardt," she said.

He raised himself on his elbow. "How's she doing?"

"Terrible," Susan said. "She can't believe what's happened. She's really beside herself."

She lay looking at Michael. "She depends on Danny for so much. With three children to think about . . . and they don't have much money."

"They never did," Michael said. "Danny was never interested. All he ever wanted was a steady salary. He used to joke about it."

Susan nodded. "Pam is frantic. I think she didn't realize at first how serious it is. Apparently the doctors haven't given her any news she can hang her hopes on. She's thinking of getting consultations with some new specialists."

"I doubt that that's necessary," Michael said. "They'll throw in everything but the kitchen sink at Walter Reed. Danny is a national figure."

"Poor Pam . . ."

He touched Susan's shoulder.

"Uh-oh," he said. "Are you identifying again?"

"Afraid so."

This was an old habit of Susan's. She always identified strongly with people she knew who suffered misfortunes. When one of Michael's Maryland constituents made the news on the basis of some horrible tragedy, Susan could be counted on to write the victim personally and often to visit. Her mail was full of heartfelt thanks from people she had touched in this way.

The Everhardts had been entertained in this house many times. Dan and Michael had served on committees together when Dan was a senator, and both were, of course, involved in party strategy meetings. Over the years the two couples had become good friends. Susan looked up to Pam as a sort of older sister. Pam had been in the political wars longer than Susan, though Pam, an overweight, rather homely woman, had never known the burden of visibility the way Susan had.

"If only they knew what it was," Susan said. "It's not knowing that makes it worse."

Michael nodded. "I spoke to her myself today."

"Really?" Susan asked.

"I've been calling her every day, just to see how things are going."

Susan smiled. This was typical of Michael, this thoughtfulness for a colleague in trouble. A few years ago Dick Friedman, a senator from Colorado who had started the same year as Michael, was injured in a hit-and-run accident that nearly killed him. Michael took personal charge of a bill that Friedman was working on and spent countless hours doing research and making phone calls to potential supporters, without ever asking for thanks or even telling anyone. Michael was loyal—a quality that had made him many friends in Congress.

"Danny doesn't even know who Pam is now," Susan said. "That's what's really killing her."

Michael hugged his wife.

"I know," he said. "It's bad."

He smiled. "Maybe he'll come out of it just as quickly as he got sick. You've heard of people coming out of comas after a long time."

Susan didn't answer. She was lying on her side, her face buried against his chest.

"Michael," she said.

"What?"

She chewed her lip nervously. She was wondering whether to share her fears with him. It might make his own burdens worse.

"Michael, do you feel safe?"

"Safe?" He smiled. "Of course I feel safe."

"It's just—everything seems strange," she said. "Those sick people out in Iowa. And now Dan Everhardt . . . everything seems so sinister."

He petted her gently.

"Bad things happen in the world," he said, "but that doesn't mean the sky is falling. Just hang in there, babe. That's all we can do. Everything will be all right."

"Do you think so?" Susan asked.

"I know so." His smile was confident and even playful, as though he knew a secret and was teasing her with it.

She raised her face to kiss him. She breathed in his warmth. There was a long pause while they lay in silence.

"Do you forgive me?" she asked at length.

"There's nothing to forgive." He kissed her lips. "Everything is going to be fine. You're going to be fine."

She nodded. "Thank you, Michael."

She didn't really feel reassured. But she did feel better. Michael always made her feel better.

The phone rang while Michael was in the shower. Naked, Susan darted into the hallway and picked it up.

"Hello?"

"Susan." The voice was female, low and somewhat husky.

"Yes?"

"Susan, I just wanted to let you know something."

"Who is this? There must be a mistake . . ."

"Susan, Dan Everhardt is not going to get well."

"I'm sorry? What did you say?"

"You heard me. Everhardt will not get well. The president is going to have to appoint a new vice president."

Susan saw herself in the hall mirror. Her hair was awry, her breasts still moist from her sex with Michael.

"I really don't understand . . . Who is this?" she asked.

"*Your husband* will be the president's choice, Susan."

"My husband? What are you talking about?"

"I just wanted you to know. We'll talk again soon."

"I—who is this? What are you talking about?"

A low laugh sounded on the line.

"You'll understand everything, Susan. In time."

The caller hung up.

Susan put down the phone. She stood for a moment looking at her naked image in the mirror. She crossed her arms over her breasts as though to hide them. Then she felt a sudden chill, and hurried back to the bed to wait for Michael.

9

Manchester, New Hampshire
November 24
11:30 A.M.

HIS NAME was Erroll, like the pianist.

They called him "Radio Flyer" because he was always talking about radio waves. Feeling them, hearing them, even seeing them.

He had been homeless for eleven years now, since they closed the state hospital. He slept in abandoned buildings, ate at shelters, and drank everything from Ripple to lighter fluid.

He carried an old Walkman he had found in the trash years ago. He was rarely seen without the little earphones in his ears. He usually had an intent, busy air about him as he dug into garbage cans, bent to collect scraps of newspaper, or, quite often, stood outside appliance stores staring at news broadcasts on display TV sets.

There were those who wondered if there was any sound coming through his famous earphones. "He doesn't need sound," said some. "He's got plenty of voices in his head."

Today, though, the twenty-four-hour all-news station was actually penetrating to Erroll's brain, for he had put new batteries into the Walkman two weeks ago and they were still running. He nodded knowingly as he listened to the news.

The two beat cops in their cruiser smelled him almost before they saw him. He had an unforgettable odor of stale sweat, urine, alcohol, and tooth decay. They were never glad to see him, for he was full of garbled stories of aliens who were bombarding him with waves.

"They weren't supposed to radiate me," he would say, "but there was a mix-up. They got the wrong guy. Now these rays are killing me, and I can't get them to stop."

Usually the cops took him to a shelter whose personnel then escorted him to a clinic where he got medication. But more often than not he didn't take the medication. He said it made him drool.

Today he shambled toward the cruiser with a bit more purpose than usual. As he approached the car he took off his earphones.

"Morning, Erroll," said the driver. "What's on your mind?"

"I found a dead body," he said.

"You found a body?" the driver asked.

"A dead person," he said. "Smells, too. Maybe a few days. Wait till you see the hands and feet."

"Hands and feet? What are you talking about, Erroll?"

The bum was visibly excited.

"I keep telling you guys. The men upstairs are making changes. I'm not the only one. Wait till you see the hands and feet."

"Where is it, Erroll?"

"In a Dumpster in the alley off Chestnut Street. Been there all morning."

The two cops looked at each other. They had long since learned not to attribute any truth to Erroll's pronouncements. But a body in a Dumpster was something that had to be checked out.

"Are you sure about this, Erroll?"

"As God is my judge. I told you there would be changes. I'm not the only one. Just wait till you see."

The driver sighed. "Okay, Erroll. Get in and you can show us."

They both wrinkled their noses at his smell after he got into the backseat. He gave them directions. They knew the alley well. Traffic was light, so they would be there inside five minutes.

The younger cop was in a happy mood and decided to make conversation with Erroll on the way.

"How've you been, Erroll?"

"Not so good this week. This pain in my joints . . . It's just arthritis. But the waves aggravate it."

"What waves?"

"The radio waves." Erroll took on a brooding look. "You can't just bombard healthy tissue with them. It plays hell with arthritis. I told them it can damage tissue. But nobody listens to me."

"Who did you tell, Erroll?"

"The new doctor over at the clinic. I'm sending some circulars around to the state health authorities, too, but I have to get a stamp first."

"What kind of stamp, Erroll?"

"A rate stamp. It tells your rate so they know how to sort the mail."

The cop turned around. "Rate? What sort of rate?"

"Your rate in the organization," Erroll explained. "I'm 513, but that's only because I missed my last review. You guys, you have it made. You're set for life. A cop, that's 915 or better. What I couldn't do with 915!" Erroll looked moodily at the buildings passing by the window.

"Uh-huh," the cop said, glancing at his partner with a meaningful look.

"But I'll get my rate back and more after today," Erroll said. "Just wait till you see. I told you there'd be changes."

"What kind of changes?" asked the driver.

"All kinds of changes," Erroll said darkly. "I told you, I'm not the only one. Everything is going to change."

The cruiser pulled into an alley between two rows of very old office buildings. The Dumpster was about halfway down.

"Is this it, Erroll?" the younger cop asked.

"Yeah. Let's go, let's hurry."

They stopped behind the Dumpster. Sighing, the two cops got out of the cruiser. One of them turned to Erroll when the smell hit his nostrils.

"Looks like you hit the jackpot, Erroll," he said. "I smell a popper, or I'm a monkey's uncle."

His partner looked nauseated. They approached the Dumpster. One cop lifted himself up to look inside while the other scanned the windows along the alley.

"Did you see anybody else?" he called to Erroll.

"Nobody. Not a soul."

The cop began shoving garbage out of the way, breathing through his mouth. He nodded to his partner. "Yeah, we got a cold one."

The second cop came to stand next to the Dumpster while the first one threw more garbage out of the way. Erroll could hear him sighing and gasping for breath. Something was clinging to his uniform, and he threw it off with a curse.

Then he stopped cold. He looked closer at the corpse.

"Jesus Christ."

"What's the matter?" asked the second cop.

"There's something wrong with the hands. Wait . . ."

He looked deeper, gasping in disgust. More garbage was thrown aside. Uncovered, the corpse filled the alley with the stench of decay.

Both cops looked somewhat sick, but Erroll breathed in the smell without blanching.

"Look at the feet," he said. "Go on."

The cop in the Dumpster rooted deeper and paused once again. He came up with wide eyes, looking at his partner.

"Look at this," he said.

The partner stood on tiptoe to look over the edge of the Dumpster. He took a long look, then looked back at Erroll.

"You saw this?" he asked.

"Of course I saw it," Erroll said. "Saw it first thing. That's why I came to get you. I told you there'd be changes. Didn't I? Didn't I predict this? You can see he's changed. Just look."

Both cops looked closely at the body. "Holy shit," one of them murmured.

Then the younger one got out, went back to the cruiser, and got on the radio to call for an ambulance.

"See?" Erroll said to the other cop. "Didn't I tell you? I told the docs too, but they wouldn't believe me, they just smiled. But you can see with your own eyes that it's the truth, can't you? Come on. Say so." Erroll was almost jumping up and down in his excitement.

The cop had finished on the radio. A distant siren was heard.

"What time did you say you found this, Erroll?" the older one asked.

"First thing this morning. Six, six-thirty."

"And you didn't see anyone around?"

"No one."

The other cop had returned. Both of them stood by the Dumpster, looking at each other and at Erroll.

"Did you ever see a thing like that?" the younger one asked.

"Never." The older cop was as shocked as the younger.

Erroll stood talking to them until the ambulance came. A paramedic got out and came up to them.

"What have you got?" he asked.

"Dead body," said the younger cop. "Discovered by this man early this morning."

"Is there something unusual?" the paramedic asked.

"Take a look at the hands and feet." The older cop stood back to give the paramedic room.

The paramedic stood on tiptoe, just as the cops had done. He took a long look, then turned back to the cops.

"Jesus Christ," he said.

"I told you," Erroll said happily.

The two cops and the paramedic glanced at Erroll. Then the paramedic called the emergency room at the hospital.

"We have a corpse with an odd deformity," he said. "I'm heading for the medical examiner's office. You might want to send someone over to observe."

They asked him something over the radio.

"The hands and feet don't look right," he said. "They're enlarged and deformed. You have to touch them to really see the difference. To me they don't even look human."

Erroll nodded, giggling. "I told you there'd be changes," he said, putting on his earphones.

10

Gary, Indiana
November 24

IN 1984 Colin Goss, already a giant in the pharmaceutical industry, found
that leftist terrorists had closed down his newest factory in Costa Rica. They
dynamited one of his buildings, killing twenty workers on a night shift. They
also threatened the local workers he had hired.

Goss had the manager of the facility complain to the authorities. They
promised to safeguard the security of the plant. Their promises were empty.
New terrorist attacks followed. The plant manager himself was kidnapped
and held for ransom. The leftist guerrillas demanded that Goss pay the ransom and take his business elsewhere.

Goss took matters into his own hands.

Two weeks after the kidnapping of Goss's plant manager, a group of
commandos led by professional soldiers whom Goss had hired at twice their
usual fee assassinated the leaders of the local guerrilla movement. All but
one, that is. The last was kidnapped from the small rural compound he used
as his hideout. His name was Gabriel Cabrera. A legend among local leftists,
Cabrera was the driving force of their movement.

The next week Cabrera was exchanged for the manager of Goss's plant.

From that time on the Goss operation was allowed to function in safety. A small army of security men, all trained commandos, remained in place to assure the plant's security and the safety of the workers.

One year to the day after the original assault on Goss's plant, Gabriel Cabrera was run over by a laundry van in San Isidro. The driver of the van disappeared before police arrived at the scene.

No leader of similar force was found to lead the guerrilla movement, which was set back a generation by Cabrera's death.

The Costa Rica episode had come to be known as "Colin Goss's *Godfather* story." He never mentioned it in public, and denied it when reporters asked if he had killed the terrorists intentionally. But it had assured his public image once and for all. Goss could accuse anyone he wanted of being soft on terrorism and know that the charge could never be leveled at him. He had paid his dues on that score.

Rumors still circulated to the effect that after the World Trade Center attack, Goss had offered to send a group of his own commandos to Afghanistan to locate and capture Osama bin Laden. His offer was refused, because the White House did not trust Goss to keep quiet about his role in the mission if it was successful, and because the political consequences would be terrible if Goss became a hero to the public. Not even the life of bin Laden was worth the risk of positioning Colin Goss to become president himself one day.

Tonight Goss arrived at a noisy rally being given for him in Gary, Indiana. The unruly crowd was made up largely of steelworkers, many of them out of work due to the deepening recession.

Goss's advance men had made no effort to quiet the crowd. On the contrary, the Goss people had projected images of chaos, violence, and hunger on huge video screens, so that by the time Goss was announced the mob was almost out of control.

This was a different Colin Goss from the mild, fatherly figure appearing in broadcast ads this fall. The only common link was the dark suit Goss wore as he strode quickly to the microphones.

"Goss! Goss! Goss!" the crowd roared. The rhythmic shout sounded like the pumping of a huge engine, pistons forcing out a hiss as steam escaped.

It took Goss several minutes to quiet the crowd sufficiently to make himself heard.

"We all know why we're here tonight," he said. "This is a new millennium, but the values we cherish haven't changed. We're here to remind ourselves about who we really are, and what kind of life we want for ourselves and our children. It's hard sometimes, isn't it? Hard to remember."

The crowd was silent now, listening intently.

"Hard to remember a time when neighbors lived in peace and helped each other when help was needed," Goss said. "A time when we could walk our streets in safety and enjoy the bounties of the greatest nation on earth. A time when love for one's fellow man was rewarded by peace and prosperity. That seems a long time ago, doesn't it?"

The crowd murmured its agreement.

"That was a wonderful world," Goss said. "It was built by people who loved freedom and wanted happiness and fulfillment, both for themselves and for their children. These people were builders. They still exist, all over this great country. But today they are besieged by another kind of human being. The kind that has no interest in building, but only in destroying. Do you know who I am talking about?"

"Yes!" The crowd answered in one voice.

"These people are not smart," Goss said. "They are not brave. They are not good. They don't know how to build or to create. But they do know how to hate. Do you know who I'm talking about?"

"Yes!" The crowd's response was louder.

"You know their faces," he said. "And you've heard their voices. They brag about the thousands of innocent men, women, and children they've murdered with their terrorist bombs. Even today, on your television screen, you can see them dancing in the streets carrying signs to celebrate the slaughter of eight hundred innocent children on an educational cruise."

As though on cue the screen behind Goss displayed the infamous mushroom cloud rising above the sparkling Mediterranean after the destruction of the *Crescent Queen*. The image was quickly followed by a now-familiar picture of pretty Gaye Symington, the most famous of the victims, standing on a diving board at a junior high school swimming meet. Water dripped from the curves of her blossoming adolescent body, making her look strangely vulnerable.

Goss paused to let the crowd remember the *Crescent Queen*.

"Why, these people have never built a thing in their lives. They've never created a thing or had an individual thought. Yet they take pride in murdering free people. The blood of innocent children is on their hands, but they're not ashamed of it. They're proud of it. They think their God is going to reward them for it. Do you know who they are?"

"YES!"

"They are cruel and brutal and heartless when they kill women and children," he said. "But they are cowards. What happens when you put them on a field of battle, with men to fight, instead of women and children? Watch them cringe, watch them hold up their hands, watch them run!"

A roar of anger surged through the crowd. The memory of surrendering Iraqi soldiers in Kuwait was fresh enough in American minds to join the image of Arab fanatics calling for the terrorist murder of civilians.

"And what happens when we capture them and drag them into our courts?" Goss asked. "They demand justice and mercy, in the name of our constitution and our laws. The same justice and mercy they denied their helpless victims."

He paused, surveying the crowd with his sharp eyes.

"And in this they remind us of our own terrorists," he said. "The ones you've seen in dark alleys, demanding your hard-earned money at the point of a gun or knife. The ones you've seen on street corners, too lazy to work for a living, waiting to corrupt your children. The ones you've seen cruising through poor neighborhoods in their gaudy cars, spraying bullets at imaginary enemies and killing the innocent. What do these people say when they are arrested and called to account for their crimes? They demand justice, they demand mercy."

A twisted smile curled Goss's lips.

"I wonder if the word *people* is really justified as a description of these creatures," he said. "For one thing, they are far too cruel to be called *people*. For another, they are far too cowardly to be called *people*. And they are certainly too dirty to be called *people*. Are they really human at all?"

"*NO!*" The crowd roared the word in one voice.

"Don't you find it funny, in a tragic sort of way, that we have allowed these animals to terrorize us, simply because we are *civilized*? That we have turned into lambs waiting for the slaughter, simply because we are too *civilized* to strike back at an enemy who wants to destroy us? Our own compassion has blinded us to the truth about these cowards. They take their courage and their swagger from our own weakness. At the first sign of strength from us, they run squealing for cover. For too long we've been too *civilized* to take a stand against them."

An invisible electricity held the crowd in silence.

"But that's all over now, isn't it?" Goss concluded. "The age of fear, the era of trembling, is over. No longer will we go about the business of freedom like victims. No longer will we wait like sheep in a pen for the wolf's next attack. This time it will be *us* attacking. And when the butcher runs for cover, we will run faster. We will catch him and destroy him. And when he falls to his knees and prays for mercy at the eleventh hour, what will we do to him?"

"KILL! KILL! KILL!"

"GOSS! GOSS! GOSS!"

The crowd surged this way and that, held in check with difficulty by the local police who were working alongside Goss's security staff. They shook their fists at the cameramen and reporters on the periphery of the crowd. Decades of downsizing in American business, along with the recent recession, fueled their rage. So did countless headlines about terrorist attacks, gang warfare, street crime, welfare fraud, school shootings, illegal drugs, and sexual permissiveness. Not to mention six months of nuclear terror on a scale not seen since the worst days of the Cold War.

The crowd did not have to sort out the manifold sources of its rage. Colin Goss focused it for them. With a sure touch developed over many years, he aimed their anger at a faceless mass of dirty, lazy, selfish, violent, and ultimately inhuman creatures who were responsible for the ills that beset society in the new millennium.

"*GOSS! GOSS! GOSS!*" came the chant, louder than ever now.

At the end the chaos was so great that Goss had to be escorted to his limousine by security men. It took forty-five minutes to disperse the crowd. Scattered incidents of violence would be reported in the nearby inner-city neighborhoods overnight, all of them directed at minorities.

Colin Goss was gone now, en route to his private jet and a speaking engagement in another city. But his message of hate remained behind him, as he knew it would. The legend "Time for a Change" loomed on the enormous video screens.

———

IN A pickup truck on a back road in rural Tennessee, three men were listening to Goss's speech on the radio.

"Fuckin' A," the driver said.

"No shit. Put that fucker in the White House and our problems are over." Rafe, riding shotgun, said this.

"Fucker knows what's happening," said the passenger in the middle, a slender out-of-work auto mechanic named Donny.

They were all unemployed, though Donny had been laid off only last month. Dick, the driver, was a construction worker who had not earned a cent in over a year. Rafe was an air conditioner repairman, out of work since the end of summer.

"Look," said Dick. "Look at this."

A young black boy, perhaps fourteen or fifteen, was walking along the shoulder of the road. He wore overalls and oversized running shoes. As the truck approached he looked over his shoulder without much interest.

Dick brought the truck to a sudden halt on the shoulder, scattering gravel into the weeds.

"Fucker," he said.

"Fucker!" his friends echoed.

They were all drunk. They had spent the night pouring down boilermakers at a country tavern. Their search for girls had been fruitless, and they had left in the truck with a bottle of cheap vodka and some Cokes, in time to hear Goss's speech on the radio as they cruised the farm fields.

They didn't need to talk over what was to happen. Rafe leaped from the passenger's seat and seized the black boy by his shoulders. Donny kicked the boy between the legs, whooping excitedly as a cry of pain came from the boy's lips.

"What did I do to you?" the boy cried. "Leave me alone."

Donny's fist crushed the boy's nose before he could say another word.

The boy fell to the gravel shoulder. Donny and Rafe crouched over him, fists flying, while Dick aimed kicks at his crotch, one after the other, methodically.

"Nigger."

"Fucker."

They would not have done it if they had been sober. Even drunk they would not have taken the risk had it not been for Goss's speech and their frustration at the tavern. But now they were out of control, beating the boy with all their strength. He squirmed and flailed under the blows, his struggles already getting weaker.

"Kill the fucker," said Dick.

The boy's eyes were beginning to glaze over. Rafe aimed a powerful kick at his undefended temple. Dick was kneeling to undo the boy's fly.

Then something happened.

Dick's hands froze in midair. His face, contorted in a grimace of hate, suddenly went blank. Off balance, he teetered and fell to the ground, his arms and legs rigid.

"Dick? Are you all right?"

Rafe and Donny paused to look at him. Rafe, assuming the black boy had injured Dick in some way, aimed a hard punch and hit his unprotected stomach. The boy screamed.

Donny bent to look at Dick. "Fucker passed out on us."

Rafe pushed Donny aside to get a better look at Dick, whose eyes were wide open. They were not the glazed eyes of a drunken man.

"Bullshit," Rafe said. "No way. He's not passed out."

The two men stood swaying over their friend, swearing inconsequentially as they wondered what had happened. They did not notice the black boy as he crept away into the thick brush.

"You don't think . . ." Rafe was scratching his head.

"Come on, don't bullshit me."

"You know . . . that thing . . . that sickness."

Donny looked closely at Dick's eyes. "Jesus."

"Let's get him to a hospital."

Rafe had jumped back in alarm. He seemed afraid of the inert body of his friend. He shook his hands as though to rid them of a contagion. "Fuck that. Let's get out of here. We'll call an ambulance."

They hopped into the truck, suddenly sober. Rafe gunned the engine. Spinning the wheels on the gravel, he got the truck onto the road and hit sixty within a few seconds.

The roar of the engine subsided. The only sound was the wind in the weeds. The black boy was nowhere to be seen. The motionless white man lay on the shoulder, where a passing farmer would notice him before dawn.

Rafe would fall into drunken sleep before dawn. When he failed to awaken by mid-afternoon, his brother would become alarmed and call 911.

By then Donny would already be in the hospital, a victim of the mystery disease like his two friends.

Washington
November 25

KAREN EMBRY was waiting for a news conference to be given by the director of the CIA.

The director was a political appointee who had played a crucial fundraising role in the president's narrow election victory. His background was in business and advertising. He had not expected to end up on the hot seat in his new job, though he was aware of the embarrassments suffered by the intelligence community over the past decade.

But the *Crescent Queen* explosion changed all that. The public held the CIA responsible for not anticipating the terrorist threat and taking steps to prevent attacks. The agency's fecklessness was one of the key issues cited by those who wanted a new administration in Washington.

So the director was on the defensive today as usual.

Karen had arrived at CIA headquarters a half hour early, and she studied her notes as other journalists set up video cameras and joked with each other. She had dressed carefully for the news conference. She knew the director liked women. She wore a fitted blazer with a short skirt. Her legs were her best feature, along with her eyes, and she knew how to show them off.

The director began the news conference with some routine details about the population of terrorists in European jails. His voice was hard to hear, and his syntax was slightly garbled as usual. Evasiveness had become part of his persona, like the character in Proust who became deaf when unwelcome things were being said to him.

He droned on as long as he dared and finally threw the session open to questions. Karen was the first reporter to raise her hand.

"As you know, sir," she began, "the intelligence community has not gotten to the bottom of the *Crescent Queen* disaster."

This question was not a surprise. But it was a sore point with the director.

"All I can tell you about that," he replied carefully, "is that we're investigating. We will bring those responsible for the attack to justice."

"All the major known terrorist organizations have denied involvement in the attack," Karen said. "Isn't that true, sir?"

"Yes, but we suspect their denials are in bad faith," the director replied.

"The intelligence services haven't been able to prove that any terrorist group had either nuclear weapons or the missiles to deliver them, isn't that true?" Karen asked.

"That's true."

"Have you considered the possibility that someone else was behind the attack?"

The director raised an eyebrow.

"What do you mean?" he asked.

"If we suppose for the sake of argument that none of the known terrorist groups was behind the incident," Karen said, "wouldn't it be possible that someone else built and delivered the bomb, knowing that the existing terrorist groups would fall under suspicion?"

The director did not know how to answer.

"We have no evidence that such a scenario is the correct one," he said.

"But if it were," she pursued, "how would you proceed?"

The director was thrown. His professional role was to sift through data and find the most clear and obvious answer. He had no time for unlikely hypotheses, and didn't really know how to deal with them.

"All I can tell you is that we're investigating all possibilities," he said. "The very fact that an outlaw organization possessed the technology to use a nuclear weapon"—he pronounced the word *nucular*—"against innocent civilians is a monstrous thing, a totally unacceptable thing. I guarantee you we will find out the truth behind the *Crescent Queen* disaster, and those responsible will be punished to the full extent of the law."

Karen waited while he answered a softball question from another reporter. Then she raised her hand again.

"The wire services are reporting an outbreak of illness in southern Tennessee that has features in common with last week's outbreak in Iowa," she said. "You're familiar with that, sir?"

"Yes, I am." The director had been informed as a matter of routine about the outbreaks in Iowa and Tennessee but had not given the matter much thought, since it was outside his field of expertise.

"Do you consider the outbreaks to be a public health concern?" Karen asked.

"Certainly. The public health people are looking into it."

"But not a terrorism concern."

"We have no reason to suspect that."

Karen pushed an errant lock of her dark hair away from her eyes.

"Let me ask you hypothetically, Mr. Director—suppose that terrorists possessed a chemical or biological weapon capable of affecting large groups of people in a short period of time. Do you think the radical terrorist organizations would shrink from using such a weapon on a mass scale?"

"I couldn't say for sure," the director replied. "But I would not like to find out. I want to be sure that none of the terrorist groups ever develops that capability."

"Do the outbreaks in Iowa and Tennessee put thoughts like this into your head?"

The director thought for a moment.

"They would if the disease we found there could be linked to any known toxin or pathogen."

"And it has not?"

"No, it has not."

"Are you saying, sir, that it is the same disease in both locations?"

"No, I'm not," the director replied with some irritation. "I'm only relating what I've been told by the public health authorities."

"You're saying that neither disease presents symptoms associated with known pathogens or toxins?"

"To my knowledge, neither. That's correct."

"What if a toxin or pathogen *as yet unknown* to the authorities had in fact been used?"

The director shrugged this off. "You're talking about a hypothesis for which we have no evidence. It's hard for me to comment about such things."

He made a point of calling on other reporters for the next several minutes. Karen let him get away with it, for she was confident he would look at her sooner or later. He had noticed her beauty.

When his eyes darted to her she pounced. "You're aware, Mr. Director, that Vice President Everhardt's illness is baffling the physicians at Walter Reed," she said. "Are you concerned that a man so important is ill, and nobody knows why?"

The director was taken off guard.

"I don't know that to be true," he said. "The doctors are evaluating the vice president's condition and giving him the best possible treatment. I don't know that they are 'baffled,' as you put it."

"But no one at Walter Reed or in the White House has been willing to comment on the situation," Karen said. "Don't you think the public has a right to know what the vice president is suffering from?"

The director frowned. "I'm not really the person for you to be asking about that," he said. "I'm not a physician, and I'm not close to the situation. I'd suggest you speak to the doctors."

"They're not talking."

The director was ruffled by Karen's questions. It had been a long time since he had been grilled this way by a reporter. Her questions were maddening because he didn't have good answers to any of them.

"Sources have told me," she pursued, "that the vice president's illness has features in common with the outbreaks in Iowa and Tennessee. Is there any truth to that?"

"None at all, to my knowledge," the director replied. "Miss Embry, at the risk of offending you, I think we should stick to the topic at hand."

"The topic, as I understand it, is terrorism," Karen countered. "It seems clear that terrorism and public health are two issues that can't be separated easily."

"Nor can they be connected easily," the director said. "Not without hard evidence."

He did not call on Karen again. The news conference petered out amid questions about the ongoing Chechen uprising in Russia and the India–Pakistan conflict.

As the reporters were packing up their equipment the director's press secretary appeared at Karen's side. A tall, handsome man who looked strikingly like a male model, he had kept a low profile during the news conference.

"I'm Mitch Fallon," he said, extending a hand. "Why haven't we met before?"

"I moved here from Boston last spring," Karen said. "I'm doing a series of articles on politics and public health issues."

"Well, it's good to have you here," he smiled. "However, I must say you seem to have a slight tendency toward the hypothetical."

She smiled. "Back in the eighties, who could have guessed that the money being used to support the Contras in Nicaragua was coming from Ronald Reagan through the Ayatollah Khomeini? Sometimes the wildest hypothesis is less strange than the truth."

"I have to agree with you there."

He studied the young reporter. Her look of permanent skepticism seemed superimposed over a face that, at rest, would have communicated something quite different. Something soft and even girlish that she had long since renounced.

"Do you have any evidence for your theories about the *Crescent Queen*?" he asked. "I mean, about terrorists having the capacity to make and deliver nuclear weapons."

There it was again—*nucular*. Karen had to suppress a smile. Was Fallon mispronouncing the word out of loyalty to his boss? There was no way to know.

"No." She shook her head. "It's just a possibility I've been wondering about. I thought it was strange that all the known terrorist organizations denied being involved. Something about that had a ring of truth. They're ruthless people. They don't care about public opinion. They wouldn't lie about a thing like that."

"What about the illness in Iowa, and the Tennessee problem?" he asked. "What got you interested?"

"I try to keep tabs on the news from the various public health organizations," she said. "I just thought the stories sounded strange. I've done articles on the major viruses, HIV and Ebola and Marburg and so on. I flew out to Iowa a couple of days ago, by the way."

"Did you learn anything?"

"A little, here and there."

He was looking at her with apparent admiration for her beauty, though she sensed a harder scrutiny behind it.

"What evidence do you have that such a thing might be intentional?" he asked.

"None," she said, not taking her eyes off him.

"What makes you think the connection is even possible?" he asked.

"It seems to me that it's just a matter of time," she said. "If you look at the terrorist activity over the last couple of decades—Lockerbie, Oklahoma City, the World Trade Center, and of course the *Crescent Queen*—it's obvious that the terrorists have been coming into possession of better and better technology. They're not the old-fashioned bomb-in-the-suitcase types. They're twentieth-century men, like everybody else. And with countries like Iraq and Libya stockpiling chemical and biological weapons, it seems to me almost inevitable that sooner or later we're going to see a terrorist attack employing such weapons."

"A scary thought," he said.

"But not unrealistic," she replied. "The terrorists don't care much about human life. They do what they think they have to do to achieve their ends. As I say, some things are only a matter of time."

"But you don't have any evidence that the time is now," he probed.

"No." She shook her head.

There was a pause. Fallon nodded to a female reporter who was hurrying past with a cameraman in tow. Something about the nod seemed a bit too familiar for a high-level official's press secretary. Karen suspected Fallon was a ladies' man. She filed away her intuition for future reference.

"Well," he said. "Nice talking to you."

"If it was possible to make a person sick for political purposes," she said, "Vice President Everhardt would probably be a good choice, given the current circumstances. Don't you think so?"

Fallon smiled. "You certainly do have a tendency toward the hypothetical," he observed.

"Think about it a moment," she went on, undaunted. "Everhardt was the ideal running mate for the president five years ago. He was chosen over a lot of other possible candidates, and the process of selection took a long time. Now, just like that, he's out of the picture."

"That's true."

"The administration has been struggling in the polls, with all these calls for the president to resign," Karen said. "Now, with Everhardt removed, the pressure will probably increase. The administration looks weaker than ever."

Fallon nodded. "Maybe."

"Suppose for the sake of argument that Everhardt was eliminated intentionally," Karen suggested.

"That's a heck of a supposition," Fallon observed.

"Far-fetched or not," the reporter said, "suppose it was true. Unlikely things happen in the world, don't they? Think of the Kennedy assassination. Nobody saw it coming. And the ripple effect was enormous. The whole course of our history . . ."

As a CIA man Fallon bristled at the mention of the Kennedy assassination.

"I'm afraid I'm out of time, Miss Embry. I wish you good luck with your theories."

"Call me Karen." She held out a hand. Mitch Fallon was a person she had to be nice to.

"Karen, then. Call me Mitch. Keep in touch. Nice to meet you."

"Same here," she smiled. "I'll be around."

He watched her walk away from him. She moved with firm strides, her body lithe and athletic. *The young female animal at the peak of her powers and her attractiveness,* he thought. If she was this intense on the job, what must she be like between the sheets?

He stopped in at the director's office on his way back to his own office.

"Did you talk to her?" the director asked.

"Yes."

"What does she have?"

"Nothing, except an overactive imagination. As far as I can see."

"Keep your eye on her."

"I will, sir."

The director turned his back.

Karen arrived home an hour after the news conference. Before turning on the computer to write down her notes, she rewound the tape on her office VCR and checked the last hour of news. An item immediately caught her eye.

"Health authorities in Australia are concerned about a tiny Aborigine village deep in the outback where a strange and crippling illness has broken out. Over a hundred villagers are unable to speak or move. Others, according to doctors on the scene, have died of the disease, which was apparently not reported at first because of the remoteness of the village."

A video image of one of the victims was displayed behind the commentator. It was a close-up, surprisingly eloquent, of an Aborigine girl, perhaps seventeen years old, whose eyes looked unseeing into the camera. The eyes were macabre. They looked hypnotized from within.

Karen dropped her notes and looked long and hard at the TV screen.

She had seen that look before. On the face of a six-year-old child in Iowa.

THE GIRL is bound to an apparatus which resembles a couch or examining table, tilted sharply toward the floor. Her skin glows against the black leatherette, the more so because of the light shining down from above. Her eyes are open, but she seems to sleep like the princess in the fairy tale. Her hair is blond. It is in disarray and hangs over her left cheek, obscuring much of her face.

Her hands are bound by rings fixed under the seat. Her legs are not bound, but because of the shape of the apparatus she assumes the crouch as a natural position. Her knees are bent, the thighs approximately vertical, the calves angled toward the floor. It is just possible for the eye to see that her toenails are painted, though the color does not come through from this vantage point.

Her left breast is clearly visible, pushed against the leatherette. The outline of her ribs is seen under the skin of her side. Her arms are long and slender.

There is something pathetic about her bound posture, but also something provocative. Her pelvis is the center of focus. The gradual upward thrust of the back leads to it, as does the vertical line of the thighs. The curve of her buttocks is given optimum shape and tension by her bound posture. She looks like a princess, but not one garbed in silk and brocade. Hers is the nobility of nudity.

There is movement, there is sound. A shadow approaches from the right, moving slowly. The girl sees nothing. As the shadow comes closer there are calls from the distance, and laughter. She does not hear. Or rather, if she hears she does not move a muscle to show that she hears.

The shadow is next to her now, a hand outstretched. The music builds toward its crescendo. The voices call out urgently.

Now the hanging cord is seen, dangling from the other hand. Slender, tufted at the end, it moves along the wall, swinging slightly as it approaches her. The voices call out encouragement. Uncertain, hesitant, the shadow dangles. Then it falls over the naked buttocks. The girl's empty eyes do not say whether she is aware of the approach or not. Is it obliviousness or terror that freezes her?

The shadow swings this way and that. The voices call out. The female flesh waits passively.

Suddenly everything stops. The poised shadow does not move. The girl is a statue. The voices are cut off. The hanging tail is an inch from her crotch. But nothing moves. All is still.

A sound is heard. A gasp, perhaps a cry of anguish.

Darkness falls. Girl, shadow, wall, disappear like magic.

The scene is ended, until next time.

1 3

Sydney, Australia
November 27

KAREN EMBRY'S plane landed at four-thirty in the morning, Australia time, after a total of twenty-three hours spent in the air.

It had taken lengthy politicking with her agent to get him to agree to this journey. She had told him much—but not all—that she had learned about the mystery illness. Sensing a book in the offing, he had finally given in.

Karen could not sleep on airplanes. By the time she arrived she had not slept in a day and a half. She had powerful uppers in her purse, given to her by a fellow reporter who was a speed addict. But she hadn't taken any. So far the scent of a story was enough to keep her alert.

She took a local flight to Perth, and then a chartered Cessna into the outback, landing on an airstrip seemingly a thousand miles from nowhere.

According to the reports she had read, the mystery disease had gone undiscovered for a couple of months or more. It had not spread beyond the small tribe of Aborigines, but it had killed most of them and incapacitated the rest. There were only about fifteen survivors, most of them quarantined in a health clinic.

The reports about the illness were garbled, no doubt because of the remote location and the victims' suspicion of the authorities. However, in one somewhat obscure report an Aborigine from a neighboring village had said, "When the people neared death, their feet and hands became hard and large, like the hoofs of animals." This had made Karen decide to see the syndrome for herself.

This would make a tremendous feature story, she thought. She could scale it up for the scientific journals, and simultaneously hype it with more dramatic wording for the popular media. If it was true that the disease involved bizarre deformities, the story could be important.

In the Land Rover Karen gazed for a few moments at the vast expanse of scrub land, punctuated by eucalyptus and occasional acacias. Then she opened the report, which included the testimony of the neighboring villager.

"The people became silent and rigid. Those who were standing up remained standing until they fell. Those who were sitting did not move until fatigue and weakness made them fall over. They would not speak. They seemed stubborn and did not move. Then they became sick."

Karen furrowed her brow in concentration. She twirled a strand of her dark hair with a finger. She barely noticed the exotic scenery around her, or the bumps and lurches of the Land Rover on the dirt roads.

The driver dropped her at the tiny hospital where the sick Aborigines were being treated. It was a battered old frame building that huddled under a shabby growth of gum trees. Emus languidly patrolled the scrub in search of small rodents. It was incredibly hot.

The doctor in charge was a tired-looking man in late middle age. His name was Dr. Roper.

"Thank you for seeing me," Karen said. "I hope my timing isn't too terrible."

"I'm glad you got here quickly," he said. "I'm afraid there isn't much time left. Of the fifteen villagers we brought in, twelve are already dead. The three still living are critical."

"Can I see them?" Karen asked.

"Sure. But you'll have to put on a hot-zone suit. We're still not sure whether the disease is communicable, and we're not taking chances."

He sent her to a nurse who helped her put on a decontamination suit. She accompanied the doctor to a quarantine ward where the three remaining patients were being kept. All were attached to life-support systems, tubes connecting them to electronic machines of surprising sophistication for this remote region.

"They're completely comatose and unresponsive," the doctor told her. "They were that way when they came in. The vital signs have been steadily weakening. We've been concentrating on keeping them breathing and supporting the heart rate, but there's nothing more we can do. They're simply dying."

The faces of the three Aborigines, one woman and two men, were wasted. Their dark skin seemed gray as death approached.

"As far as we can tell," the doctor said, "the progress of the disease was much faster in the children than in the adults, and slightly faster in the women than in the men. But it's hard to speculate with any accuracy. No one reported the outbreak until almost everybody was dead."

Karen was looking at the sheets covering the hands and feet of the dying Aborigines. They were suspiciously distended.

"May I look?" she asked.

"Get ready for a shock," the doctor said. "This isn't easy to look at."

He pulled back the sheet from the female patient. The hands were grossly distended and distorted. It looked as though the fingers had fused together in a gelatinous mass. But when Karen touched the left hand on the invitation of the doctor, it was hard. It had the appearance of amber, but darker, more opaque.

"We've done biopsies," the doctor said. "It's not like anything I've ever seen before. The cell structure looks human, but the tissue is a morphological monstrosity."

He pulled back the sheet to show Karen the foot. It was even more distorted than the hand. The toes were fused, and the front of the foot had pulled back toward the heel, creating a bizarre hooflike impression.

"Apparently the distortion comes on not long before death," the doctor said. "Those who died the quickest had less deformation than those who lasted longer. Whatever the cause and mechanism are, we haven't got a clue. My colleagues are talking along the lines of Elephant Man's disease, acromegaly, things like that."

Karen was looking more closely at the distorted foot. "Or some sort of scleroderma," she said. "Or perhaps one of the collagenous tissue diseases like dermatomyositis or even lupus erythematosus."

The doctor raised an eyebrow, impressed by Karen's knowledge.

"Are you a physician yourself?" he asked.

"No."

He took her to a makeshift pathology lab in an adjoining building. There were bodies of several villagers there, women and children as well as men. The macabre hooflike fusion and distension of the hands and feet were obvious in all the cases. In the two children it looked particularly cruel and unsettling.

"Were there other physical changes?" Karen asked. "Internally, I mean." Karen knew enough physiology to know that a change as bizarre as the distorted extremities of these victims had to be accompanied by some sort of massive anomaly at the cellular level.

"We're not equipped to deal with that here," the doctor told her. "The pathologists in Adelaide are working on the two patients we sent there. I'll give you their names. They're doing complete autopsies with cell studies. They may have something for you."

Back in his office the doctor showed Karen a strange object, apparently fashioned out of clay. It was a doll or talisman in the shape of a person with enlarged hands and feet.

"This was made by the medicine man," he said. "It was found by one of the health officers in the village. We think it represents the illness. Apparently the medicine man tried to use the icon to propitiate the gods."

Karen held the object in her hands. Though crudely designed, it radiated a sort of force, born obviously of the medicine man's intense faith. The creature held out its oversized hands as though in a gesture of acknowledgment, or perhaps prayer.

"Have you ever seen an icon like this before?" she asked.

The doctor shook his head. "Never."

He wrote down the names of the physicians in Adelaide who were working on the bodies. Karen thanked him and went to a small lodge that catered to hunters, hikers, and the occasional brave tourist who came to this remote area. On the way the driver pointed out a wombat that Karen was not quick enough to see as it waddled out of sight in the brush. Rock wallabies, some carrying infant joeys in their pouches, were surprisingly plentiful.

Her exhaustion and jet lag were catching up to her now. She had difficulty filling out the guest form. By the time she reached the little cabin where she was to sleep, she was moving slowly and her eyelids were drooping.

She left her overnight bag and briefcase unopened on the floor and lay down on the bed. The old comforter that covered it smelled of mothballs and stale food, but to Karen it felt wonderful. The minute she closed her eyes dreams began to crowd against the conscious thoughts in her mind. She breathed deeply, floating mentally over the impressions of the last ten days. It had been a busy time, full of breaking stories, garbled rumors, and well-kept secrets.

A distant motor coughed into life. A dog barked. The calls of strange birds sounded far away. Dream thoughts transported Karen to the bed of her childhood, with its colorful afghan and stuffed animals. She reached out reflexively for the blue teddy bear that no longer existed.

She plummeted quickly toward deep sleep. Her dreams took her further and further from this time and place, as though she were on a magic carpet. But something woke her up suddenly. She lay rubbing her burning eyes and looking at the unfamiliar room. What had awakened her?

Hands and feet.

She got out of bed with a sigh and went to her briefcase. She took out the portable computer and turned it on. She clicked through the various folders, searching for something she could not quite remember. She cursed herself for not finding better titles for her icons. It was time consuming to open them one by one, searching for a mere hint or an overheard clue.

Then, fighting off sleep, she remembered. She closed a folder, opened another one, and found the icon she was looking for.

"Jesus," she said.

She called the airline, made a reservation for tomorrow night, and made a note of it on her computer's desktop.

She would go to Adelaide first thing tomorrow morning and see what she could learn from the pathologists there.

Then she would fly to New Hampshire.

After looking at her watch she lay down under the comforter and closed her eyes. There was time for a few hours' sleep.

Hands and feet, she thought. *Hands and feet.*

Exhaustion put her under before the thoughts in her mind could produce insomnia. But the dreams that filled her sleep were cruel and frightening.

Atlanta, Georgia
November 27

DAMIAN LIGHTFOOT was cleaning up the trash.

Not physical trash, of course. Damian was a computer technician hired by the Corporation to assay and discard the vast amounts of unneeded and out-of-date files that collected in the company computers. It had to be done carefully. Ninety-five percent of the time the files and documents earmarked for trashing by the various research departments were useless. But once in a while a file or group of files found its way into the trash by accident and had to be double checked with the department concerned. More than once a crucial bit of research had been saved in this manner, either by Damian Lightfoot or by his predecessors.

The trash-management job was not very high paying, and was certainly not fun. It was pure drudgery. You assayed the vast quantities of trash, looking for markers that had been agreed upon in the current quarter to identify outmoded files to be trashed. When you found a file that wasn't clearly marked you saved it in a special quadrant and queried the departments involved. Usually it took them days to answer you, for the scientists looked upon the computers as their slaves, and the computer techs as idiots. Sometimes you had to send a dozen memos before they bothered to acknowledge you.

Of course you had to clear every major decision with Security. The Corporation faced stiff competition from other companies around the country and overseas. The research files were a key target, and computer invasion was the preferred line of attack. A computer security firm revamped the entire system every three months, and their staffers were always available for advice or clarification.

Damian was drinking his ninth Coke of the day and listening to Metallica through his earphones when he found the file with the strange name. Project 4. He had never seen it before.

He held the file and tried searching through various sectors of the database for the name. A drug? A chemical? No dice. No trace of it anywhere.

He didn't trash it. He was paid to always hold back until he got confirmation.

Out of curiosity he tried to open the file. A message appeared on the screen: THE FILE YOU HAVE TRIED TO OPEN REQUIRES SECURITY CLEARANCE. PLEASE TYPE IN YOUR NAME AND DESIGNATION.

Shrugging, Damian did as he was told.

PLEASE WAIT FOR SECURITY ACKNOWLEDGMENT, said another message.

Damian turned up the music and waited, sipping at his Coke. It was lunchtime, and he was hungry. He had a date to go out for lunch with one of the girls from the front office, a girl who was too new to know about Damian yet. Had she had one more week she would have been warned off him, but he had gotten to her while she was new.

Personally he didn't think he was that strange. True, he had certain tastes in food and music that made others uneasy. But he led a comparatively normal life, and he didn't want anything sexual that was different from what anybody else wanted. He still didn't understand why that girl Cynthia, from accounting, had taken such a dislike to him on their one date. She had badmouthed him to everybody within shouting distance. In a company of this size, that was quite damaging.

He waited in front of the screen, sighing, listening to his stomach grumble. This had to be an error. They had probably misnamed the file.

He finally decided to get a bag of potato chips from the machine next door. He would simply leave the computer waiting. It would only be a minute or less.

He got up, still wearing his earphones, and went to the door. It opened before he could touch the knob. A man in civilian clothes—dark suit, tie, brown shoes—stood in the doorway.

The man said something, but Damian couldn't hear him because of the music.

"What?" Damian asked, pulling one of the buds from his ear.

"Are you Damian?" asked the man. Damian noticed now that he wasn't wearing a company badge.

"Yeah. What can I do for you?"

"You found a file?"

"Yeah." Damian turned to gesture at the screen. "Can't open it. Never saw the name before. Are you security?"

"Yes."

The man had closed the door with a glance into the corridor.

"Show me," he said.

"Here." Damian leaned over the screen. "Look for yourself. It's not in any of the directories."

The man leaned over Damian's shoulder. He gave off a faint scent of after-shave and tobacco. The name *Project 4* was in the middle of the screen.

"Are you sure?" the man asked. "Did you try QPC?"

Damian laughed. "What's QPC?"

But the man's arm had curled around Damian's neck while he was turning to ask the question. The breath was squeezed out of Damian's body. He felt his muscles tense, his arms and legs flailing this way and that. Then there was a sharp *crack!* as the arm broke his neck, and a spreading red wave swept over his vision, blinding him.

He was dead before he hit the floor.

1 5

November 28

THE SUBJECT was in a traditional hospital bed set up in a special room full of monitors, not terribly different from a room for a patient on the critical list in any modern intensive care unit. Monitors for the usual vital signs— blood pressure, respiration, pulse rate, and so on—were against the walls, connected to the subject by wires. In addition, however, there were more sophisticated machines that monitored less obvious physical processes. There were also video cameras timed to keep a constant watch on the subject's physical appearance.

Two men in white coats were standing beside the bed. Both wore stethoscopes. The younger man had surgical gloves on.

"How are we doing?" the older man asked.

"Vital signs slowly decreasing," the other man said. "He's in coma now. Respiration shallow, heart rate uneven. I suspect heart failure may be the proximate cause of death."

"Other vital signs?"

"Liver and kidney function well below normal. Hematocrit reflecting cellular and other changes."

"What about the EEG?"

The younger man held up a printout. "Brain waves are our best signature," he said. "The spikes and valleys form a definite pattern that never seems to vary. It's clearly not a healthy pattern, yet it's quite consistent."

The older man looked for himself. "Interesting," he said. "I wonder what's going on in there. What kind of mentation, if any."

"There's no evidence of any sense perception," the younger man said. "No response to sound, touch, or anything else."

"But there was in the early phase."

"Oh, yes." The younger man nodded. "Perception was virtually normal at that point. As to what kind of thinking went on, that we can't measure, because the subject is paralyzed by the changes."

"How does he fit the time frame?"

"From intake? A textbook case," the younger man said. "The onset of symptoms was within twelve to fifteen hours. Then the first phase of the syndrome lasted pretty much unchanged for about two to three weeks. Then we had the dramatic dip in brain function, leading to coma after another week. The first physical changes didn't occur until coma was well under way."

"I find that fascinating," the older man said. "How do you account for it?"

"I can't," replied the younger man. "Not even our own research explains the details of it. The precise curve of the paralysis, the changes at the cellular level, and their sequelae—it will take a lot of research to objectify all that."

"Well," the older man said thoughtfully, "that's the way it goes sometimes. Most of the time, in fact. Psychiatrists never did understand why shock treatment works as it works. Most drugs, too—you get your desired result, you watch for side effects, and sometimes you never know the real mechanism."

The younger man nodded. "In any case, we're seeing a great consistency in the timing of the onset and progress. Almost like clockwork. Faster in children, somewhat faster in women."

"Let's look at the main map."

The younger man turned on a video monitor connected to a mainframe computer. A special program had been designed to assay the various tissue groups, always with specific reference to one molecular factor. The present display showed the bone marrow.

"As you see," the doctor said, pointing to the screen, "our change is in place."

"Excellent," the older man observed.

"The modifications are reflected clearly at the cellular level. You can't entirely extrapolate from this to the symptoms—our knowledge doesn't extend that far—but a glance at the numbers makes it obvious. The body is giving itself different instructions. The cells are trying to follow them, but of course the body isn't made to do that. So you have massive dysfunction, starting at the cognitive level and spreading through all the systems."

"I see." The older man looked from the screen to the experimental subject in the bed. "The skeletal was affected from the start, but not visible until now."

"That's correct. The biopsies we did on this subject made that very clear."

"Fascinating," the older man said. "The mystery of life."

"Yes, sir. Life's attempt to adjust itself to changes."

"Kind of makes you wonder whether there is a God after all," the older man said. "Only a transcendent power could design something so subtle."

The younger man nodded a bit uncomfortably.

The older man pointed to the sheet. "Let's have a closer look."

The younger man pulled the sheet up from one side, folding it over the subject's chest. The left hand was revealed, grossly distended and already considerably distorted. The skin was darkened, and already harder than healthy cartilage.

The older man lifted the arm from the elbow to get a better look. The fingers were still identifiable, though they were losing definition. What had once been the fingernails seemed to have fused with the hardened skin tissue.

"Amazing," the older man said. "Like chitin, isn't it?"

"To the touch, yes," the younger man said. "But the cell structure is closer to what we see in human bone or cartilage."

"An amazing effect," the older man said. "Let's see the foot."

He bent to look at the left foot, whose distention and distortion exceeded that of the hand. The toes were enlarged, hardened, and beginning to lose definition. The heel and toes were being pulled together by the progressive deformation, fusing gradually into a single hard platform.

"Pretty clear morphological difference from the hand," the older man said.

"Definitely," nodded his companion. "Just as you will see a differentiation in any hoofed animal from the rear to the front."

The older man tapped the sole of the foot with his knuckle. A dry, hollow sound emerged.

"Fascinating," the man observed, "how consistent it is, from subject to subject."

"Oh, yes. It never varies. It's the signature of the syndrome," the younger man said. "Quite amazing."

The older man smiled. "I wonder what they'll call it," he said. "When they get around to it."

The younger man shrugged. "That's not my department."

"I hope they pick something with a little poetry in it," the older man said with a smile. "Something people will remember."

"Yes, sir." The younger man nodded a bit weakly.

"By the way," the older man said, "I heard we had a small accident yesterday."

"That's right." His companion nodded. "It was a computer glitch. One of the special files leaked out into the network."

"What was the young man's name again?"

"Lightfoot. Damian Lightfoot."

"He wasn't security, was he?"

"No, sir. Just a computer tech. Trash management. He reported the file because he wasn't familiar with the name."

"No problem about disposal?" the older man asked. "Family? Colleagues?"

"Security took care of it already. There won't be a body. He simply disappeared."

"Good." The older man was shaking his head. "But we can't allow leaks, no matter how small. I want the system redesigned immediately. An accident like that should have been discovered within the loop. Company population is just as dangerous as general population." He gave the younger man a sharp look. "Get on it with your people this afternoon."

"I'll do that, sir."

The older man stood looking at the subject in the bed. His frown faded, eclipsed by his enthusiasm for the project.

"Something with poetry," he repeated. "Like the Black Plague . . ."

1 6

The White House
November 28

A MEETING was held Monday evening in the Oval Office.

Present were the president and his top aides, along with chief of staff Dick Livermore, who had been the president's campaign manager in the general election two years ago. Also present were the party chairman and the majority leader.

The president greeted those present with an uncharacteristically grave face.

"I know you're all concerned first and foremost about Danny," he said. "I saw him this afternoon at Walter Reed, and I spoke at some length with Dr. Isaacson. There isn't any good news to report. Danny's condition hasn't improved. His vital signs are still okay, but mentally he's nonfunctional."

The president had taken off his suit jacket and was resting his muscular forearms on the table. He did not like jackets or long-sleeved shirts; they made him feel constrained. For nearly twenty years his campaign ads had shown him in short-sleeved shirts with his tie loosened. Though some thought it was a PR gimmick intended to make him look hardworking, the fact was he actually dressed that way.

In answer to the polite murmurs of inquiry from those present, the president shook his head.

"I think we'd better look to the bottom line on this," he said. "There may be hope for Danny from a medical viewpoint, but even if he gets better, this episode will be too great a negative for us to overcome, given the polls and our other problems."

The chief PR consultant raised a hand. "I'm afraid you're right," he said. "The media are already on to the fact that Danny is catatonic. We couldn't overcome that in a fight against Goss."

The president nodded. "The first order of business, then, is for me to choose someone else as soon as decently possible. With Goss gaining in the polls we can't let the grass grow under our feet."

It was well known that the president loathed Colin Goss and would do anything in his power to keep Goss out of the White House. The president couldn't say anything publicly about Goss at this sensitive time, but he had told more than one close associate that he believed Goss was a potential Hitler. "If he ever gets into the Oval Office," he once said, "he'll make Nixon look like a wise king."

A few moments were spent discussing when and how to announce the dropping of Dan Everhardt as vice president and the selection of a replacement. Then the real problem came to the fore. Who could replace Everhardt?

The president turned the floor over to Bob Corrigan, the party chairman.

"I have a list here," Bob said. "We've gone over this with the president already, but I want your collective take on it. I give the names in no particular order." He cleared his throat a bit nervously. "The first is Kirk Stillman."

"Isn't he too old?" someone said.

There was a silence. Kirk Stillman was one of the most distinguished statesmen alive. A cabinet officer under three presidents and currently ambassador to the United Nations, Stillman was the Averell Harriman of his time. A specialist in foreign policy with superb contacts in all the major European governments, Stillman was all but indispensable to his party.

But Stillman was sixty-four years old, and looked it. With his silver hair and elder-statesman demeanor, he seemed more an icon of the past than a leader for the future.

"He's respected," someone said unenthusiastically.

"But he's a little too old." It was Bob Corrigan who said this. "It would send the wrong message."

Heads nodded in agreement. Stillman was associated in the public mind with the policies of the past. Policies that had failed to anticipate or prevent the current crisis.

After a few minutes Stillman was ruled out. Though he would make a superb vice president and could, in a pinch, ably take over as an interim president, he would be a public relations liability. The president needed a nominee with a more aggressive image. Someone younger, stronger.

"The next name," Corrigan said, "is Cary Hunsecker."

There was a beat of silence.

"He's a good man," someone said.

"Solid," echoed another voice.

Those present seemed troubled. There was good reason for this. Cary Hunsecker, serving his second term as governor of Rhode Island, had the image of strength and dash that a man like Kirk Stillman lacked. An avid sailboater who had competed in the Americas Cup and nearly won, Hunsecker was tanned and handsome.

But Hunsecker had sexual skeletons in his closet. His marriage to the daughter of a wealthy Rhode Island industrialist was emotionally barren. Hunsecker had had many affairs over the years, and showed a preference for younger females. A former campaign worker had threatened to file a paternity suit against him a decade ago, but had been talked out of it by influential Hunsecker friends.

So far the public knew nothing of this aspect of Hunsecker's life. But it would be foolish to suppose Hunsecker could face the cruel spotlight of the media as a potential vice president without having his past exposed. The press was not as easy to manipulate today as it had been a generation ago. The experiences of Bill Clinton, Bob Livingston, and others left no doubt about this.

"Too dangerous," said someone. Heads nodded in assent. Hunsecker was out.

"Okay," Corrigan said. "Before I proceed to the next name, I wonder if any of you has a suggestion."

"What about Mike Campbell?" one of the staffers threw in.

"In eight years," someone replied immediately.

"I'm not so sure," the staffer said. "He's solid with the public, and he's got so many positives . . ."

"You mean the Olympics?" someone asked. Michael Campbell's heroism in winning two Olympic gold medals despite serious back problems was universally known.

"And his wife," someone else added. Susan Campbell was the darling of American women. No other American politician had a wife whose own popularity could help as much at the polls.

"She could detract just by being so visible," a third voice added. "And don't forget, they're childless. That could be a negative at this level."

"Yeah, but she's kept her figure."

"I'll take that negative any time." Laughter greeted this remark.

The president was shaking his head. "Goss would label him a punk," he said. "I don't think we could get away with it."

His comment brought general assent. Michael Campbell was simply too young to take over as vice president. His youth would be perceived as a weakness, and would be sold that way by the Goss forces. The nominee had to project strength, experience, and wisdom.

"I like Mike," said the president, "but putting him up too early might be as bad for his future as for us. It's too risky."

Heads nodded in agreement. Campbell was out.

"There is only one name left," Corrigan said tiredly. "Tom Palleschi."

The others brightened. Tom Palleschi was the current secretary of the interior and former governor of Pennsylvania. Palleschi had been a cabinet officer under two presidents, one from each party. That was part of his appeal, the fact that he had served both parties successfully over the years. He got along with everybody, was a hard worker, and enjoyed excellent popularity with the public.

Another plus for Palleschi was that he was a self-made multimillionaire in business. He had built his father's one-man metalworking business into a precision tool empire before selling it to a German consortium when he first went into politics. He could credibly compare his own business experience to that of Colin Goss. No one could accuse Palleschi of being a bleeding heart.

Palleschi was a strong man of fifty-two with lively salt-and-pepper hair, a thick wrestler's body, and a winning smile. He could be seen jogging around Washington every morning from six to seven, sometimes with a friend or colleague but often alone. A few years ago he had endorsed an orthopedically advanced running shoe in a series of TV commercials, donating the money he made to a children's hospital in his hometown of Scranton.

Had it not been for the great popularity of Dan Everhardt, Tom Palleschi might have been the president's choice for his running mate five years ago. True, Palleschi was a bit too ethnic in his appeal. A Catholic, he was the father of six children and devoted a lot of his time to Italian-American causes. Not that this was a serious negative, but it did limit his performance in the demographic polls. He was a bit more popular with ethnic minorities than with WASPs. He knew little about terrorism and was not thought of as politically "tough." He was a peacemaker, appealing but not quite as forceful as the party would have liked.

Palleschi would make a fine choice to replace Dan Everhardt. He projected not only wisdom and experience, but also physical strength—a necessity at this moment when fear of illness was sweeping the nation.

"I like this choice," said Corrigan.

"So do I," the president agreed. "I've worked with Tom in the past, and he's steady as a rock."

These remarks brought general assent. Tom Palleschi was like another Dan Everhardt, but with a slightly different profile. He looked the part of a popular vice president. He also looked the part of president of the United States, if one added a brush stroke or two to his image.

Best of all, there was not a breath of scandal about Palleschi. His business career was spotless, and so was his personal life. He was faithful to his wife and devoted to his family.

For the next twenty minutes Palleschi's strengths and weaknesses were weighed by those present. But the palpable air of relief in the room left little doubt he would be the president's choice. A good choice.

"Let's float it around town," the president concluded. "Meanwhile I'll call Tom and bring him in."

On this note the meeting ended. The White House strategists were pleased. It was possible to chalk off Dan Everhardt's illness as a medical emergency and a personal tragedy. But Everhardt's loss need not cripple the administration. Palleschi made up for Everhardt.

That is, assuming Palleschi accepted the job.

Manchester, New Hampshire
November 28

THE HEALTH authorities in Adelaide refused to talk to Karen, despite her recommendation from Dr. Roper in the outback. They seemed cold and evasive, and distinctly unhappy to have heard from her.

This made her next mission all the more important. She retraced the route of her daylong flight to Australia, with one key difference. Instead of returning to Washington she flew to Boston and took a commuter flight to New Hampshire.

The connection she was pursuing was tenuous. Tenuous enough, she hoped, that the American authorities would not have followed it up yet. It came from an online service she subscribed to that collected police reports on homicides, suicides, and unexplained deaths from all over the United States. The deaths were cross-indexed under various headings, including parts of the body. Karen's routine search of "hands and feet" had rung a bell in New Hampshire.

She was right. When she arrived at the small city hall office of the chief medical examiner, she found him willing to talk about the body that had been discovered a few days earlier, and even willing to show it to her.

His name was Dr. Waterman, and he was surprisingly young and handsome. She saw photographs of an attractive wife and two young daughters on the bookshelf behind his desk. He offered her coffee, but she refused.

"I've been on airplanes most of the last few days," she said. "I've had enough coffee to last me a year."

"I was thinking that you looked tired," the doctor smiled. "I kind of assumed you journalists don't get a lot of sleep."

"That depends on the journalist," Karen said. "As for myself, I don't sleep much. You're right on that score."

"I sleep almost eight hours a night," he said. "No medical examiner is in a great hurry to get to his office in the morning, as you might imagine."

"Tell me about the body we talked about on the phone," Karen said.

"It's strictly a John Doe," he said. "No trace of identification. The few distinguishing marks, moles and such, were no help. We took impressions of the teeth and sent them off to the computers, but there wasn't a match."

"Who found the body?"

"A local homeless man named Erroll. A mental patient who was thrown out on the street when they cut back at the state hospital. He found the body in a Dumpster. At first the police weren't inclined to believe him. He's severely delusional, very florid. He thinks Martians are sending messages through his skin, stuff like that. But the body was right where he said it was. When the cops saw the deformations, they called me right away."

He stood up. "Want to see it?"

"Absolutely." Karen got up to follow him.

"You're not squeamish about bodies, are you?" he asked.

"No problem."

He took her to one of the autopsy rooms. He left her to wait alone while he went to find the body. He returned with an assistant who was pushing a gurney.

The assistant unzipped the body bag. Thankfully, the smell that emerged from the corpse when he pulled down the zipper was essentially formaldehyde, reminding her of her lab days at college.

The face of the body was like that of any cadaver, gray and expressionless, the features slack.

"Caucasian male, about forty," Dr. Waterman said.

As he pulled the bag aside, Karen saw the distorted hands.

"Hardened, fused," she said.

"Correct. More like modified cartilage than skin." The doctor picked up one of the hands. "I've never seen anything remotely like it."

I have. Karen was thinking that the corpse's hands were almost identical in appearance to the hands of the victims in Australia. She did not volunteer what she knew.

"Have you done tissue studies?" she asked.

"Informally, on my own, yes. I probably shouldn't have—the big shots in Atlanta will want complete control—but I couldn't resist. It's not normal tissue. I'm not enough of a cell biologist to understand it, but I do know that in all my years of tissue biopsies I've never seen changes like this."

He showed her the feet. Just as in Australia, the digits were distorted and partially fused, and the heel and sole had pulled together in a hooflike shape. Death had done nothing to alter the distinctive, troubling look of the foot.

"I've checked my medical books," he said. "No luck. I can't find a disease, no matter how rare, that has this feature."

Karen felt a suspicious throb of lightheadedness as she studied the corpse. It occurred to her rather remotely that she hadn't had much to eat in the last three days.

Before she could complete the thought her eyes began to roll up in her head. Her lips and hands tingled. She tried to steady herself against the gurney, but failed.

The doctor caught her before she could fall to the floor.

She came to in his office, lying on a deep leather couch. He was standing over her with a glass of water in his hand. She felt horrible. Her head ached intensely, her stomach was queasy, and she felt too dizzy to sit up.

"I'm embarrassed," she said.

"Don't be," he smiled. "It happens all the time here."

"It really wasn't the body, so much," she said weakly. "I've been on airplanes for the last three or four days. I'm jet-lagged."

He smiled indulgently. "Yes, that would do it too."

He revived her with water followed by strong coffee. He insisted that she remain lying on the couch. He was surprised to see her pursue her story even in her weakened state.

"You reported this to the state health authorities?" she asked.

He nodded. "I copied my e-mail to the CDC in Atlanta. Nobody got back to me. Either they're swamped, or it's a bureaucratic thing. A snafu."

"I'd like to ask you to do me a favor," Karen said. "Can you keep a lid on this for another twenty-four hours while I check out a couple of things?"

"Well, I don't know," the doctor said. "We're supposed to report anything out of the ordinary."

"You've already reported it," Karen said. "All I'm asking is that you sit tight for one day. There are people at the federal level who need to know about this."

"Which people?"

Karen was thinking of Joseph Kraig. But she didn't want to mention any names. She knew this story was in danger of being classified within hours. She needed to get to the core of it before that happened.

"I'd better not mention any names," she said. "But I promise to get back to you by tomorrow at this time."

He shrugged. "All right. I can wait."

"And put this body somewhere safe," Karen said. "Don't let it disappear."

"Aren't you being a little paranoid?" he asked.

Karen smiled. "Humor me. There may be aspects of this thing that could be embarrassing to some people. You never know."

"All right," he said. "I'll put it somewhere safe."

"I'll call you tomorrow," Karen said. "I promise. Right now I have to fly back to Washington."

"Are you sure you're well enough?" the doctor asked. "You look like you could use a night's sleep."

"I'll sleep on the plane."

"Let me get you something to eat before you go. Honestly, you look pretty weak. There's a restaurant right in the next block."

Karen realized he found her attractive. He was a young man, after all. No doubt her fainting spell had endeared her to him. In his specialty he would not often have the opportunity to take care of living people, much less young and attractive women.

If she agreed to go with him it would delay her departure for Washington by an hour. On the other hand, it might bind the handsome young doctor to her sufficiently to make him keep his word about the body.

"All right," she said. "That's nice of you."

She felt a bit woozy as she got to her feet.

"Careful," he said, taking her arm. "Let me help you."

18

Plainview, Texas
November 28
12:40 P.M.

THE RESERVOIR was controversial.

Its maintenance was paid for by state taxes as well as local fees, but local residents felt the state could not be trusted to maintain it properly. Leaks had been discovered in some of the retaining walls since the last election, and the state had been slow to repair them. Experts hired by the county government determined that the purification equipment was out of date. The state sent in its own experts, who held that the equipment met all federal standards and would not need to be replaced for twenty years.

The reservoir was crucial to the community because rainfall was an irregular thing in these parts, and drought could hit when it was least expected. Farmers joined local homeowners in putting constant pressure on both the county and state to enlarge and modernize the reservoir.

Today three small boys, all fifth-graders, had climbed the fence and were sailing toy boats on the rippled surface of the water. They had observed the maintenance building long enough to determine that the staff was out for lunch.

The boats floated jerkily on the water, pushed this way and that by gusts of wind.

"I dare you to jump in," said the tallest of the boys, whose name was Ethan.

"You're crazy," said the others. "It's freezing."

"If I go first," Ethan said, "that means you two have to go too."

"Bullshit," said the boy named George. "Does not."

"Does too."

"Does not."

The smallest boy seemed impressed by the dare, but not willing to jump into the frigid water.

"There, look." Ethan was pointing at his sailboat, which was floating away toward the deep center of the reservoir. "If I jump in, you two have to go too."

He pulled off his jacket, slipped out of his running shoes, and leaped into the water.

"Jesus!" he cried as the coldness enveloped him. But he began to swim toward the drifting boat, his arms flailing.

"Get out of there!" the other two shouted. "You're crazy!"

"You faggots!" Ethan called. "You pussies! I'm gonna sink your boats."

He had almost reached the boat when he saw the object.

It was transparent, a globe about eight inches in diameter. It was floating a few feet from him. It would have been invisible had he not chanced to come directly upon it. The blue sky was reflected on its upper surface.

"Hey," he said, more to himself than to the others. He treaded water, edging closer to the floating globe. The others, on shore, could not see it.

"Hey, this is cool," he called, turning to look at his friends. "Hey, I found something."

George and Andrew shouted in unison, "What?"

"A thing—a globe." Ethan stretched out his right hand to touch the object, still treading water. His finger, already chilled by the water, touched the globe's surface. It felt like plastic.

"Hey, you guys," he called. "Wait till you see what I found. If you only had the guts . . ."

He swam behind the object and gave it a push toward shore, intending to guide it to his friends. To his surprise, the surface of the globe was brittle and seemed to crack at his touch.

"Hey!" He patted the globe again to push it toward shore. The outer surface crumbled like a layer of ice. For an instant he saw something inside and reached to touch it. It was a viscous mass, colorless. Even as he felt it on his hand it dissolved. The shards of the globe were nowhere to be found. They also had dissolved.

"Damn it," Ethan said. "Fuck."

"What is it?" called George. "What's going on?"

Ethan now remembered his mission and made a show of sinking his friends' boats. Claiming that he was used to the water, he swam around in front of his friends for a good five minutes, pushing the boats this way and that as he shouted insults at those less brave than he.

Then the chill of the water began to penetrate his young body, and he came in to shore.

"There's no towels or anything," said George. "You're gonna get sick."

"Fuck you," said Ethan. "I'm not going to get sick."

A few moments later the boys were gone, their cries echoing over the water.

———

Cuernavaca, Mexico
6 P.M.

STRAY DOGS were everywhere.

They clustered around the tourist buses in packs, whimpering for a handout. The tourists, all Anglos, watched with distaste as ragged children kicked and punched at the dogs to get at the bus windows.

"Señor, Señora, money, money, money!"

"*Amigos, bienvenidos!*"

"Layee, give me money!"

The contrast between the crisp mountain air of the town and the fetid odors of dirty children, pariah dogs, and cooking was bizarre. In the distance the snowcapped peak of Popocatépetl could be seen, pine forests gracing its slopes. The other volcano, Ixtacihuatl, was hidden by clouds.

The tour company had obviously picked one of the most squalid tourist areas to stop at first. One good-humored woman was pointing a video camera at the children, who laughed in delight and cut capers before her. The other tourists, tired from their voyage, sat dully, their eyes half closed.

The tour director made a halfhearted effort to shoo away the dogs and children, then began herding the tourists off the bus and toward the restaurant, which was incongruously named Le Café Américain.

The restaurant's owner had come out to greet the tourists. A short, heavyset man wearing a white apron, he was the first to see the plane.

It was a small one-engine plane, apparently a crop duster. It was flying back and forth over the valley, the drone of its engine almost drowned out by the clamor of the children and the barking of the dogs.

A couple of the tourists followed the direction of his gaze and looked at the plane. Then, like the others, they were distracted by their own concern to get into the restaurant without being besieged by the children.

The driver, a mustachioed Mexican wearing a faded dungaree jacket despite the intense heat, waved the children away halfheartedly. He stood by the door of the bus, helping the female passengers down onto the dusty street. He kicked savagely at a stray dog, which yelped and limped away.

"Watch your step, please."

He noticed the plane, which, crisscrossing the valley, was now emitting a trail of spray that settled languidly onto the fields. He reached into his pocket reflexively for a cigarette, then remembered the passengers and waited until the bus was empty.

The driver and the restaurant owner fought off the dogs and children until the last of the tourists was inside the restaurant. Then the driver offered the other man a cigarette. They used the same match. For a moment they stood side by side in silence, gazing out over the valley.

"*Chingar,*" said the driver. "What's with the plane?"

"Government bullshit," replied the restaurant owner. "Trying to impress the gringos, something."

"Crop duster," the other man shook his head. "There are no crops where he is except cactus."

"And the arroyo."

"The last part of it, *sí*. Hardly more than a trickle at this time of year."

"Another way to waste our money." The restaurant owner took a long drag on his cigarette, then unwillingly threw it in the gutter. "*Hasta luego, amigo*. Have to feed the animals," referring to the tourists.

The driver watched the children converge noisily on the discarded cigarette. Then he climbed into the overheated tour bus to get out of the sun.

The plane had banked toward the town and now circled above the narrow streets in the thirsty dusk, occasionally trailing threads of mist.

Alexandria, Virginia
November 28

KAREN GOT back to her apartment late in the evening. She had left her car in the long-term lot at the airport and driven home through light traffic.

She was drained. Her jet lag had reached incalculable proportions, and the mental exhaustion of pursuing such a difficult story was taking its toll.

She was beginning to wonder whether it was all real. Perhaps she was tilting at windmills again. True, a lot of people were sick, including the vice president of the United States. Others were dead. But were they all victims of the same disease?

The symptoms of the illness were bizarre. So was the pattern of the spread. It didn't make much sense. But did that mean there was a conspiracy afoot? Perhaps there was a simple and logical explanation for everything.

Karen poured herself a drink—the first really stiff one she had had since she left home—and took a long swallow before peeling off her clothes. She left the drink on the kitchen counter and unpacked her suitcase. She emptied the hamper, threw all the dirty clothes into the washer, and started the cycle. She walked naked into the bedroom and looked in the drawer where she kept her bras and panties. No panties—they were all dirty.

"Shit," she said.

She caught a glimpse of herself in the closet mirror. She was too thin. Her ribs stood out under her pale skin, and her shoulder blades were too salient. She had good shoulders, she thought. Good breasts, too. Small but firm and well shaped. But her legs were her best feature. They had garnered her more than one confidence from sources who wanted to remain off the record. She had a large collection of short skirts, including several leather ones.

She took a bath while waiting to switch the clothes to the dryer. She filled the glass to the rim with ice and took the bourbon bottle with her. As she poured more booze into the glass the pile of ice cubes gradually shrank, and her drinks grew stronger.

She was almost too tired to think. She listened dumbly to the swish and thump of the washer, her eyes growing heavier and heavier. She studied the pretty color of the liquor in her glass. Almost the color of tea, she thought. Iced tea. Didn't they use iced tea to represent liquor in the movies?

In any case there wasn't enough. That was the problem with liquor when you got deep enough into the addiction. A glass simply could not contain all the booze you needed. So that any glass—not only the little drinks they gave you in bars, but even your own bigger glasses at home, filled to the rim with straight liquor, not a drop of water—any glass was too small. An element of frustration accompanied the relief you got when you raised the glass to your lips.

And of course that was what booze was all about, wasn't it? Frustration. People drink to make up for holes in their lives. By drinking they deepen the holes. What sort of holes? If the people knew the answer to that, they wouldn't have to drink.

Karen was the sort of problem drinker who never touched liquor during the day. She rose early, did her work carefully and well, made sure her evening was free before she started on the sauce. Then she put away half a bottle of whiskey before bed. Half a fifth, sometimes half a quart, depending on what was on sale and how bad she felt. She woke up with the same headache every morning, fought it off with Advil and a milk shake that included a raw egg and some herbs, and went off to work.

She didn't drink socially. At parties or restaurants she ordered mineral water. When she could not avoid accepting a drink, she took a glass of white wine and left half of it. She didn't want to see hard liquor in front of her, it was too frustrating.

She kept her problem very secret. Not even her reporter friends knew about it. They thought she held her liquor well and drank in moderation.

Troy had known about it, of course. He had lived with her for two years, so she could hardly hide it from him. But Troy would never tell anyone about it. He was a failure in a lot of ways, but he was not a gossip. They had parted friends, each relieved to be free of the unhappiness of living together.

The wash cycle was finished. How had it gone through so fast? Not for the first time Karen's drunkenness had made her miss a fugitive block of time.

Instead of getting up to put the clothes in the dryer she turned on the boom box she kept in the bathroom. It contained an old CD of Mozart piano sonatas, Claudio Arrau in the early 1980s. She clicked forward to the slow movement, sat back, and closed her eyes.

There was nothing in the world so peaceful as the slow movements of those Mozart sonatas. When guests came into this apartment and heard the piano they would exclaim, "It's so quiet in here!" It wasn't really. The andantes brought their own silence, their own peace to the place.

By the time she emptied her glass she was almost too drunk to stand. She got up uncertainly and toweled herself off. The wet clothes in the washer were forgotten now. She staggered toward the bedroom. On her way she noticed the local newspapers, which were piled just inside the front door. They had collected in her absence, and she had dropped them unceremoniously on the foyer floor. They could wait until tomorrow, of course, but her journalist's scruples about missed stories would not let her go to bed without quickly checking the headlines. If anything new had happened while she was gone, she should know about it.

She sank down unsteadily to the carpet, a terry cloth towel wrapped around her, and unfolded the papers. Inside the front page of Thursday's *USA Today* she saw something pasted to the newspaper. It was a Post-it note bearing a handwritten message.

She had to struggle to read the scrawled words, her exhaustion joining the overdose of liquor to make her see double.

Get off this story, said the note. It was stuck to a photograph of Vice President Everhardt on page two of the newspaper. *Or you'll end up like him.*

The note was unsigned.

Karen sobered up instantly. She pulled off the note and took it to the kitchen, where the light was brighter.

Get off this story. The note was written in felt pen, all the words underlined.

"So," she said aloud. "You're worried enough to threaten me."

Leaving the note on the counter, she went to the bathroom for three preemptive Advils to fight the hangover she would have tomorrow morning. She lay down in bed and thought back over her travels. Iowa, New Hampshire, Australia. Something was definitely up. And those who knew about it were desperate to cover it up.

She felt no fear. What could they do to her? She had already lost everything in life that had value to her. She was alone in the world, and not particularly attached to anything but her ability to find the truth. Let them do their worst, she thought.

Tomorrow she would think of a way to add fuel to the fire.

Restored to alertness by the challenge ahead of her, she suddenly remembered the wet clothes. She threw them in the dryer and turned on the cycle.

Five minutes later she was fast asleep. The smooth rumble of the dryer was the only sound in the apartment.

2 0

DOCTOR JAY Waterman sat in his office at the Manchester city hall. He was smoking a cigarette and thinking.

He glanced at the clock on his desk. Seven-fifteen. Time to call it a night.

He took a drag from the Camel Filter and watched the smoke billow under the light from the desk lamp. His wife didn't allow him to smoke at home. He was trying to quit, so he limited his smoking to a cigarette in the morning on the way here and sometimes a cigarette in a bar on the way home. He rarely smoked here in the office.

The reporter, Karen, had smoked like a chimney when he took her for lunch after her fainting spell. He had not been able to resist bumming a Newport from her. The chill, acrid taste of the menthol on his lips had been a bond with her.

She was very attractive, of course. There was something tight and tensile about her that he found irresistible. And she was so slim. His wife had become slack and overweight after two pregnancies. It was quite a while since he had been in close proximity to a girl as pretty as Karen Embry.

He closed his eyes and allowed himself to undress her mentally while the nicotine throbbed in his veins. Small breasts, no doubt, but firm. Ribs visible under her skin, a flat stomach. Good hips, rich despite their smallness and—he had not failed to notice—a nice ass. Very nice. She must look spectacular in a swimsuit.

He felt the heat of the ash approaching his fingers. He opened his eyes and stubbed out the cigarette. He made a mental note to buy a pack of Newports tomorrow.

He sighed, turned out the light, and locked the office. He had worn his down jacket—the cold weather was here to stay. Carrying the jacket in one hand and his briefcase in the other, he started down to the parking lot.

On an impulse he pushed another button and took the elevator to the basement. He had put the corpse under a John Doe in the second cooler, the rarely used one. He thought he would take one more glance at it.

It was a bizarre syndrome, that was certain. His degree in pathology had brought him into contact with some weird anomalies at the tissue level, not to mention the cellular. And many major deforming syndromes, like Elephant Man's Syndrome, remained a mystery, in terms of both cause and cure. But this was even more strange. Strange because the deformed tissue did seem to make a kind of sense. Not in a human, of course . . .

It was just like the CDC to lose his e-mail and not respond. He had been on the point of giving them a piece of his mind, and even of calling the press to embarrass them. But then the girl, Karen, had showed up. She seemed as interested in the body as he was. She seemed to understand.

He reached the basement room and turned on the lights. He had to fumble through his keys to find the unfamiliar one that opened the door. He didn't have to search for the drawer; this was the only body in here.

He pulled it open. From the weight he knew right away something was wrong.

The drawer was empty.

"Jesus Christ," he said aloud.

2 1

Washington
December 1

MICHAEL CAMPBELL was looking at his wife's face.

Susan's latest ABC interview was on the television screen. Susan was laughing at something the interviewer had said to her. Michael did not hear the words.

His eyes half closed as the sensation between his legs quickened. The girl bending over him knew him well. Her fingers were in places that never failed to excite him. Her mouth was making slow circles over him, the tongue darting subtly in strokes that made him gasp.

She stopped when she felt that the end was near. Wanting to excite him more, she reared back to let him look at her. The room was dark except for the blue glimmer of the TV screen. He looked up admiringly at her square shoulders, the lean silhouette of her rib cage. She was sleek, almost reptilian in her smooth firmness of line.

"More?" she asked.

He groaned in response. She bent down to take him in her mouth again. The long fingers were all over him, stroking and probing. The center of him began to strain.

"Wait," she murmured.

She leaned back to let him have a last look. The long hair framing her face, the firm thighs, the small breasts, the smile he felt more than saw in the darkened room.

She had him in her hands, feeling the pulse of him. She measured his excitement.

"Now," she said.

With a lithe movement she came astride him and guided him inside her. The feel of her sex around him was almost more than he could bear. He strained quickly as the hands came to pat his chest.

"Come on," she whispered. "Come on . . ."

Her fingertips found his nipples and squeezed gently. Her hips moved expertly to bring him to the crisis. He heard a low sweet sound in her throat, a sort of purring.

"Come on," she said. "All the way . . ."

He groaned, thrusting hard into her.

"All the way, Michael. Come on . . ."

He came with a great burst, gasping. She rode the spasms easily, enjoying the power of him. Her eyes rolled up toward the ceiling. The warm knees embraced him. For a moment his passion seemed to transport him to another time and place. He was literally beside himself. She looked down happily, pleased with her work.

It took him a long time to come to himself. She lay down beside him, stroking his cheek, kissing his chest. His breaths came more slowly now. He took her hand and held it, trusting as a child.

She glanced at the room around them. Her suit was hanging in the closet, alongside his own clothes. The garments had been neatly disposed of before they started. A throw pillow was on the floor where it had fallen a couple of minutes ago. Near it, forgotten now, was a scarf-sized piece of silk knotted at two of the corners.

They had done it this way many times. They knew each other's rhythms and susceptibilities. Sometimes it was quick, violent, sometimes slow and languid. But she never failed to give him the pleasure he sought.

He looked at the TV screen. Susan was nodding at something the interviewer had said, pushing a lock of her hair away from her cheek as she did so. Her expression was deferential, innocent. Sometimes, with her blond hair and her big candid eyes, she looked like a little girl. Indeed, there were ways in which she had never entirely grown up. She was softer than other women. More vulnerable. This fact never failed to charm him, though it played a part in the distance between himself and her.

Leslie was looking at him now. She leaned back on her arm, her breast rounded against the sheet.

"So," she said. "Did you miss me?"

Michael smiled. "Not a bit."

"Your nose is getting longer," she said. "Are you telling a lie?"

It was true. He had missed her terribly. Events of recent days had put him in the spotlight, not only with the public but with the White House and the party leaders. He had given three speeches and done a dozen interviews. He had met with the president four times, once alone. So much responsibility, so much tension . . . He had been thinking of Leslie for days, fighting to find time to see her. His pent-up need had been almost unbearable.

"My nose is getting longer?" he repeated.

"It was a while ago," she teased, letting her fingers graze him between his legs.

They lay together, enjoying the silence. He did not know whether she had noticed Susan on the TV screen. She ran her hand gently along his stomach.

"They're keeping you busy, aren't they?" she asked.

He nodded. "Never a dull moment. With all this bad publicity, and Danny Everhardt in the hospital . . ."

"How is he?" she asked.

"Not good. No change since he got sick."

"Do you think it's hurting the president?" she asked.

"It certainly doesn't help," he said. "But Tom Palleschi is a good man. He'll do all right."

He looked at her. "How about you? How are things?"

She shook her head. "Same old," she said.

He admired her smooth body. The legs were hard, the stomach firm. "Still in great shape," he said. "How do you do it?"

She laughed. "Men," she said. "You think what you see is all there is. You don't know what we go through for you when we're out of your sight."

She rarely talked about her life apart from him. She considered it worthless drudgery. He thought of her in her solitude. Dieting, working out—seeing other men? Could one know a person as intimately as he knew her and perhaps know almost nothing about her?

Yes, it was definitely possible. Come to think of it, that was part of the excitement he felt when she came to him. That shadow of the unknown behind her smile.

He let her hold him for a long time. Her hand was on his chest. She felt him breathe. Then she kissed his cheek.

"Time for you to go," she said.

"Already?" he complained lazily.

"Miles to go before you sleep," she smiled.

"And promises to keep."

He got up. She watched his legs disappear into the dark trousers. Hard thighs, swimmer's thighs . . . As he got his shirt off the hanger she looked at the long scar on his back. It ran from the mid-thoracic vertebrae all the way down to the lower spine. She knew it very well, having caressed it along with the rest of him countless times. She had grown to like it. It had an odd silky feel. It made him look vulnerable. In many ways he was.

"I don't want it to be as long next time," he said, buttoning the shirt. His voice sounded young and needful.

She beckoned to him to sit beside her.

"You're getting to be a very busy fellow," she said. "And visible. It won't be easy."

"I do miss you," he said, letting his hand rest on her hip. "When I can't see you, it doesn't feel right."

"Well, that's nice," she said. "I can see you'll just have to make room for me."

"What will you do?" he asked.

"When? Tonight?"

"Yes." Again there was that candid, trusting note in his voice.

"I'll go home," she said. "I have work to do. Then I'll watch TV, or read. If I get lonely I might call a friend."

He grimaced.

"Are you trying to make me jealous?"

She laughed. "A little jealousy might be good for you, my friend."

He stood up. She watched from the bed as he combed his hair and studied himself in the mirror. He would take his shower later, at his office. He said he liked to keep her smell on him as long as possible. She told him it was danger-ous—secretaries have sharp antennae—but he had a reckless streak in him.

By the time he got home, though, there would be no trace of her. In his profession, discretion was crucial. The public knew only one face. The other must be kept invisible, always.

He kissed her a last time and let himself out of the room. She lay quietly for a while, savoring the lingering throb in her senses. Then she got up and went into the bathroom.

The sight of her body pleased her, as always. Her skin was brown, her hair sandy. Her eyes were golden. She had straight shoulders, long arms and legs. Long fingers, even. When she went to her health club to work out, women looked at her almost more than men. Most women would kill for a body like hers, so lean and trim. Her walk was erect and easy, but sinuous. More than one of her lovers had told her she had an androgynous air, both male and female. She sometimes played to this perception. Sexually she knew how to make the most of it.

She got into the shower, unwrapping the hotel's little bar of soap. She soaped the parts of her body Michael had enjoyed in the bed. Her nipples stood up as the bar passed over them. She used the little bottle of shampoo to wash her hair. She smiled as her fingers slipped between her legs. His seed was inside her. She liked that.

They had been lovers for six years. She had no illusions about the future. He would remain with his wife for the sake of his political career. By all ac-counts Susan Campbell was a fine person, sensitive and interesting. Michael never said a word against her. His attitude toward her was one of fierce loy-alty and veneration.

He had confided to Leslie that Susan was frigid with him. Her frigidity made him feel terribly inadequate as well as sexually unsatisfied. But this did not attenuate his love for her.

Leslie sympathized with Susan. Michael Campbell was not an easy man to know. In the very act of giving himself physically, he withheld something deeper. And in their conversations, which had become quite intimate over the years, he left something unstated. Something that, at first, seemed like a tiny blind spot in her knowledge of him, but that now seemed more like an entire unseen world, a netherworld down a rabbit hole.

It could not be easy to be married to him. Such men were not really cut out for marriage. They slip through your fingers like quicksilver. In your closest moment with them you remain alone. A tough spot for a wife. Tough enough to make any woman frigid, come to think of it.

But for a mistress it was different. Leslie knew what turned him on. She knew she satisfied him in bed. Their fucking made her feel proud of her own attractions, her skill as a lover. Knowing this, it was easier to let go of the rest. All that was necessary was to make sure she never fell in love with him.

And she never had. Not quite.

A lot of women would have allowed their need to coil itself around that hidden core in him, would have become insatiable. But Leslie was too strong for that. She could endure the loneliness he made her feel. Perhaps because she was used to being lonely. Or perhaps because she had something else in mind for herself.

Leslie came from a small Kentucky town where, long ago, she had played with other children on her block on hot summer mornings and dreamed of being a mother like her own mother. Life had taken her far from that dusty street, but not from the dream it represented.

Some day she would take a gamble for that kind of life. She would leave this city. She would find a place for herself in the real world. A man who wanted her. A child of her own.

But somehow she could not make up her mind to do it. Not yet.

Perhaps because she didn't want to lose Michael yet.

She put on the suit she had worn. Glancing for a last time around the room, she saw the knotted piece of silk on the floor and retrieved it. She put it into her briefcase—she had come here dressed as a businesswoman on her way to a meeting—and gave herself a last look in the mirror.

As she left the room, the face of Susan Campbell was still on the TV screen, smiling at her host with the hint of involuntary distress that was her trademark. The public had come to expect and admire that look.

Susan was loved for the weakness that made her human.

Leslie would never know that feeling.

2 2

Washington
December 2

KAREN'S AGENT exploded when he saw the article she proposed to publish.

"Are you out of your mind?" he asked. "Thousands of people getting sick because some sinister conspiracy is deliberately making them sick? Political candidates neutralized by a conspiracy? You're insane, Karen."

"Was it insane to speculate that Kennedy's assassination was not the work of one man?" Karen asked. "Was it insane to connect the Watergate burglars with the Nixon campaign? How about Iran-Contra?"

"You're mixing apples with oranges," the agent said. "It's one thing to report an outrageous thing when you have facts to back up your story. It's another thing to feed the public innuendo and paranoia when you can't prove what you're saying."

"I have facts," Karen said. "Maybe not enough to send people to jail, but enough to make any reasonable person suspicious. The syndrome is not behaving like a normal disease. The illness of Vice President Everhardt, an isolated case in the middle of a big city, does not make sense. Not when the pattern of the other outbreaks is considered."

The disease had now been reported in eleven states, with several thousand victims officially identified. It was common knowledge that the cause and cure were unknown. Yet in the Washington, D.C., area there was still only one victim, Dan Everhardt.

"Those may be facts," the agent said. "But they don't justify your conspiracy theory."

"They are consistent with it," Karen countered. "That's the only point I'm trying to make. I'm not reporting the conspiracy as a fact, I'm just asking the reader to keep an open mind."

"Listen, Karen," the agent said. "It's not just the content of your piece. It's the climate out there. People don't want to hear this just now. They've got friends and loved ones who are victims of the disease. They're terrified for themselves and their children. This is the worst possible moment to start talking conspiracy."

"Which would be worse?" Karen asked. "A mystery disease about which we can do nothing, or a conspiracy we can stop once we identify it?"

The argument went on for almost an hour. In the end the agent agreed to submit the piece to newspapers, but only for publication on the opinion page. He would agree to explicit disclaimers by editors who wanted to alert the public to the fact that the theory expressed in the article in no way represented the view of their newspaper.

Karen agreed. She knew her article was speculative in nature, and did not want people to think it was being presented as hard news.

She did not mention to her agent that she had been threatened. She kept that detail to herself.

She also did one important thing without her agent's knowledge. On her own she leaked the article to several influential website proprietors who specialized in alternative news. She could be sure that the piece would be widely read. Her theory would be talked about. The authorities would have to comment on it sooner or later. They would be embarrassed, would feel pressured.

Karen was sure she was doing the right thing. The truth about the mystery disease was hidden behind a cloud of ambiguity, evasion, and perhaps misinformation. Sometimes the truth needs some help to see the light of day.

Karen intended to keep the pressure on.

23

Georgetown
December 2

SUSAN WAS getting ready for her workout.

She tied her hair back in a ponytail, her breasts standing up under the support bra as she raised her arms. The spandex shorts hugged her hips and thighs, showing off a lean female body that lived up to the fantasies millions of men had about her.

Michael would be late again tonight. She had turned on the TV, intending to watch the news, but had changed her mind. The news shows were full of reaction to the selection of Tom Palleschi to replace Dan Everhardt as vice president. The president's supporters were saying the selection was a stroke of genius. Colin Goss's supporters were saying that the choice indicated desperation and proved the administration was desperate and intellectually bankrupt. According to their statements Palleschi was the very embodiment of "a party that lives in the past," and the choice facing the American people was now clear.

The media were also devoting considerable time to the mystery disease, which had now claimed enough victims to make national headlines every day. Some of the outbreaks involved many hundreds of victims, some were inexplicably limited to a few dozen or less. Rumors were flying about more dramatic outbreaks abroad, and about bizarre and frightening physical symptoms that appeared late in the progress of the syndrome. Most of all people were terrified by the news—never confirmed officially by any health authority—that the disease was untreatable and always fatal.

Susan could not get Dan Everhardt out of her mind. It was an open secret in Washington that Dan was a victim of the disease. Susan had called Michael's sister Ingrid earlier and chatted for half an hour. She confided her worries about Dan Everhardt and her fears for Michael's safety. Ingrid, though sympathetic, did not seem worried. As a trained nurse she felt she had seen everything, medically speaking.

"It's probably a stroke, or something functional like a nervous breakdown," she said. "Don't worry about Mike, he's as strong as an ox. Except for that back problem he hasn't had a sick day in his life."

Ingrid was glad for the chance to reassure Susan. She enjoyed mothering her, and was as fiercely devoted to her as to Michael. They often went shopping together. Ingrid loved to help Susan pick out clothes, and insisted on doing the alterations herself. She understood Susan's figure in its tiniest details, and got vicarious pleasure from seeing it graced by beautiful outfits. Susan's somewhat fragile personality was a good fit for Ingrid's maternal instinct. The two were close friends.

The phone conversation did calm Susan's nerves, but its effect wore off after a while—like that of every reassurance she received these days.

Susan put on her running shoes and set the treadmill's timer for forty-five minutes. More and more, in the last few years, she had taken to using exercise as a way to control anxiety. When she got on the treadmill or the exercise bike, earphones on, an old videotaped movie on the VCR—never a talk show—she felt insulated from the real world. Her long exercise routines took away her desire to take a tranquilizer.

Today she was watching *Force of Evil* with John Garfield. It was a slow, overly talky movie, but she loved Garfield. When she watched his movies, or those of Bogart or the young Ray Milland, she wished she could get into a time capsule and go live in that world. Wisecracking heroes in suits and fedoras, beautiful women with sleek hair and dark lipstick who talked in sensual drawls, menacing bad guys with cigars and gutter slang.

The evil in those movies was so much more straightforward, so much more *clean,* than the evil in the real world. Evil in the real world was complicated, hard to grasp. Today's villains came with friendly smiles, soothing words, and fine résumés that proved competence and expertise. Gone were the days when George Raft and Edward G. Robinson telegraphed their bad intentions with snarling grimaces.

Susan had been told more than once that her beauty was akin to that of the great film stars of the past. She had been compared to Grace Kelly and Catherine Deneuve, among others. A special photo layout in *Vogue* had exploited this quality, showing Susan in slinky dresses and dramatic hairstyles. One of the photos hung upstairs. Michael had insisted on having it framed, because it had captured an aspect of Susan's charm that was normally kept in the background.

The TV was on, John Garfield was on the screen, and Susan was just fitting the earphones when she heard the phone. She ran to pick it up, thinking it was Michael.

"Hello?"

"Hello, Susan." It was the voice again. Susan turned white.

"What do you want?"

"Just you."

There was a strange intimacy to the voice. A confidence, almost a trust. Now she heard the modulations better. She guessed the caller was a woman older than herself. Fortyish perhaps.

"Please," Susan said.

"It's all right, Susan. I'm not here to hurt you. I'm on your side."

Susan thought for a moment. She could see herself in the large mirror on the wall of the walk-in closet where the treadmill was kept. In her tight leotard she looked almost naked. Childishly defenseless, her eyes frightened and guilty.

"Please," she heard herself say. The cordless phone trembled in her hand.

"You know about Palleschi, of course," the caller said.

"Tom Palleschi. Yes." Susan hated to encourage the caller by responding, but she couldn't help it.

"He will not be the vice president, Susan."

Oh, my God.

"What are you talking about?" Susan said aloud. "Of course he will. It's been announced."

"Michael will be the president's choice. Not Palleschi." The husky voice sounded pitilessly omniscient, yet still there was that undertone of sympathy.

"You're crazy," Susan said.

"I understand how you feel," said the voice. "The truth can be very painful."

"But it's *not* true." Susan grimaced to hear herself debating with this crank, but she could not listen to these things without protest.

"Give it time." The caller sounded calm. "One of the peculiarities of the truth, Susan, is that it comes slowly. It insinuates. You can't be ready for it in advance. But once it arrives, it's like a forbidden fruit that you've already tasted. It's too late to stop it."

The caller let these words sink in before saying, "In any case, when Michael is chosen, I'll be there for you. You'll know that I was right, and you'll need a friend, Susan. That friend will be me."

Susan sighed. "Why are you doing this?"

The caller said, "At some time in our lives, Susan, we are called upon to stand up and fight for who we are. Your time is coming. When it comes, you won't be alone. I'll be there to stand beside you and give you strength."

"Strength for what?" Susan asked.

"To stop him."

"Who?"

"Michael Campbell, of course."

Susan sighed deeply. "You're crazy," she repeated, a bit more weakly.

Then, gritting her teeth, "What happens if I don't answer the next time you call?"

"You'll answer," the voice said. "You've already answered. The truth is inside you, Susan. You can't unhear it."

Susan gritted her teeth, fighting to gain control of the situation.

"You're wrong," she said. "You're wrong about all of this."

"When Palleschi is removed, you'll know I wasn't wrong. In the meantime there is something you can do that will help."

"Me? What do you mean?"

"Ask your husband one small question, Susan. Ask him what happened at Harvard."

"At Harvard? What are you talking about?"

"When he answers, watch his eyes."

The line went dead.

2 4

PERHAPS THE only person who disapproved of the selection of Tom Palleschi as Dan Everhardt's replacement was Judd Campbell.

Judd regarded Palleschi as a fine public servant but a political nonentity. Palleschi was a born follower, not a leader. In a fight against Colin Goss, the president needed a much stronger man. Someone with talent and guts, someone with proven appeal to the public, and with the ability to become president himself if the need arose.

Someone like Michael Campbell.

Tonight Judd was sitting in an easy chair on the heated porch of his house on the Chesapeake Bay. His daughter Ingrid brought him a bottle of Guinness stout and a glass.

"You know," he said as she bent to put the ale on the table, "it's no wonder the president is in so much trouble. He's badly advised, and he doesn't have the guts to do the aggressive thing."

"Uh-oh," Ingrid smiled. "Here we go again."

"Here they are picking a nobody like Palleschi to replace Everhardt, just when things are going bad. And the man who can save the day for them is right in front of their noses."

"Dad, your ambition is showing."

Ingrid stood looking down at the father she loved. Judd was a strong man, but his fatal weakness was his utter inability to bend. Once he got an idea in his head there was no reasoning with him. And no idea was more fixed than his desire for Michael to become president of the United States.

Ever since Michael entered politics Judd had always counseled the most ambitious course for him. "Why waste more than one term in the House when you can run for the Senate right now?" he advised. "Why languish on lesser committees when you can get the majority leader to give you Appropriations?" And again, "Why serve on committees when you can head your own?"

Judd wanted Michael to be on the fastest track possible toward high national office. "You've got what it takes to run this whole country," he said. "As much as people like Kennedy or Johnson or Nixon, and a hell of a lot more than Carter or Bush or Clinton. Why sit around waiting twenty years for what you can have now, if you just reach out and take it?"

Michael tolerated his father's imprecations because he knew they contained a grain of truth. It was important to be ambitious. There was no denying that Judd's philosophy had had positive effects on Michael over the years. How else, indeed, could his Olympic victories be explained? No man was likely to accomplish great things in this world without being driven by the need to excel.

But Judd pushed too hard. Michael had been forced to learn the subtle art of seeming to agree with his father while secretly going his own way. It was not an easy task, and it was getting harder as Michael's stature grew among his political colleagues.

"Palleschi is a good man, Dad." Ingrid thought highly of Palleschi, as did Michael and Susan. "He's dedicated and he's honest."

"There are good men everywhere," Judd retorted. "We need something more than a good man. We need the *right* man."

Ingrid sighed. "Go on. Turn the record over and let me hear the other side."

"Goss is up in the polls because of the *Crescent Queen* and this Everhardt business," Judd said. "He's trying to ride the people's fear right into the White House. And if he gets in, it will be impossible to get him out. That's what the voters don't understand. They're flirting with dictatorship."

Father and daughter were silent as the waves crashed against the beach outside. The emptiness of the house loomed behind them, a painful reminder of happier days when the busy Campbell clan filled the place with noise and activity.

It was in this house that Judd's wife had died. He still kept her bedroom exactly as she had had it when she was alive. He never let a week go by without entering it to sit by the window in the rocking chair and to murmur a few loving words to Margery. The chair was too small—it had been built for her body—but it made him feel close to her.

Judd looked past Ingrid at the wind-whipped bay. He was thinking that he had his own reasons for hating Colin Goss.

Nearly thirty years ago Judd's conglomerate had locked horns with the growing Goss drug empire. Colin Goss wanted to take over a nationwide chain of pharmacies that had financial links to Judd's own network of companies. For a while there was talk of an amicable partnership between Goss and Judd. The two men even had a series of dinners together. One of these included their wives. Judd was shocked by the way Colin Goss looked at Margery, who at that time was an auburn-haired Irish beauty barely out of her twenties. Goss did not even try to conceal his covetousness. He flirted blatantly with Margery, who seemed embarrassed by his attentions.

A jealous husband despite his own infidelities, Judd saw red. He used his superior financial leverage to cut Goss off at the ankles, and acquired the pharmacies himself. The deal set Goss back by at least a year in his rise to supremacy among pharmaceutical giants. Goss and Judd never spoke again.

In later years Judd had watched with contempt as Goss went into politics and made himself a national figure. The very notion of a scoundrel like Goss in the White House was outrageous. Not only was the man a blatant racist; there were sexual skeletons in his closet—ugly ones—that the public knew nothing about. He would be a national disaster as president. But he was a fighter, and a patient one. He had endured three electoral defeats, knowing that some day the right circumstances could give him a chance to slip into power.

Now, by a twist of fate, his chance had come. And Michael was one of those who stood between Goss and his goal. Once again it was Campbell versus Goss.

Ingrid was gazing through the jalousie windows at the choppy bay. She wore her usual spinsterish outfit, a dark skirt and a sensible jersey with heavy low-heeled shoes. She seemed even more massive and stolid than usual. Her eyes, at rest, were ineffably tired and sad. She was a woman who had long since surrendered her own identity to her devotion to others. She had never had a boyfriend. Judd suspected she was a virgin, even now.

"Well?" Judd prodded. "Am I right?"

"It's beside the point," Ingrid said. "Palleschi is the man. And even if he wasn't, the president wouldn't ask Michael. Michael is too young, and that's all there is to it. He's only thirty-four."

"JFK was only thirty-eight when he campaigned for vice president in 1956," Judd said. "Nixon was thirty-eight in 1951. Dan Quayle was only thirty-three when he ran with Bush." Clearly Judd had done his homework on the ages of past vice presidents. "And if the president serves out his term Michael will be thirty-seven when he becomes president. That's plenty old enough."

"You know what would happen if the president picked Michael," Ingrid said. "Goss would say he was wet behind the ears and that the administration was desperate. That might make things even worse than they are now."

"And it might make them a lot better," Judd countered. "Your brother is a national hero, is case you'd forgotten, Ing. And remember, the brass ring may only come around once. There's no telling what may happen in the next eight or twelve years. There might be an unbeatable incumbent in the White House when Michael's day comes. There might not even *be* a White House. I never heard it said that the way to get something you want is to wait for it. You take it."

Ingrid sighed. "I don't know what we're arguing about. Tom Palleschi has the job. There's nothing we can do but wish him the best."

Judd Campbell said nothing. He brought the glass of dark ale to his lips, gazing out pensively at the waves.

Ingrid left the porch without a sound. She moved well for a big woman.

2 5

BY THE New Year the mysterious syndrome that had felled Dan Everhardt had spread around the world.

Outbreaks of the illness had been observed in Europe, Asia, Africa, and North and South America, with a slight preponderance in North Africa and the Middle East. The World Health Organization estimated the total number of victims at over 75,000. In the United States alone some 6,500 people had been affected.

Public health authorities were working overtime to identify the pathogen behind the disease. The media were full of reassuring stories from medical experts and government officials who promised a prompt offensive against the epidemic.

The stories were planted to prevent panic. In reality the authorities had no clue as to the cause of the illness, or how to treat it.

A paramedic in Australia had come up with the grim nickname "Pinocchio Syndrome," which referred to the victims' initial appearance of mulelike stubbornness, and to the horrifying metamorphosis of their hands and feet into hooflike appendages not long before death. The media had jumped on the name. The Syndrome was capturing the public imagination as no disease had done in a century.

The president could not give a news conference without having to answer a dozen questions about the sickness. His stock answer was to defer to the doctors and public health specialists in charge of investigating the epidemic. He expressed deep sadness and concern over the thousands of families affected, and strongly advised Americans not to panic.

"We will lose a lot more by giving in to fear than by continuing to lead our normal, productive lives while the experts find a cure to this disease," he repeated.

But the spreading illness had spawned an epidemic of fear. Parents were keeping their children out of school and away from public areas like shopping malls and movie theaters. Families were drinking bottled water and avoiding fresh food from supermarkets. Restaurants were losing business because potential customers were afraid of exposure to tainted food and to other customers.

People were wearing surgical masks when they went shopping or to work. The more hypochondriacal were staying at home entirely. Some of the affluent were studying the map of the world and moving their families to areas that were not yet touched by the disease, like Hawaii, the southern tip of South America, and Greenland.

The public was aware that no medical treatment had been found that could slow the relentless progress of the disease as it killed individual victims. From diagnosis to death the Syndrome took between seven and nine weeks, with coma supervening after the first month and the hideous physical changes appearing during the last weeks of life.

The AIDS epidemic had planted in the public mind the fear of a "Doomsday Disease," incurable and always fatal, that would find a more universal and unstoppable means of transmission than mere sexual intimacy. A disease you didn't have to court through behavior or choice. A disease that would find you wherever you were, whoever you were. A disease that would wipe out the human race. This fear, having lurked beneath the surface of public awareness for a generation, now exploded uncontrollably.

Coming on the heels of the *Crescent Queen* attack, which had been neither explained nor punished, the epidemic had an apocalyptic quality. The memory of the fatal mushroom cloud over the Mediterranean mingled in the public mind with images of Pinocchio victims with their rigid bodies and their fixed visionary stare. It did not require much imagination these days to fear that the end of the world was at hand.

The political effect of this panic was unfortunate for the president. As the incumbent he was perceived as the man who had allowed the chaos to happen. The same went for his party, whose influence nationwide was at an all-time low.

The administration's denials that Dan Everhardt had the dread disease had not kept rumors at bay. There was a public perception—not echoed out loud by the media, but trumpeted on countless websites—that Everhardt was a victim of the Syndrome.

Colin Goss, in radio and TV ads that played in prime time across the nation, announced that it was "time for a change," that the current administration followed a "policy of failure," that it was past time for Americans to cease living under a "politics of fear." Goss's ads exploited the epidemic without alluding to it directly. The technique was effective.

Goss's face, shorn of its old hateful expression and carefully modeled in a paternal look of competence and strength, was to be seen on billboards across America. A face that had once frightened many, it now reassured people. And they expressed their feelings in opinion polls that showed Goss well ahead of the president in popularity.

Like the despair that had swept Franklin D. Roosevelt into the White House during the Depression, and Ronald Reagan into office after the oil crisis and hostage crisis of the late 1970s, the current hysteria was making Colin Goss's campaign into a snowball that might be impossible to stop.

Time for a change, said Goss's ads. Their subliminal message was all too clear. The change had already occurred. The question was how much time remained.

IN THIS climate of intense anxiety Karen Embry's article about the disease sparked a firestorm of condemnation.

Though the article was entitled "What If . . . ?" and appeared only on editorial pages, it brought countless outraged letters to the editor. Readers felt that things were bad enough already without irresponsible reporters cranking out paranoid ramblings about conspiracies. Public outrage was so vehement that the editors who had published the piece had to print apologies.

"Our goal as journalists," wrote one editor in a published retraction, "should be to report things as they are in a constructive fashion. To invoke far-fetched scenarios at a time when they can only cause great distress is not responsible journalism."

So intense was the outcry that even the president's press secretary felt compelled to respond publicly.

"We are at a difficult moment in our history," he said. "The president feels it is vital that all Americans pull together in the face of this public health challenge. We need to believe in ourselves and in each other, now more than ever. The president deplores those irresponsible rumormongers who, for the sake of their own self-interest and with no sensitivity to the pain and grief of the victims and their families, are making a stressful situation worse."

No further mention of Karen's article or its contents was to be found in the media. Every editor in the nation cooperated in covering the embarrassing episode with silence.

However, the Internet was subject to no such scruples. Chat rooms around the world buzzed with excited talk about the conspiracy theory. Web surfers, who tended to be paranoid in any case, leaped on the theory hungrily. They blamed the spreading epidemic on the Russians, the Chinese, the CIA, the Martians, the Venutians. In her attempt to get at the truth Karen Embry had unwittingly tapped into the most primitive level of human fear. Her article was now a tool of the lunatic fringe.

Karen now found herself persona non grata in Washington. No elected official would talk to her. Even those in government who privately sympathized with her were too frightened to open their doors to her. The sources who had helped her when she first moved to the capital now dried up.

Her agent strongly suggested she move away, perhaps to the West Coast, and publish under a pseudonym from now on. Privately he thought it was time she abandoned journalism altogether and found a new profession.

———

THE CIA director called in Mitch Fallon, his press secretary, in a rage.

"I thought I told you I didn't want to hear from this bitch again," he said.

"It's a free country," Fallon shrugged. "I did what I could. No one on the federal level cooperated with her, I can guarantee you that. But we can't stop newspapers from printing whatever they see fit. And the Internet is—well, the Internet. They do whatever they want."

Fallon had never seen the director this angry. His eyes were bulging, his face red. "I'll make her regret this," he said, "if it's the last thing I ever do."

"Cheer up," Fallon coaxed. "No one printed it as news. It only appeared on the opinion page, and only in a handful of newspapers at that."

"That's not the point," the director said. "I knew that bitch was trouble the minute I laid eyes on her."

"What can we do?" Fallon asked.

"Tail her," the director replied. "Bug her apartment."

"Do you really want to bother?" Fallon asked. "Her name is already Mudd all over town."

"I want to make sure it stays that way."

"That's harassment," Fallon argued.

"No, it's not," the director fumed. "It's protection of the national security. A paid agent of a hostile power couldn't be more dangerous than she is. The last thing we need in this country is panic. She's a menace."

Fallon said, "Okay." He left without another word.

The director looked at the small photo of Karen's pretty face that had been published alongside her article in the *Post*. His eyes lingered on her delicate features for a moment. Then he crumpled the article and, with a single expletive, threw it into his wastebasket.

———

THE NEWS from Walter Reed was that Dan Everhardt was near death from the Pinocchio Syndrome. Dan would be the first famous person to die of the disease here at home. His death would come as a symbolic blow to the authorities' claim that the situation was "well in hand." Now everyone would know that even the famous and powerful were not immune. It was a chastening realization.

For Tom Palleschi, the situation was worrisome. Not on his own behalf, but because of his wife.

From the outset Theresa Palleschi had been against Tom replacing Dan Everhardt. She was worried for his safety.

"There's something wrong about this whole thing," Theresa told Tom. "Colin Goss, and this epidemic, and Dan Everhardt getting sick that way . . . Something is wrong, and I don't want you involved in it."

Theresa had always been philosophical about being a political wife. She understood that Tom was devoted to public service. All these years she had tolerated his long hours, his occasional preoccupation, and sometimes mental exhaustion, because she knew he loved his work. She listened willingly to his passionate conversation about the issues of the day, and shared his pride when he contributed to solving some of the problems facing the country. Tom Palleschi was a born public servant, and a gifted one. Theresa accepted this.

But the illness of Everhardt and the spreading epidemic had changed her attitude.

"Your children need a father," she told him. "They're more important than any job."

"Terry, the president needs me. Can't you see that?"

"They needed Everhardt, too," she retorted. "And where did it get them?"

"Terry . . ."

"It's not worth it," she insisted. "I was willing to share you with the federal government when it was just a question of long hours and overwork. But I'm not going to let you get yourself killed just to make things easier for the administration. They can find somebody else."

"Terry, I have an obligation here," he had remonstrated.

"You have an obligation to your children," she insisted. "And to me."

"What about my country?" he asked. "Doesn't that mean something?"

To his surprise, Theresa was unmoved.

"Your children mean more," she said. "Let the president find another partner and fight off Goss if he can. Then they can offer you whatever job they like, and I won't say a word. But I don't want you on that hot seat with all this other stuff going on. There's something evil about this business."

She would not listen to his arguments. She was scared for him, and for their six growing children if anything happened to him. The Palleschis were hardly poor—Tom's business successes had left them well fixed financially—but the children needed a father. Theresa was convinced Tom would be in real danger, physical danger, if he became vice president.

In the end Tom had to refuse her. He accepted the president's offer and was currently awaiting Senate approval as vice president.

On the night before his return to work after the holidays, Tom tried to make love to Theresa. She refused.

"I can't take you for granted when you might not be here next week," she said. "I can't have you touch me when those are the stakes."

"Terry, you're exaggerating. For God's sake, there are Secret Service agents watching everybody in the executive branch."

"Did they help Dan Everhardt?" she asked.

Tom sighed. "I admit, there's been some bad luck. But you can't build it up into a conspiracy without evidence."

"There is enough evidence for me," she insisted.

She turned away from him and closed her eyes.

Tom lay beside her, waiting futilely for sleep, until the clock on his bedside table said four-thirty. Then he gave up and decided to go out running earlier than usual. He did his best thinking while running. Perhaps things might seem clearer if he did six or seven miles before breakfast.

He brushed his teeth quickly and put on sweats and running shoes. He wore out a pair of good running shoes in two or three months. Theresa worried that he would have a heart attack while running. To oblige her Tom had regular cardiovascular checkups. He was in perfect health, of course. Running all those miles for so many years had helped.

He passed the hall mirror and looked at his face. It was more lined now, and somewhat heavier. The eyes were worried. But there was also a barely disguised look of excitement. Could this be the face of the next vice president of the United States?

He put some food in the dog's bowl and looked out the front window. A car was parked on the street in front of the house. Secret Service. He recognized the agents, and nodded to them as he jogged past the car.

After checking his stopwatch he took his usual route through the suburban streets, planning to end his run at the 7-Eleven on the corner of Waldron

Avenue for a cup of coffee. He enjoyed chatting with the owner, a feisty Italian immigrant who considered Tom his *paisan*. The fellow had a large family, like Tom, and enjoyed discussing the issues of the day. Unfortunately, he was a rabid Colin Goss supporter, and believed that only Goss could "save the country" in this perilous time.

The government agents following in their unmarked sedan were talking politics as they shadowed Palleschi. Both men liked Palleschi and had been invited in for a drink by him when they were first given this assignment. The more liberal of the two thought Palleschi should be president. The other agent, though he could not say it out loud, intended to vote for Colin Goss if a special election was called. The country needed a strong leader right now. Goss was the strongest man available.

As he started the fifth mile Tom felt a pulse of weakness, barely noticeable, in his midsection. It spread slowly upward toward his chest. There was a ringing in his ears.

He decided not to do the last two miles, which would have taken him around his favorite group of blocks one more time. Perhaps the stress had taken its toll. He did not feel as strong as usual.

He looked at the 7-Eleven down the block, which was just coming into view. For an instant it seemed the building cringed away from him, shrinking in upon itself. *Strange,* he thought. Then the store's lights, reflected by the wet street, seemed to be crawling up his body and into his mouth. He choked, coughed, shook his head to free his lungs, but it was no use. Even the sky was coming down upon him, slithering into his mouth, leaving no room for air.

He stopped, leaning an arm against the brick building next to the 7-Eleven. He wanted to call out to the agents following in the car, but the words would not come. Nor could he now move his arm.

"Hey, look, he must be tired," said the younger agent.

"I thought he was in better shape," his companion said. "He cut two miles off the run. Maybe he's got a hangover."

"Are you kidding? On one glass of wine a day?"

Palleschi did not move. His posture looked less natural now. The agents pulled their car up and got out. The Italian proprietor of the 7-Eleven was just coming out the door to greet Palleschi.

"Hey, your coffee's not ready yet."

The agents met the proprietor at the wall against which Palleschi was standing. They were already worried.

They became more worried when they saw the look in Palleschi's eyes.

"Mr. Secretary?" asked the older agent.

Palleschi did not respond. The agent tried to take his arm, but Palleschi was rigid. He seemed stubborn in his immobility.

"Jesus," the younger agent whispered.

"Get on the radio," barked his colleague. "We need an ambulance."

2 6

Georgetown
January 15

THE MEDIA reacted to the news of Tom Palleschi's illness like sharks smelling blood.

The White House was besieged by reporters demanding to know whether Palleschi had fallen victim to the Pinocchio Syndrome, like Dan Everhardt before him.

White House spokesmen, aware of the potentially disastrous fallout from the story, denied emphatically that Palleschi had the Syndrome. His illness, they insisted, was hypertension related and already under control. A quick recovery was expected.

The president's poll numbers immediately plummeted. Nothing could have been more damaging to his administration's image than the specter of illness. Deliberation in the Senate over Palleschi's confirmation ceased. In its place came heated debate over whether to pass a constitutional amendment allowing for a special election to name a new president.

So great was the embarrassment caused by Palleschi's incapacitation that thought was given to confecting a Boris Yeltsin–style video to prove that Palleschi was not seriously ill. But in his paralyzed condition Palleschi could hardly feign normality. File tape would have to be used for the video, and the media would certainly see through it. In the end it was decided to do nothing but wait and hope for the best.

During this tense period Joseph Kraig took an hour off from his busy schedule to pay a visit to Susan Campbell at her Georgetown house.

She had asked him to come in the middle of the day, when Michael would not be home. On the phone she wouldn't say what it was about. Kraig had agreed, wondering what she could possibly want to talk to him about.

He did not relish the idea of being alone with her. In the years since his divorce he had avoided the Campbells as much as he could. Being around Susan was painful for him.

Kraig had been Michael's close friend at Harvard, and his roommate freshman year. Kraig had been present on the sidelines when Michael was courting Susan. He had met her at the hospital when Michael was having his second surgery, and had had many a heart-to-heart talk with her about Michael and about herself.

Even in those days Kraig had not lied to himself about his feelings for her. Her softness, her fragility, the passion under her cautious exterior—these qualities brought out a deep longing when he was with her. He coveted his times with her unscrupulously. When he was not with her he thought about her. His loyalty to Michael deepened during that time, not only because of Michael's painful surgery and convalescence, but because Michael was now Susan's lover. That fact exalted him in Kraig's eyes, and made him seem more precious as a friend.

Kraig did not get over his love for Susan. He correctly sensed he would never have such feelings for another woman. Years later, when he met and married Cathy, his attraction to her, though sincere, was a pale shadow of what he felt for Susan. He tried to deny this, and gave a great deal of effort to his marriage. But when it went sour and he ended up divorced, he couldn't help wondering if he had chosen Cathy in bad faith, and thus doomed their relationship.

Indeed, during the last painful stages of their marriage Cathy often accused him of never having loved her in the right way.

"You picked me out because you thought it was the right time for you," she said. "Not because you really believed I was the right girl." Kraig denied this hotly, but he came to wonder whether his denials had the force of truth.

In any case, he had never stopped thinking about Susan during his marriage. He carried her image inside his brain like a guilty secret. And when he and Cathy broke up, he found it hard to be with Susan. His old feelings for her returned with a force magnified by his unhappiness.

Susan was waiting for him when he got out of the car. She was wearing a soft wool dress, perhaps a bit too conservative for her, but she looked magnificent in it. Her long hair was down over her shoulders. Her sensitive fingers nestled in his as he shook her hand.

"Welcome, stranger."

"It's good to see you, Susan."

She took his coat and watched him precede her into the house. She had not seen him in a year or more. He had not changed all that much. A little heavier and stronger looking, a little gray at the temples now. His skin, always ruddy, was a bit more lined. He gave the impression of a great deal of masculine force, combined with a secret sadness that made him attractive.

Susan knew that Kraig was not a happy man. His divorce had left scars, probably very deep ones. He had not had a serious romance since Cathy left him. He lived for his work, but he did not seem to enjoy it.

"How is your daughter?" Susan asked.

"Fine. She's in sixth grade. I have now attained the status of creep as far as she's concerned. She can't stand to have her friends see her with me."

"Oh, it can't be as bad as all that," Susan said.

"I suppose it really isn't," Kraig said. "I've got time on my side. She'll outgrow this phase."

Susan nodded, hoping that Kraig could not see the jealousy in her eyes. She would give her right arm to have a young daughter like his.

"And you?" she asked in a hospitable tone. "How are things?"

Kraig's look was friendly but evasive. "Oh, same old thing," he said. "Too much work, and not much results. Some day I'll probably get out. Practice law or something. Far from here."

"I sympathize," Susan said, gesturing for him to sit down. "Some days all

I think about is starting over someplace far from here. But I don't have that choice, unfortunately."

Kraig nodded. He was aware of her dilemma. He knew she hated politics and had never gotten used to it. The falseness of it offended her, as did the exposure. But she was trapped. Michael was working his way up the ladder to greater and greater visibility. One day she might have to assume the unenviable position of First Lady. That would be agony for her.

"I saw you on *Good Morning America* last week," he said.

She blushed to think of the fluff interview she had done. "Why did you want to tune in a thing like that?"

He shrugged. "Business, I suppose. You're pretty visible lately."

He wasn't about to admit that he always set up his machine to tape anything that had Susan in it. Or that he watched every appearance she made a dozen times, and had great trouble convincing himself to erase any of the tapes.

"A lot more visible than I'd like," she said. "Would you like a drink?"

"Whatever you're having."

"Coffee?"

"Sure."

"Still milk and Equal?"

He smiled. "You've got a good memory." He was touched that she remembered. A long time ago they had drunk many a cup of coffee together. He had sometimes left her with caffeine jangling in his ears, because he had not been able to tear himself away from her.

When she came back into the room her face was serious.

"What's up?" he asked.

"I've been getting some strange phone calls," she said. "Crank calls, I guess you would call them."

"Why did you pick up?" Kraig asked. "Don't you have an answering service?"

"We do, for business. I also have a machine here for personal calls. Sometimes I pick up instead of monitoring—when I'm expecting a call from Michael. That's what happened in this case."

"What did the caller say?"

"It was a woman," Susan said. "She said that Michael will be chosen as vice president this year."

"This year?" Kraig raised an eyebrow. "That's crazy."

"I told her it was impossible," Susan said. "But she seemed absolutely sure. She told me I wasn't willing or able to see the truth yet, but that soon I would be convinced. She seemed—it was as though she knew something I didn't."

"A woman," Kraig said. "How was the voice?"

"Husky. Strange. She sounded sort of faraway, and yet there was an intimacy about it. As though she knew me. As though she knew what I was thinking before I myself did. A step ahead."

She thought for a moment. "And there was another aspect. A sort of sympathy. As though she was my friend, and wanted to help me."

"Help you?"

"She said that when it happened—when Michael was chosen—it would all be up to me. And that I would need a friend. She said she would be that friend."

"What would be up to you?" Kraig asked.

"To get him not to take the job," she said. "I think that's what she meant."

"Was she threatening?" Kraig asked.

"Yes and no. It was frightening, but she didn't actually threaten. She just assured me that Michael would be the president's choice, and that when the time came no one could stop him but me."

"When did you get these calls?" Kraig asked.

"The first one was before the holidays, last fall. She called me right after Danny Everhardt got sick. She told me he would not get well, and that Michael would be the nominee. Then, after the president chose Tom Palleschi, she called again. She assured me that Tom would not become vice president."

Kraig reddened a bit. The caller had been right about Palleschi, who was now gravely ill, probably from the Pinocchio Syndrome, and would certainly not become vice president this year.

Kraig looked skeptical.

"Sounds like your garden-variety crank caller to me," he said.

Susan was silent, thinking.

"Why?" she asked.

"What you have to understand, Susan, is that there are cranks who spend the whole day on the phone, all day every day. A single crank will call a dozen well-known people, or their families, with vague threats. Usually the caller will mention some kind of conspiracy. The phone company deals with them all the time. They're usually paranoid schizophrenics. They're completely harmless, though they're a nuisance."

Susan was listening intently, as though eager to grasp at any crumb of reassurance Kraig could offer her.

"Why Michael?" she asked.

"Mike is the ideal choice for a crank," Kraig said. "For one thing he's been a household name since the Olympics. For another, he's widely thought of as a potential presidential candidate. He's handsome, he's charismatic—he's got it all. He's a crank's dream."

He thought for a moment. "And there is another aspect. Mike wasn't just another Olympic athlete. Those two back operations made him look vulnerable. His public image combines vulnerability and heroism. Like Kennedy with *PT-109*. A crank will fantasize on that kind of image."

Susan nodded. "I never thought of it that way."

"Then there's you," Kraig said. "You're very beautiful. Your face is all over the media. You're a made-to-order tabloid star in your own right."

A pang of familiar pain made itself felt inside Kraig as he referred to Susan's beauty. He forced himself to continue in a clinically impersonal voice. "You're known as a vulnerable person yourself because of the things you've said over the years. Also, there is the childlessness angle. A crank will get off on a thing like that. He'll think you don't have children because of some sort of plot or conspiracy. Communists, Martians, Venutians—you name it. Conception and pregnancy is one of their fetishes."

"I see." Susan was thoughtful. "I guess you've dealt with a lot of cranks," she said.

"Dozens. Hell, hundreds. I've worked with the phone company and the FBI on them. It's so predictable that you get hardened to it."

Susan nodded uncertainly.

"I see what you mean," she said. "But she seemed so sure . . . It was scary."

Kraig smiled. Susan's neurotic personality again. She was too thin-skinned to be able to laugh off a crank. In this way, as in others, she was not cut out to be a political wife.

"What is it you're afraid of, Susan?" Kraig asked.

"This disease," Susan said, avoiding his eyes. "When Danny Everhardt got sick, that was bad enough. But Tom Palleschi too . . ."

Kraig looked at her steadily. She had touched on a sore point with him. He could not confirm that Palleschi suffered from the same disorder as Dan Everhardt. On the other hand he did not want to lie blatantly to her. She had asked him here because she wanted to confide in him. He did not want to destroy that claim to closeness with her.

"I keep thinking about how closely Michael worked with Danny, and with Tom," she said. "I mean, if there is a problem of exposure, Michael must have been exposed."

"I've talked to the public health authorities," Kraig said. "They have no evidence that the disease is communicable from human to human. If Michael could have caught it from Everhardt, he would have been sick a long time ago."

Susan tried to take comfort from his words. But the voice of the crank caller came back to her, speaking with an eloquence all its own. *Palleschi will not be the vice president. Michael will be chosen.*

She looked at Joe Kraig's tanned face and calm eyes. She trusted Kraig as much as any man alive except Michael. She had known him for fifteen years and never heard him say a word that wasn't true. Yet her own fear had more power than his reassurances.

"What if Tom Palleschi doesn't get better?" Susan asked. "What if the president asked Michael to become vice president?"

Kraig smiled. "He won't. Michael is too young. He's out of the running, Susan."

"But . . ." Her words trailed off.

"Tell me what's scaring you, Susan," Kraig said gently.

There was a silence.

"Joe," Susan said, "what if someone was able to make people sick? Deliberately, I mean."

"What are you saying?" Kraig asked. "That Everhardt was eliminated by someone?"

Susan thought for a moment, chewing her lip nervously. "When she called the second time, she said *when Palleschi is removed*. Those were her words. *When Palleschi is removed.*" She was looking intently at Kraig. "And now—now Tom is sick."

Kraig did not flinch. "You said the first call came after Everhardt got sick. Right?"

Susan nodded. "That's right."

"The caller was just trying out a theory on you," Kraig said. "She's paranoid, and she's trying to make you paranoid. No one is being removed, Susan. That simply doesn't happen in politics."

"But she was right," Susan hazarded.

Kraig kept his face expressionless. Susan was very close to the painful truth. The intelligence agencies were working overtime with the health authorities to discover how Everhardt and Palleschi, two isolated cases, had been infected by a disease that always claimed multiple victims.

"It was a shot in the dark," he said. "She was just trying to scare you."

Susan nodded uncomfortably. Kraig could see she wanted to believe him, but her fear was strong.

Kraig decided to be firm with her.

"I want you to do two things for me. First, stop answering the phone. You've got answering machines and answering services for that. Second, stop worrying about this. You can't let a crank caller give you sleepless nights. That's what she wants, you know. That's how they get their kicks."

Susan weighed the look in Kraig's eyes—serious, firm—against the tone of the voice on the phone. It was a close call. The conviction in the caller's voice had been every bit as strong as Joe Kraig's conviction that it was all nonsense.

Kraig had one advantage. He enjoyed Susan's confidence, and had for many years. No human being alive had a stronger claim to her trust. But the caller also had an advantage. Her prediction had come true. Tom Palleschi was sick, and would almost certainly not replace Dan Everhardt.

Susan gave a weak laugh. "You probably think I'm completely off my rocker, don't you?"

Kraig shook his head. "This is a very tense year. The president is under attack, and so is everyone close to him. The *Crescent Queen* has left everyone afraid a nuclear bomb is going to fall on them at any moment. With Goss doing so well in the polls, a lot of things we once took for granted don't seem so sure. And Michael is on the front lines of all this. No, Susan—I don't blame you a bit for feeling tense. And the caller knew that. She used it, too."

He stood up to leave.

"Do you have to go already?" Susan asked.

"Afraid so. Duty calls." Kraig was lying. He could have stayed with her another hour if he wanted. But he could not bear the pain of prolonged exposure to her.

"Thank you for coming," she said. She stood up. The sight of her slender legs and delicate shoulders, in the soft dress, made him feel weak.

"No problem," he said. "Call me if you have any more trouble. Have you told Mike about this, by the way?"

She shook her head. "He has enough on his mind."

"You should tell him," Kraig said. "He'd want the opportunity to reassure you."

"He does enough of that already," she said. "I want him to keep his mind on his work. I don't want him fretting about a neurotic wife."

Kraig did not reply.

She walked with him to the foyer.

"We don't see as much of you as we'd like, Joe," she said.

"Well, you know how it is," he said. "Business is business."

She knew he was keeping his distance intentionally since his divorce. She wasn't sure why, but she knew Kraig well enough to know that the best way to be a friend to him was to give him plenty of space. He was a very private man.

They went into the foyer, and she helped him on with his trench coat. She noticed the gray in his hair as she stood close to him. It made him look handsome, but it saddened her, because she knew Kraig lived alone now with no woman to share his life. He was growing older without a wife.

She went out onto the stoop with him. The sky was gray, the wind brisk. He turned to say his good-bye.

She hesitated before saying, "Joe, there's one more thing."

"What is it?"

"The woman on the phone . . . She told me to ask Michael about what happened at Harvard. Do you have any idea what she might have meant?"

"What happened at Harvard?" Kraig asked. "Nothing happened."

Susan was looking at him in silence.

"You were there," Kraig said. "You were his best girl. I was his best friend. I guess one or the other of us would know. Don't you think?"

Susan frowned. "I guess so."

"I'll tell you a secret," Kraig said. "Mike led a very boring life before you came along. I know. I was his roommate."

Susan smiled.

"Well, then," she said. "I guess you'd know."

He could see from the look in her eyes that she was less reassured than she pretended to be. The temptation to protect her, to comfort her, was strong.

"Call me if anything worries you," he said. "That's what I'm here for."

"I will," she said. "Thanks. And don't be such a stranger from now on."

He got into his car and started the engine. The car was chilled already by the cold sunless air. As he drove off he saw Susan in his rearview mirror, smiling and waving. She looked very natural, framed that way against the cheerful red brick of Michael's house. She grew smaller and smaller as he drove away. He couldn't stop looking back, though, and saw her turn to go back into the house just before he reached the corner.

27

Alexandria, Virginia
January 15

LIQUOR HAD been with Karen Embry all her life. She used to hate the sweet smell of the booze on her mother's breath when the mother came in to say good night. That cloying odor symbolized her mother's absorption in her own drunkenness and her lack of interest in her daughter. Usually she interrupted an argument with her husband for the good night kiss, and resumed the argument in slurred words as soon as the little girl's bedroom door was closed.

When Karen's father left, the quarrels ended. There was only the sound of the TV from the other room, and the clink of ice in her mother's glass. Karen found herself missing even the ugly quarrels, because they at least meant she had a father.

She never saw him again. He was killed in a one-car accident two years after he left. He drove off a quiet country road straight into a thick oak tree at eight o'clock in the morning. His blood alcohol was five times the legal limit. "Serves him right," Mother said.

A series of boyfriends, all alcoholics, followed the father. One of them sexually abused Karen repeatedly over a seven-month period, until her mother threw him out for "spending all her money." Karen told no one about what had happened. She didn't trust the world of adults.

From the time Karen entered junior high in Waltham, Massachusetts, her efforts in school were devoted to the single purpose of getting her out of her mother's house. She became a reporter even then, working for the school newspaper. In high school she found part-time work at a suburban weekly and acted as a stringer for the *Globe*. As a junior she applied for early admission to Northwestern and was admitted to its prestigious journalism school.

She was never at home. She filled her time with clubs, reporting, the lacrosse team (until she injured her knee and had to quit)—and, when that wasn't enough, boys.

She slept with a half dozen of the boys in her own class and the class ahead of hers. She was attractive, a slender, nubile teenager with black shining hair and bright eyes. She could have any boy she wanted.

She felt nothing in these encounters. Somewhere deep inside herself she knew she was not ready for love, would perhaps never be ready. But she was learning the art of manipulation, an art she knew she would need as a journalist.

At Northwestern she did a grueling double major in biochemistry and journalism. She slept with a visiting professor who was a columnist for the *St. Louis Post-Dispatch*. He had many contacts throughout the profession and helped her get summer jobs in Chicago at the *Tribune*.

One winter evening, as Karen was leaving her dorm on Sheridan Road to fight her way through the vicious Lake Michigan wind to the library, she was stopped by a friend with a message. Her mother had been found dead in her bungalow back in Boston, apparently the victim of a heart attack brought on by years of alcohol abuse.

Karen flew home to dispose of her mother's few possessions. The house was so full of empty liquor bottles that her aunt and uncle had to carry them out in cartons with a hand truck.

When the lawyer had finished his work and the house was empty, Karen stood alone in the living room at midnight. She filled a glass with straight bourbon and drank a toast to her past.

"On the house," she said, pouring the dregs of her drink on the pockmarked hardwood floor.

Her first serious job was as a political reporter for the *Tribune*. After two years, fed up with the lake wind and Chicago politics, she took a job at the *New York Post*. She would have stayed, but the *Globe* offered her a job as an investigative reporter. Her major in biochemistry came in handy as she began to specialize in public health stories. Her series of articles on toxic waste resulted in billion-dollar lawsuits against four New England manufacturers. She also did features on negligence in the HMO industry. These played well in the Sunday magazine section, for health issues were always popular among readers.

As the years passed she grew more cynical about power and its uses. People in high places told the truth as seldom as possible. They sought only to protect their own asses and to increase their influence. Whether they worked in government or in the private sector, they cared little for the human race. Karen enjoyed cutting them down to size.

By now her paranoid "hunches" about wrongdoing in high places had become well known to colleagues. "Embry sees conspiracies in baseball scores and wind chill factors," joked one editor. Sometimes her hunches were wrong. But when they were right she got to important stories weeks or months ahead of other reporters. And her stories rated headlines.

Her search for the truth had become a thinly disguised vendetta against a faceless adversary. Karen was a crusader who believed in nothing. The awards she won were like so many shields covering her own emptiness. The liquor she drank was the elixir that allowed her to make believe she was happy.

She thought she would go on this way forever. Absorbed in her work, she had lost the impulse to know herself. She was living with Troy, who was as bad a workaholic as she and had his own substance abuse problems.

Then the thin ice she was walking on collapsed under her.

First Troy dumped her. He told her he could no longer stand the burden of her depression added to his own. "We're a bad combination," he said. Karen let him go without hard feelings, but he left a gap. Not only in her apartment, but in her sense of her own possibilities.

A month after their breakup Karen became convinced through some subtle hints that a major hospital supply company in downtown Boston was a front for an illegal drug operation. Though it was only a hunch, she pressed her editor for additional manpower to pursue the story. The editor sent two reporters to surveil the location overnight. No drug transaction took place. But by an unfortunate happenstance one of the reporters was killed in a drive-by shooting at two o'clock in the morning. It turned out the supply house was located on gang turf.

When the editor went to Karen's apartment to tell her the bad news, he found Karen passed out drunk on her living-room floor.

Karen's hunch had been wrong. The hospital supply company was innocent of any wrongdoing. A reporter was dead for no reason.

Karen immediately tendered her resignation. It was accepted. She moved to Washington as a freelance reporter.

She intended to work alone from now on. She felt responsible for the disaster in Boston. She was fed up with editors anyway. The politics of print journalism were too turbid for her, and the salary was too low. She wanted to write feature stories that would evolve into books.

Karen was starting over in more ways than one. Her first months in Washington were productive. The entire city seemed populated by informed sources eager to leak everything they knew about sensitive topics. She made friends quickly, doing favors for those she courted and getting favors in return.

Then came the Pinocchio Syndrome. No topic could have been more perfect for her. A worldwide crisis of monstrous proportions, it would spawn dozens of books, perhaps hundreds. She wanted hers to be the first.

But the inflammatory effect of her article on the Syndrome had made her an overnight pariah among D.C. journalists. Reeling from the setback, she did not know what to do next. If she gave up on the Pinocchio story, she would be throwing away many weeks of backbreaking work. If she pursued it, she would be beating her head against a brick wall. In her frustration she drank more than ever. Her hangovers were monumental. But the river of cheap booze running through her veins did not give her an answer.

Then something happened.

On a frigid Tuesday night, after a fruitless cocktail conversation with a supervisor at the surgeon general's office who had formerly been a friend,

Karen got home at eight. Tired, she peered into the freezer in search of something to eat. She found a tuna casserole and stuck it into the toaster oven.

Peeling off clothes as she went, she headed for the shower. On the way she poured herself a stiff bourbon and sat down at the computer in her bra and panties. She got online and checked her e-mail. There were the usual messages from friends, editors, and other reporters.

A message with an odd title caught her eye.

PINOCCHIO'S NOSE.

She clicked on the message and saw a brief e-mail appear on the screen. The return address meant nothing to her.

The text of the e-mail made her sit up straight.

I READ YOUR ARTICLE. YOU HAVE GOOD EYES. GOOD ENOUGH TO SEE THAT PINOCCHIO'S NOSE IS GETTING LONGER.
IF LONELY WRITE TO GRIMM, PERSONALS COLUMN POST.

Karen sat looking at the message. She took a long sip of her bourbon and set the glass back down. Then she read the message again.

PINOCCHIO'S NOSE.
GRIMM.

Karen did not feel the night air that chilled her scantily clad body. She had forgotten about her shower. She sat with the bourbon in her hand, pensively studying the screen.

Gaithersburg, Maryland
January 18

SECURITY AT Walter Reed remained tight. Now that Tom Palleschi had fallen ill, public curiosity about the Pinocchio Syndrome was out of control. Palleschi's whereabouts were classified information, known to only a handful of high-level Washington people. As for Dan Everhardt, he was under twenty-four-hour guard in his hospital room.

Karen knew she could not get to Palleschi. But Everhardt was another matter. It was time to take risks.

She arrived at the hospital at 3 A.M., wearing a doctor's scrub suit, a stethoscope, and a name tag that identified her as Dr. Dase. The name tag had cost her a lot of money. It bore the army designations and codes required of all Walter Reed physicians, and a photo of her taken under conditions identical to those of the hospital's identification photo studio.

She emerged from the parking lot, moving without hurry despite the cold night air, and breezed through the empty lobby to the elevators. She went up to the fourth floor, where an enlisted man stopped her at the entrance to the ICU.

"At ease, Private," she said. "Dr. Dase to see Vice President Everhardt."

The enlisted man ran a tired eye down his list of authorized names and found that of Dr. Dase. The presence of her name on the list had cost Karen three times as much as the identification card.

"Yes, ma'am. The room is—"

"I know where it is." Karen nodded to the soldier and moved down the corridor without hurry. She looked like any doctor on call at three in the morning. All business, but not happy to be awake at this hour.

Everhardt's room was at the end of the hall, for purposes of privacy as well as comfort. Karen approached it cautiously, surprised to see that there was no guard on the door.

So much for military efficiency, she said to herself.

Without knocking she pushed the door open. Everhardt was lying with his eyes closed on a modified hospital bed with an extra-long mattress. The bed must have been chosen to accommodate his height.

There was a cot by the window. Pam Everhardt, the vice president's wife, lay asleep, her mouth open wide, snoring gently. Emotional exhaustion made her face look sallow and deeply lined.

The most striking thing about Everhardt was how much weight he had lost. He looked wasted, skeletal. In the media he had always seemed huge and athletic. Clearly the disease had destroyed his normal metabolism.

Karen did not need to use her stethoscope to listen to Everhardt's heart. A monitor against the wall showed a slow, irregular heart rate. Another monitor showed dangerously low blood pressure, with the diastolic well below sixty.

Looks like I made it in the nick of time, she told herself.

She moved on tiptoe to the cot where Mrs. Everhardt slept. Something about the woman's face made Karen suspect she was sedated. It was doubtful that any small sounds Karen made would wake her up. She must be accustomed to a steady stream of physicians in the room.

Karen moved to the vice president's bedside. She stood listening to his shallow breathing, alert to telltale sounds from the corridor that would indicate someone was coming. There were none.

She looked again at the monitors against the wall. One of them showed an EEG that looked severely abnormal to Karen. Another was connected to the IV that led to the vice president's arm. Karen had never seen one like it.

Gingerly she pulled back the sheet from his left arm. The mystery line led to a patch attached to the back of the patient's hand. Monitoring cutaneous circulation, she guessed.

The hand was visibly deformed. It was at least twice the size of a normal hand, and the skin tone was darkened and unnaturally shiny. Karen touched it gently, recoiling when she felt the chitinous hardness.

Poor guy. Her heart went out to him, pity eclipsing horror over the grotesque symptoms of the disease. She had seen Everhardt in dozens of interviews. He was a nice, down-to-earth, simple man. He did not deserve this.

The lump under the sheet at the end of his right arm left little doubt as to the condition of the hand, but she took a look anyway. Then she undid the bottom corners of the sheet and looked at his feet. The distention was significant, but even more striking was the pulling back of the toes toward the heel in a hooflike shape.

Karen forced herself to feel the hardened skin. She used a penlight to take a closer look at the partially fused digits of the hands and feet. The deformation was identical to that of the victims she had seen in Australia and of the body in New Hampshire. The syndrome was unquestionably the same.

After another long look at Mrs. Everhardt, Karen removed a tiny camera from the pocket of her scrub suit. It was a Pentax 749, developed specifically for night photography without flash. It bathed the subject in a brief flare of infrared light and produced images that could be corrected by computer enhancement to reproduce natural light. Developed for the intelligence services, it had been discovered by journalists a decade or so ago.

She took photos of Everhardt's hands and feet, close up and at a distance of eighteen inches. The shutter was almost completely inaudible, but she hurried her shooting anyway. She finished with a full-length shot of Everhardt, with face, hands, and feet visible. Then she put away the camera and replaced the sheet.

As she was bending over Everhardt his eyes opened.

Startled, Karen recoiled. Then she forced herself to bring her face close to his.

"Mr. Vice President?" she whispered.

He didn't answer. His eyes were pointed at her, but they seemed to see past her or through her. This was the look she had seen in Iowa, the inward hypnotized look of the Pinocchio victims.

"Can you hear me?" she asked. There was no response.

She rested a hand on his arm, hoping for a flutter of recognition. But the eyes did not focus on her, and there was no indication that he knew she was there.

"Mr. Everhardt, who did this to you?" Karen asked. There was no response.

She glanced at his wife. The sleeping woman had heard nothing.

It was time to go. Karen peeked out of the room. The corridor was empty except for two nurses who were talking quietly at the nurses' station.

Karen left the room and went across the corridor to the staircase. She walked down the four flights to the ground floor. Making notes on her pad like a preoccupied physician, she left the hospital without hurry and walked through the brisk night air to her car.

Dan Everhardt was a dying man. He was being killed by the Pinocchio Syndrome. The first prominent man in America to fall victim to the disease, he would not be the last.

Shaking her head, Karen turned the key in the ignition. The Honda coughed into life. It needed a tune-up, she knew.

But not as much as she needed a drink.

She eased the little car out of the parking lot and headed through the empty streets toward home.

2 9

DAN EVERHARDT lay in his bed, his eyes pointed at the soundproofing tiles on the ceiling.

He could hear his wife snoring softly in her chair. He wished he could call out to her, signal her in some way to come to his side. He felt lonely. More so now that death was approaching.

The illness had many wrinkles, many resonances. The colors that became flavors, the sounds that coiled around one's insides like snakes, the memories that flew up suddenly like birds and were lost. These last two months had not been without events for Dan Everhardt, even adventures.

But the essence of the disease was the separation from those one loved. To hear Pam's voice and to be unable to acknowledge her, and then to see her move away, crushed by his silence. The children, too, bending over their father to comfort him and be comforted—and then moving away disappointed.

It was like Scrooge's visit to his own early life in the company of the Ghost of Christmas Past. Here were the people he loved, close to him, desperate to contact him. And it was he who shut them out.

Or rather, it was the disease, the monster.

He wondered who the girl was, just now. She had bent over him like all the others, asking him if he could hear her. Like all the others she had gazed straight into his eyes, giving him a chance to answer. A chance he could not take.

Unlike the others, she was beautiful. Clear eyes under fresh dark hair, shapely lips, a milky complexion. Something about her reminded him of his youth. There was a time in his life when he idolized girls, put them on a sort of sexual pedestal, as though they were princesses rather than mere human beings.

He used to watch them walk through the hallways of his high school back in New Jersey. The purses they carried, the book satchels, the sweaters or blouses they wore—all their accessories were like sacraments. Coveting them sexually was like worshiping them. If they were princesses, then he was the frog who did not deserve to touch the hem of their garments.

Though he was a football player and had lots of popular friends, he was too shy to be promiscuous. He did not even lose his virginity until he got to college. When he met Pam, an overweight but charming sorority girl, he was all thumbs. He had to call her half a dozen times to make lame small talk before he finally asked her out.

He never entirely lost his adolescent attitude toward women. As a politician he had had many opportunities to be unfaithful to Pam, but he never was. He respected women too much to take their favors lightly.

This girl, the one tonight, looked like an angel. The angel of death? Why not? There was no reason to suppose that death could not take the form of a beautiful young woman. The sight of her had filled him with an almost prayerful yearning.

A religious man, Dan Everhardt now wondered whether God was, in His vast and inscrutable way, similar to her. Perhaps God was bent over mankind, tender and inquiring, waiting for a prayer He could understand and would surely grant. But the human creature was a prisoner inside his own spirit, and could not frame his pleas for help in a language God could comprehend. So God could only look down, eager to redeem and to save, and watch in sad perplexity as man destroyed himself.

The girl had asked, "Mr. Vice President, who did this to you?" Dan Everhardt, a simple man, pondered this question with his dying mind as his eyes closed. Who had done it?

Certainly not God. Not a being who cared about man's redemption and wanted to purify him.

The devil, perhaps? Dan did not know. But if it was true, then the devil was an angel of silence. The death that came closer with each uncertain breath was like a final silence, coming to take him away from Pam forever, and from his children, and from himself.

30

Atlanta
January 19

"We have sad and troubling news from Washington. Vice President Dan Everhardt died early this morning at Walter Reed Army Medical Center. The vice president had been ill for two months. The White House had denied that his condition was serious, but anxious rumors about his health had spread through the nation's capital and beyond."

The doctor sat at his computer screen watching a succession of graphs and tables that displayed the latest quantifications of chemical analyses being updated each day.

At the top of the screen was the title, NUCLEOTIDE FIELD 3AB Δ QPC. The extra heading in the top left corner read: Project 4.2 System 6 CLASSIFIED EYES ONLY.

The doctor's hand shook as he moved the mouse. The movement was rather like that of an eraser being wiped along a blackboard. He missed the line he wanted, tried again, missed again, and finally had to use two hands to steady the mouse.

"Damn," he muttered.

He was wearing cordless headphones on which today's news was playing. The images on the screen were so familiar to him that he did not need to concentrate on them to the exclusion of everything else. He was, after all, the designer of the system on which the displays were based.

His white lab coat bore the same identity card as his civilian jacket. A photograph of his face was outlined by a thick red bar indicating Level Four security clearance. His name, Dr. Easter, was printed in large letters. His first name was Richard. People called him Dick. In high school his friends had made fun of his name, calling him Dick Keester.

The tremor in his hand was not a new problem. However, it was probably exacerbated by what he was hearing.

"Vice President Everhardt would have been fifty-four years old this October," said the cable anchorwoman. "His wife, Pam, was at his side when he died, as were his children and his brother and sister. The president himself made the announcement to White House reporters at eleven o'clock."

The doctor adjusted the volume on the headphones and closed his eyes.

"Dan Everhardt was one of the finest, most dedicated public servants I've had the privilege of knowing," the president said. "But more than that, Danny, as we all called him, was a human being. A warm, lovable, imperfect human being whose devotion to his family far exceeded his political ambition. He will be sorely missed by his many friends and his constituents. I feel this loss personally, because Danny was more than a colleague and support to me. He and I were close friends."

The doctor opened his eyes and turned his swivel chair around so he could look at the TV screen on the other side of the room. A family picture of Everhardt with his wife and children had appeared. The doctor let his eyes linger on it for a moment, then looked away.

"The funeral will be at St. Luke's Church in New Brunswick, the town where the vice president was born. He will be buried with full military honors, since he was a decorated veteran with a distinguished record. The president himself will be one of the speakers."

Confused shouting was heard—the questions of reporters, called out on the White House lawn after the president's address.

"I can't answer that," he said. "You'll have to ask the public health authorities."

The doctor paused. They must be pressing for confirmation that Everhardt died of the Syndrome. He listened more closely.

"I've been assured that the situation is well in hand," the president said evasively. "I really can't tell you any more. This is a day for mourning, not for discussions of epidemiology."

No, the doctor thought. They still wouldn't admit it. They would never admit it. Like Kennedy . . . They would hold out until the public stopped waiting for an answer.

He picked up the mouse again. The tremor in his hand was worse. Cursing his own frailty, he got up from the computer and moved to the closet where he kept his civilian clothes. He fished in the pocket of his jacket for the small bottle of pills. The bottle was opaque, like a film can, with no prescription label or other marking. He took out a pill, popped it in his mouth, and swallowed it dry.

The drug was an antidepressant with powerful antianxiety features, thoroughly tested though not yet available to the public because of the bureaucratic vagaries of the FDA. In clinical trials it outperformed every other medication in its category. Side effects, such as the tremor in his hands, came only with overdose.

The drug's key disadvantage was that it was supremely habit forming. Worse than heroin or morphine. That was why the FDA people were dragging their feet. Too many pharmaceuticals had followed in the footsteps of Quaalude, pentobarbital, PCP, and others, becoming drugs of choice for addicts here and abroad. Drug abuse in the new century was turning out to be even worse than it had been at the end of the twentieth. The pace of life, the frightening changes, were too much for people. Emotional disorders were cropping up everywhere in new variations, quicker than the psychiatrists could learn how to name them for classification in the DSM.

This drug was still known only by its development designation, 246FT. The marketing department was playing with names.

Gritting his teeth, he moved back to the computer. He clicked on the world map screen. There they were, the locations on all the continents with estimates of the number affected. Death tolls were shown in brackets. He clicked on "Zoom" and navigated to the Washington area. Two cases were shown by little animated stickpins. One of them was red already. So they had punched in Everhardt's death, he thought.

He closed his eyes and listened to the hum of the PC. It had a peculiar throbbing quality, like a bell tolling one long, incessant gong of destruction. How had he ever come to this point? A life like anyone else's—plans, ambitions, hard work, marriage, and children—how had it all turned into this horror?

Well, the facts were clear enough. The insanity of malpractice insurance, the thankless job of being a doctor in the age of HMOs. Divorce. Then a period of drifting, a couple of unsuccessful relationships, the struggle with chemicals. Then the unexpected offer of this job. Amazingly lucrative, totally secure. Challenging.

It made sense, the progression. But it was a peculiar kind of sense, leading from the sane to the insane across an invisible boundary. He was a doctor, and now a murderer.

As a child he had been taught that the Nazis used doctors to perform their hideous experiments on Jews and others, immersing them in freezing water, starving them, even carrying out experimental surgery. Where did they find doctors to do such things? A doctor's vocation was to save lives, to comfort the sick. Hippocrates left no doubt: *First do no harm.*

How did such things come about? Now he knew the answer.

He began to feel a faint chill in his stomach. That was the first sign of the drug's action. In a couple of minutes the chill would spread to his chest, and the edge would be taken off his anxiety. Late tonight he might need another dose for sleep. Habit forming, indeed: he needed three pills to get through a day now. Two months ago a single pill would last a day and a night.

When he left work tonight the world would look subaqueous and peculiarly gastronomic, like a sea of honey through which he navigated uncertainly toward his car. The steering wheel would feel like moist clay in his hands. Driving the expressway would be like plunging through layers of jello. The world was an oozing plate of food presented to an invisible giant who would soon spoon it all into his wet, waiting mouth. But the food was not fresh. It spoiled before the eye, sending macabre vapors into the air. And the invisible giant liked it that way. He fed on the sweetness of putrefaction.

"Vice President Dan Everhardt," concluded the reporter. "A well-liked public servant and a man who might well have become president of the United States one day, had his future not been cut off by an illness that remains a mystery."

A knock at the door made the doctor jump. He turned to see Colin Goss smiling at him.

"Ready, Dick?"

The doctor tore the earphones off and stood up. "Ready, sir."

THEY WALKED down the silent hall side by side. Goss seemed excited, full of energy. They paused at the viewing room, where another experimental subject, a woman, was being monitored. Goss listened to her heart and lungs before leading the way to the conference room where the overhead displays were kept.

Goss sat down at the long table and motioned the doctor to a chair.

"How are things going?" he asked.

"Very well, sir. Everything is on schedule."

"No more security problems?" Goss asked.

"None at all. I made the changes you suggested. The network has been entirely rebuilt. It is now impossible for a leak to occur such as the one we saw."

"Good work. Let's review the overall," Goss said. "Start with Everhardt."

"Decease from cardiac failure," the doctor said, looking at his notes. "Right on schedule, nine weeks and two days after intake."

"How about Palleschi?"

"A textbook case, from what I've seen. Vital signs still strong after three and a half weeks, but EEG and other tests show incipient coma."

"What is the thinking at Walter Reed?" Goss asked. "Are they connecting this with Everhardt?"

"They can't help but do that," the doctor said. "The symptoms are unique in medicine, and Palleschi presents the same initial picture as Everhardt."

"What about the other victims, here and abroad?"

"They're thinking epidemic, external pathogen," the younger man said. "They're putting pressure on the CDC to find an organism. But our CDC source tells me they've made no progress."

"What about the health people overseas?"

"Same thing. They're thinking in terms of an unknown pathogen that spreads in a way we don't understand. Quarantine is their main concern."

"And the geneticists?" Goss asked.

"There is a body of opinion to the effect that the disorder is a mutation—because of the bizarre aspect of the changes and the irregularity of the spread. Especially in England and in Australia. But they're not getting support from the public health authorities because the concept is too negative. The governments want to hear pathogen and quarantine."

"Good. That's the way we want it." Goss looked thoughtful. "A quasi-epidemic that has broken out in disparate localities. Cause and cure unknown. Vector unknown. Two important men affected, along with a lot of ordinary citizens."

He looked at the doctor. "How are we on the antidote?"

The doctor shook his head. "The work is slow going. It may be months. I can't predict."

Goss frowned. "What's taking so long? You understand the mechanism, don't you?"

"We do, yes," the doctor said. "But with this kind of intervention, the change is too massive to simply be reversed. A microorganism leaves the cell structure intact. So does an ordinary toxin. This is different. After exposure the basic structure is radically metamorphosed. The body is following a new set of instructions. That's a hard thing to correct."

"Well, it doesn't matter," Goss said. "If we're careful, it shouldn't come into play in any case."

The doctor nodded in silence.

"All right," Goss said. "It's time for the next phase."

For the first time the doctor dared to object.

"Are you sure?" he asked. "Can't we go with what we already have?"

Goss shook his head. "No. It won't work. Without more coverage, we're going to have scientists sniffing our trail. They're thinking epidemic, and that's what we want them to think. We have to give them data to support that."

The doctor sighed. "Are you sure, sir? We're talking about an awful lot of people. Human beings."

Goss's eyes narrowed.

"I beg your pardon?" he asked.

"I just meant . . ." The doctor's assurance had collapsed at the sight of Goss's eyes. "It's a great deal of destruction."

Goss shook his head. "That's not your concern."

"I'm a physician," the doctor said.

Goss gave him a dark look.

"The purpose here is higher," he said. "I was given to understand that you knew what you were getting into. I can get another man if you're not comfortable."

The look in the younger man's eyes made clear he knew what Goss's words really meant.

"I'm sorry, sir. I have no problem. I can continue."

Goss gave him a long assessing look.

"All right," he said. "We'll start at the agreed time. Keep me informed."

He stood up and moved to the door. With his hand on the knob he looked back at the doctor, who seemed wilted and depressed.

"Cheer up, Dick," Goss smiled. "You're saving the world."

The doctor nodded. "Yes, sir."

Without another word Goss left the room.

The doctor stood looking at the world map as Goss's steps echoed in the corridor. He waited until he heard the elevator door open. Then he took another pill from his pocket and brought it to his lips.

"Jesus Christ," he said. It was a curse, but also a prayer. He had been brought up Catholic. He knew about hellfire.

Hell was in the distant hum of the elevator that bore Colin Goss upstairs to his penthouse office. Hell was on the map in front of him, filled with numbers being constantly revised to quantify mass murder. Hell was in the shaking of this hand, which was making it difficult for him to place the pill on his tongue.

Two doses in a half hour, he thought. This is the end.

He tasted the acid chemical. It was strong. More than strong enough to kill, in sufficient quantities.

The last shall be the first, he mused, watching the numbers dance before his eyes.

3 2

The White House
January 22

IN 1968, three months before his decision not to run for a second term, Lyndon Johnson flew into a rage at the sight of a thousand antiwar demonstrators outside the White House and threw his orthopedic desk chair through the south-facing window of the Oval Office.

The Secret Service suffered considerable embarrassment at the chief executive's ability to shatter a window that had been considered bulletproof. New panes were installed in all the White House windows, made of state-of-the-art shatterproof, bulletproof glass. Two of the sills were damaged during the work, and were replaced with walnut from Maryland forests.

It was on one of those sills that the president now leaned, his eyes closed, as his chief of staff and the party chairman waited behind him in respectful silence. The majority leader was standing across the room, his back turned.

"Poor Danny," the president said.

The others echoed his words with a sigh.

"How is Pam?" the president asked.

"Pretty much destroyed," Dick Livermore said. "She knew he was critical, but I don't think she ever really thought it would end so soon, just like that. Dan was such a strong guy."

"How about Tom? Are they sure it's the same disease?" the president asked.

"The symptoms are identical," Dick said. "They won't confirm anything—I suppose that's natural enough."

"And they still don't know how to treat it?"

"Not at all. They're monitoring all his vital signs. They're normal—for the moment."

"When did you last see him?"

"Day before yesterday."

"Have you talked to Theresa?"

"Nearly every day."

"How's she doing?"

"Not well. She's got a lot of anger. She didn't want him to get involved."

"I don't blame her." The president shook his head. "God damn this thing," he said. He himself sounded angry.

There was a pause. The four men in the room seemed oblivious to each other. Each was wrapped up in his own struggle.

"All right," the president broke the silence. "We can't delay any longer. We have to choose another man. We can't leave it the way it is. The public will turn its back on us."

Heads nodded in agreement. The president was clinging to office by a slender thread. The movement in Congress for a constitutional amendment mandating a special election was gaining strength by the day. Colin Goss was giving statesmanlike interviews to political journalists, for all the world like the presumptive president of the United States. There was no time to lose.

"Who shall we tap?" the president asked.

"Kirk Stillman," the majority leader said. "He's the best we have left."

His choice of words was infelicitous. But he was right. Kirk Stillman was the only man the party had left who could help the president fight Colin Goss.

"I agree," Dick Livermore said.

"Have you called him?" the president asked.

"I spoke to him last week, and again yesterday," Dick said. "He understands the situation."

"And?" the president asked.

"He'll do anything that's asked of him," Dick said. "Anything *you* ask, anyway."

Dick's implication was clear. Kirk Stillman was getting on in years. The notion of a political war against Colin Goss—a war that might be unwinnable, and that might be hazardous to his own health—would not be to his liking. But Stillman believed in the president. He would sacrifice himself if necessary.

"Where is he now?" the president asked.

"Out for the evening," Dick said. "I spoke to his wife. She's expecting him home by eleven."

The president looked at those present, one by one.

"Find out where he is," he told Dick. "We can't wait until eleven."

As the president showed his visitors out of the Oval Office, Kirk Stillman was reluctantly taking leave of his longtime mistress in her Alexandria apartment.

She was a lobbyist for the tobacco industry, and had been Kirk Stillman's lover for nearly twenty years. Her name was Gabrielle Arendt. A well-preserved woman in her late forties, she knew Kirk Stillman well, and knew how to satisfy the needs of his aging body as well as the chronic need for love that afflicts all political men.

Kirk Stillman had an idea of what was in store for him. He had been waiting for Dick Livermore's call since he first heard the horrible news about Dan Everhardt. There was no doubt in his mind that Tom Palleschi had the same disease and was therefore probably down for the count. That put Stillman himself on the hot seat.

Kirk Stillman was frightened. Not for himself so much—after all, at age sixty-four he had tasted most of the glories and most of the pleasures available to any civilized man—but for the country.

The public knew Goss was a potential dictator. But fear was pulling the wool over people's eyes, making Goss look like a savior instead of a menace. Voters were ready to follow Goss anywhere, like the children in the Pied Piper story.

Stillman had seen this happen before. He was in Congress in 1968 when Richard Nixon, his true colors already known to every American, managed to get into the White House anyway. It had taken Vietnam and Lyndon Johnson's withdrawal to make the cards fall Nixon's way. Two years earlier Nixon's election would have seemed unthinkable. But it happened.

Today it was the *Crescent Queen* and the Pinocchio Syndrome that were spreading the fear, and Colin Goss who was the beneficiary. In the past this kind of blindness had caused world wars. In today's world it could cause something worse.

Gabrielle sent Stillman off tenderly, having rubbed his back and drunk brandy with him after they made love. She was like a second wife to him now.

"Call me," she said at the door.

"Tomorrow," Stillman promised. Touching her cheek with a tanned hand, he smiled and moved away down the hall.

His Mercedes was parked in the lot across the street. He took the back stairs, grimacing slightly as the impact of the steps reminded him of the arthritis in his hip. He was not worried about muggers; this was a safe neighborhood.

He took the rear exit of the building and walked east. The night was still and cold. He breathed in the crisp air gratefully. A political man who spent most of his life in meeting rooms and offices, he did not get as much fresh air as he would have liked.

He was crossing diagonally to the tree-lined park when he heard the engine. It was being pushed hard, so hard that it sounded more like a small truck than a car.

By the time he turned to look into the headlights, the front bumper was already crushing his legs and hips. He fell to the pavement, the chassis of the car pushing him along the ground.

The car backed up and struck him a second time, then a third. The impact sounded like a chicken being deboned by an expert butcher. A man got out to check the pulse in Kirk Stillman's neck. There was none. The car drove away, obeying the speed limit. The handful of witnesses to the accident would remember it as a large car of American build, dark in color.

No one saw the license number.

33

Washington
January 22

THE DEATH of Kirk Stillman shook the executive branch to its foundations.

The president, who had been expecting a call from Stillman at any moment, was in his private study when the news came. Within an hour he met with the Secret Service and representatives of the FBI, and separately with the majority leader, the party chairman, and several key senators.

By 9 A.M. the cover story was in place. Kirk Stillman had been killed in a freak traffic accident on a suburban Alexandria street. Stillman had been visiting friends in the neighborhood. He was killed instantly.

The announcement would be made by a District of Columbia police spokesman. No one in the White House would comment, except to praise Stillman for his many valuable contributions to the party and the nation over the years.

Thankfully, Stillman's selection as vice president had not been made public before his accident. The pattern of death haunting the administration was already a national scandal. The death of a third nominee would have been the final straw.

The First Lady was with Stillman's wife at her Maryland house, waiting for the Stillman children to make their way home from the cities where they lived. The children were all grown, and had given Kirk Stillman and his wife seven grandchildren.

At noon the president met with Dick Livermore in the Oval Office. Both men's faces were grave.

"Are you sure he was run down intentionally?" the president asked.

"There's no doubt about it. The car must have been waiting for him when he left the apartment building." Dick looked at a note in his hand. "Whoever it was knew when Kirk visited his lady friend, and what time he would come out. It seems they used street grime to obscure the license plates. All anyone could say was that the car was black."

"What about physical evidence on Kirk's body?" the president asked.

Dick shrugged. "The D.C. police chief told me they have forensics people working on it. They'll probably find traces of paint and other things. But if the car was hot, they'll never trace it." He looked at the president. "I suspect it was hot. This was no accident. They ran him over three times, to make sure."

Dick breathed a long sigh, his eyes closed. Then he looked up to see the expression of defeat on the president's face.

"I'm beginning to doubt we can hang on after all," the president said. "These misfortunes are too big a negative."

He stood up and went to the window. Gazing out at the morning sky, he spoke as though to himself. "I never thought it was really possible, but I begin to see Colin Goss in this office, behind this desk."

"I hope you're wrong," Dick said.

"So do I," the president agreed. "But things are out of control. Maybe it's too late to stop them." His lips curled in a grim smile. "Shakespeare had it right. The gods play cruel games with us sometimes. They kill us for their sport."

Dick seemed pensive. Noticing his troubled look, the president asked, "Is something on your mind, Dick?"

Dick looked out the window at Pennsylvania Avenue. "Has it occurred to you that the talk about a conspiracy might be right?"

The president raised an eyebrow. "You mean that reporter, and all that noise on the Internet?"

Dick nodded. "I wouldn't have said anything if it hadn't been for Kirk. But Kirk's death is too much. And it was obviously intentional. Someone wanted him out of the way. Anyone who knows our party would have known that after Palleschi we would choose Kirk."

"You mean someone made Dan and Tom sick?" the president asked. "Is that what you're saying?"

Dick sat on the arm of the heavy sofa. "I'm not saying anything for sure. But it doesn't feel right. There are only two victims of the Pinocchio Syndrome in Washington. One was your vice president, the other your first choice to replace him. And now, the last realistic choice . . ."

He shivered at the thought of so much death in proximity to this office.

"But we have no evidence that the Syndrome can be caused deliberately," the president said.

"And no evidence that it can't," Dick replied. "That's my point. It's as though someone fed us Danny and Tom in order to provoke us and to test us. They knew we would leave no stone unturned in our effort to find out what made them sick. And we have. Without success. We just don't understand the Syndrome."

"To test us," the president said. "But also to hurt us. To drive us out of office."

Dick nodded, perplexed. "I know. It sounds crazy. It's insane. Who would have such power? And why would they want to?"

He sighed. "Perhaps we should do something drastic. Declare a state of martial law . . . while the situation is investigated."

The president shook his head. "No. We can't allow the whole country to be held hostage by our own problems. Life has to go on. This is a democracy, and I'm sworn to keep it that way."

Both men were silent. They were thinking about the arduous campaign that had put the president in the White House five years ago. A highly respected leader who came from an old political family, he had nevertheless been an underdog in that campaign. It had taken more than just hard work to get him elected. A combination of political circumstances had been necessary—as it is for every man who becomes president.

And now a combination of circumstances, bewildering in its violence, was threatening to destroy his presidency.

The president looked at his old friend.

"I love this country, Dick," he said. "It's done a lot for me, and I've done what I could in return. I believe it's the greatest country in the world. My instincts tell me it's in trouble. The worst trouble in a hundred years, maybe the worst in our whole history."

Dick Livermore nodded. The president turned to look into his eyes.

"Are you afraid?"

Dick was silent. He had never been so frightened in his life.

"Well . . ." The president shrugged. "They think they can make us curl up and play dead. We're not going to. We're going to fight back."

"Yes, Mr. President."

The president sat down. On the desk before him was a list of names. Dick could not read them upside down, but he could see they had all been crossed out. Except one.

"The way I see it," the president said, "we have only one realistic choice left." He looked at Dick. "Do you know who I'm talking about?"

Dick nodded. Then they both pronounced the same name, in one voice.

———

MICHAEL CAMPBELL had canceled the remainder of his speaking tour of California when he received Dick Livermore's call about Kirk Stillman. Summoned by Dick to meet with him and the president, Michael arrived at the White House just after dawn. The meeting was held in Dan Everhardt's empty office.

Michael had been here before. He recognized the photos that documented Dan's college football career, his marriage to Pam, and the growth of his three children. There were also photographs of Dan with various party luminaries and foreign heads of state, and a couple of tasteful reminders of awards Dan had won.

Dick Livermore came to the door himself to usher Michael inside. The president was standing by the window.

"Mike, how are you?" he said, coming forward to shake hands. "How's Susan?"

"We're fine," Michael said. "Worried, I guess, like everyone else. How is Johanna Stillman?"

"The news hit her hard, but she's bearing up well," Dick said.

"It's a terrible thing," Michael said. "Kirk Stillman was a hero to me."

The president shook his head. "This is a dark time. I can't think of a moment as painful as this since—well, since Kennedy died."

Michael had not thought of it in that way, but he saw that the president was right. The Kennedy assassination had brought multiple disasters in its train. First the accession of Lyndon Johnson, a legislator with no executive experience, to the presidency. Then the escalation of the Vietnam War, which really happened because Johnson didn't know how to say no to the Kennedy eggheads who remained in his cabinet. Then Johnson's refusal to run in 1968, and the election of Nixon. Then Watergate. Then the oil crisis, then the inflation. And on and on.

Most observers believed that if Kennedy had served out his eight years, none of those things would have happened. Kennedy might have escalated in Vietnam for a while, but he would have seen the Viet Cong doing to his American boys what the Viet Minh had done to the French ten years before. Kennedy was a historian. He would have seen history repeating itself. And he would have gotten out.

But Johnson was no student of history. Johnson was a backroom politician who knew how to get out the vote, but not much else. That was why Vietnam destroyed Johnson.

Of course, other disasters might have come on the heels of a successful Kennedy presidency. Disasters perhaps worse than Vietnam. The Russians, for example, rattled by American superiority in the arms race, might have lost their heads and pushed the nuclear button.

That was the essence of fate, wasn't it? The burden of wondering whether our own tragedies were the only tragedies possible.

"Michael," the president said, "Dick and I have asked you here today because Kirk Stillman left a big hole in our plans, and we're out of time. We have to pick up the pieces right now. If we don't, Colin Goss might succeed in forcing a special election. If that happens, this whole country could go down the tubes."

"I understand," Michael nodded.

"Michael, I want you to take over as vice president," the president said without further ado.

He was looking steadily at Michael, who seemed stunned.

"Me?" Michael asked. "I—what brought you to that decision?"

The president sat on the edge of his desk, both legs dangling. It was an oddly childlike posture for such a dignified man. "Mike," he said, "we feel that you're the best man for the job."

"I don't see how you figure that," Michael argued. "I'm too young, Mr. President. I don't have the right—well, the right image."

Between them was their own silence about Stillman, a man of stature who would have looked the part of a respected vice president, and who was dead, perhaps for that very reason.

"We have spin people who can handle that," Dick said. "Mike, the president and I have thought a lot about this. You're young, that's true. But you can do the job. You understand the issues. You have a superb voting record. Most importantly, perhaps, you know how to fight Goss."

Michael was shaking his head slowly.

"I'm not a match for Goss. He'll use me as an issue, Dick. He'll say I'm wet behind the ears, a punk . . . and, in a way, he'll be right." He looked at the president. "I'll hurt more than I'll help."

"Let me be frank about image," Dick said. "True, you're young. But you're a hero to a lot of people. No one has forgotten the Olympics. You have terrific name and face recognition. You're thought of as a competent person, and as a physically courageous one. We need that now."

The president added, "Those things will outweigh the age factor. Also, Susan is well liked and admired. People will accept you as vice president. You look the part. And don't forget that I'm not an old man. I'm not going to drop dead of a heart attack in the next couple of years. People aren't going to make that connection."

"They will if Colin Goss makes it for them," Michael objected.

There was a brief silence as all three men thought of the Pinocchio Syndrome. Two important men had already fallen victim to the dreaded disease. Why not the president? Unthinkable as it seemed, such a thing was possible.

Dick Livermore broke the spell by changing the subject. "Mike, you're a perfect partner for the president. You're competent, you're popular with women as well as men. And you've got guts. That's the main thing."

Michael was chewing his lip nervously.

"I appreciate your confidence," he said. "But I don't know if I can do it."

"You can do it." It was the president who said this.

Frowning, Michael said, "Susan is going to split a gut."

Dick nodded. "Susan will be upset, naturally. But she'll come around. She knows what is at stake."

Michael looked skeptical. "You may have to talk to her yourself," he said. "She may not accept this coming from me."

"You underestimate her, Mike. She'll be fine. As you will be."

Michael looked from the president to Livermore. "You really think it's that important," he said to both of them.

The president responded in a harsh voice, almost impatient. "The course of history will be affected by what we do. We have to give it our best shot."

The president and Dick Livermore were watching Michael closely. Both noticed that something had hardened in Michael's face. His normally friendly expression was eclipsed by a look of icy determination that was almost frightening.

"All right," he said. "I'll do it."

"Way to go, Mike." Dick moved forward as though to clap Michael on the shoulder.

"But there's one more thing," Michael said.

"What?" asked the president.

"What if *I* don't live long enough to take office?" Michael asked. "Look what happened to Danny, and to Tom Palleschi. What makes you think I'm less vulnerable than they were?"

The president was impressed by these words. Michael was not so much afraid for himself as worried that he would let the president down by dying.

"Michael, there will be the tightest security in the history of presidential politics," Dick assured him. "You won't make a move without Secret Service protection. And neither of you is going to get sick. I guarantee that." The confidence in his own voice surprised him.

Michael nodded. For a moment he looked depressed. Then he came out of it as though by an effort of will.

"All right," he said. "There's nothing more to say, then."

Dick's face lit up. He looked at the president, who was already coming to shake Michael's hand.

"Good man," the president said. "I knew we could count on you."

Michael returned the firm handshake. "What happens now?"

"We'll make the announcement together tomorrow," the president said. "I want to be there personally, as the leader of our party. After that, we'll send the nomination over to the Senate and wait for confirmation. It may take a while, but I have no doubt we'll get you confirmed."

Dick lifted a finger to interrupt. "With that in mind, Mike, we should ask you now whether there is anything that could be used against you by people who are against your nomination. Anything in your past, I mean."

Michael thought for a moment. "You mean, like cheating on exams in college?"

"That sort of thing, or—anything sexual," Dick nodded. He was watching Michael closely.

"There's nothing," Michael answered. "Susan and I had sex before we were married, but I think she's already told the world that."

The others laughed. They were charmed by Michael's candor.

"Good," the president said.

Michael knew the two men would want to talk alone, so he stood up.

"I'd better get home," he said. "I should tell Susan."

"Do that," Dick said. "And tell her everything is going to be all right."

"Convincing her of that may be the hardest thing I do today," Michael smiled.

The president walked Michael out.

"Don't worry about Susan," he said. "She's a fighter too. With her on your team, you're halfway into the White House already."

"I'll tell her you said that."

Michael moved off along the corridor with firm unhurried strides. The president watched him recede. More acutely than ever he felt destiny hovering over his decision and Michael's. At election time people tended to take vice presidential candidates for granted as mere running mates. But history showed that the fate of the nation depended on the men who took office as vice president. Men like Harry Truman, Richard Nixon, Lyndon Johnson, George Bush. For good or for ill.

Michael disappeared into the elevator. Dick Livermore appeared at the president's side, ready to accompany him to the Oval Office. There were a lot of phone calls for both of them to make.

Dick noticed a spring in the president's step that had not been there in recent weeks. The president was a fighter as well as a statesman. He was drawing energy from the battle to come.

———

KAREN EMBRY lay in her bathtub, a half-empty glass of Early Times in her hand. She had the all-news station playing on the portable radio she kept in the bathroom. The announcer was talking about Kirk Stillman. Between brief interviews with political veterans who praised Stillman's distinguished career, there were updates on the freak accident that had taken his life.

Karen knew it was no accident.

When she heard the news about Stillman this morning she drove immediately to the Alexandria neighborhood where the accident took place. The police roadblocks were enormous, five vehicles thick. A cordon of uniformed officers, numbering in the dozens, blocked the neighboring houses from the street.

Sensing that the security was too tight for a mere accident, Karen made a call to a contact within the D.C. police department, a homicide detective who owed her a favor. After swearing her to secrecy he told her about the skid marks that indicated repeated assaults on Stillman after the initial impact.

"Whoever did it wanted to make sure," he said. "It's a hit-and-run homicide, for sure. Not an accident."

Karen spent the rest of the day trying to learn more about Stillman's death through government sources. It was no use. No one in an official position would talk to her. Not anymore.

By day's end Karen had decided to sit back and wait. The president would have to announce a new vice presidential nominee. Now that it could not be Stillman, who would it be?

Karen wasn't sure. But she knew one thing. The president's selection would tell her a lot about who stood to benefit from the events of the last two months. First Everhardt, then Palleschi, now Stillman . . . The dominoes were falling, and the direction in which they fell would indicate the direction from which they had been pushed.

Karen lifted her foot from the bottom of the tub, for no reason, and looked at the bubbles clinging to her toes. The water level fell slightly, and she felt her nipples tense as the foam touched them with little pops of exploding bubbles. The ash on her cigarette was about to fall into the water. She swung her arm and tapped it into the ashtray on the floor.

Pinocchio's nose is getting longer . . .

"Now you get to play the game," she said to the air.

3 4

FORTY MINUTES after Michael's meeting with the president and Dick Livermore, Colin Goss sat in an orthopedic chair in his Washington office, a glass of his favorite Italian mineral water in his hand. His cigar lay smoldering in the ashtray. The cat was in his lap, purring softly as his fingers rubbed her haunches.

Goss was lost in thought, so much so that he did not even hear the door open. The footsteps on the carpet were intentionally light, and Goss's hearing was not as acute as it had once been. He had no clue he was not alone until a pair of hands came to rest on his shoulders.

"Who is that?" Goss leaned back.

"Surprise." The voice was a whisper.

"Ah. It's you." Goss's face softened into a paternal smile. "Sneaking up on me, eh?"

"Sneaking up on you." The voice was gentle, loving.

"I missed you," Goss murmured.

"Missed you, too."

Goss got a hand around Michael's wrist and pulled him downward.

Michael let himself be drawn into the older man's embrace. Goss curled an arm around Michael's shoulder and squeezed gently.

"What's the good word?" he asked.

"It's settled," Michael said. "I just met with Dick Livermore and the president. They want me to be Dan Everhardt's replacement."

"Ah, good. Good." Goss had taken Michael's hand and was holding it affectionately. "What did they say?" he asked. "How did they put it to you?"

"They said I have the right image for the job. They say we're the only thing standing between you and the White House."

Goss smiled, nodding. "Well, they have a point there, don't they?"

"Yes. They have a point." Michael smiled.

There was a silence. Both men were pondering the gravity of this moment.

"It's been a long road, hasn't it?" Goss asked.

"Long road. Yes." Michael smiled.

"The road less traveled," Goss said. "Not quite the conventional route to the Oval Office."

"You could say that."

Again there was silence. Goss squeezed Michael's hand.

"I'm very proud of you, son."

"I'm glad."

"Nothing can stop us now, can it?" Goss touched Michael's cheek.

"Nothing."

The cat dropped from Goss's lap and twined itself around Michael Campbell's legs. Its tail joined the two men briefly, then flicked away.

The frog said, "You must let me eat at your table." And when the princess had lifted him onto the table he said, "We must eat together off your plate." The princess shared her plate with him despite her disgust. "Now I am tired," said the frog, "and want to sleep. Take me to your bedroom." Reluctantly the princess took him to her room and put him down in a corner. "I must sleep in your bed with you," he said. The princess was revolted by the idea of letting the cold wet creature share her bed. But she could not disobey the King's command. With thumb and finger she picked up the frog and settled him next to her between the silken sheets . . .

—"THE FROG PRINCE"

35

February 25

THE OBSCENE icons of the infidels have been destroyed by Allah's loyal soldiers. Muslims all over the world are called upon to celebrate this cleansing fire, and to set fires of their own wherever infidels worship unclean images.

O Allah! We pledge every Muslim heart in the battle against Jewish expansion and Satan's messenger, the unholy United States. Every Muslim should consider it his duty to martyr himself in the cause of annihilating the infidel state of Israel and especially its unclean ally and accomplice, the evil United States of America.

O Allah! We thank you for your blessing of the sacred attack which has destroyed the unholy icons of the infidel. May all Muslims everywhere prepare themselves for similar attacks, until the infidel is driven forever from your holy lands.

The cave was guarded by mujahideen armed with automatic weapons and grenades as well as rocket launchers and antiaircraft guns. It had been prepared in the late 1980s for precisely the purpose it was now serving. No outsiders knew of its existence, including the government of the country in which it was located. Only the innermost circle, made up of bodyguards, high-ranking lieutenants, and family members, was permitted access to it.

Outside was trackless desert, untouched by roads. A caravan route ran along the nearest crest, used by bedouins who knew how to mind their own business. The busy helicopter and truck traffic that had once broken the silence was gone now. Only the hot wind and the shifting sand remained.

In the innermost of the inner rooms, Ayman al-Zawahiri stood looking down at a bed on which a motionless figure lay. The air was deathly still. It was cold down here, the cavern untouched by the torrid Saharan heat above. Space heaters hummed in the corners, powered by the generators located in the main cavern.

"Shaykh," al-Zawahiri said. "I bring good news."

There was no response. The eyes stared at the rock ceiling, a look of deep preoccupation in them.

"Shaykh," al-Zawahiri said, "the plan will be carried out soon. Everything is in place. The text will be read on Al-Jazeera while your photograph is shown. We will say you cannot take the chance of being videotaped while the infidels are pursuing you. Here, let me read it for you."

He read the text aloud, his lips widening in a smile despite his fear. This would be the greatest attack on the infidels since the World Trade Center. This time the target would be spiritual and esthetic rather than financial.

"The Louvre, Shaykh," he concluded. "The greatest treasure trove of the infidels' art. It will all go up in smoke. All their heroes, Shaykh—Michelangelo, Rembrandt, Vermeer, Picasso—they will all burn to ashes. And it will be in your name, Shaykh, with the blessing of Allah."

The figure in the bed was silent. Al-Zawahiri's eyes were full of tears as he looked down at the unseeing eyes.

He is my son, he thought. *He is my life.*

So many heroes had died already. Abdul-Majid, Zandani, al-Masri. Turabi in Sudan, Kaddafi in Libya, Khamenei in Iran. Arafat too. And Hussein . . .

Why had Allah brought this scourge on his best people, his most faithful followers? Why would Allah annihilate his own soldiers?

There was only one answer: to martyr them. To make them immortal in the eyes of Muslims everywhere, Muslims yet unborn. To prepare for the day when the jihad would be won.

But that day would not be soon. The bravest and the strongest were dying. This generation of soldiers would have to accept martyrdom as their lot. Al-Zawahiri, who had devoted thirty years of his life to the struggle against the infidels, would not see victory in his lifetime.

He touched the hand of the silent man in the bed. The hardness, the deformity was palpable. He looked down at the beloved face, the beard now completely white like that of a saint. Looking back on his education, he dared to quote the infidel Shakespeare as he looked down on his friend.

"Goodnight, sweet Prince, and flights of angels sing thee to thy rest."

He closed his eyes and knelt before the bed. He spoke directly to Allah.

"Why?" Al-Zawahiri asked. "Why have You murdered us?"

There was no answer.

He held the hand of bin Laden and wept.

36

THE GIRL is strapped to the apparatus, her naked loins exposed. Her eyes are empty. The time is now, the event is at hand.

The shadow comes across her. The slow silhouette, the dangling tail, approaching, approaching. There is a change in her eyes. Is she aware? Have the shouts awakened her to what is about to happen?

The camera zooms in until the girl's naked pelvis occupies most of the image. The shadow falls over it, swinging hesitantly. Then the tail itself grazes her buttocks, and the shadow stops. He has felt the tap of it against her skin. He reaches out with his other hand. The fingers find her pelvis, the fingertips graze the blond nexus where the thighs meet the derriere.

He reaches down and fixes the tail to her tailbone. It hangs between her legs. There is applause. The camera pulls back. He is naked, too, and aroused. He is almost completely bald. The rolls of fat around his waist look grotesquely sensual as he drops to his knees beside her. The contrast between his bulbous flab and the girl's firm young body is striking.

He has removed the blindfold and can see his prize. He smiles. He begins to caress *her. Once again, for a brief instant, her eyes seem to register awareness of what is happening to her. Then their deathlike glaze returns.*

It is monstrous, a frog mounting a princess, as the steaming male crouches spoon-fashion over the girl. The cries from the others are louder, the applause crashes off the walls.

It takes him a long time to finish. When he does he moves away along the stage. The princess remains alone. The girlish back, the creamy thighs, the grace of youth bestow themselves on admiring eyes. The shouts have died down, the laughter has stopped. In the murmur of the voices one senses admiration for her innocence as well as for the violation that has sullied it.

She is alone now, motionless.

A princess with a tail.

37

BY THE end of February the Pinocchio Syndrome had claimed millions of victims. Not since the influenza epidemic of 1918 had a disease spread so quickly and destroyed its victims in so summary a manner.

Of interest to the World Health Organization was the fact that the biggest outbreaks seemed to be centered in North Africa and the Arabian Peninsula, including Algeria, Libya, Morocco, and the Sudan, as well as Syria, Iraq, and Jordan. Iran and Afghanistan were also heavily affected, as was Pakistan. The health experts were at a loss to explain this central focus of the Syndrome.

The developing countries lacked the hospital facilities to deal with the crisis. Victims of the Syndrome, paralyzed and silent, were to be found lying in the streets, on sidewalks, and in public places, slowly starving to death while frightened pedestrians and motorists gave them a wide berth. Public health workers were reduced to a clean-up role, removing the sick from public places and concentrating them in makeshift quarantine areas like sports stadiums, abandoned warehouses, schools.

The quarantine imposed on affected areas was no longer as stringent as it had once been. Health authorities had come to realize that each outbreak was short-lived and self-limiting, lasting twenty-four hours or less. There was no spread of the disease in a given area after the first flash.

There was also no evidence of human-to-human spread of the disease. The wide berth given victims by passersby was an emotional reaction, not a rational one. It would have been perfectly safe for them to touch the victims, even share their blood or saliva.

By now there was no doubt that an external pathogen of some sort was involved in the disease. This was proved by the fact that leukemia patients in sterile bubbles were spared by the outbreaks. But scientists who suspected a genetic etiology of the disorder were not willing to abandon their theory on this basis alone. It was possible, they argued, that exposure to something in the environment triggered a bizarre mutation in the human constitution, a mutation that had been waiting for just this exposure, perhaps for thousands of years.

But the best efforts of public health authorities and environmental experts had failed to isolate an element in the air, water, soil, or food in the affected areas that was not also to be found everywhere else. The "trigger theory" of genetic response to an environmental toxin remained just a theory.

In the meantime the Pinocchio Syndrome struck like lightning, plucking its victims from life like an invisible hand. This fact became part of the mythology of the disease. The victims were "chosen," it was believed, because of some spiritual or other taint that made them vulnerable to the disease. Perhaps, it was thought, they were like weak members of a herd who are weeded out by the predator, the better to safeguard the long-term viability of the herd as a whole.

Devout believers of various faiths did not hesitate to interpret the spreading illness as a sign from God. The staring eyes of the victims, and their unresponsiveness to other people, proved that their vision was fixed on God, they were no longer "of this world." They were preparing for their ascension into a higher sphere.

The macabre metamorphosis of the victims' extremities as death approached was also accounted for by believers as proof of divine purpose. Muslim scholars found obscure texts in the Koran that hinted at a metamorphosis of certain men into hoofed beasts in ancient times. Not to be outdone, Bible scholars pointed to Old Testament sources suggesting that the hoofed hands and feet were God's punishment for original sin. Talmudic scholars were not far behind. Hindus unearthed passages in the Vedas that referred ambiguously to the donkey or ass as a holy avatar of the human spirit. Similar hints could be found in the sayings of Buddha.

Indeed, the religious controversy took on unintentionally comic dimensions as believers of different faiths claimed the disease as a visitation foretold in their own scriptures. Was the malady a Christian scourge, a Muslim scourge? This question was debated endlessly.

Some splinter religious groups even brought the disease into their rituals, creating icons depicting the metamorphosis of man into a hoofed beast, and even outfitting priests with oversized hands and feet. The somewhat vaudeville aspect of these rituals was not lost on outside observers, but the practice spread nonetheless.

Many Muslims and Christians in the Arab countries had stopped fleeing the affected areas. They substituted prayer and acceptance for escape. Flight was impractical anyway, for there was nowhere to go. Neighboring countries refused to let in refugees from the illness. Immigration policies around the world had tightened due to fear of the scourge.

In America, surprisingly, the spread of the disease seemed to have stopped. Few new cases were being reported. Health authorities could not account for this reprieve, but it had a powerful effect on the public mind. The climate of panic that had existed in the fall gave way to something less desperate. Perhaps, thought many, the disease was self-limiting. Perhaps after ravaging certain areas for weeks or months, it moved on or even disappeared altogether. Many epidemics in past centuries had followed such a pattern.

People's faith in their institutions began to return. The world was not so different from what it had been in the past. True, the continuing fear of nuclear terrorism, spawned by the *Crescent Queen* attack, made life difficult. But there was reason to hope that the authorities would eventually find the perpetrators of the act and prevent a recurrence.

This change of mood redounded to the advantage of the president and his administration. The selection of Michael Campbell as the new vice president seemed like a lucky charm. The president's poll numbers rose steadily, while Colin Goss, for the first time in a year, lost ground. Americans, less terrified of the future, saw past Goss's message of hate to the commonsense levelheadedness of the president and embraced Michael Campbell like a returning hero.

Debate over Michael's nomination was proceeding in the Senate, with token resistance from senators loyal to Goss. But there was a pro forma quality to the sessions, and Michael's ultimate confirmation seemed a foregone conclusion.

Michael's selection finished the process his Senate years had started. He was now seen by voters and political pundits as another John F. Kennedy, a charismatic leader on a sure path to the presidency. His speeches were attended by thousands of excited supporters, and his television appearances garnered ratings not attained by any politician in a generation.

As for the president, he did not mind being upstaged by his nominee, for the public relations bounce from Michael's selection was working against Colin Goss and in favor of the administration. The president enjoyed sharing the spotlight with Michael, for it was a spotlight that showed Colin Goss in ugly colors.

———

JUDD CAMPBELL was thrilled for Michael. His excitement was such that he himself seemed to have a new lease on life and youth. His arthritis hurt less, his heart felt stronger, his mind seemed sharper than it had been in years.

His weekly dinners with Michael and Susan had become celebrations. The only problem was that Michael, more often than not, could not attend. He was too busy being briefed by White House and state department people about his upcoming responsibilities as vice president. Judd, of course, accepted his son's enforced absence graciously, for it was all part of a dream come true for him.

On a windy, unseasonably warm February evening Susan came over alone for dinner. The conversation was all about Michael. Susan found Judd and Ingrid almost unnaturally excited. Ingrid looked ten years younger and seemed to have lost weight. Judd could hardly sit still. He kept jumping up from his chair to glance at the TV, tuned to CNN, on which Michael's face seemed to appear every few minutes.

After dinner Judd excused himself and went up to his office while the two women did the dishes. He sat for a few moments looking out the window at the waves, which were high under the gusty wind. Then he got up and removed a videotape from the small safe in his office and put it into the VCR. He sat back in his orthopedic chair and turned off the desk lamp so he could see the TV image better.

The videotape had been recorded at the Olympic games.

"Campbell is swimming the anchor lap for the Americans. The switch was just a bit ragged, leaving Campbell a second or two behind the West Germans. He is swimming with powerful strokes . . ."

Judd knew every word of the announcer's commentary by heart. That did not stop him from sitting up straighter, his adrenaline flowing.

"Michael Campbell has amazed the world this week," the commentator continued. *"After a second serious back operation that left him all but incapacitated, he came here as a dark horse, not taken seriously by most observers, and shocked the world by winning the men's 100-meter freestyle in world-record time. Now, twenty-four hours later, he is swimming for a second gold medal. But it looks as though he's going to have to get over a major hurdle in this race."*

Judd leaned forward. His son was a blur of angry splashes and pumping arms, his face invisible. But the long scar down his back could be seen as he churned his way madly through the water, still half a length behind the West German anchor. Judd stopped the video briefly and rewound it a few seconds. This was the moment, the moment he had watched hundreds of times.

"But I spoke too soon," said the commentator. *"Campbell seems to be gaining—no, wait, he's tied Schuller for the lead. I can't believe what I'm seeing. In an*

amazing burst of speed Campbell has caught up to the West German. With one lap to go they're neck and neck. This is going to be a thriller . . ."

In the space of two seconds Michael had poured it on and caught the West German, a young man considered at that time to be the fastest swimmer alive. The gain had taken place just as the commentator was saying Michael was at a disadvantage.

Judd Campbell never tired of viewing that moment. It symbolized for him the essence of competition, that split second of absolute fury and commitment in which an athlete overcomes his own limitations and the power of the opponent to win.

"They've started the last lap. Schuller and Campbell are still tied—no, wait, it looks like Campbell has a tiny lead. Yes, they're coming in, they're coming in . . . Campbell wins it! The Americans have won the gold medal!"

Pandemonium reigned as the winning time was posted. The American relay team and coach held up their hands in victory and rushed to besiege Michael, their hero. The commentators' voices were tumbling over each other as they exclaimed over the Americans' incredible victory.

And now came the second moment, the one Judd lived for almost more than the first. Michael remained in the water at the finish line. His coach was leaning over to talk to him. The coach signaled for the trainer, who came quickly to his side.

"There seems to be a problem here with Michael Campbell. He's not getting out of the pool. The American coach has approached the judge. It appears Campbell has a back spasm so painful that he can't lift himself out of the pool."

The American swimmers and coaches converged on Michael, and after a few moments' consultation he was lifted from the pool by his relay teammates, who were assisted by Jürgen Schuller, the German champion whom Michael had just defeated. The picture of the four swimmers struggling to help the incapacitated gold medalist would become one of the most famous images in Olympic history, and the one that forever established Michael in the public mind as a man of almost unbelievable physical courage.

The picture hung today as a still photograph on Judd's office wall. Judd never let a day go by without looking at it and drinking in its eloquent combination of pathos and triumph. His son looked so vulnerable as his teammates pulled him out of the water. Yet Michael was their leader, their hero. A winner to the marrow of his bones.

Judd looked out the window. Dusk was gathering over the windblown ocean. The moon was bright. On an impulse Judd decided to go out for a walk on the beach. He wanted to pursue the thoughts evoked by the video of Michael's Olympic achievement.

At the bottom of the stairs he heard Ingrid and Susan laughing in the kitchen. He took his leather jacket from the hall closet and slipped out without telling them he was going.

The beach was somewhat narrow in front of the house, but a hundred yards down it became quite vast. The waves in that area were larger than elsewhere because of a relatively deep bottom. Judd walked along slowly, feeling the rhythm of the waves penetrate his emotions.

Thirty years ago he had chosen the beach before building the house. The real estate was expensive even then, though by today's prices he got the land for a song. He had intended the house to be a sort of hideaway for himself and the children. Michael was only five at the time. Ingrid was ten and Stewart was an already rebellious twelve.

Michael had taken to the place immediately, running along the beach in his shorts or swimsuit, making castles in the sand, chasing sand crabs and hunting for sand dollars with his mother. Judd, walking now, reflected that it was precisely on this sand that those happy early days had been spent. He used to sit here with Michael and tell his son to count the waves coming in to shore.

"Count the waves and tell me how many there are," he would say.

"One, two, three, four . . ." And the little boy would smile and hit his father on the arm when he realized the waves went on forever.

And it was here that the first omen of Michael's special destiny had appeared, marking Judd himself forever.

Judd had been alone with Michael that day. Margery had taken the older children shopping in the village. Judd was sitting on the sand with a cigar in his mouth (ah, the good old days of those Italian panatellas!), squinting into the bright sun and watching Michael run back and forth along the beach.

After a while, tired of squinting, Judd sat back on his elbows and closed his eyes. The sound of the waves, punctuated by Michael's little feet running along the sand, lulled Judd into a noonday languor.

A small cry of alarm pulled him from his reverie. What he saw horrified him. A freak wave had surged up the sand at least fifty yards ahead of the others and swooped Michael up like a predator. The event was so bizarre that Judd was taken off guard. Before he could react, the little boy had been carried off into the ocean. Michael must have swallowed some water already, for he no longer cried out. An eerie, terrible silence covered the scene. Only the rhythmic breaking of the waves was heard.

By now Judd had leaped to his feet, throwing away his cigar, and rushed into the water without removing so much as his shoes. Pumping madly with his strong arms, he fought the waves. Michael was somewhere ahead of him, invisible in a trough between the foaming crests.

Judd was too panicked even to call Michael's name. He surged forward, slamming his arms into the waves, which seemed to rear deliberately before him, battering him backward and sapping his strength. Maddened by their stubborn interference, he fought with a physical fury he had never possessed before or since. (Indeed, it was from this day that Judd would later date his heart trouble. He never felt the same after that desperate struggle.)

At last, in the trough ahead of him, he saw Michael floating, an unconscious little body whose shorts and T-shirt clung to his white skin like rags. Judd swam through the crest of the wave and caught Michael around the neck. Pulling the boy, he swam back toward the shore. The current seemed determined to hold him back. When he finally reached the sandy bottom, unusually strong waves pummeled him from behind and sucked at his legs as though to hinder his progress. Twice he was knocked over, crashing to the wet sand on his back as he held Michael aloft.

Finally he reached safety and began giving the little boy mouth-to-mouth resuscitation. It was difficult, for his own scalded breaths were coming so short that he lacked the wind to fill the boy's lungs. Michael looked oddly peaceful as he lay on the sand. Weeping in his anxiety, Judd forced his own breath into the small body. He moved Michael's arms, held his head back, slapped his little face.

"Please," he begged, not knowing who he was talking to. "Please don't let him be dead. I'll never ask you for anything again."

Judd's own tears were falling on Michael's face when, at last, Michael began to breathe, then to complain and whimper. "Thank God," Judd said aloud through rasping breaths. "Thank God."

Judd had called the local hospital and taken Michael to the emergency room by the time Margery and the two older children returned from their shopping. Having found no note from Judd, Margery was beginning to worry when she saw her husband and son come through the door, Michael eating an ice-cream cone, both looking surprisingly normal except for their sand-covered clothes.

Judd had never forgotten that day. The bright sun, the feeling of odd tranquility before the freak wave suddenly reached out to snatch his son. The frantic rescue, and Judd's occult impression of the ocean's ill will as he fought his way toward shore.

Judd believed that Fate had intended to end Michael's life that sunny day, and that he, Judd, driven by his desperate love for his favorite son, had frustrated Fate. The price he paid was his own heart condition, which was discovered not long afterward and persisted to this day. It was a price he paid gladly.

He also felt that Michael's precocious rendezvous with death had thrown a special halo over his life and destined him for great things. Judd tried his best to prepare Michael for that special fate, encouraging him always to do his best, always to win. Over the years, as Michael's achievements became more and more stellar, Judd felt confirmed in his superstitious belief. His own greatest achievement as a man consisted in having given Michael this second chance at life.

"Why am I thinking of this now?" he wondered, strolling along the shore as the moon hovered above the waves. Suddenly he saw the connection. Michael's furious strokes on that last lap of the Olympic relay had been an echo of Judd's frantic strokes when he fought his way through the waves so long ago to save his son. Michael had swum that relay as though death were at his back. And, in a way, it was.

Memory had combined with the night air to chill Judd's hands and feet, so he turned to go back home. He saw Susan coming toward him along the beach. She was wearing jeans and a sweater. Her blond hair was blowing in the wind. He smiled, pleased by the sight of this sweet nymph coming toward him under the tempestuous sky.

"There you are," she called. "Ingrid was worrying about you."

She curled her arm inside his and they started back toward the house.

"What were you doing out here?" she asked. "Aren't you cold?"

"I'm not so decrepit that I can't take a walk on the beach after my dinner," Judd growled. But his eyes were tender as he looked at Susan.

"Come on in and have a Guinness," she said.

"If you think Ingrid is going to let me have a Guinness without a fight, you're wrong," Judd said. "No wonder I can't stand to be in my own house."

Gusts of wind blew their hair this way and that as they walked. Warmed by Susan's touch, Judd was already shaking off the effects of his painful memory on the beach.

"Michael called," Susan said. "He was sorry to miss you."

Judd felt a pang of loss. His devotion to Michael was such that he even regretted small losses like missing phone calls.

"How is he?" Judd asked.

"*Terrific* was the word he used," Susan smiled. "I believe him. I've never seen him so excited."

"Well, it's an exciting time," Judd said, patting her hand. "Did he have any message for me?"

"Just that he loves you."

Judd smiled gratefully. As the house came closer, he felt as though Michael's words were incarnated in the warm touch of the beautiful girl on his arm. After a lifetime of waiting, everything was in place. Fate was smiling on the Campbells. And Michael had made it all possible.

3 8

Georgetown
March 5

IT WAS against the heady background of Michael's nomination that Susan Campbell accepted a request from Karen Embry for an interview.

Susan had never met the reporter before. Karen had explained that she was working on a freelance series of feature articles about the Pinocchio Syndrome. In answer to Susan's question she explained that her special area of expertise was public health. The series of articles she was preparing would deal only tangentially with politics. It was essentially a story of the epidemic and its effects on people's lives.

"Now that the worst seems to be over, at least in America," she said, "I want to get some perspective on the disease's impact on people. Since it obviously had a significant effect on your own life, due to the illnesses of Mr. Everhardt and Mr. Palleschi, your reaction would be very helpful to my readers."

Susan had hesitated at first. She had given so many interviews recently that her own words were a jumble in her brain. But the reporter had pressed her. "You're one of the most articulate political wives around, and also one of the most honest about your ambivalence about your role and your husband's role. I'd like to hear your views on the current situation, the more so since you're in a particularly important position now."

It was the reporter's display of sensitivity to Susan's personality that made her give in. She expected the interview to be short. She agreed to do it in her own house in Georgetown. She felt safer there, and more sure of herself.

The doorbell rang at the appointed time. When Susan opened the door she saw a young woman of about her own size and age smiling at her. Karen Embry was very pretty. She had milky skin and large, intense eyes. Her fingers were electric with energy as she shook Susan's hand.

"Thank you for seeing me. I know how busy you must be."

"No problem. Come on in."

Susan led the way to the living room, where coffee was waiting. As Karen Embry moved through the room Susan could see she had a lovely figure, though she was too thin. Her manner was slightly tense, suggesting overwork and lack of sleep. The latter, of course, Susan could relate to quite well.

The little makeup Karen wore seemed in need of retouching. Her black hair, naturally sleek and full-bodied, had been brushed in haste. On the whole she gave the combined impression of a girlish freshness and of a certain seediness. Susan liked her instinctively.

"Would you like some coffee?" Susan asked.

"Well," the reporter smiled, "I'm over my limit already, but why not? Sure."

Susan brought coffee in ceramic mugs. Karen had removed a small cassette recorder from her briefcase and was attaching the microphone.

"Shall we get started?" she asked.

"Fine."

"Let me begin by asking how your life has changed in the last few months." Karen Embry gave Susan an even, attentive look as she picked up her coffee mug.

"Well," Susan said, "it's kind of like my life from before, only more so."

"Reporters? Interviews? Public attention focused on your husband?"

"Exactly. I'm used to it, to some extent. Michael has always gotten a lot of press, and so have I. Obviously, more is at stake now, so we feel on the spot."

"How about the public health situation?" the reporter asked. "It has changed greatly since your husband was selected as vice president."

"That's true." Susan nodded. "There's a sense of relief. That combines with the excitement of Michael's work. I feel a lot better than I felt a month ago."

Susan was not being completely truthful. In reality she had never recovered from the deaths of Dan Everhardt and Kirk Stillman. The condition of Tom Palleschi, which had worsened since January, only made things worse. Susan lived with constant anxiety about Michael's physical well-being.

"How do you feel about your husband assuming the vice presidency at such a young age, and in such a tense political climate?" the reporter asked.

"I'm not completely comfortable with it. But the president asked Michael to take the job, and I do believe Michael can handle it successfully."

"How does the rest of his family feel about his selection?"

"Oh, they're thrilled," Susan said. "No second thoughts at all. They're not like me."

Susan smiled to think of Ingrid, who was already busy boning up on the wardrobe and accessories her brother would need as vice president of the United States. Judd, of course, thought of nothing else but his son's ascendancy to high political office. Even Stewart Campbell, the cynical historian who hated politicians, was caught up in the excitement about Michael.

"This is the greatest thing," he kept saying. "The greatest thing that could have happened. Mike is going to be president some day. I know it."

Susan now realized there was something in the Campbell psychology that she had not understood before. The Campbells were hungry for a kind of success and recognition that had escaped their clan not only during Judd's ambitious business career, but throughout many impoverished generations back in Scotland. They felt cheated by the world. Michael had changed all that. Michael was their torchbearer, their official representative in the competitive arena of worldly success. His triumphs in the Olympics had proved to the family that he was marked for an exalted career. His years in the Senate had built their hopes up higher. But only the White House could truly wipe out all the generations of Campbell frustration.

Choosing her words carefully, Karen said, "The death of Vice President Everhardt and the illness of Secretary Palleschi hit you close to home, I believe." Karen could not explicitly say that either Everhardt or Palleschi had been victims of the Syndrome, for the government had never officially admitted as much.

"It was terrible. It still is," Susan replied. "I knew Danny Everhardt well. Michael and I got together socially with him and his wife, Pam, over the years. Danny was the kind of sweet, down-to-earth man you don't meet often in politics. To me he always seemed more like a school principal or a football coach than a famous political leader. I liked him a lot." Her eyes misted. "I still can't get over what happened to him."

Karen said, "I get the feeling you identified with Vice President Everhardt because you yourself are something of a fish out of water as a political wife."

"That's true," Susan said. "When Michael and I got together with Danny and Pam, we never talked about politics. I think I pretended that we were ordinary working people enjoying a Sunday barbecue. Danny created that feeling. It was good for me."

Karen took these words in thoughtfully. Susan Campbell was a warm, charming woman. Yet she was smart, and experienced in interviews. She created a mood. One hesitated to shatter it.

But Karen was paid to push. She decided to probe a weak spot.

"Mrs. Campbell," she said. "There is an obvious progression in the series of men chosen to replace Vice President Everhardt. That progression leads to your husband. Does this worry you?"

"I don't understand." Susan seemed perplexed.

"The progression leads from the most obvious to the least obvious," Karen said. "Secretary Palleschi had a lot in common with Vice President Everhardt, in terms of personality as well as qualifications. He was an almost perfect replacement. Mr. Stillman, though less similar to the vice president, was a man of unquestioned competence and experience. Then we come to your husband. Until the events of recent months, no one would have thought Michael Campbell old enough or experienced enough to assume the vice presidency."

"That's true," Susan said. "Michael is young for a vice president. But he is experienced, and he is competent. He knows the issues."

"Yes, I know that." The reporter was implacable. "But the fact remains that your husband would never have been seriously considered had it not been for these untoward events."

"I guess that's right," Susan admitted.

"Don't you find something odd in all this?" the reporter asked.

"Everything about this last year or so is odd," Susan said. "The *Crescent Queen* disaster, the epidemic . . . If you're asking whether I would prefer that none of this were happening, the answer is yes. I would have preferred to go on with life as it was before. I would have helped Michael in supporting the president, and I would have expected Danny Everhardt to serve out his term as vice president with distinction. I would have continued my life as a senator's wife, and never would have asked for anything more." Susan heard the defensiveness in her own voice, but could not help herself. Karen Embry was more than direct. She was pushy.

"Do you feel less confident about Michael Campbell when you consider the unusual circumstances that have put him in the position he's in now?" Karen probed.

"Not at all," Susan said firmly. "I have great confidence in Michael. I've never doubted him. But I'm worried about our political process. I'm worried about the state of the world."

"Worried about our political process?" The reporter raised an eyebrow. "What do you mean?"

Susan resolved to choose her words carefully. Pushed by the reporter, she had strayed into dangerous territory. It was not her place to give political opinions.

"Well," she said, "to be honest I'm worried about Mr. Goss. The things he says are so full of hate, and he talks about his political opponents as though they were enemies of the nation. The situation around the world is so tense that I think that kind of rhetoric is dangerous."

She sat back, rather pleased with herself for having enunciated a position that few responsible leaders would disagree with.

"Mr. Goss views your husband and the president in a similar way," the reporter observed. "He thinks the world situation is so dangerous that their brand of political moderation is nothing less than criminal."

Susan nodded. "I guess he's entitled to his opinion. But I don't like political leaders who talk in terms of hate and revenge. I think we need to talk in terms of consensus, of responsible cooperation. Of building for the future."

The reporter was regarding Susan steadily.

"But I thought we weren't here to talk about politics," Susan said. "I thought the topic was the epidemic and its effects on people."

"Well, in your case the two areas overlap," Karen countered. "You're a woman whose friends have been affected by the disease, and a political wife whose life has changed course because of it."

"Yes, I guess you're right," Susan admitted.

"The spread of the Pinocchio epidemic seemed to favor Colin Goss, at least in the public opinion polls," Karen pursued. "The apparent cessation of the epidemic in America has had a dramatic and positive effect on the president's performance in the polls. Interestingly, this happens to coincide with the president's choice of your husband to replace Mr. Everhardt. Does any of this worry you?"

"What do you mean by 'worry'?" Susan asked.

"Does the involvement of the disease in the poll results worry you?"

Susan was thoughtful. "Yes," she said. "So did the involvement of the *Crescent Queen* disaster. It's rather macabre to see political candidates rising and falling in the polls when lost human lives are the cause."

Karen was impressed by the subtle combination of candor and evasion in Susan Campbell. She was not like other political wives. She was more sensitive, more communicative. Yet she was hiding something. And that deception was at the core of her charm and her likability.

Karen's instincts told her an unpleasant truth was somewhere close by. She decided to take a chance on chasing it.

She turned off the tape recorder. "May I ask you something off the record?" she said.

"Sure. Of course."

"Did you ever speculate that the removal of Everhardt and Palleschi and Stillman was not accidental, but was specifically designed to put your husband where he is today?"

"What do you mean?" Susan asked.

"I mean that somebody got the other three out of the way so that Michael Campbell could become vice president ten years sooner than he would have otherwise."

Susan turned white. "No, that has not occurred to me," she said. "Not once. I don't know why you think it should have."

Three denials, Karen thought with an inner smile. *Three denials makes an assent. She has been worrying about it.*

Karen turned on the tape recorder, then turned it off again.

"I'm terribly sorry," she said, "but would you mind if I smoke?"

"Not at all," Susan smiled. "You should have asked sooner. I hate to think of you being uncomfortable." She got up and brought an ashtray from the lowboy against the wall.

As Karen lit her Newport she smiled inwardly at the other woman's hospitality. Susan Campbell seemed relieved to be able to offer creature comforts to others. She was the kind of woman who had spent her whole life leaning over backward for other people. This was a self-destructive posture, in psychological terms. She did not respect herself enough to put herself first.

Karen was trying to think of a softer question to ask as a segue into more on-the-record dialogue. Before she could find it the telephone rang.

"Would you excuse me a second?" Susan asked with an apologetic smile. "I forgot to turn the machine on. Let me just pick it up."

She left the reporter smoking her cigarette in the living room and hurried into the kitchen. She removed the cordless phone from its wall mount.

"Hello?"

"Hello, Susan." It was the voice she had come to know all too well. Her hand trembled as she held the phone. She ducked into the pantry, where she could not be overheard from the living room.

"I—can I call you back?" she asked. "I'm in the middle of an interview."

"You sound frightened, Susan."

Susan was silent. She heard a low laugh, strangely sympathetic, on the other end of the line.

"You're frightened because what I predicted has come to pass. The others were eliminated to make room for Michael. You know something bad is happening, and you know he's involved."

Susan reflected that these terrible words echoed the question the reporter had asked her only moments ago.

"And now that Michael has been chosen to be vice president, the epidemic has stopped. At least here." The voice sounded confident, sure of what it was saying.

"I don't understand," Susan said.

"You will."

"I really can't talk," Susan said weakly.

"It's not over, Susan. Nothing is over. You realize that, don't you?"

"What do you mean?"

"Doesn't it strike you as odd that the epidemic is suddenly sparing the United States of America? And of course you've noticed the effect of this on your husband and the president in the polls. The deaths of Everhardt and the others were only the beginning."

"You're crazy."

"Susan, Susan. Don't you know that the truth burns at first, only to heal later on? It's just like a disinfectant poured onto a wound. At first it seems like the worst pain in the world. But it kills the infection, which otherwise would have grown and grown until everything was dead."

Susan sighed deeply. She closed her eyes, unable to speak, unable to hang up. She smelled the smoke of the reporter's cigarette from the living room.

"Susan," said the voice, "did you ask him about Harvard? Did you ask him what happened there?"

Susan sighed. "No, I didn't. He's been so—"

"It doesn't matter. You haven't lost anything by waiting. Ask him now. Look into his eyes when he answers. You'll see the truth there."

"Please stop . . . What truth?" Susan's resistance spoke in one voice, her desperate curiosity in another.

"Ask him now. After he's answered, you'll want to talk to me."

"I was there," Susan said. "I was there the whole time. Nothing happened. I know that. I was with him every minute."

"Not quite. He was away for weekends at a time. Remember?"

Susan was silent. Her eyes were closed. Her hand was shaking harder now.

"He gave you excuses," the voice said. "You believed him. In reality you had no idea where he was, did you? Whole weekends out of your sight."

"I know where he was."

"You know what he told you. That's all."

"What is it you want?" Susan pleaded. "I've listened to you, I've let you go on . . ."

"I'm proud of you for that, Susan. You were brave enough to listen, when you knew the truth was going to hurt. You're a strong woman, no matter what you may think of yourself."

"Is he in danger?" Susan asked. "Is that why you've called me? Please, tell me so I can help him."

"Poor Susan. You still haven't understood, have you? He's not in any danger. He won't get sick like the others. No car will run him down."

Susan grasped at these words as a lifeline. But already she sensed the menace behind them.

"Susan, are you there?" the voice asked.

The only response was Susan's exhausted sigh.

"Susan, I'm going to give you the medicine that will kill the germs once and for all. The medicine that will heal you."

There was a pause. Susan rested her head against the pantry shelf, feeling the odd intimacy of the voice.

"The medicine is a question," the voice said. "Ask him what happened at Harvard. Ask him about the Donkey Game. When he answers, watch his eyes."

"I . . ." Susan felt too exhausted to frame a reply.

A click sounded on the line. The caller had hung up.

It took all Susan's strength to pull herself together. She emerged from the pantry and hung the phone on its wall mount. She paused in front of the hall mirror to see whether her emotion was visible on her face. Amazingly, she looked almost normal. She went back into the living room wearing a brittle smile.

"I'm very sorry," she said. "I don't know when I'm finally going to learn to turn on that answering machine."

"You should be like me," Karen smiled. "I never answer my phone. I have an answering machine at home and a voice-mail service. I check them when I feel like it. Anybody who has a legitimate reason to call will leave a message and a number. The cranks and salesmen always hang up."

The word *cranks* unsettled Susan. But Karen had done Susan a favor by talking about herself. She had given Susan an extra minute to compose herself. Her armor was back in place.

"I'm sorry, but I've forgotten the question you asked," she said.

"I hadn't asked it," Karen said.

"Oh."

"But I will now, if that's okay."

"Sure." Susan awaited the question fearfully. The reporter turned on the tape recorder again.

"I was wondering what you think would be the worst thing about becoming the vice president's wife at this particular time, and what would be the best thing."

Susan breathed a sigh of relief. The question was harmless.

"The worst thing is easy to answer," Susan said. "Being in the public eye. I'm a very shy person. Every public appearance is a struggle for me."

"What about the best thing?" the reporter asked.

Susan thought for a moment. "Working side by side with the president and the First Lady. They're both very good people. They work hard, but they're fun to be with. I respect them both enormously."

Karen noticed that Susan had not said the best thing about being in the White House would be the joy of being Michael Campbell's wife. Her husband was noticeably missing from her answer.

The interview concluded with a series of easy, almost caressing questions about Susan's hopes for the country and herself. When the tape recorder was turned off the two women exchanged pleasantries about life in Washington. As Karen packed up to leave Susan recalled her expertise in medical matters.

"Do you think the disease is really gone from here?" she asked.

"The Pinocchio Syndrome? No one knows for sure," Karen said. "It isn't well enough understood. But it's possible. Remember how long the AIDS epidemic was concentrated in Africa? Even intensely contagious diseases sometimes stay within circumscribed areas. And don't forget, they never could prove the Pinocchio Syndrome could be passed from human to human."

"I hope we never see it again," Susan said.

"Me too," Karen said.

She got up to leave. "I appreciate your finding time to talk to me. You must be terribly busy."

"It was a pleasure." Susan was lying, but she had found it interesting to meet this bright young reporter. Karen Embry reminded her of herself, but in different colors and with a different psychology. Where Susan was soft, Karen was aggressive. Where Susan was smooth, Karen was messy. Yet they had something in common, something Susan could not name.

"May I call you if I need clarification of any of the details?" Karen asked.

"Sure thing," Susan smiled, walking the reporter to the door. "I'd be glad to hear from you."

"That's a new one," Karen said. "Most people aren't glad to hear from me."

Susan wondered why she had said she would be glad to hear from Karen. Perhaps it was because Karen seemed too blunt, too remorseless to be untrustworthy. Susan felt in need of someone she could trust.

Susan watched from the doorway as Karen moved on brisk legs to her car, a relatively new Honda that had not been washed in a long time. The engine sprang to life. The car did not move, though. The reporter must be checking her notes or looking at her schedule for the rest of the day.

Susan closed the door and disappeared into the house.

Inside the car Karen was scribbling as fast as she could on her note pad, trying not to forget what she had heard on the phone.

3 men eliminated to make room for Michael.
Truth like medicine . . . kills germs . . .
Michael will not get sick. No car will run Michael down.
Odd that epidemic now spares USA.
"It isn't over."

Karen thought for a moment, her eyes closed tight. "Damn," she said out loud. "Come on. Come on."

Ask him what happened at Harvard.
Ask him about donkey game.

With a sigh she wrote down the last words.

The minute the phone had started ringing in Susan Campbell's kitchen Karen had glanced around the living room in search of an extension. It was on the table by her side. She had heard the whole conversation between Susan and the caller.

"Okay," she said to herself now. "Okay, kid. You've got something to run with."

She had interviewed Susan Campbell in order to hear her lie. She had hoped that by measuring the shape and tenor of Susan's lies, she could glimpse a shadowed profile of the truth. This was the vocation of any reporter who interviewed important people—especially a Washington reporter. To catch the hints and connect the dots.

But thanks to that phone call, Karen had learned far more than she expected from this visit.

She closed the notebook and put it into her purse. As she did so she noticed a folded piece of printer paper that had been in the purse for two weeks.

She unfolded the paper and looked at it. The message was brief.

AFTER CAMPBELL SELECTION THE EPIDEMIC SPARES UNITED STATES.

The message was signed GRIMM.

Of course the epidemic did stop after Michael Campbell was selected by the president. The words in the note were perfectly true.

But Karen had received the e-mail a week *before* Michael's nomination. Six days before the untimely death of Kirk Stillman, which brought about that nomination. Thus Grimm had predicted the future on two counts. Whatever was wrong in Washington, Grimm knew the people who were behind it.

She had been putting personal ads to Grimm in the *Post* every day since. But Grimm had not answered.

She looked at the cryptic words. She thought about the voice on Susan Campbell's phone.

Could they be the same person?

Karen folded the note and put it back in her purse. She lit up a Newport and watched the smoke billow against the dirty windshield.

Harvard.

She turned the key in the ignition. The engine sprang into life. A burst of dust came from the vents.

Impatiently she threw the car into gear. She hit the gas too hard, and the front wheels skidded as she hurtled into traffic.

Ask him about the donkey game.

39

"Despite the reassurances of health authorities to the effect that there is no danger after the initial outbreak, a taboo seems to attach to the affected areas. They are like ghost towns. The houses are empty, the streets are silent. It is an unsettling sight. Looting is a serious problem . . ."

Colin Goss was sitting at the desk in his penthouse office, watching a tape of a CNN report on the worldwide effects of the Pinocchio Syndrome epidemic. Goss leaned forward as the image of an abandoned neighborhood in suburban London filled the screen.

"Fanciful cures and preventions for the disease are being hawked to an impressionable public by unscrupulous entrepreneurs," said the reporter. *"Exotic herbs, organic foods, and vitamin supplements are being sold at health food stores and homeopathic mail-order houses for inflated prices. Some of these products are not even what they claim to be, like the pulverized beef bones being sold as the tail bones of rare Brazilian monkeys. Health authorities have tried to warn the public against*

such fraudulent cures, but rumor and the Internet seem to have outstripped their warnings."

Colin Goss smiled. He had wanted the Pinocchio Syndrome to appeal to the public imagination. He was not disappointed. The terror spawned by the Syndrome, unequaled since the great smallpox epidemics and the Black Plague, was causing civilized people to become as primitive in their thinking as the uneducated masses in Third World countries.

"We're seeing a huge increase in suicide, street crime, and domestic violence. But perhaps worst of all, John, is the ethnic violence spawned by the Syndrome. Not only is there fighting among groups thrown together by history and geography, such as the Indians and the Pakistanis. There are even signs of vast, bloody migrations like the Aryan invasion of the Near East in the second millennium B.C., or the Germanic invasions of the Roman Empire after the birth of Christ. It's as though the human race had been set back a thousand years."

There were now over eleven million victims of the Syndrome in sixty countries. About six million had died. The authorities had long since given up trying to hide the victims' macabre physical deformities from the families. The image of a dying human being with distended and distorted hands and feet had now become the official nightmare of the age, replacing the buboes of Plague victims, the pocked skin of smallpox, the baldness and telltale emaciation of cancer and AIDS victims.

Goss poured himself a glass of his favorite mineral water. The water had the tang of juniper berries, a result of the vegetation in the vicinity of the Tuscan springs from which it originated. Goss was in excellent humor, so excellent that when the phone rang and he heard the worried voice of his public relations consultant, he was unfazed by the man's bad news.

"I'm afraid we lost another two points in the past week," the consultant said. "I just don't understand it. Your speeches in Detroit and Scranton were well attended, and you got good press all week."

"Don't worry about it," Goss said. "Let's just keep the pressure on."

"Yes, sir." The man did not seem encouraged. "We might think about changing our focus a bit. Since the epidemic has stopped in America, the public mood isn't the same."

"No, that won't be necessary," Goss assured him. "Everything is under control."

Everything was going according to plan. Goss's message of hate was playing poorly to a public whose fear of the epidemic had abated since January. The further Goss slipped in the polls, the higher the president rose—and with him Michael Campbell.

"Don't worry about it," Goss said. "Everything will work out fine. You'll see. Don't lose sleep over it, Ron."

Goss hung up and took another sip of the tangy water. He glanced at the now-silent TV screen, on which news film of terrified Europeans and Arabs was being shown. Outside the window the great American heartland basked in the relief procured by its freedom from the spreading illness. With this relief came renewed optimism and hope for the future.

This was exactly as Goss had planned it.

A timid knock at the inner office door interrupted Goss's reverie. He went to the door and opened it. A girl entered the office. She seemed younger than her eighteen years. She wore a skirt and blouse, and low-heeled shoes. Around her neck was a delicate gold chain. She wore no bracelets or rings. She looked diffident and a bit unnerved.

"Don't be shy," Goss smiled. "Come closer so I can look at you."

She came toward the desk like a frightened child. She was a bit overweight, perhaps ten or fifteen pounds for her height. Baby fat, Goss thought, noting with approval the budding breasts under her blouse.

"I'm glad you could come," he said. "Please sit down. Can I get you something to drink?"

"No, thanks."

He motioned to a large leather armchair. The girl perched nervously on the oversized cushion. Goss took a sip of his mineral water and sat down opposite her.

"So," he smiled. "You're here on a mission of rescue."

She nodded. "I hope you didn't tell anyone."

"Of course not. This will be just between us." Goss studied her for a moment. She had blond hair and a fair complexion that accentuated her innocence.

"You look pale," he said. "You should get more sun. But I suppose school doesn't leave you enough time for that."

She said nothing. She chewed her lip nervously.

"Don't be nervous," he said. "There's nothing to be nervous about. Everything is going to be fine."

She gave him a pleading look.

"I need to be sure nothing else will happen," she said.

"On that you have my personal word," Goss said. "Our little transaction today will end the entire business. You will never see me again. Your father's sins will be wiped out, and it will be business as usual from now on."

The girl's father owned a large software company that Goss had tried to acquire for one of his subsidiaries a year ago. The father, a self-made man, had refused to be bought out. Routine intelligence had unearthed a crime that could put the proud entrepreneur behind bars for a dozen years, and ruin his reputation forever. Goss had discussed the case with his people and found out about the daughter. She was her father's only child and his pride and joy.

Goss had his people working on cases like this all the time. Their work, however, did not always bring results as fetching as the beautiful child before him.

She nodded uncomfortably. "He'll never know, will he?" she asked. "It would kill him if he knew."

"He will never know." On this one point Goss was lying. But the rest of his statements were true.

There was a pause. Goss looked at her calves, which tapered to delicate ankles.

"If he did know," Goss smiled, "he would be proud. You're making a sacrifice to save your father's good name. Not to mention his livelihood."

She nodded.

"Are you sure you wouldn't like a drink?" Goss asked. "Perhaps a little wine, to steady your nerves?"

She took a deep, nervous breath. She shook her head.

"Fine. Let's get started, then. Take off your blouse."

She hesitated for a long moment, looking away. Goss watched her closely, as though measuring her distress.

Then she did as she was told, her fingers trembling as she touched the buttons.

"Good girl. Now the bra."

The little bra came undone, revealing breasts that did not seem full grown. She had very much the look of a schoolgirl. This delighted Goss.

"Leave the skirt on. Take off the panties."

She had to stand up to slip the panties down her legs. Goss watched with interest.

"Bring them to me."

She brought the panties and held them out. Goss took them and held them to his lips. He sniffed them appreciatively.

"Your father made a mistake," he said. "Didn't he?"

Her arms were crossed over her breasts. She nodded.

"Put your arms down at your sides," Goss said.

She did as she was told.

"Your father made a mistake for which he might be severely punished in the courts," Goss said. "Thanks to you, and to me, that mistake will be wiped out. Isn't that right?"

She nodded, a hopeful look on her face.

"He will never know, but you will know," Goss said. "You will always remember this. It will be a memory that will make you proud."

She was looking at him fearfully.

Goss studied her for a moment. "Step out of your shoes."

She removed her shoes, which looked expensive and stylish. Why not? Her father was wealthy, he could afford to clothe her in fine things.

"Take off the skirt and lie down on the couch," he said.

There was a low couch at right angles to the desk. It was backless, like a chaise longue. The girl looked at it uncertainly.

"On your tummy," Goss said.

The girl took off her skirt and lay down somewhat clumsily. Goss admired her derriere and the fresh expanse of her skin.

"Very good," he said. "You're really quite lovely."

He came to her side.

"Don't be afraid," he said. "There's nothing to be afraid of."

He stroked the small of her back. She shuddered.

"Stop that," he said.

"I can't," she replied.

Goss pushed warningly at her spine. "Stop that!"

"I can't. I can't help it."

"One phone call from me, and he's ruined. Everything he's worked for. Is that what you want?"

She shook her head. Goss saw, and savored, a tear which flowed from underneath her face and down the leather of the couch. There was a forlorn quality to her posture, an aloneness as she prepared to face her ordeal. Goss noted this with satisfaction.

"All right."

His hand moved lower.

"No!" she cried.

"It's you or him," Goss said. "Which will it be?"

Sobs shook the girl's shoulders. Her hands were clenched. The intoxicating aroma of youth and fear reached Goss's nostrils.

"You or him. Make up your mind!" he hissed.

A siren sounded suddenly on the street far below, like a cry of pain.

"Me," said the girl.

"Good," Goss smiled, bending to kiss her. "Good."

40

Alexandria, Virginia

AT EIGHT o'clock on a windy March evening Karen was sitting at her computer as usual, her legs crossed under her, wearing cutoff jeans and a T-shirt, when the doorbell rang.

A Newport was sitting in the ashtray beside the computer. Behind it was a small cocktail glass half filled with straight bourbon. The glass was positioned so that if Karen knocked it over with her left hand when she was drunk, it would fall away from the keyboard.

She crushed out the cigarette, padded to the door with her pencil in her mouth, and opened it to see Joe Kraig standing on the stoop.

"Agent Kraig," she said. "What can I do for you?"

"May I come in?" Kraig asked.

"Sure." She stood back to let him pass. He entered her foyer, not taking off his mist-soaked trench coat.

"Sorry," Karen said. "Let me hang up that coat in the shower."

He let her take the coat. The apartment stank of cigarette smoke. It looked as though it hadn't been cleaned in six months. It was far dirtier than his own place.

As she came back from the bathroom he noticed that Karen was thinner than ever. Her shoulder blades were salient under the T-shirt. If she were to take it off he guessed he would see her ribs.

"Don't you ever eat?" he asked. "You look worse than the last time I saw you."

"No time to eat," she said, motioning to the couch. "Want a beer? A drink? Bourbon? Vodka?"

"Nothing." He was sitting stiffly on the couch, as though about to get up and leave.

"What's on your mind?" she asked. "You don't look happy."

Kraig grimaced. "You had an interview with Susan Campbell last week."

Karen nodded. "Yeah, I did. So what?"

"What did you talk about?"

"What do you think? Her husband's selection as vice president. The Pinocchio Syndrome. Her fears. Her concerns. Stuff like that." Karen shrugged. "It was human interest. Reactions of the families. That kind of thing."

"I wish you had seen fit to leave her alone," Kraig said.

"Why? She didn't seem unhappy to see me." Karen had stubbed out the cigarette beside the computer and was lighting another one from a butane lighter. She flopped down on the battered armchair across from Kraig, her slim legs extending straight in front of her.

"She was upset by your questions," Kraig said.

"How do you know?"

"I keep in touch with her and with her husband," Kraig said, watching the smoke plume around the reporter's head. "I don't think you really needed to talk to her, did you?"

Karen was perplexed and intrigued. Why would a man as busy as Kraig go out of his way to come here and upbraid her for doing her job? What was he trying to hide?

"She was helpful and forthcoming," she said. "We parted on good terms. She even asked me to keep in touch. I think she likes me."

Kraig watched sourly as Karen picked a piece of lint off her shirt. Her easy informality in the midst of this mess irritated him.

"Look," he said. "Oh, hell. Get me a drink."

"Bourbon?" she asked.

"Whichever bottle is the fullest," he said.

"Ice?"

"And water. Yes."

She got up and poured a stiff shot of Early Times over ice with a splash of water. She padded back into the living room on bare feet and put the drink on the table before him.

He sipped the bourbon. He didn't like liquor anymore. It gave him headaches. He had only asked for the drink to try to forge a small bond of hospitality between himself and Karen.

"Let me explain something to you," he said.

"I'd like that." She regarded him steadily over her joined knees.

"I've known Susan and Michael since college," he said. "I've known Mike since we were together at Choate."

"Prep school buddies," Karen observed with a small grin.

"Susan has never really gotten used to the political life," Kraig said. "As a matter of fact, she hates it. They have a good marriage, I think, but the public part of their life is hard on her. She doesn't sleep well. She's—"

"Unhappy?" Karen offered.

"I wouldn't go that far." Kraig was lying. He believed Susan was in fact unhappy in her life. But it was a life she had chosen. She would never give it up.

"She's fragile," he said. "Permanently so. At least that's my opinion of her. The last few months have been hard on her nerves. It would help if she wasn't bothered any more than absolutely necessary."

"If she doesn't want to be bothered, she shouldn't be married to a man who is about to become vice president of the United States," Karen said.

Kraig nodded grimly. He took a sip of the bourbon, whose flavor reminded him faintly of furniture polish.

"I respect your job," he said. "I can understand that you wanted reaction from her about the things that have been going on. I'm just wondering . . ."

"What?" Karen asked, puffing at her cigarette.

"Did you say anything, or ask anything, that might have upset her?"

Karen smiled. "What are you, her keeper?"

"No. But I'm responsible for the people who are keeping an eye on her husband," Kraig said. "Her state of mind can have an effect. She sounded upset when I talked to her after your interview."

Karen looked at Kraig. "Yes, I asked something that might have upset her."

"What?"

"I asked her if it had ever occurred to her that Everhardt, Palleschi, and Stillman were removed so that Michael Campbell could become vice president this year."

Kraig's dark eyes flashed. "Christ!" he said. "What a thing to ask her."

"I didn't get an answer," Karen said. "The phone rang. She went to answer it. When she came back I backed off and threw her softballs for the rest of the interview."

"Why?" Kraig asked.

"Why what?"

"Why did you let up?"

"She seemed upset," Karen said. "I could see she didn't know anything that might help me, so I saw no reason to upset her further." She blew smoke out the side of her mouth. "I liked her."

Journalists, like politicians, have to be adroit liars. Karen's bland look gave no hint of the crucial phone conversation she had overheard at Susan Campbell's house. Karen's own questions could hardly have upset Susan as much as that phone call.

Kraig looked displeased. "That was a stupid thing to ask."

Karen shook her head. "No, it wasn't, Agent Kraig. It was the perfect question."

"To ask a woman like her?" Kraig shook his head. "Christ. Do you have to float your conspiracy theories to innocent people who are worried enough as it is?"

Karen smoked in silence, looking at him.

"Well?" he asked.

"I have to push buttons," she said. "It's my job. I wanted to see her reaction."

"But you backed off."

"Yes. I backed off."

Kraig thought for a moment. "Who was on the phone?"

"I don't know. She took the call in the kitchen."

"Was she upset by your questions or by the call?" Kraig asked.

"I'm not sure. Probably by me."

Kraig took another cosmetic sip of his drink. Then he stood up.

"Thanks for the drink."

"You didn't finish it."

"I'm not much of a drinker. I never was, to tell you the truth."

"I forgive you." Karen smiled. Her face looked younger in that instant, framed by her dark hair.

"Will you do me a favor?" Kraig asked. "Bring your theories to me. Let me answer you. Don't bother Susan Campbell."

"Bring them to you? That would be a first," Karen said. "I haven't been able to get a foot in the door with any government employee since my article came out."

"I make my own decisions about interviews," Kraig said.

"All right, then I'd like to hear your answer to the question I asked Mrs. Campbell," Karen said. "Right now."

Kraig looked for his coat. He didn't see it.

"There is no evidence that anything that has occurred this winter was deliberate," he said. "No evidence that anyone is behind the epidemic, or that anyone made Everhardt or Palleschi sick."

"What about the hit-and-run that killed Stillman?" Karen asked.

"That's exactly what it was," Kraig replied angrily. "A routine hit-and-run by a drunk driver."

"You believe that?" Karen asked.

"Yes!" Kraig raised his voice to cover the lie.

Karen was looking steadily at Kraig. "Are you relieved that the epidemic stopped in America?"

"Obviously."

"You don't see anything odd about the fact that it stopped right after Michael Campbell was chosen to replace Vice President Everhardt?"

"Jesus!" Kraig exclaimed. "You stop at nothing."

The note of dismissal in his voice annoyed Karen.

"If I were you, Agent Kraig, I wouldn't be too quick to breathe a sigh of relief about this."

She got up and went to the bathroom for his coat. Her slim thighs moved delicately under the wrinkled shorts. She had pretty feet, he observed, like her pretty hands.

She helped him on with the coat. He paused to look at her.

"You're a bright girl," he said. "When are you going to give up?"

"When I get some answers that make sense," she said. "So far things don't add up. It's a reporter's job to pursue that."

He sighed. "Do we have a deal about Mrs. Campbell?"

She chewed her lip ruminatively, studying his face.

"I can't make that kind of promise," she said.

"If I catch you around her uninvited, I'll pick you up for harassment," he said.

"I won't come uninvited," she said. "That I will promise."

"Fair enough." He turned to leave.

"Agent Kraig." Her voice stopped him.

"What?"

"You don't really believe it yourself, do you? Everhardt, Stillman, Palleschi . . . That's no coincidence."

"It is until we can prove otherwise."

"What are you trying to prove?" she asked. "That it is, or that it isn't?"

Kraig shook his head. "Good night, Miss Embry."

He let himself out and moved quickly along the sidewalk to the parking lot. He got into an unmarked government sedan. Karen heard the engine roar. He must have gunned it angrily as he was turning the ignition key.

She watched him drive away. She wondered why he had come. His mission as Susan Campbell's knight in shining armor didn't ring true. He had another reason, one he wasn't saying.

Karen closed the door and returned to her computer. A faint smile played over her lips as she looked at the screen.

Kraig headed for home, cursing at the traffic that surged under the rainy sky.

He had learned what he went there to learn. Karen Embry did not know who telephoned Susan Campbell during their interview.

Kraig did know. It was the crank Susan had been worrying about. Susan had told him so.

What Susan had not told him was that the reporter had dared to float her conspiracy theory to Susan herself. No wonder Susan's nerves were frayed, Kraig thought.

He would not tell Susan about his conversation with Karen. There was no point in bothering Susan any further about it.

As for the reporter herself, Kraig could not stop her from seeking the truth. After all, the constitution he was sworn to uphold guaranteed the freedom of the press. But he could punish her if she used her power unscrupulously. There were ways. A free press was one thing. An irresponsible press was another.

She knew a lot already. She was sharp, all right. But she didn't know about that phone call.

"Thank God for small favors," he mused, nosing the sedan into the ugly traffic.

4 1

MICHAEL CAMPBELL was in the weight room.

He was finishing his bench presses. Two hundred eighty pounds, eight repetitions. He had started at 180, then moved to 220. Then 250, then 280. He had found a few years ago that he simply lacked the muscle bulk to handle more than 280.

His arms were burning after the last rep. He sat for a long time, waiting for his rasping breaths to subside. Then he lay down on the mat for some stretching. His physical therapist had taught him long ago that with his back problems, frequent stretching was a must. He could not afford to have his back muscles stiffen up on him.

He lay on his back and turned both legs to the left, stretching the base of his spine. Then both legs to the right, then bridging and catbacks to stretch the spine forward and backward. He was wearing cotton shorts over a weightlifter's supporter, and a Baltimore Orioles T-shirt. The shirt was soaked already from his curls and presses.

Lying on his back he thought of Susan. One of the first times they made love, after his second operation, he had been on his back. She took off all her clothes as he watched, and came astride him, her beautiful breasts poised above him, her warm knees caressing his ribs. When she lowered her fanny to guide him inside her, he had an orgasm despite himself, spilling his seed on her fingers. His embarrassment had been intense.

But Susan had smiled and said, "I'm flattered that you want me that much." Her generosity had touched him.

Later on, when he was fully recovered, they made love with her on her back. She liked the deeper penetration he could achieve with her legs pulled up and wrapped around him. She wanted to feel all open to him, possessed by him as completely as possible.

Nowadays he usually lay on his back when he made love to Leslie. With Susan he stayed on top. In a way the difference of position symbolized the different relationships he had with the two women. Susan wanted to be passive, wanted him to take charge. Leslie liked to dominate him, using her wiles to force him to come when she wanted it.

Sighing, Michael got up to do the Nautilus. Squatting under the bar, he started at 175 and worked his way slowly up to 250. This was the core of his routine. The weight went right to his back. Where the back was permanently weakened by his scoliosis and the two surgeries, his legs made up the difference.

Eight reps. Then rest, then eight more. He had to be careful. He had to *think* the distribution of the stress. If he allowed the wrong muscles to take on too much, his lower back would go out and he could be bedridden for weeks.

Michael had a near-perfect body for a man of his age. His shoulders were a bit larger now than they had been when he did his competitive swimming. So were his biceps. The rest of him looked like a twenty-one-year-old athlete. Women raved about his pectorals, his washboard stomach, his long legs. Two years ago a photographer got a picture of him sweeping Susan up into his arms on the beach in Hawaii, and it had made all the wire services. *Beautiful couple at play.* Michael did not mind being hyped for his physical attractiveness. In politics one learns to use what one has. Even now his athletic body was being used by the White House PR people to project an image of health and strength.

But Michael did not work out just to look good. He needed to feel strong.

The political life made him feel more vulnerable than other people. Exposed. Endangered, even.

He thought about Dan Everhardt. Dan had been a good friend and a dedicated colleague. Now he was dead. Soon Tom Palleschi, one of the most athletic men in Washington, would die too. Kirk Stillman, a legend among diplomats, was buried in his hometown of Glenview, Illinois.

The world was not a safe place. Security was not a thing one took for granted. It was a rampart one built with the strength of one's hands and maintained by the force of one's will. And force sometimes meant violence.

Violence, Michael believed, was not an accident or an aberration. No matter what the political scientists and historians said. One look at the history of international relations left no doubt that the waves of violence that swept over the world at regular intervals arose from something deep in man's nature. Something he must express every few years, in some part of the world, simply to show that he was human. Africa, the Middle East, the Balkans—sooner or later it touched everyone. Civilization was man's way of bottling up the violence inside him. War was his way of letting off the steam, getting the bad blood out. War, and genocide.

Violence could not be stopped. But that did not mean there was nothing to be done. One could fight to prevent the violence from touching one's own family, one's own country, during this generation. One could take precautions, be cunning, have foresight. If one did a good job, the violence might take someone else this time. Not my wife, not my child, not my loved ones.

Michael thought of Susan. She was so delicate, so vulnerable. He felt a husband's fierce need to protect her against harm. Because they had no children, this need was focused entirely on Susan herself. The world was so cruel, he had to shield her from its dangers.

But he could not accomplish it by hiding his head in the sand. He had to put himself on the front lines and do the difficult and painful things necessary to protect his country. Because, in the last analysis, that country was the vessel that contained Susan, the rampart that protected her life.

Difficult and painful things. Sometimes ugly things. The world was not a kind place.

Thirty-five years of life—almost twelve of them in public service—had taught Michael that the United States of America could not survive if it continued to follow its present course. The senseless murder of three thousand people in the World Trade Center had made that abundantly clear. So had the bombing of the *Crescent Queen*. Civilized countries could no longer stand by passively and watch terrorists and terrorist nations destroy their institutions.

It was time for a change. Michael would be part of that change. So would Colin Goss.

Judd Campbell had said it best when Michael was still a boy. "Sometimes the only way to survive is to win." A few more months, a few more difficult battles, and the struggle would be over. In the meantime, as Colin Goss had told Michael so often, one must keep one's eyes on the prize, and not allow oneself to feel anything.

The sexual thoughts that had come to Michael during his workout stayed with him all afternoon. He kept thinking of Leslie's smooth body, and of Susan's sensual blond softness. He knew he could not slip away to see Leslie today or, for that matter, this week. There was simply no time.

He got home by seven despite the rush-hour traffic. Judd and Ingrid were there for dinner. Michael made the drinks while Susan and Ingrid baked the hors d'oeuvre, a special recipe of Ingrid's for scallops casino, handed down from Michael's mother. Then they all sat down to a rib roast made by Susan. Dinner was amicable, but Michael was eager to get it over with and be alone with Susan. He was grateful when Ingrid insisted that Judd get home for an early bedtime.

Judd and Ingrid left at nine for the long drive home, with Ingrid behind the wheel of Judd's Cadillac, looking very much like the boss as her father slumped sleepily against the side window.

Michael curled his hands around Susan's waist when the door had closed.

"Let's make love," he whispered in her ear.

He pulled at her zipper even as she was closing the blinds, and had her dress down around her waist by the time they got to the top of the stairs. He picked her up and carried her to the bed, ignoring her remonstrances about his back.

"I want you so bad," he said, kissing her and feeling her breasts swell under his hands.

Their lovemaking was quick and breathless. Susan's panties were barely off before Michael was inside her, thrusting quickly, his face buried in her hair. Infected by his excitement, she wrapped her legs around him and squeezed hard.

"Oh, Michael," she whispered.

"You're so beautiful . . ." He had his hands under her, glorying in the satiny skin of her loins. Her tongue was in his mouth, caressing, stroking. A groan sounded in his throat.

He pulled her harder onto his penis, feeling the last wave rise inside him. She was so sweet and pure, a blond princess . . .

He heard his name on her lips as his semen burst into her.

They lay for a long time, feeling the gradual ebb of their scalded breaths. He stayed very hard inside her as he kissed her cheeks and hair. He loved the smell of her, a composite aroma that combined the innocence of a child with the subtle pungency of the female animal.

They lay in silence for a few moments. Then Michael got up to take his shower. Susan would shower much later, as usual. Her insomnia kept her awake late, while Michael usually went to bed by eleven.

Michael returned to the bedroom and found Susan lying under the sheet, still naked, the outline of her nipples visible under the fabric. He lay down beside her.

"That's my girl," he said.

He buried his face against her breast, which still smelled of their sex.

"Michael," she said.

He could feel that the languor of lovemaking was gone. She was tense.

"Yes?" He looked into her eyes.

"Did something happen at Harvard?" she asked.

"What?" He looked amused. "What do you mean, did something happen?"

"Was there a game?" Susan asked.

"Game? What game?"

"Something about a donkey." Susan's voice was steady, her hands at her sides. "A donkey game."

Michael sat up. "What? What did you say?"

"A donkey game," she repeated.

"Babe, I don't know what you're talking about," Michael said. "Is this some kind of riddle?"

She lay with her head against the pillow, looking into his eyes.

"You don't know what I'm talking about?" she asked.

"No." Michael looked perplexed, uncomprehending.

"You're sure?"

"Of course I'm sure." His tawny eyes bore a look of the most complete innocence.

"Never mind," Susan said.

He bent to kiss her lips. Her eyes, wide open in the shadows, half closed as she felt his touch.

4 2

"The White House counterattacked today after Colin Goss's inflammatory speech to the VFW in Chicago last night. Press Secretary Anspach said the president would stand on his record as an opponent of terrorism and as a public servant, and dared Colin Goss to do the same. The press secretary hinted at shady business practices on the part of Goss's huge business empire, without being explicit."

The woman paused in her cleaning to listen to the news item. She looked at the screen, hoping for an image of Michael Campbell, but the news broadcast was interrupted by a commercial.

She turned on the vacuum cleaner and finished cleaning the living room floor. She used the attachment to get the drapes, which were somewhat dusty. Then she turned off the vacuum and surveyed the room.

The bookshelves held inexpensive copies of her guest's favorite authors, including Ann Tyler, Sue Miller, and Agatha Christie. There was also a compendium of Somerset Maugham's short stories, and a complete paperback set of Jane Austen. She knew these were her guest's favorites.

Vanity Fair, Cosmopolitan, the *New Yorker.* Several issues of each, in the magazine rack. Each morning there would be a copy of the *New York Times.*

Alongside the small TV, on which the commercial murmured, were about a dozen videotapes and DVDs bought at considerable expense. These included Bogart films like *Dark Passage, The Big Sleep,* and *The African Queen,* as well as Ray Milland films from the 1940s, including *The Big Clock* and *Lost Weekend.* Also some John Garfield, including *Force of Evil* and *Gentleman's Agreement,* and a few others, recorded off TV, that featured Charles Boyer, Gary Cooper, James Stewart, and other stars of the thirties and forties.

In the kitchen were low-fat foods, including Jenny Craig meals, vegetables, skim milk, granola. Diet Coke in the refrigerator, bottled water in the pantry. In the bathroom were hypoallergenic cosmetics—her guest suffered from allergies—and a supply of Alfred Sung perfume. The soap in the bath was Camay. The shampoo was Pantene.

There were pajamas, workout clothes, and informal wear in her guest's size. There was an exercise bike, but no treadmill.

The commercials were over. The woman paused in front of the TV, listening. A plane was coming in overhead, so she had to turn up the volume to hear.

The commentators were talking about the debate in the Senate over Michael Campbell's nomination as vice president. There were more than enough votes committed to confirm him, but senators loyal to Colin Goss were slowing the process with long speeches and parliamentary delaying tactics.

There was a sound bite of Michael Campbell, taken from his speech at the University of Illinois last night.

"Now more than ever, we need a man in the White House whom we can trust," he said. *"A man who has earned our trust over twenty-five long years of public service. A man whose judgment we do not doubt and will never have to doubt. I'm proud to say that the president is that man. I'm proud that he has chosen me to work with him as vice president. I'm looking forward to working alongside him as he finishes out his term."*

She sat down on the rug, studying the youthful handsome face, whose smile broadened as the audience applauded. A candid face, innocent, too

fresh for his years. It was attached to a body millions of women had fantasized about, a body whose scars attested to the heroic physical feats he had
accomplished.

She nodded slowly. She rocked slightly back and forth. A low sound came
from her throat, a wordless murmur or moan. Outside the windows another
roar sounded, this time a large jet taking off. She didn't hear it.

Suddenly she sat up straighter. Susan Campbell had appeared on the
screen, talking to an interviewer. She was wearing a bright blue dress and
gold loop earrings. She wore an expectant half smile as she listened attentively to the interviewer's question.

"Are you getting ready to move into the White House?"

*"Oh, I don't think that far ahead. If Michael is confirmed I'll do whatever he
asks me to do."*

"Do you see yourself as First lady of the United States after the next election?"
Susan blushed.

"Oh, no, I don't think about that."

Predictably, the media spiced every report about Campbell with sound
bites of Susan. She was news, of course, because she was the wife of the presumptive vice president. But she was a commodity as well. A sex symbol.
Every time her face appeared on a TV screen or a magazine cover, women
took notice.

Thus the media were the unwitting tools of the White House, offering
Susan's face and voice like a tempting appetizer every time an item about the
vice presidency was shown. They were literally selling Susan as an eventual
First Lady. So much for the objectivity of the press.

Now the press secretary's face appeared again as he completed his news
conference. The woman turned the volume back down. She stood up and
moved slowly about the apartment. Food, music, books, entertainment.
Clothes. Television. A comfortable double bed. A clean, simple environment.
Suitable for an extended stay if necessary.

She sat down on the couch, hearing the muted sounds of the traffic outside. Another plane took off, its vibration rattling the windows slightly.

"All right, Susan," she said. "I'm ready for you."

43

Georgetown
March 28

IT WAS a Friday. Michael was spending the weekend in California at a conference on environmental issues. Susan would be on her own until Tuesday.

Susan had been scheduled for an interview this morning with Gail Osborne, the doyenne of Washington social interviewers. Now that Susan was the wife of the probable vice president she was hotter than ever.

However, Gail had come down with a bad flu, and the interview had to be canceled. The show's producer called to apologize to Susan and ask her to reschedule. Susan agreed.

When she hung up the phone Susan looked at her calendar. Surprisingly, she had no other commitments for today. Her dinner with the leadership of the Junior League had been postponed, and her speaking engagement at the Baltimore Chamber of Commerce was not until Monday.

Naturally the phones were ringing off the hook with requests from journalists for interviews or with urgent messages from political people about one thing or another. But Susan did not have to answer the phone unless she wanted to.

This was a golden opportunity to get a dose of real solitude, real relax-ation. All she had to do was leave the house. Disappear for a day. Or even for the whole weekend.

Susan thought about it for a few minutes. Then she called her secretary, Deborah, and told her she had a migraine. She would have to spend the afternoon in bed.

After hanging up Susan went into the bedroom closet and opened a box kept on an upper shelf. It contained the dark wig she wore on visits to her psychiatrist in Baltimore.

She sat down before her vanity mirror and put on the wig. As usual, it had a dramatic effect. It called attention to itself, and away from Susan's features.

Susan completed her disguise with a tight pair of jeans, a tight T-shirt, a tiny leather jacket, and a pair of mirrored sunglasses.

She packed an overnight bag and, leaving no message behind her, left the house.

She was heading for the little cottage in rural Pennsylvania that Michael had bought not long after their wedding. The cottage was on a tiny lake deep in a forested area in the southern part of the state. It was easily accessible from Washington, but quite secluded. There were only a dozen other cottages on the lake, so the place was always tranquil.

It had been nearly two years since Susan had even been up there. Her schedule, like Michael's, was simply too hectic to allow a weekend off. Often she had longed for the rustic little cottage, with its propane heat and its spring water, without being able to make the trip. Today she was going to drive there alone.

She took the little MG, which was almost never driven, and headed out of town. She took the expressway to 270 and drove for an hour before stopping. She got her lunch at the takeout window of a McDonald's on a crowded frontage road. Then she pressed on.

On an impulse she stopped in Hagerstown for a matinee of the new romantic comedy *Right of Way,* which she had intended to see with Michael but had little hope of doing. She bought popcorn and a Coke, and again was not recognized.

After the movie she drove Interstate 81 into Pennsylvania, then took the local roads that led to the lake. She avoided listening to any news on the radio, or noticing newspapers anywhere she went. She was fed up with the world's realities, at least for today.

The afternoon light was beginning to wane as she reached the bumpy dirt road that led to the lake. The hollows were filled with muddy water that splashed over the little MG. She turned on the windshield wipers, which only spread the muck over the glass, making visibility poor. It took her six or seven lurching minutes to get to the cottage.

The place looked neat and well kept. The caretaker kept an eye on the exterior of the cottage, pulling branches off the roof, checking the dock, and so forth. But no one cleaned the interior. It had not been touched since Susan and Michael were last here.

Susan parked the car on the steep driveway and walked to the cottage, her overnight bag in her hand. Her keys worked smoothly in the two locks, and she went in and locked the door behind her.

The place was freezing cold inside. She turned on the furnace, shivering in her skimpy clothes. She found a sweater in the bedroom closet and put it on. She put the kettle on the gas stove for tea.

She intended to spend the night here, sitting in front of the fireplace and drinking toddies. There were some old CDs and a player here. She would listen to music. She would make a supper of canned food from the pantry; she would not chance going to the local grocery, where she might be recognized.

Her plan was simple: to play hooky. She was going to take a vacation from her life for at least twenty-four hours. Tomorrow she would call Ingrid, tell her where she was, and decide whether to spend Sunday as well. She needed this respite desperately.

The cottage was beginning to warm up now. She opened the cabinet under the TV and looked at the small collection of videotapes that was kept here. She saw *A Room with a View*, a charming romantic comedy from the 1980s, from the E. M. Forster novel that Susan had never read. She decided she would watch it tonight.

She looked at the fireplace. There were fresh logs and kindling in it, left from their last visit. Michael always liked to have the fire cleaned and ready to go for their arrival.

Susan opened the flue, sprayed some lighter fluid over the logs, and held a burning length of newspaper inside the chimney. Then she lit the kindling and stood back to watch the fire get started.

The leaping flames delighted her. Here in this remote place, so far from the burdens the world reserved for her, she had made herself a hearth. She sat down before the fire with her legs crossed, closed her eyes, and basked in the heat that caressed her cheeks and legs. She was so lulled by it that she almost fell asleep sitting up. She realized how deep her fatigue was. It had been months since she had had a truly refreshing night's sleep. Perhaps tonight would be different.

She was beginning to think about supper when a small knock sounded at the door. Susan stood up with a start. She caught a glimpse of herself in the mirror. She was still wearing the curly wig. She looked very strange, she thought.

She could not very well refuse to answer the door. Her car was right outside, and the smoke going up the chimney left no doubt someone was at home.

"Who's there?" she called.

"It's Mrs. Bender, your neighbor," came a woman's voice. The voice said something else, but Susan couldn't hear it.

"I'm sorry?" she said, opening the door a crack. A woman was standing outside, looking chilly in a sweater and jeans.

"Hi, I'm your new neighbor from across the way," she said. "I didn't think anyone was home, but I saw your smoke so I came over. Would you by any chance have a tank of propane that I could borrow? I just ran out this second and my husband isn't home."

Susan did not recognize the woman. On the other hand, she hadn't been up here in nearly two years.

"Sure," she said. "Come on in while I look."

"I'm terribly sorry to bother you like this." The woman obviously didn't recognize Susan, which cheered her considerably.

"Did you move in just recently?" she asked as she opened the pantry door.

"Yes, just this fall. We're retiring here, at least for the moment. My husband—"

"I'm sure I have some extra propane," Susan said. "I don't know how full it is."

"Oh, I don't need a lot. I'll pay you back tomorrow. If only I had that damned cell phone, I could have him pick some up right now. But I never could get used to them."

"Oh, I know how you feel." Susan smiled. Her own hatred of telephones had a different basis, of course.

She saw the little tank of propane that was kept in the pantry for emergencies, along with the spare batteries and lightbulbs.

"Here it is."

She was bending to pick it up when she realized there was something familiar about the woman's voice. Before she could weigh this thought she felt something wet close over her mouth and nose. The powerful odor of chloroform shot through her senses.

Susan was taken completely by surprise. She tried to get to her feet, but she was pushed down toward the floor by surprisingly strong arms.

"Wait," she cried against the wet cloth. But the fumes were overcoming her already. She turned her head this way and that, trying not to breathe. It was no use. Her legs buckled under her and she slumped slowly, dreamily, toward the floor. She felt the warm breast of a woman against her head. It seemed as though she was being cradled protectively as she fell.

A brief image of her mother, from very long ago, rose before her mind. Mother at the dock in Massachusetts, holding out the beach towel as Susan climbed out of the frigid water. Her enfolding arms, her soothing voice. "That's a good girl . . ."

The words ran together as Susan lost consciousness.

44

NOMINEE'S WIFE VANISHES

March 30

In the latest of a series of disturbing events haunting the vice presidency this year, Susan Campbell, the wife of vice presidential nominee Michael Campbell, disappeared Friday while on an apparent visit to her cabin at Green Lake, Pennsylvania.

Law enforcement authorities are investigating . . .

Such was the *New York Times*'s understated announcement of a piece of news that was to overwhelm the media.

Had she been an ordinary citizen Susan Campbell's disappearance would have brought bored and unwilling attention from the Pennsylvania state police as a routine missing persons case. But Susan was not an ordinary citizen. She was a high-profile political wife whose face was known and admired by millions around the world. She was also the wife of a nominee for the White House in what was proving to be the most troubled political season in modern history.

For this reason the FBI immediately took over the investigation. Susan's disappearance would be treated as a kidnapping until reason was found to treat it as something else. The search for her would be intense.

The Secret Service was deeply embarrassed by Susan's disappearance. Its operatives had been keeping loose surveillance on her as a matter of routine, but the central focus of their effort was Michael himself, not his wife. Thus Susan, in her disguise, had easily slipped past the agents responsible for keeping an eye on her.

Susan's disappearance had been noted by her secretary as early as Friday evening. When Susan did not check in as usual, the secretary called Ingrid Campbell, who immediately became worried. Not wishing to alarm Michael prematurely, Ingrid telephoned all Susan's friends as well as Michael's campaign associates. No one had heard from Susan.

It was Ingrid, covering all bases, who telephoned the caretaker at Green Lake in Pennsylvania in the wee hours of Saturday morning. The caretaker drove his Jeep along the muddy lake road to the cabin, where he found Susan's little MG in the driveway, its engine cold.

The caretaker used his key to enter the cabin and found evidence of Susan's presence there Friday evening. The furnace was still running. The fire in the fireplace had burned down, but the caretaker knew it had been lit during the past few days because Michael and Susan always left fresh logs and kindling in the fireplace so they could start a fire when they arrived. The blinds over the windows were still closed. Susan's overnight bag was not found.

Ingrid accompanied the FBI to the Georgetown house, to which Michael had now returned, and made a careful study of Susan's clothes and cosmetics. She knew them better than Michael did, so she went through the closets and medicine cabinet while a distraught Michael sat in the living room with the agents.

Ingrid was not able to identify the clothes Susan had been wearing when she left, but she did notice some missing cosmetics, and was able to describe the overnight bag Susan had probably taken with her. "That's the bag she brings when she visits us on the Bay," Ingrid told the FBI.

Ingrid was not familiar with the wig Susan had worn, so she could not note its absence from the closet. It would fall to Stewart Campbell, days later, to mention to one of the agents that Susan sometimes wore a wig to disguise herself when she visited him in Baltimore.

Stewart could not know that the real reason Susan wore the wig was to visit her Baltimore psychiatrist. Her many lunch visits to Stewart over the years had all taken place on days when she visited her psychiatrist, whose house on North Charles Street was only a few blocks from the Johns Hopkins campus, where Stewart taught history.

Thus the federal agents had no reason to think Susan's appearance was anything but normal when she left home. The APB they put out described her as millions of Americans knew her: a brown-eyed blonde, five feet six inches tall, weighing 120 pounds.

The Pennsylvania state police were kept out of the investigation from the start. The FBI's forensic techs went through Susan's Georgetown bedroom with a fine-tooth comb. They found nothing of use there. In the Green Lake cabin, however, they found prints of a man's rubber boots on the cabin floor. These were clearly visible because of the muddy conditions Friday night. Unfortunately there were no fingerprints inside the cabin other than those of Susan and Michael and the Campbell family.

Even more unfortunately, a heavy rain late Friday night had eradicated all tire marks in the driveway. The MG was found sitting in a large puddle of rainwater, its own tire marks nowhere in the drive.

The authorities easily reconstructed what had happened on Friday. The producer of the Gail Osborne show told them of her call to Susan to postpone the interview. Susan's secretary related the call from Susan about her migraine headache and her intention to stay home in bed all day.

Susan must have impulsively decided to get away to Green Lake for some much-needed solitude. Was her abductor waiting for her at the cabin? Had someone noticed her en route and followed her? Had someone who lived near the cabin taken it into his head to abduct her? The agents could only guess.

Photos of Susan were circulated, unnecessary as that seemed in light of her fame. Special emphasis was given to the route she had most likely traveled in her MG from Georgetown to Pennsylvania. A tollgate employee on Interstate 81 thought she remembered the MG from Friday afternoon, but had not recognized the driver as Susan.

Susan's stops at the McDonald's for lunch and at the Hagerstown movie theater were not discovered by the agents. Susan had not stopped in the town of Green Lake to buy groceries or gasoline. No one along the route from Georgetown to Pennsylvania had seen her pass. The trail was dry.

The agents approached the investigation with several concerns. In the first place, Susan's face was easily recognizable. It was highly unlikely that her abductors would have let her be seen. In all likelihood she was transported in the back of a van or the trunk of a car after being taken. She would not be seen anymore—not as herself, anyway.

It was the FBI's director himself, in a conference with the regional heads, who articulated the theory that would dominate the investigation.

"Look, people," he said. "Mrs. Campbell hadn't been to that cabin in two years. No one could have expected her to turn up there. I can't believe someone had it staked out. That leaves two options. First, someone along her route saw her and started following her. Second, someone followed her all the way from home. I think the second option is the best. Someone was watching her and looking for a chink in the Secret Service's surveillance. When she left home unexpectedly, that someone followed her. Whoever it was had to be in a vehicle. If we can get a lead on that vehicle, we've got a lead on the perpetrator."

The chances of finding a witness who saw not only Susan's MG but a car or other vehicle following it were one in a thousand. But the FBI has the manpower and resources to follow up slender leads. A small army of agents was assigned to scour the entire route Susan took to the cabin.

Beyond this there was little to do but wait and hope. All the signs at the cabin pointed to abduction. If Susan had been kidnapped for ransom, a ransom demand would be made in due course. If her abduction had a political basis, those behind it would make some sort of demand, either to Michael, to the administration, or to someone else.

Then, of course, there was the possibility that Susan had run away under her own power. Having driven the MG as far as the cabin, she might have abandoned it there and continued her journey using other means.

It was also possible that she had committed suicide. Whether or not her trip to Green Lake was made on an impulse, she might have suddenly decided to take her own life after arriving at the cabin. It was well known that Susan was a nervous woman, a woman under considerable stress. The FBI brought in specialists to drag Green Lake and to search the surrounding forest areas. Dog teams were also put to work. Agents were assigned to hospitals throughout Pennsylvania and adjacent states to monitor DOAs and patients with self-inflicted injuries.

Finally, of course, there was the possibility of murder to consider. Whoever abducted Susan might have done so with sexual assault and murder as a motive. This was another reason to drag Green Lake. It was also a reason to alert police forces around the country that any and all female Caucasian bodies found in the coming days or weeks must be examined with special emphasis on comparison with Susan's dental records and other distinguishing characteristics.

Beyond this the intelligence agencies were left with the unenviable task of running down worthless leads and sitting on their hands while they tried to assure the public that everything possible was being done.

Those in charge of the search for Susan took pains to express optimism—for public consumption. In private they were thinking about Kirk Stillman, the victim of a deliberate hit-and-run. There was a grisly logic to Susan's disappearance, and it did not make the agents hopeful about finding her alive.

It fell to Joe Kraig, because he was a close friend of Michael's, to visit Michael and ask him the necessary questions about Susan's personal life as it might affect her disappearance.

Kraig found the Georgetown house ringed with official vehicles. The authorities were advertising their concern to make absolutely sure that nothing untoward happened to Michael Campbell.

After greeting several agents he knew, Kraig rang the bell and was let in by Ingrid Campbell, who had taken on the role of official gatekeeper.

"Joe, how are you?" Ingrid asked, her eyes red from crying. Kraig guessed from the look on her face that she was assuming the worst about Susan.

"I've been better," Kraig said, squeezing her hand.

Ingrid looked heavier to Kraig than the last time he had seen her, more settled in her permanent spinster's role. She wore heavy shoes and an unbecoming but sensible linen dress.

For her part, Ingrid thought Kraig looked not only older but sadder. His divorce must not have agreed with him, she decided. Underneath his veneer of professionalism and focus on the job at hand, he looked empty and depressed.

"How's Mike?" Kraig asked. "How's Judd?"

"Dad is beside himself," Ingrid said. "He's raising hell with all the agencies. He's out of control, Joe. You know how he feels about Susan."

Kraig knew Judd Campbell well enough to be aware of Judd's fierce protectiveness toward Susan. Judd's tenderness toward his daughter-in-law bordered on the incestuous. His long loneliness since the suicide of his wife no doubt had something to do with this.

Predictably, Judd was furious with the federal agents for having allowed Susan to be abducted. He did not trust the intelligence agencies to conduct the search for Susan expeditiously. He had never trusted the government, which he thought of as a collection of civil service ninnies who pushed paper at their desks all day and couldn't find a Budweiser in a six-pack. He had spent a lifetime battling the IRS for his hard-earned money and watching the justice system fail to enforce laws that would have helped him run his businesses more efficiently. Inertia, apathy, and stupidity defined the federal government as far as he was concerned.

Without telling the FBI, Judd had retained the services of one of the largest private detective agencies in the nation, and was prepared to pay whatever it cost to find Susan.

"How about Mike?" Kraig asked.

"You'll see for yourself."

Michael was sitting in his den, an untouched glass of brandy before him on the coffee table. He was staring at a TV screen whose volume was turned down low. He looked up pathetically when Kraig came in.

"What's up?" he asked, his casual words sounding bizarre when compared to the stricken look on his face.

Kraig was astonished by Michael's appearance. He looked as though the life had been drained out of him. He seemed to be crumbling from inside.

"How are you doing, Mike?"

Kraig came to Michael's side and put an arm around his shoulders. For a moment Michael seemed to nestle in his friend's embrace like a needy child. Then he pulled himself together.

"No news?" he asked.

"Nothing. We're doing everything we can." Kraig instantly regretted his choice of words. Those were the words the surgeon had used when Kraig's father was in the hospital dying.

Michael said nothing. His eyes were back on the TV screen. Apparently he was hoping that an image of Susan, alive and well, would pop up as a special report and put him out of his agony.

"I saw Ingrid," Kraig said. "She seems to be holding up well."

"Oh, Ingrid's the rock," Michael said with a weak smile. "She won't . . ." His words trailed off. Anxiety made him incapable of finishing his thought.

"How about your dad?" Kraig asked, hoping to use Michael's concern for others as a way of breaking through his catatonic condition.

"He's pretty bad," Michael said. "You know how he feels about Susan."

There was a silence. Kraig was a direct man, not good at the bedside manner. There was nothing to do but get down to cases.

"Mike, how has Susan been lately? I mean, with your nomination and everything . . ."

Michael looked up. "What?"

"How has Susan been, mentally? Emotionally. Has she been depressed or worried?"

Michael nodded. "Worried, yes. About me." He laughed bitterly. "She should have worried about herself."

Suddenly Michael turned to Kraig, a look of supplication in his eyes.

"Joe, who would do this? Why would anyone do this to Susan? She's never hurt anybody in her life!"

Kraig touched Michael's shoulder again. "I don't know, Mike, but I'm going to find out."

The look of childlike trust lingered in Michael's eyes for a moment, then was eclipsed by something darker.

"This could be the end—of everything," he said. His words sounded ruminative, intended more for himself than for Kraig.

"Mike, I know how you're feeling. This is a rough time. Try to help me if you can. Did Susan mention anything in the last few months that upset her or frightened her? Other than Dan Everhardt, I mean. And Palleschi, and Stillman," he added, chagrined by the extent of the chaos that had already occurred this year.

Michael seemed not to have heard. The same hopeless, distracted look was in his eyes.

"I don't mean the politics, Mike, not per se. I mean something that happened specifically to Susan. Her own problem."

Michael looked up in perplexity. "What do you mean?"

Kraig was thinking of the crank phone calls Susan had told him about. She had seemed deeply worried by them. Kraig had concentrated on reassuring her, and had not taken the calls seriously. Now, too late, it occurred to him that he should have tapped her phone when she told him about the calls. He might have learned something.

"Something that frightened her," Kraig probed. "Enough to make her panic and run away."

Misunderstanding him, Michael said, "I wouldn't blame her . . . I haven't been much of a husband. I ask so much of her, and I don't give . . ."

Kraig sighed. Michael might be hiding something. Many married couples had secrets they would not reveal to an outsider until they had no choice. But Kraig's questions seemed to be glancing off him like tangents irrelevant to his fears.

"Did she ask you anything that seemed out of the ordinary? Anything that suggested she had something preying on her mind?"

Michael shook his head. "No. Nothing except this damned vice president thing. She was scared. Terribly scared."

"She didn't want you to take the job, did she?" Kraig asked.

Michael shook his head ruminatively. "She didn't say that, but I knew how she felt."

He turned helplessly to Kraig. "I should have listened, Joe. I should have at least talked to her. I was so wrapped up in my own work . . . I knew she was upset. I wasn't paying attention."

"Mike, I know she never liked being part of your career," Kraig said. "But it was a burden she took on gladly, for your sake. I honestly don't think her ambivalence about it would have made her run away. Not unless . . ."

Michael looked up helplessly. "Unless what?"

Kraig was thinking that perhaps Susan had a sudden emotional break-down and simply couldn't stand the pressure any longer. If that was the case, it might be easier to find her.

But then he remembered the man's boot prints at the cabin. No—it would not be easy to find Susan.

He looked at Michael, who was slowly shaking his head.

"Did she say anything, mention anything unusual that was on her mind recently? Try to remember. Did she bring up anything that seemed odd to you?"

Michael gave him a blank look.

Kraig decided to take a chance. "Did she ask you anything about the past? Your past with her? Anything that seemed weird?"

Michael shook his head.

"About Harvard, maybe?" Kraig probed.

Michael was silent for a moment, staring at the TV screen.

"What?" he asked. "What did you say?"

"Harvard, Mike. Did she ask you anything about Harvard?" Kraig was watching his friend closely.

Michael looked up at him. "No," he said. His face was as innocent as that of a child.

There was a silence. Kraig let it stretch for a long moment.

Then he decided it was time to give up.

"Mike, don't torture yourself. I'll find her." He squeezed Michael's hand. "But if you think of anything—anything at all that might help—call me. Day or night. Will you promise me that?"

Michael nodded. "Okay."

Kraig took his leave. Michael was watching the TV screen again, for all the world like a patient waiting for his doctor to tell him his illness was not fatal.

45

THE PUBLIC reaction to Susan's disappearance was extreme. Michael's residence and Senate office were inundated with cards, letters, telegrams, and e-mails expressing sympathy and hope for Susan's safe return. Surprisingly, many of these messages came from overseas. No one had quite realized how well known Susan was in Europe and Asia. The Internet having effectively shrunk the world, Susan's many admirers in foreign countries could get in touch with Michael just as easily as Americans could.

Meanwhile the FBI was besieged with phone calls from people who thought they might have seen Susan since her disappearance. Most of these were cranks, of course, but it seemed that even normal people fell prey to hallucinations of Susan in public places, usually in disguise.

The hysteria went deeper. On websites across the Internet, chat rooms and bulletin boards displayed messages from users who had theories about the cause of Susan's disappearance. Some blamed the Russians, the Iraqis, the Israelis. Others blamed the Mafia, the CIA, the National Rifle Association, or political enemies of Michael Campbell within his own party. Not a few thought the dreaded enemy behind the Pinocchio Syndrome had taken

Susan for occult purposes. Even as the authorities struggled to pick up her trail, Susan was passing into myth.

Dick Livermore conducted daily meetings with his staff to discuss the crisis. From the polls it was clear that Susan's disappearance had not hurt the president politically. At least not yet. In fact, the Lindbergh-style groundswell of public sympathy for Michael was pushing the poll numbers higher.

Understandably, there were tactful suggestions from the PR people about how to exploit the situation. Dick rejected these out of hand. He could not bear the thought of making political hay out of a tragic event.

The president himself paid a visit to Michael at his Georgetown house. He talked with Judd and Ingrid like any concerned friend, asking them how Michael was bearing up, offering his prayers for Susan's safe return.

He spent a half hour alone with Michael. He was impressed by the depth of Michael's despair. Michael looked like a man who is falling through thin ice and trying to seem casual about it. The president's comforting words had little effect on him.

Colin Goss, realizing that his public reaction to the crisis would be watched intently, made a dignified statement to the press.

"Michael and Susan Campbell are valued friends to me and to this country," he said. "If anything were to happen to Susan, I would be personally devastated. She is a beautiful person, and an important one. We need her."

Goss also cannily used his appeal as a platform to decry and deplore the violence going on in the world. "Once we get Susan back alive and safe," he said, "we must, we *must* take aggressive action to stop the kind of people who could commit an act as atrocious as this. We must, we *must* restore sanity and order to this world of ours. I will do everything in my power to see that this happens, and that events like this one are never repeated in the future."

Privately Goss was deeply concerned. Not about the standing of Michael and the president in the polls—that was part of the plan, after all—but about the fact that Susan's disappearance was *not* part of the plan, and had taken him and his people completely by surprise.

He had called Michael at home Sunday night. He knew the phone would be tapped by agents waiting for a ransom call, so he had to keep the conversation formal. Michael's replies to his questions left no doubt that Michael was as surprised by what had happened as Goss was. He had not seen it coming, and had no idea who might be behind it.

Colin Goss had some influence inside the intelligence community, and used it. From now on he would be kept informed of all progress made by the major agencies in the search for Susan.

However, like Judd Campbell, Goss did not trust the government agencies to do their job and preferred to use his own people—people whose expertise he himself could guarantee, and whose loyalty was beyond question—to get the job done. Among the many Goss subsidiaries was a private detective agency called the Beta Group. Goss ordered the agency to drop all nonessential work and concentrate on the Susan Campbell matter immediately.

So the world waited while an army of investigators scoured the nation for the missing woman. All those who searched for her were experts at their jobs. They had done investigations like this before.

They also had one other crucial thing in common. They had no clue as to what had happened to Susan Campbell. None at all.

Where was Susan? No one knew the solution to the enigma. Thus, for the first time since Colin Goss began his campaign to oust the president, there was a new player in the game, a player whose face and whose plans remained utterly unknown to all the others.

Nothing more could happen until this faceless player made his move.

———————

To Grimm: I believe in your crystal ball. Please tell me one more thing: Do you know what happened at Harvard?

This message had appeared in the personals column of the *Washington Post* since the day after Karen Embry's interview with Susan Campbell.

The enigmatic source had not replied. Karen, suspecting that she was dealing with the same person who had telephoned Susan during the interview, hoped that her own mention of the Harvard connection would break the silence.

Karen now realized that her wildest surmise about the Pinocchio Syndrome might be correct after all. The disease was perhaps being deliberately spread. The epidemic was an act of terrorism on a worldwide scale.

But who was doing it? And why? And how?

Karen had no answers to these questions.

In the meantime she continued to ponder the things that had happened, and to use her deductive powers to try to understand it all.

The Pinocchio Syndrome had removed Dan Everhardt from the White House, then prevented Tom Palleschi from taking his place. Then a very suspicious hit-and-run accident had killed Kirk Stillman. Then, when Michael Campbell was chosen to replace Everhardt, the epidemic retreated from America to increase its ravages around the world.

If one posited that the spread of the disease was a deliberate act, it made sense to conclude that its cessation in America was intentional, and was a response to Michael Campbell's selection.

Karen knew she had no chance of convincing anyone in a position of authority of this. The events taking place were simply too perverse, too insane to be believed. And people in positions of authority were the last to believe that truly insane events sometimes actually came to pass in the world. Just ask those who tried to convince the American government in 1938 that one of the world's oldest and most civilized countries was herding Jews, Gypsies, homosexuals, and Marxists into gas ovens and killing them by the millions. Try telling the Warren Commission that the most beloved American president since FDR was killed by a bungled conspiracy among anti-Castro Cubans, the Mafia, and the CIA.

People in positions of authority were in the business of dealing with the world as a sane place. More importantly, they were in the business of *selling* the world to the public as a sane, ordered place. When truly insane things happened, such people were naturally resistant to hearing the awful truth, and even more resistant to revealing it. This was, at the best of times, a journalist's cross to bear.

On a cold night three days after Susan Campbell's disappearance, Karen sat at her computer, staring at the screen saver, an M. C. Escher–style pattern that showed birds flying from right to left. When one looked at the pattern in a certain way the birds turned to fish swimming from left to right. It was a dizzying sight.

Touching the mouse Karen created a new document and wrote a single sentence on the blank page.

DISEASE CONNECTED TO VICE PRESIDENCY.

This was the first theorem. Everything else flowed from it.

INTERRUPTION OF EPIDEMIC HELPED PRESIDENT AT THE POLLS.

THEREFORE INTERRUPTION INTENDED TO HELP PRESIDENT.

Karen closed her eyes. She smelled the acrid smoke of her Newport and crushed out the cigarette.

"Connect the dots," she said aloud.

SUSAN'S DISAPPEARANCE CONNECTED TO MICHAEL'S NOMINATION.

VOICE ON PHONE SAID NOMINATION WAS CONNECTED TO DISEASE.

THEREFORE SUSAN'S DISAPPEARANCE CONNECTED TO DISEASE.

Karen shook her head, trying to clear the cobwebs of her latest hangover.

SUSAN'S DISAPPEARANCE CONNECTED TO WHAT HAPPENED AT HARVARD.

This step was pure speculation. But it was a logical bridge between the other theorems, so it had to be postulated.

She thought for another moment, then wrote:

SUSAN'S DISAPPEARANCE CONNECTED TO DONKEY GAME.

Karen did not know what the game was, or who was involved. But somehow it played a role.

The circle was almost complete. All Karen had to do was to write down one more convergence.

WHAT HAPPENED AT HARVARD—DONKEY GAME—CONNECTED TO MICHAEL'S SELECTION AS VP NOMINEE.

THEREFORE CONNECTED TO PINOCCHIO SYNDROME.

DONKEY GAME—PINOCCHIO SYNDROME.

There it was—the final link, the craziest convergence of all. Pinocchio, the wooden doll who wanted to be a boy, and the donkey into which naughty boys were transformed in the Pinocchio story.

Karen clicked "Save" and sat back with a sigh. She lit another cigarette. She poured bourbon into her glass from the bottle on the floor. She closed her eyes and sat smoking for a couple of minutes.

Part of her thought her imagination was running away with her. Another part thought she had never been so close to reality in her life.

When she opened her eyes the birds were back on the screen, flying innocently, then turning into fish without her being able to see exactly when the change took place. Then birds again, then fish. The pattern seemed to symbolize the search for truth. Truth was in the eye of the beholder. But it depended on which way the beholder was looking at a given second. Looking for fish? Looking for birds? Maybe there was no such thing as simple truth.

Sighing, Karen touched the mouse to make the pattern disappear. She saw her desktop and navigated to her online service. She got online, intending simply to check her e-mail. Almost immediately the bell rang to signal an instant message. The IM box appeared.

I'VE BEEN WAITING FOR YOU, read the message. GRIMM HERE.

Karen sat up straight. This was the moment she had been waiting for. She typed, I'VE MISSED YOU. WHY HAVEN'T YOU ANSWERED MY ADS?
There was no reply.
Karen's haze of semidrunkenness had vanished. She had to find a way to keep Grimm on the line.

I BELIEVE WHAT YOU TOLD ME, she wrote. I'M TRYING TO CONNECT THE DOTS. I NEED YOUR HELP.

There was no reply.
Karen crushed the cigarette in the crowded ashtray.

I BELIEVE DISEASE CONNECTED TO VICE PRESIDENCY, she wrote. DISEASE CONNECTED TO CAMPBELL. EVERHARDT ELIMINATED. PALLESCHI ELIMINATED. STILLMAN KILLED. EPIDEMIC STOPS IN USA WHEN CAMPBELL CHOSEN BY PRESIDENT. WHY?

There was a pause.

YOU'RE GETTING WARMER, came the reply.

Karen gritted her teeth.

NOW SUSAN CAMPBELL DISAPPEARS, she wrote. WHY?

There was a silence. Karen looked at her glass of bourbon, but did not drink. She took another Newport from the pack and lit it.

I DO NOT KNOW, came the reply.

She was on the point of asking straight out whether Grimm was the voice on the phone at Susan Campbell's house. But something told her not to crowd Grimm this way.

WHAT HAPPENED AT HARVARD? she asked.
I WASN'T THERE, Grimm answered. YOU'LL HAVE TO FIND OUT FOR YOUR-SELF.

Karen sighed. She was disappointed. She had slipped into the habit of attributing to Grimm an omniscience that could solve all her problems. Perhaps he knew less than she thought.
And there was the possibility that he was not being completely truthful about what he did know.

WHY SUSAN? she asked. WHY NOW?

There was no answer.
Karen tried to think of something to say that would keep Grimm on the line.

IF I TRY TO WRITE THE TRUTH ABOUT THIS, she wrote, NO ONE WILL LISTEN.
AGREED, came the answer.

Karen chewed her lip, thinking furiously.

HELP ME MAKE THEM LISTEN, she said. GIVE ME NIXON'S TAPES. GIVE ME LEWINSKY'S BLUE DRESS. SIMPSON'S KNIFE.

For a long moment the screen was silent.

YOU ASK TOO MUCH, came the answer. A SMOKING GUN IS THE EXCEPTION NOT THE RULE.

Karen sighed. HELP ME, she wrote.

The pause was long. When the answer came it took Karen by surprise.

HE HAS MADE PEOPLE SICK BEFORE, came the reply.
WHO? Karen wrote. WHO HAS MADE PEOPLE SICK?

Another silence.

Then: FOLLOW THE TRAIL OF THE SICK.

Karen chewed her lip nervously as she stared at the screen.

WHERE DO I START? she wrote.

The IM signal disappeared. Her correspondent had signed off.
"Shit," she said aloud. "Shit!"
She puffed at her cigarette, studying the words on the screen.

HE HAS MADE PEOPLE SICK BEFORE.

FOLLOW THE TRAIL OF THE SICK.

She took a sip of the warm bourbon. She closed her eyes, then opened them.
Then she navigated to the online reservation service and inquired about flights to Boston.

4 6

SUSAN WOKE up with a splitting headache.

She was in a small bedroom whose windows seemed to have been blacked out with some sort of dark paper. There was a tiny outline of light around the windows, but the room itself was lit only by a small lamp on the dresser.

She tried to remember what had happened. Nothing came back except the fact that she had been at the cabin. She saw herself lighting the fire, turning on the furnace, putting the water on to boil for tea. Then nothing. The headache throbbed cruelly behind her eyes, canceling memory.

At length there was a soft knock at the door, and a woman entered, carrying a TV tray.

"You have a bad headache, right?" The woman was smiling, but something about the look in her eyes was strange. She looked middle-aged, Susan thought. A young fifty or an old forty. She wore slacks and a sweater. Her brownish hair looked as though it had been cheaply dyed.

Now Susan recognized her as the neighbor who had asked for propane at the cabin.

"Where are we?" she asked.

"Here," the woman said. "Take three ibuprofen, they'll knock it out. I also brought you some coffee and some breakfast."

There was a little thermal pot of coffee on the tray, and a couple of muffins. "You do like bran muffins, don't you?" the woman asked.

Susan hurriedly swallowed the three pain pills. Noticing a little glass of orange juice on the tray, she drank greedily from it.

Almost immediately she realized she needed to urinate.

"I have to pee," she said.

"Use the bathroom." The woman pointed to a door beside the bed. Susan got up, holding her throbbing head, and went through it into a tiny bathroom with a molded plastic shower enclosure, a sink, and a toilet. There was no window.

Susan used the toilet, her head aching painfully. She heard or felt a droning somewhere behind the walls. Could this place be near an airport? The vibration made her head feel worse. She returned to the bedroom. The woman was still there.

"Eat something," she said. "You'll feel better."

Susan poured coffee and forced herself to eat one of the muffins. Her mouth felt dry. Gratefully she noticed that the throbbing in her head seemed to be getting less intense. The woman, out of tact or indifference, stood silently, watching her eat.

At length Susan stopped chewing. She looked at the woman.

"You're the lady from Green Lake," she said.

"Not really," the woman replied with a faint smile.

"Why am I here?" Susan asked.

"You've been abducted," the woman said. "The authorities are looking for you. They won't find you."

Susan sighed. "Why me?"

The woman looked at Susan intently, but said nothing.

"Is it money you want?" Susan asked.

The woman shook her head.

"Then what?"

"A demand will be made," the woman said. "A political demand. When your husband goes along, you'll be released. You may be here a week. Maybe longer."

Susan placed her hands on her painful temples. Terrorism, she thought. A political hostage. Was that better or worse than being a ransom hostage? She didn't know.

"What demand?" she asked.

"You'll find that out in due course." The woman was standing with her hands at her sides. Susan noticed there were cut marks on the woman's wrists. Seeing Susan's look, the woman turned her wrists inward.

Susan looked more closely at the woman's face. The expression was not hostile, but there was a sort of inward glare in the irises that frightened Susan. Perhaps, she thought, the woman was not as old as she had first thought. Something other than age had altered that face.

"Are you going to hurt me?"

"You won't be harmed," the woman said. "If anything happened to you, your husband would be a martyr. His political career would be assured. We can't have that."

"Who is *we*?" Susan asked.

The woman ignored the question. She gestured to the small bookcase and the TV with its built-in VCR. "I've put some magazines here for you," she said. "I know you like *Vanity Fair*. I also got the *New Yorker* and *People*. I got you some books. I know you like Sue Miller. I got you her latest."

She gestured to a copy of the *New York Times* on the table. "I didn't know what paper you like," she said. "I'll bring tapes of your favorite shows. And I have movies for you. If there are others you want me to rent, I can do that."

Susan didn't answer.

"You'll find your favorite shampoo and cosmetics," the woman said. "I got some Sung perfume, I know you like that."

Susan noticed the woman's shoes. They were sensible flats in brown leather that looked like they came from a department store. The woman's appearance was an enigma. She looked quietly respectable, but not suburban. She was well groomed, but there was something strange about her skin and above all her eyes. Was it the look of insanity? Or of political fanaticism? Susan could not tell.

"I'll try to make you as comfortable as I can," the woman said. "No one likes being abducted. If there had been any other way, this wouldn't have happened."

Susan was looking at her through narrowed eyes.

"That was you on the phone, wasn't it?" she asked. "You're the one who called me those times."

The woman smiled. A sad smile.

"Yes," she said. "Do I sound different in person?"

Susan recalled the strange intimacy of the voice on the phone, sinister and yet somehow caressing.

"What is it you want?" she asked.

"To make sure your husband doesn't get into the White House," the woman said.

Susan thought for a moment. "Why?" she asked.

"Because I love my country."

Susan thought this over.

"Are you part of a terrorist group?" she asked.

The woman gave a short, cold laugh. "Before this is over you'll understand how funny that question is," she said.

"What has he done that's so terrible?" Susan asked.

The woman looked at her. "You really don't know, do you?"

"No," Susan said. "I don't."

"I thought you didn't," the woman said. "It's amazing that you can live in such close proximity to evil, and see nothing."

"Evil?" Susan asked.

"Finish your breakfast. We'll talk later."

"I want to talk now," Susan said. "I need to know why I'm here."

"You're here to hear the truth. That takes time."

The woman got up and left. Susan didn't see her again for many hours.

47

JOE KRAIG first met Michael Campbell when they were classmates at Choate. They found themselves at the same table in the dining hall one day and struck up a conversation. Both were tennis fans, and they talked about their favorite tennis players. At the end of the meal they agreed to play tennis that weekend. They played two sets, which were closely contested. In the end Michael's quick reflexes and instinct for the game triumphed over Kraig's speed and power.

After that day they were friends. Later they competed together on the track team, until Kraig abandoned track for wrestling. By the time Michael's back problem was diagnosed, Kraig was close enough to visit him regularly in the hospital.

The two were temperamentally suited to each other. Both were well behaved and kept their own counsel. Both were hardworking athletes and high academic achievers. Kraig was attracted by Michael's charm and physical courage. Michael liked Kraig for his honesty. They hung out together and told each other the normal things teenaged boys tell. They often studied together.

They double-dated. Michael was there when Kraig broke up with his girlfriend, a pretty girl named Joy who went to Rosemary Hall. Kraig was there when Michael lost his virginity in the backseat of Rafe Johnston's 1973 Audi. He could not remember the girl's name, but he remembered the callow, frightened look on Michael's face when he said later, "I didn't know it would feel like that. I hope she's not pregnant."

One spring vacation Kraig came home to the Campbell house on the Chesapeake Bay and spent an enjoyable week with Judd and Margery and Ingrid. Stewart was off at college and had a different spring vacation schedule.

Judd treated Kraig like an adopted son. Kraig took to Margery by instinct, for Margery was much more caring and maternal than Kraig's mother had ever been.

After that spring Kraig felt a special bond with the Campbells. He wrote to Margery and sometimes spoke to her on the phone when Michael called her.

When Margery committed suicide Kraig felt as though he had lost a mother.

It was only natural for Kraig and Michael to room together at Harvard. By now Kraig felt as though he had known Michael all his life. Then Michael's second spine problem came along, and with it Susan. Kraig took a backseat in Michael's life, as male friends always do when a woman enters the picture.

Kraig watched on television as Michael won his two Olympic gold medals. He found it hard to believe that his old friend was capable of such amazing physical courage. He realized there were things about Michael that even he, a close friend, did not know. Michael was not an ordinary person. He was a hero.

In the years since then Kraig had rarely seen Michael without Susan present. This necessarily circumscribed their relationship. Kraig was alarmed by his own feelings for Susan, which had not dissipated when he married Cathy. After his divorce he saw the Campbells less and less.

It was because of his long familiarity with Michael that Kraig had not taken seriously the admonition of Susan's crank caller to ask Michael about "what happened at Harvard." Kraig had been Michael's roommate at Harvard. He had gone drinking with Michael in Cambridge, gone on double dates with him, picked up girls with him in Boston. He had listened to Michael's complaints about his demanding father, helped him get drunk the night he found out he would need another operation, watched him work with maniacal concentration on his rehabilitation. He felt he knew Michael Campbell as well as anyone in the world. Except Susan, of course.

Rightly or wrongly, Kraig had reassured Susan about the crank phone calls and given the matter no more thought. In retrospect he wished he had tapped her telephone. If the crank caller had anything to do with Susan's disappearance, Kraig would have had a taped voice to help him in his search.

But as a federal agent Kraig knew that you do not tap the home telephone of a United States senator without a powerful reason. If Michael had found out about such a thing and taken it amiss, the consequences for Kraig would have been serious.

The phone was tapped now, of course, because the agents were waiting for ransom calls. But Kraig feared the people who had abducted Susan would be too smart to use the phone for a ransom demand.

In any case, the voice on Susan's phone might well have been just a crank. The enigmatic reference to Harvard was probably the delirium of a telephone nutcase. It was well known that Michael had gone to Harvard.

There was nothing to do but pick up the pieces where they lay. And that meant following Susan's trail to the Green Lake cabin in the hope of finding a witness who saw her being followed. In the meantime the intelligence agencies would scour the ranks of terrorists, militiamen, and political radicals, hoping for the best. And they would wait for a ransom demand.

It had now been four days since Susan disappeared. The combined work of several thousand agents had brought no results. Susan had vanished without a trace.

Maybe, Kraig mused, she *had* run away. Maybe she decided she couldn't take it anymore.

Kraig shook his head: Susan was too loyal to Michael. She would never run away.

Maybe someone bad had taken her. Someone without a political motive. That was the worst thought of all. Casual rapists and killers came in all shapes, sizes, and colors. Many of them had left no trail behind them in official records, as political terrorists had. Such a man could have Susan tied up in the back of a van right now, and all the federal agents in the country would not know where to look for him.

Kraig closed his eyes as he struggled to banish the image from his mind. If Susan died, a great part of his world would die with her. And he would never be able to share his loss with a living soul.

4 8

April 2

KAREN HAD done her usual advance work before leaving for Boston.

She had sent e-mails to Boston reporters she had known over the years, asking them to check their files for instances of unexplained illness in the Boston area during the past fifteen to twenty years. The responses were interesting. Karen made an appointment with a public health officer at the Commonwealth's center for disease control. She also made some inquiries about events at Harvard during Michael Campbell's time there. ❧

She flew from D.C. in the early morning so as to allow herself a full day of work. Spring was a long way away in Boston, but there were joggers along the walkways by the river, and sailboats on the Bay. Karen recognized everything. She had grown up in this city, and perhaps inherited some of its inhabitants' ingrained caution and stubbornness. She liked the place. But she knew she would never live there again. Too many bad memories.

The national manhunt was big news. It blared from every newspaper and magazine and from every television screen Karen saw on her way through Logan airport. When she checked in at a Sleep Inn not far from the airport, the face of Susan Campbell was on the TV in the lobby.

"Where do you think she is?" Karen asked the young woman behind the motel's registration desk.

"The Bahamas," the girl smiled. "Soaking up some sun and trying to forget everything back home."

"No way," threw in the male desk clerk. "She's dead."

"Do you think so?" Karen asked.

"Sure," the young man said. "You can't hide a woman like that. Whoever took her killed her right away and either buried her or dumped her in the ocean. Something like that. Wherever she is, she's dead."

"Mark, you're crazy," said the female clerk. Karen sensed the young man was needling his colleague. Yet his logic was persuasive.

Karen spent a long day investigating Michael Campbell's years at Harvard. She found nothing that did not accord with the official history of his college years. He was a 3.9 student with a fine attendance record. Refused membership in the Porcellian Club, he belonged to a couple of lesser clubs and participated in intramural sports until his second back operation, which took place at the end of his junior year. He met Susan on the eve of his surgery, and their romance began when she visited him in the hospital and later helped him with his rehabilitation.

After his surgery Michael became a varsity swimmer, and his times in the freestyle and breaststroke were so remarkable that he began training for the Olympics. Susan continued as his companion and informal coach, timing his swim practices, rubbing his sore back, and, probably, sharing his bed.

The rest, of course, was history. Michael Campbell charged through his rehabilitation and went on to win two Olympic gold medals. The famous image of him being helped from the pool by his teammates became the symbol of that entire Olympics.

But that was later, when Michael was at Columbia Law. The question Susan Campbell's caller had asked was "What happened at *Harvard*?"

Michael's college personality was typical of a future politician. He studied hard, got good grades, was involved in student politics, and avoided the more dangerous pursuits of male undergraduates—drugs, whores, and the like. Except for the back operations and his swimming career, his was a boring story. His friends found him loyal, friendly, trustworthy. There was nothing to him except ambition, hard work, and a well-developed talent for making friends.

Karen had also researched Michael's earlier years, which were scarcely more interesting. He was the last and best-loved child of Judd Campbell, a hugely successful conglomerator who was unfaithful to his wife and demanding of his children. Judd's overbearing personality had caused a rift with his older son Stewart, who was not on speaking terms with his father. The only sister, Ingrid, was an overweight spinster who seemed to have had no love life at all, and who devoted herself to her widowed father and to Michael, whom she regarded as a surrogate son.

Michael was the family "star," the beloved youngest son whom everybody fiercely protected. By all accounts he had also been his mother's favorite, before her suicide.

Somehow this flat, dull story line made Karen's antennae quiver with suspicion. No one's life was that boring. Everyone had a skeleton in a closet somewhere. Michael Campbell was too good to be true.

Ask him what happened at Harvard. The voice on the phone at Susan Campbell's Georgetown house haunted Karen. There was something hidden behind Michael's well-documented career as a Harvard student. Her journalist's nose had never so clearly scented a story.

But she could find no answer to the riddle.

Remembering Grimm's admonition to "follow the trail of the sick," Karen made calls to her reporter friends, who informed her of a number of unusual or unexplained outbreaks of illness in the greater Boston area during the period in question. Most of what she heard was useless: an outbreak of food poisoning that turned out to have been caused by tainted seafood caught on the Maine coast after a toxic waste spill; an epidemic of typhoid that was, thankfully, contained and stopped by the aggressive and efficient Commonwealth public health authority. A remarkable outbreak of phosphate poisoning caused by a pesticide company whose formula was mixed too strong.

These were interesting public health stories, worthy of documentation by the great Berton Roueché had he still been alive to write about them. But they were not the sort of thing Karen was looking for. They were easily explained. They were mysteries that had already been solved.

The exception came to her attention when she visited Gavin Doering, a physician at the department of health who had worked as a pathologist at the chief medical examiner's office during the period in question. A native Bostonian, Doering was a walking encyclopedia of fact and anecdote about major and minor outbreaks of illness in the city since the 1950s. A smiling, somewhat fussy man in his sixties with snow-white hair and bright, inquisitive eyes, he greeted Karen with a look that told her he was not interested in women. Then he gave her a chair and a cup of coffee from the percolator in his outer office.

"I appreciate your finding time to see me, Doctor," Karen said.

"Frankly," he told her, "I didn't expect to get questions from a reporter about the episode. It was a long time ago. It's old news. The only interesting thing about it, I think, is how baffling it was."

"Baffling in what way?"

"Well, we investigated it every way we knew how, and nothing in medical science at the time shed any light on it at all. It's one of my greatest failures."

Karen nodded thoughtfully. "On the phone you said the victims were all girls."

Dr. Doering nodded. "All girls, all young. About eighteen, if I remember correctly. They came from communities in the Greater Boston area. They didn't seem to have a great deal in common except their sex and age. And, of course, the symptoms."

"What were the symptoms?" Karen asked.

He looked at a file on the desk before him. "Cognitive dysfunction," he said. "Amnesia. Motor dysfunction. Difficulty with language, suggesting aphasia. Coma, in several of the cases. Permanent disability in the rest. Of the fourteen we saw, eight are dead. The rest are in nursing homes or living at home. I've followed them up to some extent, checking in once or twice a year. There's been no change in any of the cases, except for one girl who died a couple of years ago, apparently of an organic problem unrelated to her original trouble."

"How were the initial symptoms discovered?" Karen asked.

"The girls were found in various locations around the city," the doctor said. "One was discovered on a bus. Another at an MTA station. Another was lying on the ground in a public park. Most were noticed by strangers. The police were called, or the parents. The girls were confusional, wandering, talking gibberish. Most of them ended up in the emergency room and then were taken to hospitals for observation."

"And the results were . . . ?" Karen asked.

"Inconclusive." He shook his head. "Their symptoms were suggestive of any number of things. Drug overdose was at the head of the list, but we couldn't find anything in their blood or tissues to suggest that. Exposure to some sort of organic or inorganic toxin was next in line, but we drew a blank there as well. Blood and tissue tests ruled out infection. We even gave some thought to the notion of a bizarre mass hysteria, but there was no evidence to support that theory, so we gave up. In the end the outbreak remained completely unexplained. There was concern in public health quarters for a while, because if it spread—whatever it was—we had no way of stopping it. But after that first year there were no more cases reported."

"Did you do cerebral angiography on the comatose ones?" Karen asked. "Brain imaging?"

The doctor raised an eyebrow. "I see you've done your homework. Yes, we did. We couldn't find a brain or vascular lesion. It was quite a mystery. Still is," he added.

Karen nodded ruminatively.

"What was the time frame of the episode?" she asked.

"Let me see . . ." The doctor flipped through the pages of his file. "About seven months, from October to April of that year."

There was a silence. Karen was studying the doctor's face.

"Did you consider foul play?" she asked.

The doctor nodded. "Absolutely. Almost from the beginning. The girls appeared drugged when they were found. The toxic connection seemed obvious. We worried about terrorism. Remember the Tylenol killer? That sort of thing. But as I say, the tests we did came back normal."

"No official explanation was given?" Karen asked.

"No. What could we say? We simply had no clue as to what had caused the illness."

Karen was taking notes. After a moment she looked up.

"Tell me," she asked. "Did you do the routine tests that are performed on crime victims? For instance, did you look for evidence of rape? Semen?"

The doctor shook his head. "I'm afraid not. We had no evidence for that kind of connection. And frankly, we weren't quick enough to think along those lines. By the time we tested the girls, they had already been in the hospital for a number of days."

Karen nodded.

"Have you kept in touch with the families?" she asked.

"Loosely, yes." The doctor shook his head. "It's painful. The circumstances are so tragic. Some of the families never recovered."

"Would you mind if I visited them myself?" Karen asked.

The doctor's eyes narrowed. "To what purpose?"

"To get their reaction," Karen said in her blandest voice. "To see how they're coping."

Dr. Doering was silent for a long moment, thinking her request over.

"You're not after anybody in the medical profession, are you?" he asked.

"Not at all. I'm just doing research on public health topics, with emphasis on the effects on families," Karen said. "I'm not out to embarrass the medical profession. You can read my past articles, Doctor. I'm a great fan of your profession." Karen was not lying. She considered public health professionals to be some of the most honest and selfless people she had ever known.

"It's in the public record in any case," she prodded, "but I thought I would ask you."

The doctor shrugged. "I don't see why not," he said. "I'll give you the addresses from my own file. But be gentle with them. They're still in a lot of pain."

"I understand," Karen said.

That night Karen stood in a cubicle at the Sacred Heart nursing care facility in Waltham, Massachusetts. Beside her was an exhausted-looking woman in middle age named Glenda Christensen. In the bed before them lay the woman's only daughter, Jane Christensen, who was one of the fourteen victims in Dr. Doering's file.

The girl lay in the rigidly decerebrate position of many long-term coma patients, her neck hyperextended, her hands flexed on the wrists. She was emaciated and ghostly pale. Her eyes were open and staring.

"Just look at her," the mother said. "She hasn't moved a muscle in all these years. Except for a few spasms that the doctors told us are normal. She's hardly opened her eyes in all that time."

Karen was silent, looking down at the girl. She was breathing on her own, but an IV was connected to her arm, apparently for nutrition.

"Has she been here all that time?" Karen asked.

The mother shook her head. "She was in Mass General at first. Then we put her in a nursing home near us, out in Lexington. Then my husband died. He didn't leave me much. I couldn't afford it out there anymore, so I had to look for another place. They took her in at Western Chronic Care, but after about a year they made us leave. I finally found out about Sacred Heart from a woman in our parish."

"And you've never spoken to your daughter in all this time?" Karen asked.

"Spoken?" Mrs. Christensen smiled sadly. "I speak to her every day. I tell her my news, tell her how her brother is doing, and his wife and kids. I try to make believe she can hear me. I even read to her from the newspaper. But she's never given the slightest sign she heard me. Not one sign."

Karen said, "Tell me again how it happened."

"She went out that night to meet her friend and go to the movies. They wanted to see *Terms of Endearment*. She never came home."

She shook her head. "I made the mistake of going to see that movie later. I didn't know whether she had actually seen it or not, that night. If she had, I wanted to see what she saw. It devastated me, because in the movie the daughter ended up dying in a bed with her mother looking down at her, just as I have to look down at Jane every day."

Karen nodded, looking at the ruined girl in the bed.

"Did you try to find out where she had gone that night after the movie?" she asked.

"Yes. But the police were no help. She was sick, you see. That was all there was to it. The police told me that without evidence of foul play it wasn't their problem. Later my husband went to the theater and asked the ticket seller if she had seen Jane. The girl didn't remember. I think Justine's parents went further, because she was a missing person. But even for them the police wouldn't do anything."

"Justine?" Karen asked.

The mother turned to her. "Didn't I say that? Justine was never heard from again. That's why we were convinced something bad had happened to the girls. But the police refused to investigate. They listed Justine as a missing person, and that was that."

"What was her last name?" Karen asked.

"Justine? Lawrence. Justine Lawrence."

"And you say her parents tried to find out more about what had happened?"

"For a while, yes. But they weren't successful. Then Mrs. Lawrence committed suicide. She didn't leave a note, but I've always felt certain it was because of what happened to Justine. And the father, Mr. Lawrence, he's a hopeless drunk now. He was an alcoholic even at the time, but he was well enough to work. After Justine disappeared and his wife killed herself, he fell apart. He doesn't live here anymore. I don't know where he is, to tell you the truth. We used to keep in touch, but then it just got too painful."

"Do you know where I might look for him?" Karen asked.

The woman shook her head. "You could try his old neighbors. I don't know. He was fired from his job, and then one day he just disappeared. He used to talk about going himself to find Justine, but he was too far gone to do anything like that. He was drinking himself to death, poor man."

"And Justine was never found?" Karen asked.

Mrs. Christensen shook her head. "I think she's dead. I think whoever did this to Jane killed Justine."

"What makes you so sure?" Karen asked.

The woman looked at her. "I feel it in my heart."

Karen wrote down a quick note in her shorthand.

"I'm terribly sorry," she said. "I can see what this has done to you."

The woman looked at her. "How old are you?" she asked.

"Twenty-nine."

"You're not that far from Jane's age. Is your mother living?"

Karen shook her head. "No."

"I'm sorry. When I see a young woman like you, I feel so jealous. All the things Jane would have experienced, all the things she would have told me about in these fifteen years. I could have helped her. Or listened, anyway. Sometimes I think it would have been easier if she had died. To see her this way, every day . . ."

Karen nodded. "It must be torture." She touched the woman's arm gently.

Mrs. Christensen sighed, looking down at her daughter.

"Has she ever spoken in all this time?" Karen asked.

"Only in her sleep," the mother said. "The first year she would mumble things while her eyes were open. Then she stopped." She sighed. "I ask the nurses here to listen when they're near her. But I don't think they do anymore."

"Has she ever said words you could understand?" Karen asked.

"A few times," the mother said. "Nothing that made any sense, though. Just gibberish. Just raving. Something about a donkey . . ."

With an effort of will Karen managed to put on an expression of neutral curiosity.

"A donkey? What about a donkey?"

"Nothing. Just donkey. It didn't make any sense."

Karen made a note on her pad.

"Does she still say it?"

"She doesn't say anything now." The woman shook her head. "She was so beautiful. So bright. She had her whole life ahead of her."

"Mrs. Christensen, I'm going to try to learn what I can about this whole thing," Karen said. "I'd appreciate a favor. If you remember anything else about what happened when Jane first got sick, please call me. And if she should say anything, or give you any sign of life, I hope you'll let me know. Here's my card. You can call my answering service anytime, day or night. I'll write my home number and e-mail on the back."

She knew there wouldn't be anything new. But she wanted to give the woman a small reason to go on hoping, to go on waiting.

"Thank you for helping me," she said.

Mrs. Christensen gave her an empty look. "Don't mention it," she said. In her eyes Karen could see a world where thanks and help were no longer realities, where only pain existed.

49

Hamilton, Virginia
April 2

JUDD CAMPBELL sat in the office of his Chesapeake Bay home, talking to the head of the detective agency he had hired to find Susan. The clock on the desk said 2 A.M., but Judd did not notice it. Nor did he care that he had awakened the detective with his call.

"You can't tell me that's all you've got," he said. "It's been six days."

"There's very little to go on, Mr. Campbell," the detective said. "As far as we can tell, she intended to slip away unobserved."

The FBI had interviewed a neighbor of Susan's in Georgetown who thought she saw a woman with curly brown hair driving Susan's MG the day Susan disappeared. The woman knew the little car and was about to wave when she saw that the driver didn't look like Susan.

From this the authorities deduced that Susan was in disguise when she left her house. Obviously she intended either to take a vacation from her well-known role as the visible wife of a United States senator—or to run away permanently.

The FBI had finally found its way to the Hagerstown movie theater where Susan had seen the matinee of *Right of Way*. Agents had put the two teenagers who worked at the theater under hypnosis. The boy remembered nothing, but the girl remembered an attractive curly-headed woman wearing tight jeans, a T-shirt, and a tiny leather jacket. She did not recognize the woman as Susan Campbell, but the height and weight were right.

There the trail ended. Like the FBI and the other agencies, Judd's detectives could find no evidence that Susan's MG was followed on its route from Washington to the Green Lake cottage.

"Can't you do any better than that?" Judd asked angrily.

"We've talked to everybody who lives at the lake," the detective said. "Unfortunately most of the cottages were empty. The caretaker was there in his own place, but he was asleep at the time. It turns out the fellow has a drinking problem. He's plastered most of the time. None of the other neighbors saw the MG."

"I'm paying you to find her," Judd said. "What are you doing now?"

"The routine missing-person stuff is best left to the government agencies," the detective said. "They have the manpower to scour the country for her. Our best bet is to follow up angles they don't want to pursue."

"Like what?" Judd asked.

"Runaway is one," the detective said. "Suppose she set all this up in order to give us the impression she was abducted. That would mean she had a game plan starting at the cottage. She intended to leave the MG there and vanish without a trace. If that's what happened, she had to have another vehicle or a plan for transportation from the cottage to wherever she was headed. I have men working specifically on that angle."

"What have they learned?" Judd asked.

"Nothing yet."

"They're not going to," Judd said. "That's a dead end."

Judd did not believe that Susan had plotted her own disappearance. She would not abandon Michael. She would stay at her post no matter how frightened she was.

"We have to pursue it anyway," the detective said. "Maybe you didn't know her as well as you thought you did. Anything is possible, sir."

"Anything?"

"She could be in league with your son's political enemies. She might have run away in order to hurt the administration. Don't reject ideas like this out of hand. Believe me, stranger things have happened. And this is an unusual year. There are pressures . . ."

Judd sighed. "I don't believe it. That's not Susan."

There was a silence. The detective was tired and irritable. This was the fourth or fifth time Judd had awakened him in the wee hours. Judd was a hard man to work for. He kibitzed at every opportunity, and there was a nasty, accusing edge to his questions, as though the professionals he had hired did not know how to do their jobs. A typical executive, Judd had a need to give orders, to kick ass. He didn't know how to sit back and let the detectives do their work.

"Then again," the detective went on patiently, "there is always the possibility that two unrelated things happened. First she ran away, and then she was abducted. That sort of scenario."

"Abducted by who?" Judd asked.

"Somebody who had nothing to do with the reason why she left town in disguise. Possibly even somebody who didn't know who they were abducting. Anything is possible."

"You don't really believe that, do you?" Judd asked.

"I don't believe anything. I'm not committed to anything. I just want to find out what happened."

Judd hung up without saying good-bye. He went down to the kitchen, poured himself a glass of ale, and sat down in the dark living room looking out at the moonlit waves.

He was out of control emotionally, and he knew it. In some imponderable way the torch of his late wife Margery had been passed to Susan. When Susan came into the family it was as though Judd had an opportunity to make up for Margery's loss. He had made sure Susan felt accepted by the family. After all, she needed a home after her own family splintered. But more than that, the Campbells needed her. Judd needed her.

Throughout this menacing year Judd had been essentially unmoved by what was happening in the political world. The deaths of Everhardt and Stillman played into the hands of his ambition for Michael. He was sorry they were gone, that was all. He never felt the events of the winter as a danger. Not really.

But that was before Susan disappeared. Now Judd Campbell's entire world was menaced. He had to get Susan home. If she was in danger, he had to save her. She might as well have been his own wife, or his daughter. He simply had to get her back.

A voice startled him.

"Dad?" It was Ingrid, standing in the doorway in her nightgown.

Judd gave her a sour nod. It was impossible to be up and around in the wee hours without her knowing about it. Her ears were even sharper than Margery's had been. And she was constantly hovering over him, urging him to sleep, not to upset himself.

But tonight, moved by a pitying impulse, she did not reproach him. She came forward to put her hand on his shoulder. "I could make you a toddy," she said.

"No, thanks, dear." Judd squeezed her hand. "I'm fine."

She sat down in the chair opposite the couch. The waves thumped outside the windows in the darkness. The only light in the room came from the little lamp on the piano. Susan was the only one in the family who played. She picked her way through Mozart sonatas sometimes, and the easier pieces by Beethoven and Schumann. At Judd's request she had learned arrangements of some of his favorite songs, including the Beatles' "Yesterday" and the Gershwin classic "Love Is Here to Stay."

Ingrid looked at her father. He was showing signs of old age. He napped more these days than he had in the past. He forgot things. When he thought no one was looking he would lapse into an attitude of exhausted passivity that was like a distant harbinger of the nursing home. Only when his flashing eyes were open, and his sharp tongue was lashing those around him, did he still seem youthful.

Ingrid had sacrificed her life for him. And, of course, for Michael and Stewart and Susan. She did not regret it. She had known as a young girl that something about romance simply didn't appeal to her. It wasn't that she disliked men, or liked women. It was that she felt nothing for anyone outside her family. It felt natural for her to remain within it and devote herself to nurturing and protecting it. She was a hybrid creature, part matriarch and part big sister, not cut out for the marriage bed.

"Dad," she said.

Judd emerged from his reverie to look at her. His despair was written all over his face.

"Dad, we'll get her back."

"Yes," Judd said. "Yes, we will."

There was a silence.

Ingrid said, "Remember that night, after Mom's funeral, when you and I were sitting up? We couldn't sleep, and we met right here in this room, just like tonight. And then Michael came in, and Stewie. Michael hadn't gone back to school yet, and Stewie was spending the night."

"We were so wide awake that we ended up making chowder at four in the morning," Judd said. "Your mother's recipe."

"We even laughed at what we were doing," Ingrid said. "God, we were crazy that night."

Judd nodded, smiling. "That's what grief can do."

"That was the last night we were all together, as a family," Ingrid said. "We've never been in a room together since. The four of us, I mean. You and me and Michael and Stew."

Judd's smile faded. It was true. In the years after Margery's death his conflict with Stewart had become a permanent rift. The loss of Margery had hardened Judd, made him less tolerant and perhaps less wise. He had driven Stewart away.

"But after Susan came," Ingrid said, "we felt like a family again. Didn't we?"

He looked at Ingrid. He smiled. "Yes. Susan brought all that back."

Their smiles were clouded, for they both knew that Susan might never come back. If she didn't come back, that would be the second end of the Campbell family. Judd's heart constricted at the thought.

"I wonder if Mike is burning the midnight oil like we are tonight," Ingrid said, to change the subject. Michael was in Georgetown.

Judd shrugged. "With a house full of federal agents? I wouldn't sleep a wink."

"He's a good sleeper," Ingrid said. "The only really good sleeper in the family."

"I guess you're right." Judd was wondering what terrible thoughts must be weaving their way into his son's dreams this night. Michael's love for Susan was strong. His dread must be consuming, unbearable.

Ingrid stood up. "Turn the light off when you come up," she said.

"I will." Judd was grateful to Ingrid for not hovering over him. For the first time since this vigil began, it occurred to him to wonder what it was doing to her.

But he didn't ask. Time had circumscribed their roles. Ingrid was the rock, the foundation. No one ever asked her what she was feeling.

He watched her pad out of the room in her ugly slippers, an aging woman whose body had never known the touch of a man. She was a slave to the role she had chosen for herself in life. There was nothing to be done for her, nothing to be said.

He sat in the silence, staring into space. This vigil felt for all the world like a continuation of that long-ago vigil over Margery. He had no desire to sleep. Every moment he remained awake was like a hand outstretched to Susan, wherever she was. Every moment asleep was a small betrayal of her.

He moved to the battered old couch and lay down without turning out the light. It was on these cushions that, long ago, he used to lie with his head in Margery's lap.

A few minutes later he turned on his side. His eyes closed. The thing that passed for sleep in this tortured time came slowly over him. His breathing grew deeper, its rhythm matching the thump of the waves.

Twenty-five miles away, in his Senate office, Michael Campbell lay with his head in the lap of Colin Goss.

MICHAEL'S EYES were half closed. His hand was in that of Goss. The room was in darkness.

The light in the outer office was left on for the agents who were tailing Michael. The agents, respecting Michael's grief and worry over his missing wife, would not disturb him.

Only the smoke of Goss's cigar disturbed the stillness of the room. With his free hand Goss stroked Michael's hair, his fingers gentle as those of a mother.

"There, there," he said. "It will all be all right. You're going to be fine."

Neither Michael nor Goss had any idea where Susan was or who had taken her. Her disappearance had been the only event of the winter that was not foreseen. It was also the one event that could endanger everything.

Michael was frantic. Goss, though deeply worried, was cool. He had surmounted many a crisis before, and believed in his heart that he would overcome this obstacle. The more so because Susan Campbell was not central to the plan. Susan alive was a plus. Susan dead was not really a negative. Goss had thought this through.

Michael sighed, savoring the caress that was the closest thing he had to a mother's touch. That had always been the most important thing about Colin Goss in Michael's mind. Goss was not like a father, but like a mother.

————

COLIN GOSS had come into Michael's life much as a character in a fairy tale crosses the path of a wayfarer deep in a forest. Like a mysterious stranger or a gnome, Goss had simply appeared. And by appearing he had changed the course of Michael's life.

It began when Michael was still a schoolboy. He was in the lower school at the Bryce Academy in Maryland, testing his wings as a scholar and athlete against the aggressive boys who went there. They all came from distinguished families, and all felt the silent but powerful pressure to live up to their backgrounds. It made for a curiously unpleasant experience. You never felt quite alone in yourself. You sensed a mission mapped out for you in advance. In a subtle way it left you feeling suffocated.

For Michael this situation was perhaps more painful than for the other boys. Judd Campbell was a hard, rigid man. He knew his own ideas and his own ambitions. It was obvious to his sons that they could not question them. The price of Judd's approval was obedience. When Stewart, later on, made his choice to rebel against Judd, he would have to give up everything for that choice.

But that was Stewart. Michael was different. He loved Judd Campbell and could not bear the thought of disappointing him. He excelled at everything he did. Not because he felt a natural impulse to excel, but because, in a way, the devil was at his back.

This came easily enough in academics. Michael was bright, brighter than his father. With a modicum of application he attained straight A's.

In athletics it was much harder. Michael was not strong as a child. His body was slim. His personality was gentle, not assertive. His future talent as a peacemaker and diplomat was already in evidence. He was a great communicator. Had things worked out differently, it might have been Michael instead of Stewart who grew up to become a teacher.

But on the playing fields Michael had to be fierce, aggressive. He knew his father wanted and expected this. He forced himself to comply.

One weekend he returned home from school with bruises on his legs from a collision that had occurred on the soccer field. Judd Campbell was more approving than sympathetic. "They gave you something to remember them by, did they?" he asked. "Well, think of it as a trophy."

Michael forced a smile, for the hurt muscles ached. Perhaps sensing his distress, Judd asked, "Who hit you?"

"Fred Cooperman," Michael replied.

"Is he bigger than you?" Judd asked.

"Yes." In fact Fred Cooperman was six inches taller than Michael and outweighed him by forty pounds.

"Did you give him something to remember you by?" Judd asked. "Something black and blue?"

"Not really," said Michael, who had taken by far the worst of it in the collision.

"Well, make sure you do it next time," Judd said, looking back to his *Wall Street Journal*. "Then he'll respect you." And with a final glance at Michael, "And then you'll respect yourself."

Judd Campbell meant this stern man's-man philosophy in a loving and protective way. Michael was his favorite son. He simply wanted Michael to be well armed for the struggle he would face in the competitive world. Judd meant no harm.

But the remark's effect was quite different. Michael felt there was a price tag on his father's love, and that price tag was the sternest possible definition of manhood. This demand was like a toxin injected into Michael's personality. Judd, who was not an introspective man, could not know how seriously his fatherly "encouragement" had backfired.

One day at a soccer meet with another private school Michael noticed a man watching the game from the sidelines. Michael's school won, and Michael scored one of the goals. The man came up to congratulate him. He introduced himself as "a friend of your mom and dad." He said he came to the games for old times' sake, since he himself had once been a boy here.

Michael replied with polite thanks and a smile. He did not feel he could spurn the stranger's overture, since the man apparently knew the family and was an alumnus of the school. A few weeks later Michael was in another meet and injured his knee in a collision with one of the opposing players.

He was coming out of the locker room when the stranger blocked his path.

"Are you all right?" the man asked.

"Sure." Michael's response was abrupt. He did not want to admit that he was in pain.

"Come and have a cup of coffee with me," the stranger suggested. "We can talk about the game."

Michael had nowhere to go, so he accepted the invitation. The stranger took him to the local café, where Michael ordered a hot cocoa and the man had coffee.

The man was extraordinarily gentle as he spoke to Michael about the game. He had only praise for Michael's performance on the field, and concern for his injury.

"Can I see it?" he asked.

Michael pulled up the leg of his pants and the man gently touched the sore knee, which was already turning black and blue.

"That must hurt," the man said. "You're very brave. I don't think I would have been so brave," he added, watching Michael roll the pant leg back down.

This was new to Michael, this self-effacing bestowal of praise by a man. Michael was used to a rigid yardstick by which he was expected to measure up to male standards. This man was more like a mother than a father. He was sympathetic, understanding, and completely approving.

They parted after their brief conversation at the coffee shop, but the man came back now and then to see the games, and Michael fell into the habit of having a drink or a snack with him.

The man introduced himself as Colin Goss and said he had known Michael's parents a long time ago. He inquired about Michael's mother, and listened attentively to the little details Michael provided about the Campbells and their life. Michael got the impression the stranger had a crush on his mother, for the man spoke of her with an exaggerated respect, a kind of courtly veneration.

Colin Goss explained that he was a widower whose wife had died giving birth to a stillborn child a long time ago. "A little boy," he said. He seemed to feel that Michael reminded him of the son he wanted so much and never had. The odd tenderness in his manner accentuated this impression.

He asked Michael all about his friends, the school, his feelings and opinions. Michael was fascinated by the respect with which Goss treated him. There was nothing to live up to, nothing to prove. Goss delighted in everything about Michael.

"It might be a good idea not to tell your parents about me," Goss told him. "Your dad is mad at me."

"Why?" the boy asked.

"Oh, something that happened a long time ago. Nothing for you to worry about."

Michael acceded to this request willingly. The sweet, lulling intimacy he felt with Goss was so much in contrast to the relationship he had with his father that it seemed natural for him to keep this new friendship secret.

Goss began coming to Michael's away meets, and sometimes drove him back to school. He gave him gifts, almost always books. This also was in contrast to Judd Campbell, who was not a reader, and whose gifts to Michael were always athletic equipment or hunting or fishing gear. The poem "If" by Rudyard Kipling was the only piece of literature Judd had ever mentioned to Michael. Goss introduced Michael to Jack London, to Walter Scott and Dumas, and later to writers like Hemingway and Thomas Wolfe. Goss encouraged the dreamy, reflective side of Michael, while Judd cared only to make his son a man of action. Interestingly, in later years Michael's literary knowledge would help endear him to the more intellectual people he met as a politician. Colin Goss was largely responsible for this aspect of Michael's success. It was as though Michael had two fathers, each of whom provided half his education.

Michael learned from both men how to make his way in the world, how to succeed. From Judd he learned ambition and the desire to get things done. From Goss he learned how to wait, to bide his time, to circumvent obstacles instead of trying to crash through them.

By the time Michael started at Choate he had reached the point in life where thoughts of girls preoccupied him throughout the day and kept him awake at night. Since he attended an all-boys' school he didn't have occasion to see as many girls as he would have liked. Those he did see, he fantasized about intensely. In the dark hours of the night he undressed them in his mind, adoring their soft bodies, listening to imagined endearments they murmured in his ear as he caressed them.

Judd Campbell noticed no change in Michael and seemed reticent on the subject of girls. But Goss noticed Michael's sexual maturation immediately, and discussed it with him in a delicate, almost poetic manner. "Nothing in the world is as perfect as a pretty girl," he said. "A girl's smile is worth a whole Mozart symphony. We men have poetry in us, son"—he had come to call Michael "son" by now—"but we need women to bring it out for us. We are nothing without them."

Soon after that conversation Goss took Michael to an apartment not far from the school on a rainy autumn afternoon. When they came in the door a girl stood up from the couch where she had been reading a magazine. She was extraordinarily attractive, with auburn hair and milky skin. She had slender legs and beautiful breasts whose outline was clearly visible under her blouse.

Goss introduced her as Valerie and excused himself. She took Michael into the bedroom and had him lie down on the bed. She sat and talked with him for a while, then politely asked him to help her off with her blouse. She showed him how to unhook her bra, even having him practice it a few times. "It's something you'll need to know," she said.

She seemed to understand Michael better than he understood himself. For a long time she confined herself to the things he had already fantasized about, touching, kissing, letting him look at her and caress her. Then she began to instruct him in the art of intimacy, spreading her legs to let him explore her, then exploring him in her turn, asking, "Does it feel good when I touch you here?" until his answers became moans.

Michael learned most of what a man needs to know about a woman's body that afternoon. The rest Valerie taught him in the weeks to come. She made him as subtle in bringing her to orgasm as she was in doing it for him. The clumsy experiments most young men struggle through in high school and college—usually under the influence of alcohol—were spared Michael. He became an adept of physical pleasure and an expert seducer at age fourteen.

This talent was to stand him in good stead, for Colin Goss soon encouraged him to find attractive young girls on his own and, later, to bring them to Goss himself. "You're so much better with them than I am," Goss said self-deprecatingly. "And no pretty young girl wants an old man."

Michael was happy to act as intermediary. It was a way for him to repay Goss's kindness, and to earn his gratitude and admiration. More subtly, it confirmed their loving relationship, this providing of young female flesh that made Goss so happy. Later, when Goss confided to Michael that sometimes he got from the girls a kind of pleasure that society frowned upon, a kind of pleasure that was not something young girls would give of their own accord, Michael did not object. He continued in his role as go-between, and took the special precautions Goss asked him to take. He made sure the girls never knew his real name, or Goss's real name.

Michael understood in one part of his mind that what he was doing was wrong, was bad for the girls. But on another level he felt that it was right and justifiable, for it cemented his friendship with a man who admired him and could do a great deal for him. (For by now Goss had begun to make promises to Michael, to speak to him of a future in which he would have great privileges and accomplish great things, with Goss's help.)

This moral casuistry was not new to Michael. His father had taught it to him a dozen times over. In order to be a man of action, Judd said, you sometimes had to do things that seemed repellent or reprehensible. If you lacked the courage and the will to do such things, you would inevitably be walked over by stronger men. "Nice guys finish last," Judd often repeated. You had to dare to transgress the laws that might hold you back from attaining your goal. *Winning isn't everything—it's the only thing.* The Lombardi maxim was Judd's bible in one sentence.

What Michael did not realize was that Goss had sought him out precisely with this moral blind spot in mind. Like any powerful man in charge of a large organization, Goss had to be constantly on the lookout for men who could be of use to him. As an outlaw entrepreneur he needed a steady supply of men whose moral compass was slack enough to permit them dubious endeavors on his behalf.

Goss knew Judd Campbell, had crossed paths with him. Been beaten by him, hated him. He knew how ruthless Judd was, and how incapable of imagining any point of view other than his own. Goss had suspected that Judd might raise a son who cared more for ambition than for human beings. Now, having met Michael and tested him over a period of years, he knew he was right. Michael would do anything that furthered his own ambitions. Like Goss himself.

Colin Goss had high hopes for Michael. Michael was a more subtle man than his father, a cleverer man, while equal to his father in force and determination. Michael knew how to use his charm to get other people to do what he wanted. Judd Campbell had never had that gift. Judd always made more enemies than friends. In the end that had limited him severely in his career.

Goss did not doubt that Michael would go much further in life than Judd. Michael was capable of becoming a great man, a man who could change the world.

And indeed Michael went on to greater and greater things in his young life, bringing praise and love from both his fathers as he did so. His excellence in sports brought approval from Judd, while his academic achievements and his hungry intellect delighted Goss. His success in school politics pleased Goss more than it did Judd, while his physical courage in enduring two painful spine operations touched both men.

They were thrilled when Michael won his Olympic medals. Judd was present when Michael won the relay, while Goss watched at home on TV. Both men cried when Michael, paralyzed by muscle spasms, was helped from the pool by his teammates.

When Michael married Susan, Judd was guardedly enthusiastic. She came from a fine old family whose name might help Michael in his career; on the other hand her branch of the family was impoverished, and Susan's childhood darkened by her father's disappearance and her mother's death.

As for Goss, who had not been introduced to Susan, he approved of her as a match, but worried that Michael might become too emotionally dependent on her. Michael soon showed that he was not slowed down by marriage. His early political career was marked by triumphs of strategy that matched the greatest coups of Goss's own career.

The rest was history. The official history of Michael's rise to prominence in the Senate, and the unwritten history of the master plan that took shape in Colin Goss's mind as the years passed. A master plan whose linchpin was to be Michael himself. A plan that was about to become a reality.

Until Susan Campbell disappeared.

5 1

Boston

KAREN EMBRY saw all five of the surviving girls who had been part of the mysterious series discovered by the Boston police fifteen years ago. She learned nothing new from seeing the incapacitated girls. As Dr. Doering had said, their condition was a mystery. No medical professional could have looked at thirteen healthy adolescent girls in this condition without suspecting either a drug overdose or some sort of foul play, such as deliberate poisoning. But the physical or chemical clues that might have supported such a theory simply were not there.

Whatever had happened to the girls—or whatever had been done to them—had left no trace. Except for the destruction of their capacities, that is.

Karen was also unable to learn anything worthwhile from the families of the girls. They were predictably bitter about what had happened, and deeply depressed. They knew the other victims had already died, so there was no realistic probability that their bedridden girls would recover. Yet they clung to the desperate hope that medical science would discover a new treatment that could save them.

The victims were still young, only in their thirties. They should have had their whole lives ahead of them. This was the most painful aspect of all.

Karen kept her own thoughts to herself as she interviewed the families and thanked Dr. Doering for his help. Privately she weighed the disturbing similarities between the sick girls and the millions of victims of the Pinocchio Syndrome.

The two illnesses had several things in common. Physical incapacitation. Mental incapacitation. Lack of an apparent organic or inorganic cause. Sudden onset of the disorder, with immediate paralysis of voluntary cognitive processes. Coma.

There were differences, of course. The Boston girls lacked the dramatic physical changes that overtook the Pinocchio victims just before death. Some of them were alive many years after falling ill, while the Pinocchio Syndrome left no survivors.

But one final link convinced Karen that the disorders were related—the word *donkey* that Jane Christensen had pronounced in her delirium. This convergence—though most observers might call it a coincidence—was too powerful to ignore. Karen thought it was a crucial "dot" that, when connected to its fellows, would complete the picture she sought.

There were other dots she still had to find. She began by obtaining from the girls' families the precise dates of their discovery after being victimized. The episode had occurred fifteen years ago, over the seven-month period from October to April. All but one of the girls had been discovered the day after a nighttime outing. Most had gone out to the movies or to a party. One had gone to visit a sick relative. Two of the girls, less subject to parental discipline than the others, had not told their parents their destination. They were simply out.

Karen got the impression from the parents that all of the girls had been slightly wayward. A bit rebellious. Girls who had presented slight discipline problems for their parents. It was difficult to be sure of this, because the parents were naturally motivated to idealize the girls in memory.

Also, to judge from their photographs, they were all attractive girls with good figures and pretty faces.

Only one girl was an exception to the rule of waywardness. She was an Advanced Placement math student with a 4.0 grade point average at a special school for gifted children in Waltham. Her name was Emily Koehler. A bookish girl who had never given her parents a moment's worry, she was also the only victim who had been on a daytime errand at the time of her disappearance. She had taken the bus to Cambridge to attend a mathematics clinic for high school students at Harvard.

Ask him what happened at Harvard. Karen's antennae were alert. The episode involving the fourteen girls had occurred during Michael Campbell's junior year at Harvard.

The transcripts of Harvard students were not confidential. Karen obtained a copy of Michael's transcript from the registrar and made a careful study of it. In the reference archives at the Harvard University Library she found class schedules of the courses Michael had taken that fall and spring. From the breakdown of lectures, quiz sections, and exams, it was clear that Michael had been in Boston on each of the dates when the local girls became ill.

There was another thing to consider. In February of Michael's junior year the recurrence of his scoliosis was discovered. Michael arranged to take final exams early in all his courses, and underwent his second spinal surgery on April 22. He spent the rest of the spring and summer recuperating. The next fall he was back at school. He joined the swimming team in November and was excelling at racing by the following spring.

The last of the Boston victims, a girl named Judy Luszczynski, was found unconscious in a city park on April 2 of that year. The series ended with her.

Karen filed this fact away in her memory. She sat back to ponder what she had learned. Obviously the key facts so far pointed to a connection between the voice on Susan's telephone and Michael Campbell's career at Harvard. This connection involved illness. Grimm had told Karen "he has made people sick before."

Karen decided to widen her net. She would explore the possible connections of all the major players in this year's political situation to that forgotten year.

She flew back to Washington and settled in at her computer for a long siege of research.

She began with the well-known figures. Dan Everhardt. Colin Goss. Kirk

Stillman. Tom Palleschi. Susan Campbell. And, to make the series complete, the president.

She opened her online news archive, navigated to the year in question, and searched the index for the names, one by one. All were political figures at the time except for Colin Goss, so they left constant trails of news items, large and small, in their wake. The search was surprisingly easy.

The president, then a U.S. senator, visited Boston once that year, just before Christmas. The rest of the time he was in Washington or in his home state.

Dan Everhardt, then a congressman from New Jersey, went to Boston for a weekend with his wife to visit her mother in January. That was his only visit of the year.

Tom Palleschi, who had relatives in Boston, visited his mother in a nursing home the first Sunday of every month, flying back to his then home of Chicago the same evening.

Kirk Stillman, then a cabinet officer, did not visit Boston at all that year.

Susan Campbell was in Boston as a Wellesley student all year. She did not meet Michael Campbell until the spring, just before his surgery. When she visited his hospital room, she was a new friend, barely known to him.

That left Colin Goss. Karen's news archive contained few items about him. Then, as now, Goss had been chairman and chief stockholder of The Goss Organization, based in Atlanta. He traveled widely, visiting his companies around the world and attending meetings with executives and stockholders. His precise itinerary was not available.

Karen went to the Library of Congress and began searching for Goss in the major indexes and catalogs. Her search led almost immediately to the one source she had foolishly overlooked all week.

It was a biography.

Karen had seen it before, but paid no attention to it because it was an authorized biography written by a Goss PR executive and published with funds provided by Goss himself. Clearly it was a love letter, the kind of pablum one often saw published by corporate people whose minions are paid to strew roses in their path.

But now, in paging through the book, Karen saw that it included a detailed chronology of the formation, acquisition, and divestiture of all the companies under the huge umbrella of The Goss Organization. She carefully searched the chronology for the year that the girls in Boston got sick. Her breath came short.

Colin Goss was putting together a major New England regional headquarters that year, and was involved in meetings starting in September. The new headquarters was officially dedicated on May 25. It was located in a downtown skyscraper whose striking triple towers became a highlight of the Boston skyline.

Goss must have attended meetings in Boston throughout the year. The headquarters could not have been set up without his personal supervision.

Goss, Karen thought.

It seemed as though the sun was breaking through the clouds after a long absence. She cursed her own blindness.

He has made people sick before.

Who else would have the capacity to intentionally make people ill? Who on the planet was more perfectly equipped to conduct biochemical terrorism than Colin Goss?

He has made people sick before.

Follow the trail of the sick.

Karen xeroxed the chronology before leaving the library. Her first stop was a business bookstore on M Street where she found a paperback copy of the Goss biography, which she bought and took home with her.

5 2

Alexandria, Virginia
April 5

JOE KRAIG had had a long day.

He had spent the morning on the phone with contacts from all the law enforcement and intelligence agencies. He attended a noon meeting with Ross Agnew and the CIA director, discussing the progress of the investigation. At three he attended a press conference given by the director of the FBI.

The whole day was an embarrassment. The investigation was stalemated. Though a handful of witnesses had been found who might have seen Susan's MG en route from D.C. to Pennsylvania, no one had thought to notice whether a car was following Susan. It was simply too much of a long shot.

As a potential victim of abduction, Susan Campbell had done the worst thing she could possibly do. She had slipped away from home, unseen by anyone, and led her abductors right to the one isolated spot where they could take her without anyone seeing it happen.

Not surprisingly, the FBI's director had trouble with the reporters. Their questions dripped with skepticism about the competence of the law enforcement agencies to deal with the crisis.

"This hasn't been a good year for the intelligence agencies," observed the senior CNN correspondent sarcastically. "First a deadly terrorist nuclear attack which the federal agencies have not solved or punished. Then three political leaders neutralized, under highly suspicious circumstances, without the government being able to explain why. Now the most admired and visible political wife in the nation is missing, and you can't tell us what happened or why. Are you surprised when you hear that the public's confidence in the government agencies is at an all-time low?"

The question was hard to answer, the more so since CNN had just done a poll that confirmed that sixty-five percent of the population disapproved of the way the administration was handling the crisis. The broadcast media were full of man-on-the-street interviews with citizens who complained that the abduction of Susan Campbell was part of a pattern, and that the law enforcement agencies had neither the intelligence or the sincerity to get to the bottom of it.

"They're all in on it," said one middle-aged voter, summing up the national paranoia. "I'm not sure who is giving the orders, or who stands to benefit. But this is nothing new. We've seen shenanigans like this before. Ever since the Kennedy assassination . . ."

Kraig's workday didn't end until after ten. He badly needed a hot shower and a martini. He turned into his condo complex with a sigh of relief.

Then he saw a familiar figure sitting on his doorstep.

"Oh, shit."

Karen Embry stood up when she saw Kraig emerge from his sedan. She was wearing jeans and a leather jacket, her battered briefcase by her side.

"It's old home week," he said. "To what do I owe the honor?"

"I've got to talk to you." The reporter seemed nervous, intent.

"What about?"

She gestured to his apartment. "Is it safe in there? From bugs, I mean."

Kraig shrugged. "From the occasional ant or roach, no. From the kind of bug you mean, yes. I sweep the place myself."

"Good." She kept her eyes on him as he turned his key in the lock.

He opened the door and motioned her to the living room, which looked dusty and unkempt. "Make yourself at home. Want a drink?"

"Sure. Whatever you're having."

"I'm having a martini."

"Well, maybe not that. Gin makes me fuzzy."

"Bourbon?"

"Thanks."

He took off his jacket and flung it over a kitchen chair, wrinkling his nose as he smelled his own perspiration. The shower would have to wait.

He poured a stiff Early Times for the reporter and a short Beefeater martini for himself. He noticed the answering machine blinking, and didn't bother to count the blinks. There were at least twenty calls every night by this time.

"What's up?" he asked as he returned to the living room.

"I take it you're no closer to finding Mrs. Campbell," she said.

"Off the record, no." There was no sense in denying the obvious, Kraig thought.

"Listen," Karen said. "Susan Campbell had been receiving crank phone calls from someone who wanted her to find out what had happened with her husband at Harvard," she began.

"How did you know about that?" Kraig asked angrily.

"So you knew too," she observed.

"I asked you a question. How did you find out about it?"

"Remember the interview I had with her?" Karen asked. "I told you the phone rang while I was there. She went to the kitchen to pick up the phone. There was an extension in the living room. I listened in."

Kraig let out an exasperated sigh. "Christ, you're something."

Karen lit a cigarette, giving Kraig time to cool off.

"How did *you* know?" she asked.

"Susan told me."

"When?"

"Back in January. Before any of this happened."

"You mean she had calls before?"

"Off the record, yes, she did."

"Before Everhardt?" Karen asked.

Kraig shook his head. "It was after Everhardt. That's why she was worried. She thought Michael wasn't safe." He shrugged. "As you can see, not so."

Karen saw the unintentional irony in his remark. If Michael Campbell was not in danger, Susan herself certainly was. Events had proved this.

"Did you investigate the calls?" Karen asked.

"No. I told her to tell me if it happened again."

"Did you tap her phone?"

"No."

"Why not?"

"She didn't ask me to tap it."

"And you didn't do it on your own?"

Kraig gave Karen a twisted smile. "If you were in my position, how much cause would you need to tap the telephone of a United States senator? What if Michael found out?"

Karen nodded. "I see what you mean."

"Besides," Kraig added, "that kind of crank is par for the course when you're in politics. What politician with a profile like Michael's doesn't have a hundred cranks coming out of the woodwork with stories about his secret sins?"

Karen was looking at him steadily. He wondered if she sensed the defensiveness behind his glib answers. After all, he did regret that he did not have a recording of the voice Susan had told him about.

"Did Mrs. Campbell tell her husband about the calls?" Karen asked.

"I don't know." Kraig looked impatient. "Where are you going with this? Do you think the crank on the phone is connected to her disappearance?"

Karen puffed at her Newport. "Let me start from the beginning," she said. "This business about Harvard interested me. I have another source who suggested to me that there might be a connection between the present events and the past. With a specific connection to people getting sick in mysterious or unexplained ways. So I spent some time in Boston investigating."

Kraig said nothing.

"It turns out there was a rash of unexplained illness affecting young girls fifteen years ago," Karen said. "Fourteen girls were affected. They became mentally and physically incapacitated overnight. The doctors couldn't find the cause of the problem. And, needless to say, no cure."

"Did they recover?" Kraig asked.

She shook her head. "They slipped into coma. Nine have died in the years since. The ones who are still alive are vegetables. I saw them all."

Kraig said nothing.

"Does this remind you of something?" Karen asked.

"No. Should it?"

"How about the Pinocchio Syndrome?"

Kraig thought for a moment. "Were there physical changes?"

Karen shook her head. "But the other features of the illness are certainly reminiscent of what we have going now."

"Like what?"

"Sudden incapacitation. Mental and physical paralysis. Coma. Complete absence of any trace of a known organic pathogen or toxin. Totally incomprehensible disease in a person who should be healthy. See what I mean?"

Kraig nodded. "All right. What else have you got?"

"I was concerned about this phone crank who told Susan to find out what happened at Harvard." Karen sipped at her drink. "I checked the academic records for Michael Campbell's junior year at Harvard, the year these girls got sick. Michael Campbell was on campus for every one of them."

"Why shouldn't he have been?' Kraig asked. "He was a student there."

Karen shook her head. "Listen. These girls disappeared when they were out at night, going to movies, things like that. It looks as though they were picked up by somebody. In every case but one they were found the next day. And that one exception was a girl who was attending a math clinic on the Harvard campus."

"So?" Kraig asked.

"So, Michael Campbell was on the scene for every one of those girls."

"So was I," Kraig said. "I was a junior that year myself. I was in Cambridge all year. What do you make of that?"

Karen ignored the question. "I didn't want to jump to conclusions, though the similarity between the unexplained disease then and now impressed me. So I checked out the whereabouts of everybody who's involved in this year's events, from the president on down."

"And what did you find?" Kraig's tone was patronizing, bored.

"People like Dan Everhardt, Tom Palleschi, and the others were busy with their careers," Karen said. "They spent a day or two in Boston that year, no more. But Colin Goss is a different story. His New England pharmaceutical subsidiary was setting up its headquarters in Boston that year. Goss was in town every few weeks from October to May, when the subsidiary officially opened."

Kraig was silent. He looked less bored.

"Goss was in the city on each and every occasion when one of those girls went out for the evening and was discovered incapacitated the next day," Karen said.

Kraig was looking at her steadily. "Did the Boston police check out Goss?"

Karen smiled. "Are you kidding?"

Kraig shook his head wearily. "Karen, you're tilting at windmills again."

"I don't think so." Karen was adamant.

Kraig sighed. "Colin Goss is a three-time candidate for president of the United States. Do you seriously think he hasn't been checked out every which way by the FBI over the years? Not to mention the other major agencies? If there was a skeleton in his closet, we'd know about it."

Karen held back her reply to this. She believed a man of Goss's power was more than capable of keeping the intelligence agencies out of his private business.

She was tempted to tell Kraig about Grimm, but prudence told her to keep this crucial source to herself.

"You're not impressed by the coincidence?" she asked.

"You're turning a coincidence into a conspiracy," Kraig said. "I hear you're famous for that."

Karen did not reply.

"So Goss was in Boston at the time," Kraig said. "And I was in Boston. Does that make Goss and me co-conspirators?"

"No one is telling your wife to ask *you* what happened at Harvard," Karen rejoined.

"I'm not married," Kraig corrected her.

There was a silence.

"Listen," Karen said. "The crank on Susan Campbell's phone told Susan that when the selection process was over, Michael Campbell would be the president's choice. That idea seemed incredible at the time. But consider what's happened since. Palleschi got sick. Stillman was murdered. Michael was in fact selected. And look what's happened since his nomination: the spread of the Pinocchio Syndrome in America has stopped. And the president's stock has gone up dramatically. Colin Goss has been losing ground in the polls."

"So what are you saying?" Kraig asked. "That Goss abducted Susan Campbell in order to slow Michael's momentum?" He looked at Karen. "Aren't you getting your conspirators mixed up? If Goss was in league with Michael back at Harvard, why would he hurt Michael by abducting his wife?"

Karen chewed her lip nervously. "I haven't got that figured out yet. I'm trying to put it together."

"Besides," Kraig said, "no man on earth hates Mike Campbell more than Colin Goss. Have you heard the way Goss's spokesmen talk about Michael? They make him sound like a cross between Mick Jagger and Charles Manson."

It was true. As Michael had predicted, the Goss forces were accusing him of being wet behind the ears, an ambitious punk whose selection proved how desperate the president and his administration were. *Why send a boy to do a man's job?* Such was the refrain of the Goss ads.

Karen had no response to this.

"Look, Karen." Kraig leaned forward. "Someone has got Susan Campbell. I have to find her. If you have evidence that will tell me where to look, I want you to share it. If all you have is imaginary skeletons in the closet from fifteen years ago, you can keep that to yourself. We're fighting the clock here."

Karen looked at Kraig. She knew he wasn't hearing her. He belonged to that officialdom, that establishment, which believes in the sanity of the world. She could never convince him of something as sinister as what was in her mind. Not without proof.

"Okay," she said. "I hope you find her in time."

"So do I," Kraig said.

She stood up to leave. Her slim arms looked pale and almost ghostlike in the dim light of the living room. Kraig watched her toss her hair over her shoulder. It must have been washed today or tonight. It looked fresh and fluffy. He could no longer deny that he was strongly attracted to her.

She turned at the door to look at him. "So you were there that whole year," she said. "Were you on the scene when Susan first met Michael?"

"Yes," Kraig said. "A friend of hers introduced her to him before his second operation. He introduced Susan to me."

"What did she look like then?" Karen asked.

"Young. Pretty." Kraig shrugged.

"Neurotic?" Karen asked.

"I wouldn't say so. Sensitive."

"Did you like her?"

"Sure I liked her."

"Were they sleeping together then?" Karen asked. "Before the surgery, I mean."

Kraig shrugged. "I doubt it. It was her visits during his convalescence that made them close. It's possible, I suppose, that they were intimate even before the operation. I wouldn't know."

"Why not?" Karen asked. "You were his closest friend, weren't you?"

"Sure. But you don't necessarily tell your best friend who you're sleeping with."

"So there are things even a best friend wouldn't know," Karen said. "Right?"

Kraig didn't answer.

Karen gave him a last searching look as he let her out.

5 3

ON HER fourth day in captivity Susan had her first serious conversation with her captor.

The woman came in to remove Susan's lunch tray as usual. But today she remained to talk.

"Well," she said. "Are you ready to hear the truth?"

Susan reddened. She did not like being lectured by a kidnapper.

"I know the truth already," she said.

"What truth do you know?" the woman asked.

"My husband is a courageous man who loves his country," Susan said. "He has more physical courage than anyone I've ever met. The pain he endured from the two operations on his back would have turned any normal man into an invalid. He never wanted notoriety, but he has lived with it for all these years because he wants to serve his country."

The woman nodded. "And as a husband?"

"Michael is a loving husband," Susan said. "A devoted husband. He has always respected my feelings. He loves me."

"Why don't you have any children?" the woman asked.

Susan's face flushed again. "I blame myself for that."

"Does he satisfy you sexually?"

"That's none of your business."

The woman was watching Susan closely. Her gaze was penetrating. Avoiding it, Susan noticed that the woman's arms were bare today. The traces of small burns, cigarette burns perhaps, were visible on both arms.

"And as a son?" the woman asked.

"He is the son of a powerful, somewhat domineering father," Susan said. "A father who has made life difficult for his other two children. But Michael is strong. He has a strength of personality to match that of his father. Greater, in fact. He wouldn't be bullied by Judd. He stood up to him from the beginning. And I think Judd respects him for it. Michael commands respect."

"But they see eye to eye about his political career?" the woman asked.

"No, not really," Susan replied. "For one thing, Judd's politics are much more conservative than Michael's. For another thing, Judd has always pushed Michael to be more ambitious than he is naturally. I think this is because Judd was always ambitious for himself. He's a winner. He wants Michael to be a winner. Michael understands this, but he refuses to be ruled by Judd. Michael is his own man, and Judd has learned to respect that. Michael has backbone."

The reference to "backbone" was a Campbell family joke. It was ironic that Michael, whose spine was distorted by disease, should be the one in the family with the strongest will.

"Yet Michael is a nominee for the vice presidency at a tender age," the other woman observed. "Those who oppose him point out that fact. He is too young. Why do you say he has resisted his father's pushing?"

"He has. He did. It wasn't Judd who put him in this position."

"Who was it, then?" The woman's eyebrow was raised.

Susan needed a moment to find the right word. "It was fate."

"Ah." The woman smiled. "I understand."

"I don't think you do," Susan said. "If you did you wouldn't be trying to stop him from doing what his country needs him to do at this moment."

The woman studied Susan for a moment.

"Susan—do you mind if I call you Susan?"

Susan said nothing.

"Susan, are you familiar with the parable of the elephant?" the woman asked.

"Elephant?" Susan replied. "I'm not sure."

"Two blind men are holding parts of an elephant. One is holding the tail, the other the trunk. They need to figure out between them what animal they are holding. One man thinks the animal is very thin. The other thinks the animal is large and thick and makes a trumpeting noise. Between them they can't arrive at a picture of the real animal. Each of them knows too small a part."

"Yes, I've heard that," Susan said. "What about it?"

"Sometimes the truth eludes us because we see only a part of it. You've been dealing with the trunk, Susan. You've never seen the tail. You've never seen the whole Michael Campbell."

Susan shook her head. "You're wrong," she said. "I know him better than anyone alive."

There was a silence. The strange inner glare in the other woman's eyes softened.

"I'd like you to call me Justine," the woman said. "It's not fair for me to know your name when you don't know mine."

Susan silently weighed the sound of the name. It had an interesting dignity that seemed suited to this woman. Prematurely aged by some sort of suffering perhaps beyond anything Susan had ever known, she looked like a survivor. Her external scars seemed to echo invisible ones too terrible to be seen.

"All right," Susan said. She hoped her assent would create a touch of sympathy on her captor's part. But she stopped short of saying the name out loud.

"For obvious reasons," Justine said, "you have difficulty accepting the idea that your husband is evil. I'm here to convince you. Why? Because when the time comes, you're going to have to carry the ball."

"What do you mean, carry the ball?" Susan asked. "I would never do anything to hurt Michael. You might as well know that now."

There was a silence. Justine looked thoughtful.

"Michael's mother committed suicide, didn't she?" she asked.

Susan nodded. Despite herself she felt that there was something evasive in her nod.

"The reason was never clear, was it?" Justine asked.

Susan thought for a moment. "I once heard Judd say that Margery had problems with depression. He said she had trouble growing old gracefully."

"And you believed that?"

Susan chewed her lip nervously. "Why shouldn't I have believed it?"

Justine studied Susan's face.

"During your courtship with Michael," she said, "you spent a lot of time together, didn't you?"

"Yes. At first he was bedridden. I sat and talked to him. Sometimes all evening. Afterward we used to study together. I helped him train for the Olympics. I think I spent more time with him than anyone else."

"But every week or ten days, Michael left you for a whole day or more, didn't he?" Justine asked.

Susan reddened slightly. "Yes, that's true."

"Where did he go?"

"He went to Provincetown to see Father Griffin," Susan said.

"Who is Father Griffin?"

"He was Michael's favorite teacher in the school he attended as a boy. He had to retire when he got multiple sclerosis. Michael would go and see him every ten days or so and spend the night. He considered Father Griffin a sort of surrogate father and spiritual advisor. He always called him his favorite adult."

"Was Judd Campbell jealous of this relationship with the priest?" Justine asked.

Susan pondered this. "A little bit, perhaps. Judd was in some ways a difficult father, and he recognized that Michael needed some relief from him. He also realized that Father Griffin taught Michael a more gentle philosophy. Judd was so demanding . . . But on the whole I think Judd dismissed the relationship as something Michael was doing for the sake of his mother. His mother was Catholic, you see, and it was because of her that Michael had gone to a Catholic school as a young boy."

"Did you ever meet Father Griffin?" Justine asked.

"No, but I saw pictures of him. And I saw the pictures he painted of Michael. He was an amateur painter, pretty talented, until his illness made it impossible for him to hold a brush."

Justine was looking at Susan.

"But you never met him."

"No."

"Even when you were getting engaged to Michael, he never took you to Provincetown to meet his favorite adult?"

Susan reddened. "No. He didn't. Why should he have?"

"Wouldn't it have been the normal thing to do?" Justine asked. "Since he admired the priest, wouldn't he have wanted to show you off to him? Wouldn't he have wanted to ask his approval of your relationship, at least as a sign of respect?"

Susan thought for a moment. "Father Griffin was an invalid. He hated to have people see him in his weakened state. He was too embarrassed by his illness."

"It was Michael who told you this?"

"Yes."

Justine gave Susan a look of pity and understanding.

"Susan, there never was a Father Griffin."

Susan felt anger surge within her.

"What do you mean by that?" she cried. "Of course there was. I even talked to him on the phone once."

Justine shook her head. "You talked to a man on the phone. It was not Father Griffin. There is no Father Griffin. There never was."

There was a silence.

Justine stood up. "I could prove it to you today," she said. "But you wouldn't believe it. Not even if it was documented. You're not ready yet." She smiled at Susan. "So, I'll give you more time."

"Wait," Susan said.

Justine paused at the door. Her left arm hung at her side, marked by the small burns that looked like stigmata in the dim light.

"Yes?"

The roar of a large plane taking off nearby created a pause in which Susan fought to find words for what she was feeling.

"I don't believe you," she said. She wanted it to sound like a challenge. But it came out sounding like a plea.

Nodding understandingly, Justine went out and locked the door behind her.

5 4

Baltimore
April 8

JOE KRAIG parked his sedan in front of a large house on North Charles Street in Baltimore. The neighborhood was venerable, the house well kept up. It had old-fashioned high windows, ornate gables, and magnolia trees in the yard. The morning traffic was not particularly heavy. The warm Baltimore sun gave the city a balmy air despite the brown lawns and slushy streets.

Kraig sat in the waiting room looking at the stack of magazines on the coffee table, without making a move to pick one up.

After a few minutes a small gray-haired woman opened an inner door and gave Kraig a controlled smile. "Mr. Kraig? Come on in."

Kraig followed the woman into a relatively large room with tall windows and hanging plants. She sat behind a desk and motioned Kraig to an armchair beside which a box of Kleenex sat on a small table. In a corner of the room was a leather couch with a headrest at one end.

"Doctor, thank you for seeing me," Kraig said.

"What can I do for you?" The woman placed her hands on the table. She had the deliberate calm and steady eyes of her profession.

"I won't waste your time, Doctor," Kraig said. "Susan Campbell was your patient. We know that. It wasn't hard to trace her here. She made phone calls to this number. It's long distance from Washington, so they appeared on her phone bill. I assume she paid you in cash, since there are no payments to you on her checking account or credit cards. It's understandable, of course. A woman in her position would not want it publicly known that she was seeing a psychiatrist."

The doctor said nothing, but regarded Kraig steadily.

"I don't want to pry into Mrs. Campbell's private life, Doctor," Kraig said. "But as you know, the situation is serious. Her life could be in danger. I need for you to tell me anything you know that might help us get her back."

The doctor looked thoughtful. "Mr. Kraig—"

"Agent Kraig. I'm a federal agent, Doctor, assigned to investigate Mrs. Campbell's disappearance."

"Agent Kraig, then." The doctor gave Kraig a thin smile. "I can't violate the confidence of a patient."

Her voice bore the hint of an indeterminate European accent. Kraig already knew she was a psychoanalyst, trained in Vienna. His research into her background had revealed that she was highly regarded in her profession, with all the usual honors and fellowships. She taught at Johns Hopkins and had published several books on psychotherapy. She had patients from the best families in the Baltimore–Washington area. She would not be intimidated by a federal agent's badge.

"Did she use her real name when she came here?" Kraig asked.

"I'm afraid I can't discuss my patients with you, Agent Kraig," the doctor said.

Kraig sighed.

"Doctor, let me explain something to you. Susan Campbell left home under her own power. She drove to her cottage at Green Lake in Pennsylvania. We know the cottage was opened. She lit a fire, started a pot of tea, things like that. Then she disappeared. May I tell you something in confidence?"

The doctor looked uncertain. Then she nodded. "Everything that is said in this office is confidential."

"The evidence we found in the cottage was consistent with abduction," Kraig said. "However, there are grounds for the possibility that Mrs. Campbell committed suicide. Also for the possibility that she ran away, using the cottage as her point of departure. I want to get her home safe, Doctor. The best way to accomplish that is to avoid wasting time on scenarios that didn't happen. I want you to help me in this. Help me narrow down the possibilities."

The doctor was thoughtful.

"I can't violate the confidence of one of my patients, Agent Kraig."

"Even if it's a matter of life and death?" Kraig asked.

The doctor turned to look out the side window at the pleasant wisteria arbor in the yard. The arbor had been planted there so that her patients would have something to look at from the office. Over the years she had come to use the twisted wisteria branches as a metaphor in her therapy.

"The branches have twisted to accommodate the obstacle of the wood frame," she told her patients. "If you remove the frame, the branches will begin to grow straight. But they will always bear the trace of the twist caused by the obstacle. This is the way our character works. Now that our childhood stresses and conflicts are behind us, we are free to grow in any direction we like. We will always bear the trace of those early twists and turns, but they need not determine the direction our future will take. The purpose of therapy is to teach the branches that the obstacle is gone."

The doctor turned back to Kraig. His eyes told her he was sincere in his concern for Susan Campbell. More than sincere, in fact.

"Are you acquainted personally with Mrs. Campbell?" she asked.

"We're friends," Kraig said. "I was her husband's college roommate. I was present when they first met. I've known her husband since prep school. I consider them both friends."

The doctor thought for a moment. Susan Campbell was an unhappy woman. Moreover, she was the kind of unhappy woman who needs to believe she is happy. That made the therapy difficult, for the doctor had to work on the conflicts indirectly, without forcing Susan to acknowledge them openly. It was reminiscent of the physicians of the last century who had to give women complete physical exams without removing a single article of their clothing.

In recent months Susan had been terrified of the unexplained illness that was affecting so many people, including important political leaders. She had received crank calls suggesting that her husband was part of a conspiracy or plot that was threatening the country.

Her initial reaction was extreme fear for her husband's safety. But in the course of the winter, she began to express suspicion that there was something more at stake. The voice on the phone made her feel responsible, as though the weight of the whole thing was on her own shoulders.

Like so many neurotics, not to mention normal people, Susan had a lot of guilt inside her which met the outer threat halfway. The guilt stemmed from her father's abandonment of the family when Susan was six years old, and her mother's subsequent death. She had never entirely worked through her ambivalence about this.

Her married life had complicated the problem rather than solved it. Michael Campbell represented not only respectability to her, but also family. The Campbells accepted Susan and loved her.

However, the Campbells were not a normal family. The mother, Margery, had committed suicide under questionable circumstances, and the four surviving members were both joined and torn by significant stresses. Judd Campbell, the overbearing father, was the source of much of this trouble. The Campbells depended on Susan even more than she depended on them. Judd's attachment to her was obviously incestuous.

The tense Campbell family situation was matched by the extreme exposure Susan had to endure as the wife of a famous political man. Her visibility increased her self-consciousness and endangered her self-esteem, which was already fragile. The events of recent months—the sudden illness and death of important political figures—upset her badly.

For a while the doctor had suspected that the crank caller of whom Susan spoke was merely a fantasy. But the caller's prediction that Michael would be the eventual nominee for vice president had come well before the fact. The caller was real.

When Michael's selection came to pass, like a prophecy, Susan was shaken to her foundations. Emotionally she seized on the logic that every-thing was her fault, that the responsibility for curing the evil lay on her own shoulders. She could not talk to Michael himself about her feelings, or to Judd Campbell, who was thrilled by his son's selection to be vice president.

Was there motivation for suicide in Susan's situation? For flight? Certainly. That is, if Susan were a different person. But Susan was a fighter. She was motivated to stay at her post, not only by her love for her husband but by her need to protect the life she had built with him. She would not abandon her deeper crusade to feel legitimate as a person, to feel loved. To make a long story short, she was simply too healthy to crack under the strain. She had too much ego strength to run away, or to do herself harm.

The doctor turned to look at Agent Kraig. She suspected his feelings for Susan Campbell went deeper than mere friendship and loyalty. Underneath his cool professional veneer he had the look of a grieving relative holding vigil over a loved one.

"Agent Kraig, I have no patient in my practice at the moment who would be a risk for suicide. As for flight, I can only tell you that many people flee their family situations when stresses become too great. They usually return."

"You're saying that Susan was probably abducted," Kraig said.

"I can't tell you how to do your job," the doctor said. "You are far more expert in it than I. I can only tell you my impressions as a psychiatrist."

"Has she contacted you?" Kraig asked.

"I'm afraid I can't answer that."

"Is there a place you know of that she might have gone to from the Green Lake cottage?" Kraig asked.

The doctor shrugged. "As I say, I can't violate the confidence of a patient."

"In the event she did get in touch with you . . ."

"I would certainly urge her to let her family know she was safe," the doc-tor replied. "That would be my advice to any patient."

Kraig smiled. "Then there's nothing else you can tell me." He stood up. "Doctor, I appreciate your seeing me."

The doctor came around the desk to escort Kraig to the door. Seeing how disappointed he was, she took pity on him.

"Agent Kraig, all my patients are responsible adults. I would be astonished to hear that one of them had either harmed himself—or herself—or run away. If one of them disappeared, I would be inclined to look elsewhere for the explanation."

Kraig smiled. "Thank you, Doctor. Thank you for your help." He went through the waiting room and out into the sun.

The doctor returned to her desk. If her own theory about Susan Campbell was correct, and if Susan had in fact been abducted, there was reason to suspect that the crank on the telephone had not been talking pure nonsense. It was not inconceivable that the bizarre events of this political year had something to do with Susan's disappearance.

Susan Campbell was sane. The world was not sane. Not this year, anyway.

It was not the doctor's job to evaluate things like this. Agent Joseph Kraig and his colleagues would have to get to the bottom of it. She only hoped they did so in time to save Susan.

She could still feel Kraig's warm, firm handshake. A strong man, she mused. A strong man at a weak moment. A man pursuing a woman he perhaps cared too much about, a woman he had little hope of finding.

Sighing, she looked out the window at the deceptive antebellum charm of the yard.

Where was Susan? Was she alive?

The doctor shook her head and prepared to greet her next patient.

———

AS KRAIG was leaving the psychiatrist's office, Karen Embry was online with Grimm.

He had broken in via instant messaging as she was checking the latest statistics from the World Health Organization about the Pinocchio Syndrome.

GOOD MORNING, said Grimm.

Karen immediately stopped what she was doing.

I'M GLAD TO HEAR YOUR VOICE, she wrote. I MISSED YOU.

I'M TOUCHED, came the reply. WHAT HAVE YOU FOUND OUT?

SICK GIRLS IN BOSTON, Karen wrote. 15 YEARS AGO. COMPLETE MENTAL PARALYSIS, CAUSE UNKNOWN. FOLLOWED BY COMA. 8 ARE DEAD. I VISITED THE OTHER 5. ONE GIRL MISSING WHO WAS WITH ONE OF THE VICTIMS.

GOOD FOR YOU, replied Grimm. WHAT DID THEY TELL YOU?

DOCTORS STILL BAFFLED. Karen thought for a minute. I CHECKED WHERE-ABOUTS OF ALL MAJOR PLAYERS IN THIS YEAR'S POLITICS. MICHAEL CAMP-BELL WAS A STUDENT AT HARVARD FOR ALL 14 GIRLS. COLIN GOSS WAS VISITING BOSTON THAT YEAR TO SET UP NEW ENGLAND HEADQUARTERS. GOSS WAS IN BOSTON FOR ALL 14 GIRLS.

There was a brief pause.

THAT SHOULD BE ALL YOU NEED, wrote Grimm.

Karen was tempted to tell Grimm the results of her conversation with Joe Kraig. But she didn't want Grimm to know she had shared her information with anyone. She tried to find words that would get him to help her.

NO ONE WILL BELIEVE ME BASED ON WHAT I HAVE SO FAR, she said. THEY'LL SAY COINCIDENCE. CAN YOU GIVE ME SOMETHING MORE?

The screen was silent. Grimm must be thinking.

YOU SAW THE GIRLS, AND YOU STILL DON'T UNDERSTAND? he wrote.

Karen puffed nervously at her Newport.

I WANT TO UNDERSTAND, she wrote. SOMEONE MADE THE GIRLS SICK. I'M NOT SURE WHY.

I OVERESTIMATED YOU, he wrote. I THOUGHT YOU WERE SMARTER. YOU HAVE ALL YOU NEED. GOODBYE.

WAIT! Karen typed the word hurriedly. To her relief, the IM box remained open. Grimm was listening.

Her fingers trembling, she began to type.

YOU WOULDN'T BE WRITING TO ME UNLESS YOU WANT ME TO TELL THIS STORY SOMEDAY, she wrote. I CAN FEEL TIME RUNNING OUT. I'M BEHIND. HELP ME CATCH UP.

YOU'RE RIGHT ABOUT TIME, Grimm wrote. THERE IS VERY LITTLE TIME.

FOR WHOM? Karen wrote. SUSAN? ME?

FOR ME. And after a pause: FOR ALL.

The reply chilled Karen.

ONE MORE THREAD, she wrote. I'LL FOLLOW IT TO THE END. AND I'LL TELL YOUR STORY, I PROMISE.

A long pause.

SEE PATRICIA BRODERICK. SHE WAS THERE.

The message board went dead. Karen was left looking at the name, and wondering who it belonged to.

WHILE KRAIG was on his way from Baltimore back to Washington on I-95, the ransom demand the authorities had been anxiously awaiting for eleven days came in.

It was received by the managing editor of the *New York Times*. It came in the form of a telephone message. The message was recorded.

"This is Susan Campbell," it began.

The editor's assistant, who had taken the call, frantically pushed the intercom button to get the editor to pick up. It was too late. The editor was on another line.

"I am safe and being well cared for," said Susan's voice. The recording was of poor quality, probably from a discount-house Walkman with an interior microphone. *"No one intends to hurt me, provided that my husband Michael complies with the following demand."*

The assistant was writing furiously. Before she could finish the second sentence a different voice came on the recording.

"Michael Campbell must immediately withdraw his name from consideration as vice president," said the voice. *"When Campbell has withdrawn and another per-*

son has been selected, Mrs. Campbell will be released. If there is a delay in comply-ing with this request, Mrs. Campbell will die."

Word of the call spread like wildfire through the entire floor. Computer keyboards stopped clicking, voices were stilled. A deathly silence reigned. The assistant cursed as she tried to copy down the message.

"Can you repeat that?" she said into the phone. "Please, I'm trying to write it down."

The voice of Susan Campbell returned.

"Michael, please do what they say right away," Susan said. *"They mean busi-ness. They know what they're doing. Michael, I love you."*

The recording went dead.

A small group of reporters and secretaries had gathered at the door of the assistant's cubicle.

"Did you get it all?" someone asked.

The assistant shook her head. "Just the gist. They want Campbell to withdraw. That's all."

"Whose voice was it?" someone asked.

"Two voices. Susan Campbell and someone else," the assistant said. "A re-ally shitty tape. I could barely understand it."

"Was it Susan?" one of the reporters asked.

The assistant nodded. "I recognized her voice. It was her all right."

"God damn," the editor said. "We should have got that on tape."

The assistant shrugged. The newspaper did not have facilities for taping incoming calls.

They need not have worried. The same recording was phoned in to CNN headquarters in Atlanta later that day while a report on the demand was in progress. The cable technicians got the entire message on tape, including Su-san Campbell's voice and that of her captor.

5 6

Washington

A SPECIAL meeting of the intelligence and law enforcement people was held that evening. The first order of business was to determine if the voice of Susan Campbell on the kidnappers' tape was genuine.

The FBI's director was categorical on this. "I'll have the answer to that tonight. We have voiceprints of all the major political officials. That goes for the more visible spouses like Susan Campbell. We'll do a comparison."

Few of those present had any doubt that the voice on the tape belonged to Susan. The question was what condition she was in when she made the tape, and how much duress she was under at the time.

Again the FBI director took responsibility. "Our hostage rescue guys have psychological consultants," he said. "There are ways to analyze a recorded voice so that various methods of coercion can be determined."

"What do you mean?" asked the Secret Service head.

"Whether she's reading from a prepared document," the director said. "Whether she's reading it for the tenth time. Whether certain words upset her more than other words. We can also get some profiling data on the abductor by a careful analysis of the word choice. This technique got a lot of refining when Patty Hearst was kidnapped back in the 1970s. You'd be surprised what you can learn from a recorded ransom demand."

"Except they're not demanding a ransom," threw in one of the national security men.

"True." Heads nodded at this remark.

"What about the other voice?" someone asked.

The FBI director shook his head. "We don't have voiceprints on file for the general population. If this is someone from one of the well-known terrorist or militia-type organizations, there is a chance. If it isn't, forget it."

He looked at a page in the file he had brought with him.

"Our top priority is going to be the acoustical characteristics of the tape," he said. "What sort of room they were in when it was made. Where that room might be located. Things like that. One of my guys already mentioned that he could hear planes taking off or landing. We'll try to get a fix on where this might have come from."

Joe Kraig raised a hand. "What if they recorded it in one place and are no longer in that place?"

The director nodded. "That's certainly a possibility. But we'll learn all we can from the tape and go on from there."

"What about the demand itself?" Kraig asked. "What do we do about it?"

"The first thing is to gain time. Do nothing for two or three days," the director said. "Talk to everyone concerned, starting of course with Campbell. Then, if we can, we'll try to get these people to negotiate. Get them talking."

"They didn't give us a method to get in touch," someone said.

"True, but we can offer to parley in one of several ways. An announcement to the press by me, by Campbell, maybe by the president."

"What if they won't talk?" Kraig asked.

"We'll figure out something. We may have to offer concessions in order to get Mrs. Campbell back alive. After that, we'll do whatever we have to do."

Voices spoke up around the table, offering suggestions and warnings. All those present had some experience with terrorism and wanted to put in their two cents' worth. Kraig could hear territoriality in some of the voices, ego in others. Apparently they scented history in the making. No one of Susan Campbell's fame had ever been abducted before.

The combined wisdom of those present offered little constructive help, however. It was the old story. The terrorist has the initiative. He sets the rules, defines the parameters. All the authorities can do is react. Keep him talking, stall him, while doing everything possible to find out where he is and how heavily armed he is. Then kill him or overpower him. Or, if you can't do that, give in to his demand—the least savory course for any modern government.

"If only they hadn't called the cable news," one of the national security men said. "Now the whole country knows about this. We could have controlled it better if we were the only ones who knew."

"That's true," said the Secret Service head. "But there might be an advantage to it. Someone somewhere might know that voice. We can set up hot lines and let people call in. E-mail, too. Let the public help. It might work."

Everyone seemed to agree rather grudgingly with this notion. Few things were more hateful to intelligence men than public knowledge of their doings. The cloak of secrecy was their life's blood. Exposure was anathema.

"You know," Kraig said, "it occurs to me that the people who took Mrs. Campbell must have wanted it this way. They wanted the public to know what was being demanded." He paused, looking down at his clasped hands. "I wonder why," he added.

No one took up the question.

"And what about the demand itself?" he asked. "Who would want to keep Campbell from becoming vice president?"

Heads turned to him. The faces of those present bore expressions of incuriosity and even impatience. They seemed to consider his question irrelevant.

"She could be dead before we ever get to the bottom of the why of it," said the Defense Intelligence Agency man. "We have to go with what we have."

"It seems to me," Kraig said, "that we should be thinking about who stands to benefit from this. Who would consider a thing like Campbell's withdrawal desirable or important."

"Joe, we'll learn what we can," said the FBI director. "But it could be anybody. Arabs, Serbs, Maoists, militia freaks, UFO nuts. Mike Campbell has a high profile, and so does his wife. They're perfect targets. I think *where* is more important than *who*—at least for the moment. And let's not forget, our track record in protecting important people isn't so good lately." He did not glance at the Secret Service head, who reddened at the remark. "The priority is to find Mrs. Campbell."

Kraig nodded noncommittally. He thought there was a flaw in this logic. He could not forget Susan Campbell's story of a voice on the phone, a voice that had predicted, months before the event, Michael's selection as vice president. A voice that had told Susan it would be up to her to stop Michael when the time came. Well, the time had come. And Susan was gone.

Kraig had never heard that voice. Susan had told him it was a woman's voice. The voice that had made the demand to the *Times* was that of a woman.

Kraig sat quietly through the rest of the meeting. When it ended he returned to his office. He was pensive. Not for the first time in this crazy year he felt that events were outrunning the efforts of responsible leaders to understand them. History was writing itself in a shorthand that no one understood.

Kraig wanted desperately to understand it in time to save Susan.

———

JUDD CAMPBELL breathed a gigantic sigh of relief when he heard the news about the kidnappers' demand.

In the days since Susan's abduction Judd had slept little. He was devoured by nightmares about Susan lying dead in a shallow grave or under the water of a lake somewhere. The public demand, terrifying though it was in itself, offered some comfort. Susan was alive somewhere. The people who had her were human beings possessed of reason and logic. They wanted something. They could be bargained with. Some sort of deal could be struck with them.

Judd commiserated with Michael, who also seemed relieved by the news and desperately hopeful that it meant he would get Susan back.

Yet Michael seemed thoughtful. When Judd asked him what he was thinking, Michael only said, "I'd like to be surer."

"Surer of what?" Judd asked.

"That she's still alive. If only I could talk to her myself . . ."

Judd squeezed Michael's hand. "She's alive, son. I feel it in my gut. She's alive, and we're going to get her back."

It was not until Judd had left Michael and returned home that he began to weigh the consequences of the captors' demand.

Assuming they were telling the truth, Susan might come home safe—but only on the condition that Michael abandon the greatest opportunity of his political career.

Judd knew, as a man familiar with the political wars, that too often a chance for the White House came only once. There was no way to predict what the political situation would be in two years, six years. This might be Michael's only opportunity. If Michael gave in to the abductors' demand, that opportunity was gone.

Judd worried that Michael might jump at the chance to refuse the president's nomination. Michael had always resisted Judd's relentless pressure to be aggressive, to be ambitious, to move up faster, to achieve the greatest things in the shortest space of time. Michael had always wanted to move more slowly, to enjoy life. Michael wanted to be a person instead of just a success. The kidnappers' demand might be just the escape he secretly craved.

Judd even feared that Michael would be so wounded by what had happened this year that he would never run for high office again. Like Edward Kennedy, he might want to devote himself to the Senate for a lifetime. This concept was hateful to Judd. He knew Michael was capable of more, so much more than simply voting on bills in the Senate.

Now a rare introspective thought entered Judd's head, to the effect that perhaps his own ambition for Michael was being punished by the current situation. Perhaps in some obscure way it was Judd's relentless pushing of Michael, Judd's vicarious lust for the spotlight of history, that had put Susan at risk. If Judd had allowed Michael to live a normal life like other men, none of this would have happened.

The thought was uncharacteristic, and it skipped out of Judd's mind like a stone skipping off the surface of a lake. Returning to his concern for Susan, Judd called the head of his detective force and demanded that everything be done to determine who had Susan and whether she was still alive.

"Find out who that voice on the tape is," he said. "Find out where the tape was recorded. And don't tell me you can't do it."

Having taken the only constructive action he could take, Judd could now go back to comforting Michael and, in the solitude of his bedroom, of weeping more tears over Susan.

———

COLIN GOSS'S advisors found him uncharacteristically agitated following the news about Susan Campbell.

"I'm going to make a statement tonight," he told them. "Something statesmanlike. We must put aside political differences while we make sure that this lovely young woman comes home safe. That sort of thing. Make it good, very good."

"Will do," said Goss's chief speechwriter, making a note on his pad.

Goss dismissed the PR people and had a meeting with his detectives.

"I want to know where she is," he said. "I want to know before the FBI knows. And I want to know who took her."

The chief detective looked concerned. "All we really have to go on is the phone call," he said. "We don't really have a clue to who might be behind this." His tone was faintly interrogative, as though he wondered what Goss might know on the subject.

"That's right," Goss said, pouring mineral water into a crystal glass with a hand that shook slightly. "But we're going to find out, and fast."

The detective gave Goss a slight smile. "You know, it wouldn't hurt us too much if Campbell did drop out," he said. "The president has been climbing in the polls ever since Campbell came on board. Take Campbell out and the president is very vulnerable. That could be a big advantage for us."

Colin Goss's usual composure failed him at this moment.

"Michael Campbell is going to become vice president," he said. "No matter what happens."

The security man looked at Goss uncomprehendingly.

"Michael *must* take the job," Goss said.

Seattle, Washington
April 10

KAREN ARRIVED in Seattle on the red-eye from Washington at 5 A.M., three hours behind East Coast time. She was physically exhausted but focused on her goal.

She had located the Patricia Broderick of Grimm's e-mail without much difficulty, using online address services and making a few phone calls.

Patricia Broderick's married name was Gaynor, but she still used Broderick as a professional name. She was a real-estate agent specializing in homes and condominiums. Her husband was a tax attorney. She had two children, a boy of eleven and a nine-year-old girl.

Karen had called her long distance to arrange to look at some houses and condominiums in the greater Seattle area. She told the woman she was a journalist relocating to Seattle. A crisp, intelligent voice told her what a lovely city Seattle was, and promised to meet her at the appointed time.

Karen had heard the audiotape of the demand made by Susan Campbell's captors. She felt sure the voice of Susan Campbell on the phone was genuine. That unique edge of warmth and worry so typical of Susan was eloquently captured on the tape.

As for the other voice, that of the captor—or the captors' spokesperson—
Karen had not recognized it at first. But a few repetitions and some thought
had convinced her it was the voice she had overheard on the phone at Susan's
Georgetown home.

Karen did not know exactly what to make of this. The demand that
Michael Campbell remove himself from consideration for vice president was
consistent with the vague threats made by Susan's anonymous telephone
crank. But why? Why should anyone want Michael out of the way? Who
would benefit from his withdrawal?

The first answer, of course, was Colin Goss. Ever since Michael's selection to replace Dan Everhardt, the president had been gaining in the polls,
and Goss had been losing. Goss hated Michael Campbell—that was well
known. No man in Washington stood to gain more by getting rid of Michael
than Goss.

On the other hand, Joe Kraig's challenge to Karen's logic about the
Boston episode had left her perplexed. If Goss was Michael's enemy, why did
Grimm's hints about Boston lead to a seemingly guilty link—the fourteen
sick girls—between Goss and Michael?

Karen did not know the answer. But her instinct told her to trust Grimm
and to follow the trail he offered her. She needed to know what Patricia Broderick knew. She would put the pieces together later.

Karen met Patricia Broderick at her realty office at 10 A.M. Patricia was a
handsome, well-preserved woman in her forties who might well have been
beautiful fifteen or twenty years ago. She had thick auburn hair, freckled
skin, and very large green eyes.

For a change it was not raining in Seattle. The day was chilly but beautiful. Majestic mountains graced the horizon, and the blue waters of Puget
Sound came in and out of view as Patricia Broderick drove Karen toward a
new subdivision.

Karen decided to waste no more time. "I hope you'll forgive me, Mrs.
Broderick," she began.

"Oh, call me Pat! Everybody does."

"Pat, then. I needed to talk to you alone about a sensitive matter, and I
didn't want to alarm you at long distance. I'm here as a reporter."

A wary look came over the woman's face. "I can't imagine why a reporter would want to talk to me," she said.

"Let me assure you that anything you tell me will be off the record," Karen said. "This is not an official interview. I'm working on something important, and time is of the essence. I just need as much of the truth as I can get my hands on. As quickly as possible."

"What is this in reference to?" Pat asked.

There were two names on the tip of Karen's tongue. She chose the latter. "Colin Goss."

"I have nothing to say about that." The realtor's jaw was set. A frown of distaste was on her face. Her eyes looked frightened.

"Listen, Pat," said Karen. "I don't want to threaten you. What I'm working on has nothing to do with you directly. But the press is the press. Your name could come into it. All I want is a completely confidential interview."

The quid pro quo was on the table. The woman chewed her lip nervously as she drove.

"What about?"

Once again Karen had to gamble.

"About the Donkey Game," she said.

There was a silence. Pat Broderick drove more and more slowly. At length she turned into the parking lot of a strip mall. She left the engine running as she turned to Karen.

"I don't know what you're talking about," she said.

"I'm talking about deep background," Karen said. "If any of what I'm investigating finds its way into print, you will never be identified as a source."

"I still don't know what you're talking about." Pat Broderick looked stubborn.

"Do you watch the news at all?" Karen asked. "Are you aware of what's going on?"

"You mean Susan Campbell?" The realtor's big green eyes looked pained.

Karen nodded. "I'm fighting against the clock, Mrs. Broderick. I'm working closely with the law enforcement agencies. We're trying to get Susan Campbell back alive. That's why I'm here."

Pat Broderick was silent.

"I need background that will help me find out who abducted Susan Campbell, and why. And where she can be found," Karen said.

"Nothing I might tell you would help you find Mrs. Campbell," Pat said.

"It might help in ways that have nothing to do with you," Karen rejoined. "Why not let me be the judge of that? Just tell me what you can, and I'll be on my way."

There was a silence.

"Listen, Miss Embry," Pat Broderick said. "I'm worried about more than just being embarrassed in this. Susan Campbell is a hostage. I might turn up dead."

"Why do you say that?" Karen asked.

"Colin Goss is not a man who plays with white gloves on."

"So you do know him," Karen said.

"I'm not saying I know him." Pat Broderick looked fearful.

"I know you know him," Karen said. "And if you know him, he knows you."

There was a silence. Karen studied the other woman carefully. Her crisp realtor's demeanor had vanished. She looked scared to death.

"Listen," Karen said. "If what you say is true, the safest thing you can do is to talk to me. I'm not a federal agent. I won't subpoena you and drag you in front of a grand jury. What you say to me will never be attributed to you publicly. The law enforcement people can't offer you a deal like that."

The other woman had turned a shade paler at the mention of subpoenas.

"Please," Karen said. "Help me and I'll help you. I promise."

Pat Broderick sat for a long moment staring out through the windshield, her fingers drumming nervously on the wheel of the car.

"Are you telling the truth about keeping my name out of it?" she asked.

"Absolutely. You have my word. No one knows I'm here. Not even my agent."

"Are you wired?"

"No. Feel free to search me."

The realtor ran a hand around Karen's back and between her legs, in search of the telltale battery pack that went with a wire. Her hand trembled.

"If you ever tell anyone about this, I'll deny it," she said. "I want you to know that. I will never testify about this, ever."

"Fair enough. I won't ask you to."

Patricia Broderick paused one more time, as though weighing a terrible choice.

"All right," she said with a sigh. "The Donkey Game? Yes, I know about it. I participated in it, more than once. Goss and his rich corporate friends would get several girls together and play games with them. Some of them were paid, like me, and knew what to do in advance. Others—so I heard—were lured in off the street. They were drugged before the game, and afterward they were either paid off or threatened, or—"

"Or what?"

She chewed her lip nervously. "I can't testify to this personally, it was just a rumor. I heard some of them were made to disappear. I also heard Goss used some special drugs on them, to make them unable to talk about what had happened. You probably know his company is into truth serums and hypnotic drugs, stuff like that. Well, I heard he turned a few girls into mental vegetables after he had his way with them. I never knew if it was true. I didn't want to know."

"What kind of girls?" Karen asked. "Hookers? Bar girls?"

"No." Pat Broderick shook her head. "Straight girls. Students. They had to be innocent types. That's what Goss got off on. It was one thing to pay a call girl like me to take part in a bondage game or an S&M scenario. But Goss knew I was acting. The other girls weren't acting. They were scared shitless. That's what turned him on." She exhaled nervously. "Fear is an aphrodisiac to him."

Karen nodded. "Tell me about the Donkey Game," she said.

"They would tie a girl down. Naked. With her ass exposed. They would play Pin the Tail on the Donkey. The man whose turn it was would be blindfolded. They would give him a tail made out of horsehair, with some glue on the end. He would make his way through the room, trying to find the girl. They placed bets on who would get to her fastest. Anyway, when he found her he would stick the tail to her ass. Then the reward was that he could have sex with her, right there. The others would cheer him on. Usually he would be drunk, so he needed all the encouragement he could get." Patricia's lips curled in distaste.

"Was the man naked?" Karen asked.

"Yes. The contestant was always naked. The others were dressed. They sat at tables, drinking company booze. It was like a nightclub, there was music playing."

"And you were one of these girls?" Karen asked.

Pat nodded. "More than once. Sure. I pretended I was drunk or out of it. I would just sit there passively. It didn't particularly bother me—I've done stranger things in my time. And I was being well paid for it, believe me. Colin Goss doesn't stint where money is concerned."

She thought for a moment. "My sense of it was that the other men enjoyed the betting and the idea of screwing a helpless girl. In later years I began to feel that Goss got off particularly on the idea of the girl wearing a tail. Because of some kink of his own." She looked at Karen. "He's a sick guy. That was well known. The public knows nothing about it, naturally. If they did, he would be finished. In politics, anyway." She darted a bitter glance at Karen. "But he has the press in his pocket, I'm sure you know that."

"Sick in other ways too?" Karen asked. "Other than the bondage?"

Pat Broderick chewed her lip nervously. "Yes." She glanced out the window, as though afraid her words could be heard by someone outside the car. "He likes pain. Inflicting it, I mean. He likes having total control over people. That could lead to a lot of things. He may have gotten worse since I knew him. Men, as they get older, get kinkier."

"What do you mean, worse?"

"The thing about him was, he never attached any value to other people. They were all guinea pigs to him. There was a coldness in him . . . I can't describe it. You had the feeling there was nothing he would shrink from. He didn't care how other people felt. He lived only for himself." Pat shook her head. "As I look back on it, that was the scariest thing. That way he had. That look in his eyes."

Karen was thoughtful. This was news to her, though she had heard vague rumors that Colin Goss had sexual skeletons in his closet.

"So you're saying that the Donkey Game didn't bother you particularly," she said. "You weren't physically hurt."

"Right."

"But if you were a girl off the street," Karen suggested, "a girl who had been lured there under false pretenses, and you were forced to do this against your will . . . it would be bad, wouldn't it?"

Patricia Broderick nodded. "Yes, it would be bad. Especially if you were drugged. As I say, it was only a rumor. But I wouldn't put it past Goss. He was very into pain, humiliation. And he liked young girls."

"But you never saw anyone actually harmed during these games?" Karen asked.

"Never. Not physically, anyway." Pat shook her head. "But I was only a small part of Goss's sex life. You have to remember that. What he did in other places, with other women, I have no idea. I wouldn't put anything past him."

"What was the connection of Michael Campbell to Goss in those days?" Karen asked with studied casualness. "Did he play a part in these games?"

Pat Broderick's face, which had softened a bit during the last few minutes, turned distant again.

"I don't know anything about that," she said. "I wasn't aware of any connection. I didn't know they even knew each other."

Karen nodded, mentally counting the other woman's denials. Three of them. That meant she was lying. Protesting too much. An easy denial to see through, for a seasoned reporter.

"You never saw them together?" Karen asked.

"Certainly not. Never."

"You never heard Goss mention Michael Campbell?"

"Never. Why would he?"

"You're sure?" Karen probed.

"Absolutely." Pat Broderick spoke firmly. But her eyes told Karen she knew more than she was saying.

"You've been a great help," Karen said. "As I say, I promise I'll never mention your name in connection with this. By the way, do you know any other women who took part in Goss's games? I'd like to get confirmation on deep background if I could."

"No." Pat Broderick shook her head. "No, I don't." She looked afraid.

Pat drove Karen back to her office. The two women shook hands in the parking lot.

"I appreciate your honesty," Karen said. "And I'll respect your confidences. I'll never mention your name to anyone."

A change had come over Pat Broderick's face. "I'll tell you something for your own good," she said. "If you ever got to the point of publishing any of this, especially under your own name, you wouldn't have any more chance than I would."

Karen nodded. "I'll remember it."

Pat seemed to relax slightly.

"Do you think they're going to get Susan Campbell back alive?" she asked Karen.

"I don't know," Karen replied. "I hope so. I'm trying to help. If we can find the right connection in time, it might save her."

"And you think Colin Goss is part of the connection?"

"I think he may be," Karen said. "He wants to be president, after all. Susan Campbell is the wife of a man who stands in his way."

"I'll tell you something else off the record," Pat said. "If Colin Goss ever gets his hands on that kind of power, this country will be finished."

Karen looked interested. "What makes you so sure of that?"

"This is a free country," Pat said. "Colin Goss has never believed in freedom for anyone else but Colin Goss."

She looked past Karen at the lovely Seattle skyline. "These politicians getting sick and dying . . . That could be Goss's work. There's nothing he's not capable of."

Karen said, "But it seems as though the bad things that have happened have benefited Michael Campbell. Haven't they? He's about to become vice president, isn't he?"

Patricia Broderick turned back to Karen. "Yes. You're right."

"And, to hear Goss talk, he hates Michael Campbell more than anyone alive."

The look on the older woman's face was ambiguous. "Yes, you're right. I don't know, then."

Those words were still echoing in Karen's ears as she watched Patricia Broderick walk quickly back into the realty office.

5 8

AN HOUR after leaving Patricia Broderick, Karen was on a flight to D.C. Cocktails were being served, and the tempting aromas of bourbon, blended whiskey, and gin were wafting through the cabin. Karen was trying to forget the fact that she would not have a cigarette for the next five hours. She had put down her tray table and was using it as a desk. Her pad was before her, covered with notes in her crisp, cautious handwriting.

If he ever gets that kind of power . . .
There's nothing he's not capable of.

Karen thought back over her interview with Patricia Broderick. Everything the woman said had the ring of truth. She was revealing things she had kept hidden for years. She was afraid.

The only time she had become evasive was when Karen had asked about Michael Campbell. Her denials about Michael had the hollow ring of deception.

And there was the faraway look in Pat's eyes when Karen had reminded her that the removal of Everhardt and Palleschi and Stillman benefited Michael Campbell. It was the look of a person who is hiding something and does not want to be seen through.

Karen wrote on her pad:

Colin Goss ⟵⟶ Michael Campbell

Once again she was up against the contradiction that had been pointed out to her by Joe Kraig. If Colin Goss hated Michael Campbell as much as he claimed to, why would he do things behind the scenes that had the effect of helping Michael?

And if Colin Goss was truly in bed with Michael Campbell, for reasons which were unknown to the public, why would Goss abduct Susan Campbell and demand that Michael withdraw from consideration as vice president?

Karen closed her eyes with a sigh. The key to the Sphinx's riddle was right in front of her, but she was not sharp enough to see it. Not yet, anyway.

She opened her eyes and scribbled some more thoughts at random.

Everhardt dead.
Palleschi sick.
Michael chosen by president.
Susan Campbell kidnapped.

Karen crossed out the line about Susan, but left it where it was.

~~Susan Campbell kidnapped.~~

Then she wrote:

Pinocchio Syndrome stops in USA. This benefits president.
Does not help Goss. Goss losing in polls.

She chewed her pen, moistening it with lips that wanted a cigarette even more than a drink. Then she wrote:

President likely to remain in office.
Unless Campbell withdraws.

She thought for another minute.

Goss in bed with Campbell, she wrote.

"Come on," she said aloud. "Connect the dots."
Suddenly the unseen connection popped up before her.

Goss wants Michael as VP. Hence others removed.
GOSS WANTS TO LOSE.

Karen exhaled abruptly. Her seatmate glanced at her. Karen forced a polite smile to show she was all right.
Her hand trembled as she wrote the next proposition.

Goss wants MICHAEL to win.

Karen pushed the call button. When the flight attendant came, she asked
for a double Jack Daniel's.
"Sure thing." The flight attendant bustled away toward the kitchen
area.
Karen did not move until her drink was brought. She inhaled the nutty
aroma of the liquor with a sigh of relief. This would be her only drink until
she got home tonight.
She sat back and closed her eyes.

Ask him what happened at Harvard. Ask him about the Donkey Game.
When he answers, watch his eyes.

Karen tried not to think. She did not succeed. The truth, someone once
said, is both inescapable and hard to grasp. Slipping through our fingers like
quicksilver, it seeps through our pores, into us, like a disease. No matter how
blind we try to be, we can't escape it.

Karen kept her eyes closed. The roar of the engines harmonized with the throb of the liquor inside her.

The truth hit her like a slap. She almost knocked over the drink as she grabbed the pad.

Abduction NOT part of the plan, she wrote.

Now she understood the voice on the phone at Susan Campbell's house. *When the time comes, it will be up to you, Susan.*

The person who abducted Susan was not trying to stop Michael in order to help Goss. Michael and Goss were on the same team.

The person on the phone knew something that neither Susan nor the authorities had yet suspected: that the accession of Michael Campbell to the White House was precisely what Colin Goss wanted.

Colin Goss ⟷ *Michael Campbell*

Again Karen exhaled, this time from relief. The dots were connected, the gestalt was complete. Even if she could never convince anyone else of it.

Pinocchio Syndrome ⟷ *Donkey Game*

She wanted to order another drink, to celebrate. But she knew she must wait. She had a lot of thinking to do before she hit the bottle again.

She closed her eyes. The ideas on the page before her grew dim. The voice on Susan Campbell's phone came forward, eclipsing everything.

When he answers, watch his eyes.

5 9

SUSAN WAS sitting in the little bedroom whose corners she had now come to know very well. The place was too dark and cloistered to feel like home, but there was something curiously womblike about it. She felt isolated from the world here.

Justine was seated in the rocking chair across from the bed. She had played Susan a tape of the CNN news broadcast on which the telephone demand was aired.

Susan was thoughtful.

"Why did you make it so public?" she asked. "Why didn't you just send them a cassette tape, or something like that?"

"The demand had to be public," Justine said. "I had to make the call to the media to insure that."

"Why did it have to be public?" Susan asked.

"Because now everyone will know what the demand is." Justine smiled. "If I hadn't made sure the call was recorded, the authorities would have lied about the demand. They would have said it was something else."

Susan frowned. "I don't understand."

"Now that your husband has been chosen, the president will almost certainly remain in office," Justine explained in a patient voice. "All the powers are lining up behind that proposition. They won't want Michael to withdraw, with the White House at stake. They would lie about my demand if they could."

Susan nodded uncertainly. "I still don't really understand," she said.

"Think, Susan." Justine might have been talking to a child. "Use your common sense. If none of this was public, if all of it was hushed up, it would end up like a dozen other political mysteries. Even if you died, the real reason would never see the light of day. That's how they operate, Susan. When they want things a certain way, they cover up how they did it."

"And now they want Michael to be in the White House?" Susan asked.

"Precisely." Justine smiled. "It's at times like this that the truth becomes a casualty of men's self-interest. They're getting ready to write a history in which Michael Campbell became vice president, then went on to greater and greater things, while certain minor mysteries never got cleared up. Such as the deaths of Everhardt and Palleschi and Stillman—and a disease called the Pinocchio Syndrome."

Susan's eyes were wide. "You can't mean . . ."

Justine waved away the question. "But now, Susan, now your husband is going to have to make his response to my demand public. He can't hide it. It's too late."

Susan asked, "And what will his response be?"

Justine stood up and took a brief walk around the room. She looked at the TV, which was not hooked up to the cable and could only be used to show videotapes. She looked at the small collection of videos.

"You like the old movies," she smiled.

Susan nodded, her face expressionless.

"You long for simpler times," Justine observed. "Times when good and evil were easier to tell apart. Isn't that right?"

Susan was surprised. "How did you know that?"

"Times when it was easier to love and be loved," Justine said. "You see that when you look at John Garfield's face, don't you, Susan? And James Stewart, and Gary Cooper . . . Have I understood you correctly?"

"Yes," Susan said, a bit sadly.

Justine came to Susan's side and sat down on the bed. She took Susan's hand.

"Are you ready, Susan?"

"For what?"

"To hear the truth?"

Susan looked into the tortured eyes, the face prematurely aged by pain. She did not want to hear the truth. She just wanted to be left alone, to be left in peace. But she was so tired of running away.

"Yes," she said. "I'm ready."

"I was eighteen years old," Justine said. "I was a high school senior. I was with my friend Jane. We both lived outside Boston. We took the train downtown one Saturday night. We had told our parents we were going to the movies, but we were really cruising the downtown area, looking for boys."

She paused. "We had done this before. Sometimes with other girls, sometimes just the two of us. We were a little bit wild, Jane and I. We both had trouble with our parents, and we were not very mature emotionally."

She smiled. "We weren't as daring as we pretended. We were both virgins, in fact. We hadn't had much luck in our downtown outings, but we kept at it."

"Boston," Susan said.

"Yes. Boston." Justine gave Susan a hard look.

"We hung around the downtown area for a while," she continued. "We tried to seem desirable, but not much happened. We stopped into a McDonald's for fries and Cokes. Then we began to get discouraged. We were on the point of getting the train home when a young man came along and spoke to us. He was very good-looking. He asked us if we were college girls, and we said no. We giggled, I remember. He told us he was on his way to a party, mostly college kids but some younger, and he invited us. He promised we would have a good time. He said there would be liquor there, and he hinted there might be grass. He said there would be unattached boys there."

She paused. "I've had a lifetime to think back on that moment," she said, "and to wonder why we didn't say no. We were a bit wild, Jane and I, but we were basically innocent teenagers. We were the kind of girls who would never go anywhere with a stranger."

She shrugged. "It was because of him," she said. "He was handsome, he was charming. He seemed so young, almost vulnerable. He had a way of looking into your eyes as though there was nothing so important to him as his need to impress you favorably, to gain your approval. As though your opinion meant everything. This was irresistible to two naive girls, coming from a man that handsome. We went with him."

She sighed. "He took us to a big building downtown. A new building. We went up in an elevator. It was very luxurious. Jane and I exchanged a look—we were impressed. We went up to one of the top floors. He took us down a corridor to a sort of lounge. Actually it was a billiard room. There were these two beautiful pool tables, in dark wood. There were also a couple of poker tables. And a bar, a small but well-stocked bar. Very swanky, very club-bish. He offered us a drink. Jane asked him if this was where the party was to be, and he said no, it was on the floor above."

She paused. "I remember that Jane had a daiquiri. I had cold feet, I just asked for a Coke. That might have made all the difference. Whatever he gave us might have reacted with alcohol. I never figured that out."

She shrugged. "Anyway, after a minute he excused himself, he said he would be right back. Jane and I started to get giggly. At first I thought it was just the situation, the excitement, but then we realized we were getting high on something. We exchanged a look, like 'Maybe we'd better get out of here.' Then we both collapsed. We were out cold."

She took a deep breath. "The next thing I remember, I woke up naked in a large room full of smoke. Cigarettes, cigars. Music was playing. I heard men's voices. I was tied to a strange couch or padded table. My head was down, my fanny was sticking up. My hands and feet were bound, so I couldn't really move anything but my head.

"I saw Jane. She was tied into a similar thing. She looked like she was un-conscious, but her eyes were open. A strange, empty expression. I tried to speak to her, but I was paralyzed. I couldn't move a muscle. I tried to look out into the room, but there were spotlights on Jane and me, so everything else was invisible. That's when the game began."

Susan was listening, her face expressionless. Justine herself seemed empty of emotion as she talked.

"There was a sort of fanfare. The music got louder. I could tell something was about to happen. I heard the voices of men calling out to each other. I began to get the impression they were placing bets. I heard movement in the room. I tried to call out to Jane, but my lungs didn't seem to work. It was the strangest feeling—being lucid, conscious, but absolutely unable to move.

"I saw a figure approaching from behind the glare of the lights. Voices were calling out encouragement, laughing. As he came through the lights I saw that it was a middle-aged businessman type, fat, jowly. He was blindfolded. He was naked. He was holding his hands out in front of him, as though feeling his way. He had an erection. Then I saw what he had in his hand."

Susan's eyes had opened wider. She was listening intently.

"It was a tail. Like the tail of a horse or a donkey. Tight at the top, then flaring out at the bottom. As he came closer the shouts got louder. They were shouting 'Warmer!' and 'Colder!' I realized they were playing Pin the Tail on the Donkey."

She looked down at Susan's hand, which was still in her own. On an impulse she let go and stood up. Her eyes bore the cold inward glare Susan had come to know.

"I tried to struggle, but as I say, I couldn't move a muscle. The man came gradually closer. The others were calling out to him. I think those who were betting on him were trying to help, and the others were trying to confuse him. Or maybe they were betting on which of us he would get to first. Anyway, it was Jane. He stumbled against her, then he reached out and felt her thigh. He ran his hand over her until he found her ass. He stuck the tail to her ass, I don't know how. Maybe it had glue attached to it. There was applause. The music got louder. Glasses were clinking. Some of the voices sounded disappointed in a drunken way, as though they had lost their bet."

She was silent for a moment, as though gathering her courage to continue.

"Then he took off the blindfold," she said. "He looked at Jane. He got down on his knees and started to nuzzle her between her legs. The others were shouting and laughing. His erection got harder. He—" She looked at Susan. "He fucked her. Up her ass, I think; I'm not sure. She never moved, the whole time. Her eyes were pointed at me, but there was no expression on her face. I think she saw me as I saw her, but I'm not sure. He took a long time to finish. When he finally did there were cheers. Glasses clinking, laughter, music."

Justine took a deep breath.

"I thought I had died and gone to hell. I really did. Part of me couldn't believe what I was seeing. Another part thought that this was what I had heard about all my life, this was the fate reserved for girls who were bad. I couldn't move, but I also couldn't close my eyes."

She crossed her arms over her breast. "They started playing again. Someone took the tail off Jane. There was music, and laughing. Betting. I saw another man coming forward, blindfolded like the other one. This one was taller, but like the other one he was flabby, out of shape. He came toward Jane at first, but then he came toward me. They were calling out encouragement . . ."

She looked at Susan. "Do I have to tell you the rest?"

Susan had turned pale. She shook her head.

"They kept us there until the wee hours," Justine said. "Each of us must have been raped seven or eight times. I realized they had positioned us intentionally so that each one could see what was being done to the other. My heart went out to Jane when I saw what they were doing to her. And I realized that our ability to see each other, Jane and me—our compassion, our horror—was all part of the game to them. When I understood this, I had the most profound sense of evil. Beyond anything I had ever imagined at my tender age."

She breathed in, then out again.

"The most horrible thing of all was that empty look in Jane's eyes. I kept wondering whether she was too out of it to know what was happening, or whether that empty look was because what they were doing was simply beyond anything she could bear."

She looked at Susan. Now Susan understood the reason for that strange glare in her eyes. A glare that shone eloquently to an outside observer, but that seemed directed inward above all. It was the glare of her shame at being a victim, and of her impotent rage. Susan glanced at the cut marks on her wrists.

"What happened then?" she asked.

"In the end I passed out," Justine said. "The effect of the drug, my exhaustion, my terror—I don't know."

"What about Jane?"

"I never saw her again."

There was a silence. Susan didn't know how much of Justine's story she should believe. It might be an elaborate fantasy, the product of a tortured mind.

"Did she survive?" she asked.

"Yes. But she never woke up. She's a vegetable. She's in a nursing home in the Boston area."

Susan clenched her eyes shut. Then, with an effort, she opened them. Justine was looking at her steadily.

"Did you ever see any of the—of the men again?"

Justine smiled. "Of course."

"You mean they kept you?" Susan asked.

"No. I was free when I woke up. I never saw any of them in the flesh again. But I did see two of them in the media."

Susan's voice trembled as she asked, "Which two?"

"The man who was in charge of the game. The master of ceremonies, as it were. Colin Goss."

Susan kept her eyes averted as she asked, "Who was the other?"

"The young man who picked us up on the street. The one who invited us to the party."

"Who was he?" Susan's voice shook.

"Michael Campbell."

Susan could not move. She tried to speak, but words would not come. She felt paralyzed. She thought of Justine's story, of the paralysis Justine had experienced while the game was going on. An inability not to see, an inability to close one's eyes. That was how Susan felt now.

Justine had sat down again and was looking at Susan with eyes full of pity.

"Now it comes full circle," she said. "The world is teetering on the brink of the fate your husband has planned for it. No one knows the truth. No one wants to know. The world's eyes are closed, Susan. But you and I have made them see one thing. We have made them see that Michael Campbell must choose between the White House and the wife he claims to love. The whole world has heard this."

Susan nodded, staring at nothing.

"What is he going to decide?" she asked.

"You mean you don't know?" Justine asked.

"Please," Susan said in a small voice. "Just tell me."

"He's going to refuse to withdraw," Justine said with a cold smile. "He's going to let you die."

BOOK THREE

THE EMPEROR'S NEW CLOTHES

All the courtiers were on their knees, admiring the Emperor's new suit of clothes. The commoners, assembled by the thousands, applauded him. They had never seen anything so beautiful.

But suddenly a little girl, holding her mother's hand in the throng, pointed at the Emperor and said, "Mommy, the Emperor is naked! He has no clothes on at all!"

—"THE EMPEROR'S NEW CLOTHES"

No one believed the little girl. Her mother shushed her and she was forgotten. The people went on admiring the Emperor's new clothes.

—JUSTINE'S EMENDATION, AS TOLD TO SUSAN

Boston
April 11

OF THE fourteen young girls who had been abducted in Boston, all were accounted for except one: the girl who had accompanied Jane Christensen the night she went out to see *Terms of Endearment* and did not return.

Her name was Justine Lawrence. According to Jane Christensen's mother, Justine was never seen again after the night she and Jane disappeared.

Karen Embry was at a crossroads in her investigation. She could drop the Boston connection now and concentrate her efforts on finding out where Susan Campbell was. Or she could continue her inquiry into the past—and perhaps find a more indirect route to Susan.

Karen decided to follow the instinct that had guided her journalistic career from the beginning. She would do the aggressive thing. Follow her own hunch, go for the big score, and damn the consequences.

The parents of Justine Lawrence were gone. The mother had committed suicide years ago. The father, a notorious alcoholic, had disappeared.

Karen flew back to Boston and went to the Brookline neighborhood where Justine Lawrence had lived. She talked to the neighbors. All of them remembered Justine's mother, a friendly but neurotic woman, and her father, a nasty drunk who had noisy fights with his wife. A neighbor lady recalled that the wife often bore black-and-blue marks after their quarrels.

"Justine, too, once in a while," she said. "I couldn't swear to it, but I got the feeling he hit her, too. That was why Justine was a little bit wild, I think. The family wasn't very good for her."

Unfortunately, there was no sibling for Karen to look for. Justine Lawrence had been an only child.

But Karen managed to locate a sister of Justine's late mother. The woman's name was Grace Cowlings. A widow who lived alone in North Boston, Grace was a devout Catholic still shamed by the memory of her sister's suicide and still hopeful that Justine was alive somewhere.

The Lawrences' house had long since been sold along with all the furniture, but Grace Cowlings had kept the few personal possessions her sister left behind. These included photo albums and family mementos. She let Karen look through the albums, which depicted Justine as a little girl and later a junior high school cheerleader.

"Justine was a good girl," Grace said. "She became a problem when she hit her teens, but that was mostly high spirits. And her father's troubles, of course. He was pretty much out of control by then, and there were terrible fights between the parents. Justine had good grades, she found time for her cheerleading and her studies, and she was quite religious."

"I don't suppose there are any home movies of Justine. Anything like that," Karen asked.

"Not from the later years, I don't think," Mrs. Cowlings said. "Dick broke the video camera, and they never bought another one. I might have some tapes of Justine when she was little."

She went up in the attic and returned with a couple of videotaped compendiums of the eight-millimeter home movies the Lawrences had made. The tapes showed Justine as a pretty little girl with pigtails, and later as a slightly overweight seventh-grader singing in her class's performance of *The Pirates of Penzance*. There were few close-ups of Justine's face. Her voice was that of a child.

"That was the year Dick smashed the camera," Mrs. Cowlings said with unconcealed contempt for her sister's husband. "There isn't any more."

"How about Justine's personal effects?" Karen asked.

"Yes, I have a few. I saved them in case we ever found her." Mrs. Cowlings left the room again and was gone for several minutes. Karen glanced around the sad blue-collar house with its overstuffed furniture and family portraits. It reminded her uncomfortably of the house she herself had grown up in. She needed a drink badly. She also needed a cigarette, but it was easy to see from the lack of ashtrays and the smell of the room that no one had smoked here in twenty years, if ever.

Mrs. Cowlings returned with a cardboard box full of Justine's belongings. There were dolls, a diary, some snapshots of friends, a few report cards. There were also several books, including a biology textbook that had been pointlessly saved. There was an ancient Walkman that dated from the 1980s, and a small collection of audiotapes. Most were prerecorded: Carly Simon, Blondie, Bruce Springsteen. Two were blank tapes without labels.

Karen eagerly looked at the diary. Unfortunately it was a dead end, the last entry having been made when Justine was a ten-year-old in grade school. She found a handful of letters held together by a rubber band. These also were useless, dating from the girl's junior high school years.

Karen turned to the two blank audiotapes.

"Do you know what's on these?" she asked Mrs. Cowlings.

"I have no idea," the woman said. "I don't listen to music."

Karen picked up the Walkman. "I don't suppose you would have a couple of double-A batteries around," she asked.

"Let me look." Mrs. Cowlings got up with a sigh and went into the kitchen. She returned a few moments later with a package of batteries.

Karen got the little machine working and put on the first of the tapes. It contained rock music, obviously dubbed from a friend's tape player or compact disc player.

The second tape contained what sounded like a home recording of a slumber party or other gathering. The sound quality was poor, but the voices were clearly audible. They were all girls, talking and laughing uproariously as music played in the background.

"Tell me if you hear Justine's voice," Karen said to Mrs. Cowlings.

On the tape the girls were exchanging stories and gossip. At one point the music in the background was turned off and a TV was turned on. The girls continued their conversation over the sound of the TV.

"Wait," said Mrs. Cowlings suddenly.

"Yes?" Karen said, stopping the tape.

"Turn it back a little."

Karen rewound the tape. One of the girls was shushing the others. "Shut up, you ninnies," she said. "I hear my mother. Shut *up!*"

Mrs. Cowlings pointed at the little machine. "That's Justine," she said. "I would know that voice anywhere." Tears had welled in her eyes. "Poor girl . . ."

Karen played more of the tape. The raucous slumber party went on for a few more minutes. Then more dubbed music came on. She fast-forwarded in search of more conversation, but there was none.

"Mrs. Cowlings," she asked, "would you mind if I borrowed this tape? I'd like to play it for a friend of mine who does professional sound recording. If Justine is still out there somewhere, it might help me find her."

The woman looked skeptical. "Go right ahead," she said. "That's mighty old, though."

Karen's friend, a recording engineer who often worked for news departments, had some experience in voiceprint technology. She thought he might be able to enhance the recording of Justine's voice and possibly to print it.

"Mrs. Cowlings, you've been a great help," she told the woman. "I'll get this tape back to you. If I find Justine, I'll let you know right away."

"Good luck," the woman told her. "It's been fifteen years, and the police haven't done a thing. You're the first person who's cared."

Karen took her leave with a handshake and a hopeful smile. She got into her rented car and immediately lit up a cigarette.

The car had a combined tape/CD player. Karen pushed the audiotape into the player and listened to the voices of the girls.

"Bullshit. You idiot . . ."

"Shut up, you ninnies! I hear my mother. Shut UP!"

Karen closed her eyes, inhaling the smoke with a deep sigh. Then she re-wound the tape for a few seconds.

"Jane's got a boyfriend, Jane's got a boyfriend . . ."
"Bullshit. You idiot . . ."
"Shut up, you ninnies! I hear my mother. Shut UP!"

Karen had spent her entire life as a reporter listening to voices. She had scribbled down official comments at news conferences, strained to hear snatches of overheard conversation in restaurants and hallways, importuned reluctant phone sources to repeat their mumbled, evasive answers to her questions.

Indeed, she would ask her friend to enhance the tape. But his results would only confirm something she knew already.

The voice of the giggly teenaged girl on the tape was the same as that of Susan Campbell's crank caller. Younger, more innocent, sweeter—but the same.

It was also the voice that had made the demand that Michael Campbell refuse to become vice president of the United States.

In all probability Susan was with Justine Lawrence now.

If she was alive, that is.

6 1

"I WOKE up under an underpass on the interstate, about a hundred miles from Boston," Justine said.

The roar of a plane taking off outside made the windows rattle, but Susan had no trouble hearing Justine's low voice. She had learned to tune out the continual airport noise.

"I didn't know who I was," Justine went on. "At first I barely knew *what* I was. I was like an animal, just breathing and trembling from the cold. But somehow I got on my feet and staggered to the nearest rest area. I locked myself in a stall in the ladies' room and curled up in the corner, not moving, just sitting. I drifted in and out of sleep. The drug was very powerful. I felt like an insect that somebody had sprayed with a giant can of Raid. Paralyzed."

Susan sat on the bed, listening. She had pulled the comforter over her, for she felt cold. Her eyes never left Justine.

"Eventually a janitor knocked on the stall and told me I had to leave," Justine went on. "Thank God, it was a woman. When she saw the condition I was in, she took me home with her. She wanted to call the police, but I wouldn't let her. I didn't tell her what had happened. I think she just assumed I was a rape victim."

Justine took a deep breath.

"She was very nice. She had kids of her own. She had a house in a little town not too far from where I woke up. I stayed with her for a couple of days. Her husband wasn't home; he worked on the road. A truck driver or something. She fed me soup, she helped me wash. She seemed to realize I couldn't talk, so she did all the talking. She wasn't educated, but she was quite understanding.

"If she had asked me who I was, I doubt that I could have told her. I was in a daze. That whole period is still fuzzy to me. In a sense I never completely came out of the drug. It left me changed. Why it didn't kill me, I don't know. It killed the others, or at least ruined them."

Justine looked at Susan.

"I was content to stay where I was, for the time being at least. But then I heard her talking on the phone to somebody about me. I was afraid it was the police. I ran away that night. I hitchhiked into the country. I headed south for the warm climate. I ended up in North Carolina. I was just wandering the interstates, sleeping at rest stops. It was amazing no one raped me during that time. I hitched rides with truck drivers, strange men . . . I don't know. Some sort of providence was watching over me." She shrugged.

"One day I was walking along the side of a road when a woman stopped in a pickup and asked me if I needed a ride. I still wasn't able to talk much, but she got the idea I was shell-shocked in some way. She had a small farm nearby, and she took me there. She had two daughters and a son who was in the army. Her husband had abandoned the family. They were dirt poor. I went to work for her—cleaning, working in the fields, cooking, whatever she needed—and got my room and meals in return.

"It wasn't a bad life. She was a Southerner, her people had been poor for generations. Hiring a drifter to help out was not a new thing to her. She managed to put food on the table, and she was actually rather genteel in her way. I got to know her daughters. They were nice girls."

Justine got up and stood looking at the blacked-out window.

"I stayed with them for about a year. I had total amnesia about who I was, where I had come from, what had happened to me. I kind of enjoyed it, the amnesia. I felt like I was free of the entanglement of an identity. I would joke with her children about it. They were fascinated by me. They thought I was a sort of free spirit, a freak.

"Then the husband came back and they reconciled. He didn't want me around, so I had to leave. The wife dropped me off at the bus station. She gave me a hundred dollars. I didn't want to take it, but she insisted. The money was in small bills and change, obviously taken from her cookie jar or somewhere. I was very touched by that. I couldn't express it, though. I just took the money and got on the bus."

She paused for a moment, thinking.

"I wasn't sure what I was going to do. I was beginning to have flashbacks to who I was. But every time my identity occurred to me, the memory of what had happened to Jane and me would try to come back. So I would for-get, or repress—whatever you want to call it. My mind was sort of going in and out, like one of those electric circuits that isn't quite connected."

She looked at her wrists.

"I took the bus to Charleston. I was in the bus station when I tried suicide for the first time. I was sitting in the waiting room on one of those molded plastic chairs. I saw the pop-top from a can on the floor. I picked it up and took it into the ladies' room and cut my wrists with it. I didn't do a very good job. They found me and took me to a hospital. There was a woman there, a psychiatric social worker named Marie Gervasi. She got them to release me into her custody and she took me to the clinic where she worked. It was a rape and sex abuse clinic.

"Marie was the first person who really tried to talk to me about myself. She knew something had happened to me. She tried to help me remember. She got me some counseling with a doctor friend of hers, a psychiatrist. A woman, Dr. Henley. She spent a lot of time on me, a lot of appointments. She was very kind.

"I finally remembered everything, but I didn't tell the doctor the truth. I just told her I had been raped back home. Gang-raped—I did tell her that much. She tried to help me work through it. To make me understand that it wasn't my fault. Sometimes I wish I had told her what really happened. She was so nice, so caring . . ."

Justine looked at Susan. "But I'm glad it worked out the way it did. I kept it to myself. Now the only people in the world who know about it are me and you. That's the way I want it."

Susan nodded, not objecting. She was past the point of protesting Justine's decisions. She just wanted to understand her.

"I eventually got a GED and did a program at a local junior college," Justine went on. "I saw the way Marie helped young girls who had been hurt, and I decided that's what I wanted to do."

She glanced at Susan. "This was around the time you were first becoming a political wife."

These words stung Susan. This woman had known Michael at the same time Susan knew him. While Susan was marrying a hero, Justine was fighting to survive. These were the two destinies Michael had wrought. Justine saw the distress in Susan's eyes and looked away again, at the blacked-out window.

"I got a degree. I became a counselor. I helped take care of girls and women who couldn't handle the world for whatever reason. It was good work for me. It was fulfilling. Nothing is better for your own pain than to help someone else."

Justine was looking down at her scarred wrists.

"Marie stayed with us until she got married again—did I mention that she was divorced?—to a man whose daughter had been a client of ours at the clinic. They moved away. I stayed. Then our funding dried up, and we had to close.

"I sent my résumé around to other clinics and hospitals, but it was hard to find a job. My résumé was too full of holes. I couldn't give my full history. The fact that I had been a patient and had attempted suicide didn't help either."

She looked down at her wrists. "All of a sudden the temptation to end my life came back, very strong. The pain was so great, the memories . . . I made up my mind I was going to kill myself for real. I had a little apartment with a gas stove. I sealed up all the windows and doors. I bought a bottle of vodka. I was going to get stinking drunk, turn on the gas, and pass out. Then something happened."

"What?" Susan asked.

Justine smiled at her guest's curiosity.

"I had the TV on—I was going to leave it on so the neighbors would hear the sound and think I was still all right in there—and there was a talk show on with several politicians talking about the economy. One of them was your husband. I started looking at him, listening to him.

"Then, just like that, I saw that I couldn't kill myself. Seeing Michael Campbell's face, hearing his voice, was like an epiphany to me. He was an ambitious young politician. He was charming, well spoken. Everyone admired him because of the Olympics. He was going places. He had a beautiful young wife. The sun shone on everything he touched. While I, his victim, was about to kill myself."

Justine looked at Susan through narrowed eyes. "I was going to get out of his way, just like every other obstacle that had ever stood in his path. He would go on to greater and greater things, with everyone loving him and looking up to him. And no one would know about the lives he had destroyed."

She shook her head. "I decided I was not going to go quietly, I was not going to let him get away with it. I poured the vodka down the drain. I took the sealing tape off the doors and windows. I never did turn on the gas. I had a reason to live now. I had a mission. Your husband gave it to me."

Susan said nothing. Her eyes were riveted to Justine.

"I found another job in a counseling center," Justine resumed. "I became very skilled as a counselor. There are rape victims, girls and women, who still keep in touch with me. I've worked in several places; they're always having funding trouble. Depends on who's in the White House."

She turned to Susan. "And I studied your husband. I studied him the way a biographer studies a famous person whose origins are obscure, whose private life is a mystery. I learned everything there was to know about Judd Campbell, about the Campbell family. I learned about you. About your mother, about your father abandoning you. About your courtship. About Michael's friends."

Her expression grew colder.

"Eventually I learned more about his connection with Colin Goss. I found out how far back it went, how deep it went. It was easier for me, you see, because I already knew from my own experience that they were involved with each other. I didn't have any scales over my eyes, like other people. I didn't have to overcome my own doubts. That's more than half the battle, you know, in the search for truth."

She got up and stood looking down at Susan.

"I found out that the building where Jane and I had been raped was Goss's Boston headquarters. I did some research about Goss. I learned things that shocked even me. I thought I knew most of what there was to know about sexual perversion, about abuse, about cruelty. Goss surprised me. He wrote the book on sadism."

She touched Susan's hand gently. Susan saw the burns on Justine's arm as she felt the warmth of her touch.

Impulsively Susan asked, "What about love?"

"Love?" Justine asked. "What do you mean?"

"Have you ever loved someone? Been in love?" Susan asked. Then, "Made love?"

"I haven't had sex since that night, if that's what you mean," Justine said. "I was a virgin that night. So was Jane. We were very young. Babes in the woods. As for love . . . When you go through a thing like that, especially at a tender age, you stop believing that anyone could ever love you. The taint goes all the way to your core. You don't even dream of love. That door is closed."

There was a long silence. Tears welled in Susan's eyes as she pondered the depth of the wound inflicted on Justine. The tiny cuts at her wrists, the burns on her arms were mere ripples on the surface of a black ocean of pain. They reminded Susan of the Holocaust survivors she had met in Michael's company. They looked just like anyone else, they talked in normal tones. But underneath they were scarred in a way that ordinary people could not imagine. Empathizing with them was difficult, because their suffering took you out of your depth.

Justine seemed to be reading Susan's thoughts.

"You're a good girl," she said. "You feel the pain of others. You care about people."

Susan said nothing. She was staring at the scarred hand that held hers.

"I've been watching you all these years," Justine said. "I've seen you with your husband, I've heard the way you talk about him. You're not happy with him, are you? Sexually, I mean."

Susan hesitated before answering. Then she breathed a hopeless sigh. "I'm frigid."

"Were you always?" Justine's voice was gentle.

"I don't know. I don't remember."

"Were there other men before Michael?"

"Yes. Boys, students . . . But they didn't mean anything. Michael was the first, in the only important way." Susan looked at Justine. "I was young, too," she added. "He's all I've ever really known."

Justine patted her hand. "Poor Susan," she said. "You have a lot to overcome."

She stood back. "We haven't much time. You need to know the plan."

"What plan?" Susan asked, a fearful note creeping into her voice.

"After Michael gets into the White House, the president will be eliminated," Justine said. "Michael will become the youngest president in American history."

Susan's eyes were wide. She could not take in what she was hearing. Not even after everything that had happened this year.

"Michael will replace the president's Cabinet members," Justine went on. "He will bring Colin Goss into his administration. Some sort of non-Cabinet post that doesn't need Senate approval. Foreign policy or national security, something like that. He'll use as an excuse Goss's record on terrorism. The pundits will say that Michael is trying to gain the confidence of the voters by appointing someone tough on terrorism at this sensitive time."

Justine stood looking at Susan. "The rest of the plan is too terrible for me to tell you today. Suffice it to say that the illness, the Pinocchio Syndrome, is part of it. A great many people will die if Michael Campbell becomes president."

Susan was thoughtful, staring straight in front of her.

"So that's why you took me," she said.

Justine nodded. "Michael Campbell is famous as a man who loves his wife. The kidnappers of Susan Campbell have asked him to do a simple thing in order to get her back—to refuse the president's nomination. Any loving husband would agree to that. The president can always find another man for vice president, it isn't that crucial a position.

"But Michael can't refuse. He and Goss are too deep into the plan to back out now. Everything hinges on Michael becoming vice president. Remember also that in two years, or six years, conditions may change. There could be war, a depression, whatever. The other party may be in the White House. This is the moment. Michael must become vice president. That's why Everhardt and Palleschi and Stillman were removed. That's why Michael will refuse to withdraw."

Susan was looking at Justine. "Am I going to die?"

Justine shook her head. "No. Not if I can help it. But when Michael refuses my demand, he'll *assume* you're going to die. That's part of my plan."

Susan lay back against the pillows like a very sick hospital patient. Justine's revelations were like so many body blows.

"How do you know all these things?" she asked weakly.

"I know them because I have eyes to see them." Justine smiled. "Have you ever heard the parable of the emperor's new clothes?"

Susan nodded. "Yes. The emperor has been duped into buying a suit of clothes that is supposed to be very beautiful. But the clothes don't exist. The emperor is really naked."

"And when the emperor shows off his new clothes to the courtiers and commoners of his kingdom," Justine finished for her, "they all bow down in homage to the beautiful clothes. Except for one small child who points at the Emperor and cries out, '*The Emperor is naked! He has no clothes on at all!*' That's how the story goes."

Susan nodded.

Justine smiled. "The child cries out the truth because it is naive, it is innocent. All those around it are motivated by self-interest or fear or both. That's why the cry is so scandalous."

She looked at Susan.

"But it's only a parable, Susan. In the real world, the child would be shushed by its mother. None of the commoners would heed its little voice. The courtiers would be too far away to hear. The emperor's new clothes would continue to be admired by all. That's how the story would end."

Susan was listening intently. Her eyes were locked on Justine's.

"I am that child the world will ignore," Justine said. "When I die, my voice will be silenced. No one will know the truth about Michael Campbell."

"You're going to die?" Susan asked.

"Oh, yes," Justine smiled. "I won't come out of this alive. He won't allow it. Neither will Goss. They're coming to find me right now. I'm Lee Harvey Oswald in this scenario, Susan. Jack Ruby is coming to find me, and no one will stop him. I'll be dead, my voice will be stilled."

"How can you be so sure?" Susan asked.

Justine did not answer.

Susan had now begun to understand. "And me?" she asked.

"You'll be the one to stop him," Justine said. "They can't make your voice go unheard. That's why you're here."

6 2

Alexandria, Virginia
April 12

JOSEPH KRAIG sat in the battered armchair in his living room, the day's classified briefing before him. The search for Susan Campbell was not going well. Experts had analyzed the audiotape of the abductors' demand without success. The noise of the cheap recorder had obscured much of the background sound. The voice of the abductors' spokesperson, whoever she was, had been printed. But there was no library of voiceprints to match the fingerprint files that identified millions of individuals.

A thousand terrorists and would-be terrorists had been arrested and questioned in connection with Susan's disappearance. More than a few had been subjected to rough treatment by state and federal law enforcement agents frantic to save Susan at all costs. Interpol, in conjunction with the intelligence agencies of the major Western powers, had arrested as many more, particularly in the Arab world, and grilled those already in custody, using methods the Americans did not dare employ.

The results were nil. No one with a political motive for Susan's abduction could be found. Her whereabouts remained a mystery.

The nation waited for Michael Campbell's response to the kidnappers'

demand. So far the abduction of Susan Campbell had not hurt the president
in the polls. But if Michael were to withdraw the president's stock would
probably drop again, and the Colin Goss forces would renew their assault on
the White House.

The media resounded with talking heads debating the issue and making
predictions about the outcome. Michael's image, or that of Susan, was on
every TV screen in America. But only Joe Kraig knew that Michael was sequestered in his bedroom in Judd Campbell's Chesapeake Bay house, refusing sedation, staring out the window in a daze. Kraig visited him almost
every day and found him completely uncommunicative. The loss of Susan
had left him an empty shell.

As for Kraig himself, he was having more and more trouble sleeping. Devoured by his worry about Susan, he remained awake into the wee hours. In
the past week he had taken to intentionally staying up until two or three, just
to tire himself out. It wasn't really working, but he kept at it. It was better
than going to bed at midnight and lying awake until five or six.

It was 1:30 A.M. when a soft knock came at the front door. Irritated, Kraig
strode through the living room to the foyer and flung the door open. Karen
Embry stood in the darkness. She was wearing a skirt with a cotton top, no
coat.

"What are you doing here at this hour?" Kraig asked.

"I thought you'd be up. I want to talk." The reporter's no-nonsense manner had not changed.

"Are you sober?" Kraig asked cruelly.

"Yes, but I don't want to be." She smiled.

Kraig shook his head in annoyance. Nowadays his solitude was all he had
left, and that only for a few hours each night.

"Come on," she said. "It's cold out here."

"Why didn't you wear a coat?"

"Come on, Kraig. Let me in, for Christ's sake."

Kraig stood back to let her in. She darted gracefully through the door, as
though afraid he might slam it in her face if she didn't hurry.

She preceded him into the living room, where the TV was tuned to CNN,
the volume turned all the way down.

Karen stood with her weight on one leg, half turned toward the TV. She looked surprisingly vital, even sporty. She had brought a breath of the cool night air in with her. Her hair was its usual schizoid self, full-bodied and pretty, but needing a trim.

"What are you drinking?" Kraig asked.

"Bourbon if you have it," she said.

He mixed her a stiff Early Times over ice and put it on the coffee table. She took a long sip as he opened his bottle of Guinness stout.

"Mind if I smoke?" she asked.

"Why should I mind?"

She lit up a Newport and left the pack on the table along with her small butane lighter. She sat down cross-legged on the couch, the smoke curling around her head.

"My parents were both drunks," she said. "Did I tell you that?"

Kraig shook his head. "You must have forgotten to mention it."

She smiled, taking another swig of the bourbon. "My mother was half Chinese and half German. My father was half Jewish and half Irish. They were both alcoholics. He killed himself in a one-car accident. After that she married an Italian guy, a car salesman. Also a drunk. He drank himself to death."

"And your mother?"

"Died of heart failure," Karen said. "Before she was fifty."

"I wondered what your ethnicity was," Kraig said. "You're very exotic looking."

Karen darted him a small glance. "I suppose, yeah. I always thought of myself as a mutt."

Now that she had told him about her background he saw the faint Asian tinge of her eyes, as well as the delicate Semitic undercurrent that graced her fair Irish skin. The knowledge made her seem prettier to him. More vulnerable.

"Why so much booze?" Kraig asked.

"Reporters are all drunks," she said. "With a few exceptions who are downer addicts or speed freaks. It's related to the alcoholism of writers. We are writers, in our way." She grimaced. "Frustrated writers."

She puffed at her cigarette. There was, Kraig reflected, a desperation about her far worse than his own, but so controlled, so camouflaged by her competent exterior that it was hard to see.

"I read an article in a medical journal once," she said, "in which the author argued that the gene for writing might be somehow involved with the gene for drinking. He wasn't a geneticist so he couldn't prove it, but I thought the argument had merit." She swirled the bourbon in her glass, watching the ice cubes bump against each other. "Writing makes drinking worse."

"And vice versa?" Kraig asked.

She shrugged. "Maybe."

Kraig looked at her in silence, the bottle of Guinness in his hand.

"What about you, Kraig?" she asked. "Did you ever flirt with booze?"

"Not really. There was a time when I graduated from one martini before dinner to three. Not long before my divorce. The fights with my wife got out of control, and I quit."

Karen smiled. "You're an amateur. I'll bet you never even had a DUI."

Kraig smiled. "You're right."

The reporter looked thoughtful. "The little scares," she said. "Every drinker has had them. You crack up the car, you leave the stove on all night, you forget a cigarette burning in the ashtray . . . I know my way around the rough spots. I'm very careful. I never get bombed until I'm safe at home and free of responsibilities. It's a preparation for bed, really. I get into the bath and have a few snorts. Then I go to sleep. You'd be surprised how many people have never seen me drunk. Colleagues, editors . . . They think I take a glass of chardonnay at dinner, and that's all." She grimaced. "What do we know about people?"

Kraig nodded. The words struck him at an uncomfortable tangent.

The reporter seemed to notice it.

"The girls I told you about in Boston," she said. "One girl seems to have been involved and to have escaped. Why, I don't know. I visited her aunt—her parents are dead. The aunt showed me some of the girl's memorabilia. Diaries, snapshots, things like that."

"Did it help?" Kraig asked.

"Not much." Karen dragged at her Newport, intentionally not mentioning the audiotape she had copied. She was not sure whether she should tell Kraig about it.

"So?" he asked.

"So, I think she's out there somewhere. I'd like to find her. She was with the other girl, Jane Christensen, the night Jane was drugged, or whatever. This girl, Justine, might be an eyewitness to what happened."

Kraig was looking at her steadily. "If anything happened."

Karen shook her head with a resigned smile. "You think I'm crazy, don't you?" she asked.

Kraig sat back in his chair. "I don't think you're crazy. I think you're a reporter who is after a hot story. At the back of your mind you're thinking of it as a Pulitzer Prize winner, a book. A scoop." He shrugged. "I'm a federal agent trying to get a political leader's wife home alive. That's a different thing. A different agenda."

"The truth is the truth, isn't it?" she asked.

Kraig lifted his Guinness to his lips, but did not drink.

"I'm beginning to wonder," he said. "Maybe it depends on who's looking for it. On why they care. Or who they're trying to help."

Karen stubbed out her cigarette. His relativism annoyed her. She was almost tempted to play him the tape of Justine Lawrence's youthful voice, just to get his attention. But she held back.

Kraig was watching her. He thought about the smell of nicotine, the way it must cling to her hair. He wondered how she got it out. He wondered if she even tried.

"Something happened back there," she said. "The voice on Susan's phone told her that. If it weren't for that voice, I wouldn't be pursuing the connection."

"That's your right," Kraig said. "It may make a great story."

"Don't patronize me, Kraig." Anger flashed in the reporter's green eyes. Kraig thought of her Irish blood.

"Sorry," he said. "I'm not myself."

"Anyway," she said, lighting another Newport, "it's more than you've got." She looked at him. "Isn't it?"

"Maybe it is."

"What *do* you have?"

"I'm not at liberty to tell you that."

She gave a soft laugh. "So be it."

She finished her drink and put the glass down. "I'd better go."

He guessed she wanted another drink, but was sick of his company. They were at cross-purposes, in more ways than one. She was an aggressive woman, hell bent on getting what she wanted. Her very energy tired him, filled him with depressive thoughts. Yet something about her was endearing.

He got up and went to her side. He reached for the glass as though to take it for a refill. She held it up. He put the glass on the table, took both her hands and lifted her to her feet. He kissed her. He put his arms around her, feeling the slender back under her cotton blouse. She seemed much smaller and softer than he had expected.

Her lips tasted good. The smell of tobacco mingled with something sweeter on her breath. Her hands were around his waist, holding him but not pulling him closer.

Suddenly he was very hard under his pants. It was too late to hide it from her. His breath came short.

"It's all right," she murmured, patting his shoulder. There was something tender and almost pitying in her manner. Kraig let himself be comforted by it.

She drew his face to hers and kissed him, slipping her tongue into his mouth. That was too much for Kraig. He picked her up like a doll and took her to the bedroom. He pulled the cotton top over her head and removed the skirt. Her hair tumbled over the white skin of her shoulders. She helped him with the bra, and he saw small breasts, pale, with sweet little areolas around the nipples. He kissed them.

She lay back to watch him pull the panties down her legs. In her nakedness she looked very young. He took off his clothes, fumbling with the belt and zipper, and lay down beside her.

He cradled her to his chest. She rested her head against him. Her thigh grazed his hip. He kissed her again. He was wet already—even as he realized this her hand was discovering it.

A tremor came over him, and he was inside her before he knew it, out of control and pumping madly. She wrapped her legs around him and buried her fingers in his hair. He came too soon, but she didn't seem to mind.

They made love three times. Each time he tried to let her go, and couldn't do it. He kept pulling her back, holding her head against his chest, embracing her, squeezing the slim shoulders with needful hands. He couldn't get enough of her.

She came the second time, her orgasm sounding as a soft thoughtful gasp in her throat. The third time they both savored it. Her fingers caressed him delicately, inquiringly, and he stayed inside her a long time, stroking slow and deep until the paroxysm overtook them at the same instant.

Kraig had not felt this satisfied in years. He drank in her messy unhappiness, the smell of the nicotine in her hair, the liquor on her lips. He was turned on by her loneliness and by a soft, innocent quality that hid behind it. For the first time he really liked her.

They slept in each other's arms. Kraig awoke with a hangover, though he had drunk little. He staggered to the bathroom naked and bumped into Karen as she came out wrapped in a towel.

"Aspirin," he said.

"I left it out for you," she offered with a smile.

He took three aspirin and padded back to bed. He lay with his head on her breast. She smelled fresh and sweet now. She must have showered and washed her hair while he slept. She cradled him to her breast, running a soft finger over his throbbing temples.

He indulged himself by not looking at the clock. He knew it was early. This would be a long day. He would be tired. But it had been worth it. Karen Embry was, in her way, a very beautiful woman. A man could become strongly addicted to that subtle body. He rested a hand on her thigh.

After a while she disengaged herself and went to make coffee. He lay with his eyes closed, waiting. She returned with orange juice in little glasses and coffee on a tray.

"Milk and Equal, right?" she asked. He nodded with a groan, his eyes still closed.

She stirred it for him and he drank greedily, almost scalding his lips. She turned on the little bedroom TV as though by reflex, but considerately avoided turning up the volume. Susan Campbell's face was on CNN, the same file footage Kraig had seen a hundred times in the last two weeks. The light of the screen hurt his eyes. He moved his head so that Karen's slender back obscured it.

When the cup was finished he lay back against the pillows. Karen was looking at him. She was smiling, but the softness of the night had left her eyes.

"You're in love with her, aren't you?" she asked.

Kraig narrowed his eyes. "With who?"

"Susan Campbell."

He closed his eyes. This was no time for cross-examinations.

"What made you think that?" he asked.

"Everything."

"Last night?" he asked.

"Last night, too. But everything."

He sighed. Women. Their radar was unlike anything in the arsenal of men.

She was right. But he wasn't going to admit it.

"She's a friend," he said.

"Uh-huh." Karen lay down beside him and closed his eyes with a gentle hand, as though to shield him from unpleasant truths as well as from her own inquiry.

He lay in silence, his hand still on her leg. Weak as he felt right now, his sex stirred at the contact with her.

Suddenly she tensed. "Just a minute." She had seen something on the TV and was looking for the remote. She darted off the bed, a naked Peter Pan with no shadow, and turned up the volume.

The legend "Special Report" was on the screen over the face of Michael Campbell. An anchorperson was saying, "A family spokesman made the announcement fifteen minutes ago. Senator Campbell will give his response in a public statement at his Senate office at nine o'clock this morning. For nearly six days the public and Campbell's political colleagues have waited for his answer to the abductors of his wife. It has been a tense vigil . . ."

Karen was putting on her clothes. "I have to go."

Kraig was out of bed, his head throbbing again. "Christ," he said, "why didn't they call me?"

"It must have happened just now," Karen said. "Don't worry, you'll get there in time."

Their tenderness was gone. She spoke to him as a fellow professional. Already she was pulling the blouse over her head. Her eyes were hard, her hands were quick. Kraig had sat up, and he watched as she hurriedly combed her hair.

"Jesus," she said, "I look like shit."

Kraig smiled. She was still barefoot, the pretty calves he had caressed last night disappearing now under the skirt. Her profanity was the anthem transforming her from a human girl into a hard-as-nails reporter.

"Wait." He got up and embraced her. He breathed in the fragrance of her wet hair. For a brief second he felt her hands pet him, almost as they had done last night, but not quite.

Then she was leaving.

"Take a shower," she called over her shoulder. "You'll feel better. Thanks for the bed."

He started to say something, but didn't bother. She was gone already.

In the car Karen lit up a Newport and turned on the radio. The Campbell story was the big news. She realized that since the demand came in she had been on tenterhooks, wondering how Campbell would respond. In recent weeks she had come to feel that no one really knew him after all, that his personality was a mystery on which the entire political situation turned. She knew he was a brave man. Anyone who had seen the tapes of the Olympics knew that. But was he a good man? She wasn't so sure. Her contact with Susan Campbell, convincing her beyond doubt of Susan's basic goodness, had made her doubt that of the husband. The voice of the crank on Susan's phone had increased her suspicions. Her trip to Boston had not attenuated them.

As a reporter, Karen had long since given up her instinct to trust people. Believing the worst, she felt, was rarely a mistake. It was good protection.

This morning before her shower she had watched Joe Kraig sleep. She had liked the way he made love. A passionate man, tired of controlling himself, wanting to give, wanting to trust. With him inside her she had felt less alone. That had weakened her defenses.

She was on the point of telling him about the tape of Justine Lawrence's slumber party. Once he heard it, he would know that the voice on Susan

Campbell's phone was a link to the past he had tried to ignore. He would also know it was the voice that had made the demand that Michael Campbell refuse the president's nomination. He would no longer deny the truth of Karen's arguments.

Then the news about Campbell's upcoming response had come on. Karen held back from Kraig, wanting to know how Campbell responded before she trusted Kraig with what she knew. It was only a hunch—perhaps an irrational fear—but she saw Kraig as part of the larger structure that included Campbell, the president, Colin Goss, and all those who lived by courting the favor of the public without telling the whole truth. Those who sought power, and wielded it by using only the truths that were useful to them.

For the first time it occurred to Karen that if Justine Lawrence had Susan Campbell and the authorities found out about it, the result might be disastrous. For Justine, certainly. For Susan, possibly. For the country . . .

There are moments in history, Karen knew, when those who know too much don't live to tell what they know. When the truth is buried under the fist of power, often never to see the light of day again.

With that thought in mind she had pulled back from Kraig, the man who had made her happy last night.

This was not a time for trust.

6 3

MICHAEL CAMPBELL made his announcement in a special broadcast from his Senate office. Every network and cable news station had interrupted programming to cover his speech as a special report. People everywhere stopped what they were doing to listen on car radios, TVs, Walkman radios. The broadcast was piped through speakers in discount houses, electronics stores, and even in the common areas of shopping malls.

Michael's face was drawn. He had obviously lost a lot of weight. But his eyes were clear and his voice strong.

After a brief preamble describing the abduction of his wife and the demand made by her captors, Michael described the role Susan had played in his life.

"I first met Susan Bellinger," he said, "when I was getting ready for my second spinal operation. I was a junior at Harvard, Susan was just starting at Wellesley. She was introduced to me by a friend of my roommate. She was the most beautiful girl I had ever seen. Today, after thirteen years of marriage, she is still the most beautiful woman I have ever seen."

Emotion forced him to pause.

"I have long since given up trying to put into words what it is about Susan that I find so irresistible," he said. "When you love someone, that person becomes part of you. You can't step back and see her as though she is an outsider. All I know is that Susan is the sweetest, kindest person I have ever known. She is also a quirky, exotic, funny, and supremely vulnerable person. For thirteen years I've had no more fervent wish than to grow old with her and have children with her. She is the only life I want."

He took a deep breath.

"In this country," he said, "we have faced more terror in the last few years than any nation should be expected to endure. We have seen our hopes for ourselves and our children endangered. We have seen our very institutions attacked. We have seen the world we spent two hundred years creating in this nation placed under siege. Now, through my situation and Susan's, we see our way of life held hostage once more."

Tears welled in Michael's eyes. With obvious effort he fought them back.

"I have spent the last four days asking my family, my friends, my colleagues, and above all my God what is the best thing for me to do in this situation. Obviously, this is the most difficult decision I have faced in my life, or will ever face. I would gladly sacrifice my own life to bring Susan back to her family. Certainly I would end my political career today and spend the rest of my life as a private citizen, if only I could have her back.

"But the decision I face is not a personal one. The welfare of our nation rides on it. I cannot make the choice that is natural for me, if that choice places my country at risk. And in today's violent, unpredictable world my country is definitely at risk. It is crucial that every American do everything in his power to safeguard the great experiment in freedom which our founding fathers launched, and which we have collectively pursued."

Michael paused. He swallowed. He seemed unable to overcome the catch in his throat. But he kept his eyes on the camera.

"If we have learned one lesson from the political events of the last forty years," he said, "that lesson is that we cannot negotiate with terrorists. Terrorism is more than capable of destroying every freedom we cherish, if we allow it to do so. Our free society is only as strong as the will of every American to defend it. Accordingly, I have made a difficult but necessary decision. I will not give in to the demand made by my wife's abductors by withdrawing my name from consideration for vice president of the United States. If the Senate confirms my nomination I will gladly join the president in working to make sure that our nation continues to grow and prosper as a symbol of freedom and justice in this new century."

The broadcast went on for another three minutes, but the die had been cast. Reporters rushed to get the story into early editions. Network and cable commentators launched into discussions of Michael's speech and its repercussions, not only for himself and Susan, but for the political future of America and its allies.

———

JUSTINE LAWRENCE turned off the little TV in Susan's room and disconnected the 75-ohm antenna wire she had brought in to connect the TV to the cable for the broadcast. Susan watched in silence, sitting on the bed.

Justine turned to Susan before leaving.

"As I told you," she said.

Susan was silent, looking at the dark screen.

"I recorded it," Justine said. "The tape is still in the VCR. Watch it again if you like." She thought for a moment. "Watch his eyes."

Susan said nothing.

"I'm sorry," Justine said.

Then she left the room.

Susan's eyes followed Justine as she closed the door behind her. A look of desperate longing was on Susan's face, as though Justine were the only friend she had left in a dark, indifferent world. But she said nothing.

A long time passed before she rewound the tape to watch Michael's speech again.

She spent that time thinking.

6 4

Washington
April 15

DEATH OR LIFE.

There were only two choices, Karen thought. That truth applies to everyone who has experienced something unbearable. You choose either death or life.

Justine Lawrence was alive. The proof of that was her voice on Susan Campbell's phone, and on the tape sent to the media to demand that Michael Campbell refuse the vice presidency.

The amateur voiceprint technician Karen had consulted had no difficulty in matching the prints at dozens of points on the digital oscilloscope. Justine's voice had changed greatly over the years, but its underlying profile remained the same.

Justine had not died. She had lived. But where, and in what manner?

There was one clue. Justine had been a young girl, profoundly traumatized and no doubt physically and mentally damaged, when she began her journey into the future. If she survived, that survival had to be marked by what had happened to her. The trauma gave her a direction.

Karen thought about this. What kind of a life would a rape victim choose? How would she go about surviving?

From what she knew of Justine, Karen saw her as a competent, responsible girl. True, her parents' marital problems had affected her behavior as a young teenager. She was troubled. But she was a high achiever, a serious person. Under normal circumstances she would no doubt have finished college and gone on to some sort of professional career. A lawyer, a professor, a businesswoman.

But fate had intervened to change that direction. Justine was a victim. Her life was in shambles. The proof of this was that she never saw her parents again. She was sufficiently damaged to never return home.

Where did she go?

Karen assumed that Justine must have suffered severe mental problems from what had happened to her. Very possibly she attempted suicide, perhaps multiple times. She did not succeed, though. She was alive today, as one of Susan Campbell's captors.

Karen postulated that Justine must have left a trail in some mental health clinic, state hospital, or counseling center. As a patient who had survived and gotten better, or as a chronic patient.

Karen got online and searched out the mental health clinics and hospitals in the Boston area and around New England. She began canvassing the facilities by fax, phone, and e-mail, identifying herself as a reporter who was doing a story on female runaways and what had happened to them.

The weak spot in her procedure immediately became clear to her. The mental health facilities refused to identify any of their patients, past or present. Confidentiality was a key part of their business, after all.

Karen thought the matter over. It would be both time consuming and futile to try getting mental health people to provide information that they didn't want to reveal. Even the police would face a brick wall in such an inquiry.

But there was another possibility. Suppose Justine pulled herself together. Permanently damaged, sexually and emotionally, she survived. She lived an independent adult life. Not a normal one, perhaps. A life that led through unknown twists and turns to the abduction of Susan Campbell.

What about those intervening years? Where did Justine go, and what did she do?

Connect the dots, Karen thought.

It was worthwhile to postulate that Justine became, at least for a while, a mental health professional, either as a social worker, a tech, a nurse, or a psychologist or psychiatrist. After all, the best remedy for a person with ineradicable scars is to help other people who are in pain. If Justine was the kind of person Karen thought she was, she might have left a trail in the mental health field as a counselor.

Karen took the gamble. She began querying clinics and hospitals not about a former patient, but about a former staff member. A social worker, a volunteer, a mental health tech, even an orderly. She identified herself as a family member who needed to inform Justine Lawrence of the sad news that her mother had died. As the only surviving child, Justine had to sign some papers in order for the mother to be buried, Karen said.

At first her search led to nothing. Then it occurred to her that she was wrong to limit herself to the New England area. Since Justine had suffered her trauma in Boston, she probably would have put as much distance between herself and that locale as possible. Her breakdown, if it had occurred, and her ultimate rehabilitation would have occurred elsewhere.

Karen extended her search to the entire country and to Canada. The job was far too big for her to handle alone, so she called a canvassing service her editor had used in the past and had them do the legwork.

For two days nothing happened. Karen concentrated on other things. At the back of her mind was the disturbing thought that the trail she was following would lead nowhere.

But it turned out Karen had guessed right.

The canvassing service got an e-mail from a counseling clinic in Savannah, Georgia. The e-mail was signed by the clinic's director, a clinical psychologist named Marie Saylor, who thought she might have crossed paths with Justine Lawrence. Karen called the woman an hour after the arrival of the e-mail.

"I think I know the woman you're looking for," Dr. Saylor said. "She used a different name, but she was the right age. I was a psychiatric social worker at the time, at a clinic in Charleston."

"What name did she use?"

"Theresa. Theresa Manuel. I knew her when she was about eighteen. I would never have connected her with your subject if you hadn't included the photograph with your query. The picture you sent was taken when she was younger, but I recognized her. That's Theresa."

"You knew her as a counselor?" Karen asked.

"It's more complicated than that. She was a patient. She came to us after attempting suicide in a bus station by cutting her wrists. I met her in the hospital. She had been raped. Gang-raped, I believe. When she was released she came to our clinic. She was still terribly depressed and suicidal, but we kept her going until she began to improve. I had a lot of counseling sessions with her, and Dr. Henley, our director, did too."

"Where can I find Dr. Henley?" Karen asked.

"I'm afraid you can't. She died of cancer a few years back."

Karen suppressed a sigh. "Okay," she said. "What else can you tell me?"

"Theresa—I mean Justine—was a very strong girl. She improved steadily and told me she wanted to work as a counselor. She completed her GED while she was with us, and later got a master's in counseling. She was very good. Intelligent, committed, very understanding and empathetic with our young female patients. I was proud of her. She was a special person to me. When I got married and left the clinic I was sorry to leave her."

"You left the clinic?" Karen asked.

"Yes. We moved to Atlanta, then to Savannah. My husband is a tax attorney. I ended up getting a Ph.D. in psychology and working in other clinics, until I accepted the directorship here."

"Did you stay in touch with Justine?" Karen asked.

"Loosely, yes. I called her a few times to see how she was doing. Then the clinic closed down for lack of funding. I lost touch with Theresa—Justine—after that. I pretty much gave her up. I did hear from her once, a few years later. There was an article in *Newsweek* about mental health professionals, and they included a brief quote from me along with the fact that I was in Savannah. I got a card from Theresa telling me that she had enjoyed the article and wished me well."

"Where was the card from?" Karen asked.

"There was no return address. If there had been I would have written back to Theresa. As I say, she was quite special to me."

"And you never heard from her after that?"

"That's right. Never."

"Did you ever try looking her up in the directories of mental health professionals?"

"Yes, I did. No luck."

"How long ago was it that you got this card from her?"

"About six years ago."

Karen thought for a moment.

"Did you worry that she might try suicide again?" she asked.

"Frankly, yes." The other woman sounded worried. "She was a virgin at the time of the rape, she told me. She was very disturbed sexually. I don't think she ever had a sexual relationship after the episode. Not while I knew her anyway. There was a hopelessness in her, despite her effectiveness as a counselor. Yes, I always worried about Terry."

Karen said, "I certainly wish I could find her."

"You know, it occurs to me that I might have saved the card she sent. I have a couple of old shoeboxes where I keep old cards and letters. They're not organized in any way; I just throw in anything that has some personal meaning or value. Why don't I sort through them tonight? If I find the card I'll call you."

"I would appreciate that very much. Thank you for your time."

Karen hung up expecting little from Marie Saylor. But late that night she received a call from her.

"I found the card," the psychologist said. "I remember noticing the postmark, because I was worried about Terry and wondered where she might have gone and what she was doing."

"And where was it postmarked?" Karen asked.

"St. Louis. I remember it very clearly, because the stamp she used had a picture of the Arch in St. Louis."

Arlington, Virginia
April 15

LESLIE WAS at her health club, finishing a hard thirty-five-minute workout on the StairMaster.

The machine was in a row of ten, all occupied by sweating, breathless women who were driving themselves almost beyond their limits. Of the ten, Leslie was by far the most attractive, and she knew it. Her long hair was tied back in a ponytail. She wore spandex bike shorts over a leotard and white running shoes. In the mirror along the wall she had seen herself ogled by a dozen joggers. As usual, the women devoured her with their eyes even more hungrily than the men. It was envy, she knew, and not sexual desire. Women came here in the frustrating attempt to mold their bodies to a fantasy. Leslie was that fantasy in the flesh.

She was out of breath and covered with perspiration when she got off. She wiped the machine with her towel and took a long, slow walk around the track, ignoring the joggers who shot past her. Then she went to the locker room, stripped, wrapped a towel around herself and entered the women's sauna.

She would weigh herself tomorrow morning as usual. If she was above

115 she would eat nothing but salad and come back here for another long workout.

The TV in the sauna was set to CNN. The big news was that Secretary of the Interior Tom Palleschi had died. Though government spokesmen denied hotly that Palleschi was a victim of the Pinocchio Syndrome, polls showed that fewer than twenty-five percent of the American people accepted the government's story.

Palleschi's death threw a new light on Michael Campbell's refusal to give in to the demand made by his wife's captors. With Palleschi dead, Michael was a key to the stability of the administration—what remained of it, anyway. Yet Michael's nomination was now clouded by tragic circumstances. If he became vice president, it might be at the cost of his wife's life.

CNN showed the same piece of file tape of Susan that it had been showing since the beginning: a shot of Susan smiling a bit bemusedly on *The Oprah Winfrey Show* as Oprah laughed aloud at something Susan had said. As for Michael, he was shown sitting at the desk in his Senate office, where he had made his fateful response to the terrorists.

Leslie had not seen Michael in all this time, or heard a word from him. She was not offended by this; she understood that he was in a terrible situation, and no doubt surrounded by law enforcement and intelligence people. He could not make a phone call without being monitored in some way.

Leslie wished she could comfort him. Over the years she had come to feel that this was her body's main function as far as Michael was concerned: comfort, succor. Often she would lie for long minutes with his head on her breast, stroking his hair in silence. He was like a child who has lost his mother, and Leslie the substitute for that lost mother.

The night before Susan's disappearance Leslie had shared Michael's bed in a discreet San Diego hotel. Earlier in the evening she went to the War Memorial to hear his speech on the environment. She had found herself glancing around anxiously for suspicious-looking people in the crowd. Michael looked so vulnerable up on that platform. Like a sitting duck.

But Leslie, like everyone else, had misdirected her anxiety. It turned out that Susan Campbell, not Michael, was the one in danger.

Leslie had been surprised when Michael refused the abductors' demand.

She knew how much he loved Susan, how much he prized her. She fully expected that he would take himself out of the running and let the White House find another sucker. He would not let his wife die for the sake of politics.

Michael was passionately devoted to Susan. True, there was something ever so slightly official or formal about his veneration for her. As though she were someone to whom he dedicated himself as a faithful protector, rather than someone with whom he was intimate. Absent from his remarks about her was a husband's easygoing irony about his wife's weaknesses or peculiarities. He never criticized her at all. Some would see this attitude as a lack of real affection.

Leslie chalked it up to Michael's sexual unhappiness with Susan. His intense erotic need for Leslie left no doubt that he was not getting sexual satisfaction at home. Not that this was so unusual for a Washington husband—or for any husband. But with Michael the lack seemed more deep, more painful.

Sometimes Michael would come to Leslie with a look of such pent-up hunger in his eyes that she took pity on him and pulled him quickly into her bed. He made love with furious energy, and sometimes came too soon. She did not mind this. She enjoyed being wanted, she liked the privilege of being the woman who made him happy.

At other times, when he was less famished, he was very considerate of Leslie's own needs. He would touch and kiss her in all her favorite places, knowing from the rhythm of her sighs how excited she was becoming. He would enter her gently and stroke her with himself until her sex was aflame. On these occasions she rarely had fewer than three or four orgasms.

He was in every way a fine lover. Tender, considerate, patient. Not at all like most of the men she had known, who took their pleasure so peremptorily that they might be eating or urinating rather than fucking. Michael never forgot the fact that he was with a woman who had feelings of her own.

The only remarkable or unusual thing about her sexual history with him was the blindfold.

She had been his lover for about two months when he first brought it up. She was not shy about sexual kinks. She had done a few unusual things in her time. She was surprised when what he suggested was so innocent. He simply wanted her to put a blindfold on him and hide, naked, while he searched for her.

"If it's too stupid, forget it," he had said. He explained that the request had to do with a thing that had happened in his childhood. He had played the game with some little girl friends when he was nine or ten years old, and it had left a lasting impression on him.

Leslie went along. She put the blindfold on him and hid in a corner, watching as he moved slowly around the apartment or hotel room, searching for her. Always she was naked; at first he kept his clothes on, but over time he began to play the game naked too. She found herself turned on by the sight of him moving slowly toward her, his penis erect, his fingers feeling for her in the silence. Often by the time he actually touched her she was aroused herself, hot to get into bed as quickly as possible.

Eventually the game became a favorite form of foreplay, especially when they were not pressed for time. Michael was decidedly more ardent as a lover when they played it. Leslie did not begrudge him this innocent little kink.

She missed him now. Her body needed him. She had not had sex since her last time with him. In her own way she felt she was keeping a vigil too.

Leslie knew that his decision not to trade the vice presidency for Susan's return must have cost him a great deal. Frankly, she would not have thought him capable of it. Had the president influenced him? Or his father? Or had he made the decision based on his own convictions?

She shrugged, pulling the moist towel tighter around her breasts. Michael must have had a good reason.

Michael never did anything without a good reason.

JUSTINE LAWRENCE had abandoned her assumed name of Theresa Manuel when she worked as a mental health counselor at the Webster Groves Mental Health Clinic in St. Louis. She was using the name Susan Laurents.

She spent three years at the clinic, distinguishing herself as a professional and making a lasting impression on her patients and colleagues as a troubled, sad, certainly brilliant person. By now those who knew her were characterizing her as a prematurely aged young woman who looked at least ten years older than her age. Her face was lined, her skin sallow. The scars at her wrists told the story of her tortured emotional life. But she had a melancholy strength that impressed all those who crossed her path.

She made much the same impression in Meriden, Connecticut, where she spent two years at the Cheshire Stress Care facility. Her patients thought the world of her. Her colleagues found her hard to know, but obviously expert at her work and highly committed to it. If she had not been so demonstrably unhappy, she would have been a logical candidate for the directorship of a clinic. She had an instinctive understanding of the mechanics and even the finances of mental health care.

She gave her name as Susan Lawrence.

Karen had by now seen several examples of Justine's signature on patient forms. It was a remarkable signature, the words going steeply downhill while the individual letters leaned back as though resisting the descent. Though the name was fake, the signature was full of truth. It could easily be verified from form to form.

Karen saw the significance of Justine's choice of the pseudonym Susan. Even in those years she had a secret quest.

No one at any of the clinics where she worked got to know her as a friend outside work. No one ever saw her on a date with a man. A couple of her coworkers speculated that she might be homosexual. Others were convinced she was simply celibate.

"Any chance she might have had for happiness in a relationship was burned out of her long ago," one of them told Karen. "I just don't think she had a sex life. She was too unhappy for that. Yet, in a strange way, her unhappiness equipped her to deal with the patients better than the rest of us. The patients adored her."

The director of the Meriden clinic had a photograph of Justine, a Polaroid that had been used to make her name badge. In the photo Justine looked like a woman of forty or so, with stringy brown hair and prematurely wrinkled skin. Her eyes were deep, complex, tortured as those of any mental patient. Karen shook her head as she reflected that Justine had been no more than twenty-five when the snapshot was taken.

After two years in Meriden Justine quit her job and dropped out of sight. That was five years ago. Karen could find no trace of her after that.

For a couple of days Karen was stumped. The trail she was following had been hot as a pistol. Then it had vanished. The likelihood was that Justine Lawrence had abandoned the mental health field. Why? Where had she gone?

Had she tired of the mental health bureaucracy and the insurance companies with their perennial allergy to mental patients? Had she simply decided that the profession of counselor was not for her? Or had something else happened to change the course of her life?

Karen floundered, feeling empty of ideas. She sat in her apartment, watched the news, made phone calls to this and that source, without much hope.

Then she remembered that her arsenal of facts was not as empty as it seemed.

If she did not know all the intervening steps in Justine Lawrence's journey, she did know the end point. Justine had telephoned Susan Campbell in Washington, perhaps many times. Then Justine—or people with whom she was associated—had abducted Susan. That meant that the last stop on Justine's itinerary was Washington.

Unfortunately, the efforts of Karen and her canvassing service turned up no trace of Justine, or anyone of her description, in the mental health field in the Baltimore–Washington area.

Karen had one more thought. The whole history of Justine Lawrence and her odyssey began with Michael Campbell. But not only with Michael Campbell. The starting point of the journey, if Patricia Broderick was to be believed, included Colin Goss.

Connect the dots.

The national headquarters of The Goss Organization was in Atlanta. If Justine had interrupted her career in counseling, she had perhaps done so in order to move to Atlanta. No doubt there were ideas in her mind about Colin Goss, ideas she wanted to clarify. Facts she wanted to check. Proofs she wanted to have in her hand before the next stage in her life—the stage that led to Susan Campbell.

Karen began by doing the obvious. Styling herself as a prospective employer, she sent The Goss Organization a routine employment query about Justine Lawrence, a.k.a. Susan Lawrence. She included a copy of the photo from Meriden. She called the Atlanta headquarters to try to hurry up the process. A helpful personnel director told her no person of that name or description had worked for the Organization.

Karen was back to square one.

Or was she?

There was the possibility that Justine had not actually worked for The Goss Organization, but had penetrated it in another way. Perhaps by becoming friends with someone who worked there. Perhaps by seducing someone who worked there, or someone close to Goss. Perhaps by contacting one of Goss's many corporate enemies and making some sort of deal.

The possibilities were multiple. What Karen needed was a contact close enough to Goss to be in the know about such things. Or close enough to know who to ask.

Sitting in her bathtub with a Newport smoldering in the ashtray, Karen realized she already knew such a person.

Crushing out the cigarette, she got out of the bath and went in search of Patricia Broderick's phone number.

Atlanta

2 A.M.

DR. RICHARD Easter, late of Harvard and Johns Hopkins, Diplomate of the American Board of Internal Medicine, Ph.D. summa cum laude in pharmacology from Berkeley, glided through what appeared to be an underwater tunnel toward a closed door.

He knew the door would not be locked. Security in the headquarters was so tight that it was unthinkable an intruder could penetrate to this penthouse. He himself had the run of the place because of his Level Four security clearance. The guards manning the monitors would not even give him a second look, he passed this way so often at all hours.

He let himself in and stood measuring the darkness. Waves of weakness and confusion throbbed under his skin. He had to keep telling himself, *I am here. This is happening now. This is me.* The role of medication in his life had become so great that accurate perception was no longer a given. This might all be a dream. A nightmare, certainly. After all, had he not given up his soul long ago? And the world must look different to eyes that see without a soul.

But now he was going to end it. Tonight was the first phase.

He kept the lights off, though it wasn't really necessary. There was no surveillance camera in this room, because it was here that Goss played his little games with girls and women.

Dr. Easter put on the specially designed mask and the latex gloves. His movements were slow, exaggeratedly careful, like the movements of a drunk who is trying to appear sober. He breathed out in little gusts through his nose, a habit he had picked up recently.

He made his way through the darkness to the lowboy against the wall. He took out his penlight.

He opened the lowboy carefully. The hinges were silent. Inside, the bottles stood in neat rows, their little caps bearing the smiling face of a country girl in Tuscany. The picture was crude, but there was in fact something fresh and young in her countenance, something of innocence and renewal.

He picked a bottle in the third row. He removed it carefully and set it on top of the lowboy. Then he realized he could not balance himself well enough in this position. He sat down on the floor, his back against the wall, and propped the bottle between his legs.

He took a last deep breath and held it.

He took the cap off the syringe and, quickly, remembering his days as an intern giving hurried injections to frightened children, pushed the needle through the top of the bottle. The metal was soft; the syringe went in easily.

He plunged it in, watching the swirl of clear liquid disappear into the water. He removed the needle, replaced the cap, put the bottle back where he had found it, and breathed out. A long rattling exhalation, the wheeze of an old man.

He closed the door of the lowboy and stood up, straightening himself with an absurd show of dignity, as though he were about to lead the residents on grand rounds. He walked to the door with measured steps and let himself out.

In the corridor he took more deep breaths to steady himself. He was weak, almost too weak to get back to his own office, but relief flooded through him intoxicatingly.

"The last shall be the first," he said aloud.

Seattle, Washington
April 16

PAT BRODERICK was holding an open house in the fashionable Seattle sub-
urb of Bellevue when a well-dressed woman in her thirties came in.

"This is a beautiful home," the woman said, "but I know my husband
won't like the price. He's a sales executive at Boeing."

"Oh, that's nice," Pat said, always eager to flatter a customer who seemed
to have good financial prospects.

"Well, not to hear him tell it," the woman said. "He's worried about
money. One of his friends lost his job in the layoffs last year. We need a new
house, because I'm pregnant again."

"Congratulations!" Pat threw in. "How many kids do you have?"

"We have a boy and a girl, eight and ten," the woman said. "This third
will be the last. As you can imagine, we have to have four bedrooms." She
looked around her. "This wouldn't be too much house for us, but the price
tag is too high."

"It's the address that's driving up the house," Pat said. "I'm sure I can fix
you up. I have several listings in this neck of the woods that are hardly more

than half the price. I can think of one that would be ideal. It's in a great school district, with lots of kids in the neighborhood."

"Where is it?" the woman asked.

Pat showed her the location on the map she always carried. The house was a modest four bedroom with a nice-sized lawn. It would suit a growing family perfectly.

"How much is it?"

"They had to relocate, so the price is negotiable," Pat said. "They're asking four twenty-five, but they have a new mortgage back east, so I strongly suspect they'll come down quite a bit." She didn't volunteer the fact that the house had belonged to a Boeing executive who had been a casualty of the layoffs.

"Hmm," the woman said. "It looks promising."

"I could show it to you this afternoon," Pat said. "Another realtor is going to spell me at three o'clock. What is your name, by the way?"

"Debbie. Deborah. Deborah Harding," the woman said, extending a hand.

"Pat Broderick. Delighted to meet you."

Pat had her lunch at her desk and listened to her phone messages. One of them was from Karen Embry, the reporter who had been here last week. Pat ignored the message, moving on to messages from real-estate clients. She would need to be pushed before agreeing to see the reporter again. Her sleep was still disturbed by the memories Karen had made her confront.

Pat left on schedule at three-thirty, then drove over to the empty house and let herself in. The couple was late, arriving at a quarter after four. The man was handsome, about forty to judge by the gray at his temples. He wore an expensive business suit.

"Pat, this is Tom," Mrs. Harding said.

"I hear you're going to get me this house for three twenty-five," the man joked.

"That would be quite a steal," Pat smiled, impressed by his acumen. "I don't know that we can come down quite that low, but I'll try."

"I like to proceed from the basement up," the man said. "Why don't you and Deborah look at the kitchen and the bedrooms, and I'll catch up with you."

He wants to check the furnace, Pat thought. "Sure thing," she said. "Just call out if you have any questions."

Deborah Harding seemed to love the house. She spent only a moment in the kitchen before heading up the stairs.

"You say there are lots of kids around?" she asked.

"Oh, tons of kids," Pat assured her, climbing the stairs behind her.

"Because my youngest, Robbie, is kind of shy," Deborah said. "He spends too much time on those computer games. He needs other kids to draw him out."

"That shouldn't be a problem," Pat said. "Look there," she pointed out the window. On one of the nearby lawns several children were playing a game, apparently Keepaway, with a ball. Their shouts echoed over the drizzly air.

"That's good," Deborah said. "I don't suppose there are problems with barking dogs. Tom is a light sleeper."

"They have an excellent neighborhood association here," Pat said, looking out the window. "They handle problems like that very well. People respect each other's privacy. I haven't heard a single—"

She heard the bedroom door closing. She turned to see Deborah Harding holding the knob. She was looking at Pat through hard eyes.

"What's the matter?" Pat asked, a chill going down her spine.

"What did you tell her?" the other woman asked.

"Tell who? I don't understand."

"The reporter."

The chill spread through Pat's stomach and down her legs. Her fingers trembled around the file folder she had brought with her.

"Reporter? What reporter?" she asked.

"This is a sensitive time," the woman said. "I'm sure you understand. Mr. Goss needs to be extra careful."

"Mr. who?" Pat Broderick drew on her instincts as a realtor and as a call girl to lie as convincingly as possible. But the fear in her eyes could not be concealed.

The bedroom door opened silently. The man came in. The woman gave him a brief nod. He moved toward Pat, who retreated toward the window.

"I really don't understand," she said.

"Away from the window," the man said, taking her arm.

He drew her toward the inner corner of the room while the woman stood guard at the door.

"What did you tell her?" he asked.

"All right," Pat said. "All right. She was here. I told her nothing. Do you think I'm crazy? Mr. Goss knows he can count on me. He's always known that."

The man's eyes searched hers. He said to the woman, "Go downstairs. Watch the front door."

The woman slipped out soundlessly.

"Please," Pat said.

The man smiled.

"They said to make it look like rape," he said.

"No!" Pat cried. "I didn't tell her a thing. I don't know where she got my name. I just told her to leave me alone—"

The man's arm curled around her neck, choking off her words. He pulled her toward the floor.

"Don't worry about it," he said. "You'll never feel a thing."

He squeezed harder. As he pulled up Patricia Broderick's skirt, she heard children shouting to each other in the suburban yards outside. Their cries drowned in the red wave rising behind her eyes.

6 9

Washington

ON APRIL 17, four days after Michael's refusal to withdraw from consideration for vice president, a package addressed to Michael in care of the director of the FBI was received at FBI headquarters.

There was no return address. The parcel was postmarked Washington. It was opened by FBI bomb disposal experts. Inside it was the overnight bag Susan had taken with her the day she left Washington for Green Lake. The bag contained all the clothing Susan had worn that day, from the tight jeans and shirt to the tiny leather jacket to the shoes.

Also included was the wig Susan had worn, as well as her undergarments, including the bikini panties and the bra, which was made specially for her by a designer in New York.

In the pocket of the folded jeans the agents found Susan's wedding ring, as well as the ivory pendant Michael had given her for their tenth anniversary, a token she always wore for luck. The contents of Susan's purse, including all her identification cards and credit cards, were inside a Ziploc bag at the bottom of the package.

The arrival of the parcel sent a wave of despair through all those who were hoping to get Susan back alive. It signified that Susan would no longer be needing any of these items. She was either dead already, or would never be coming back to her old life.

Of those who saw the package's contents, no one was more moved or more alarmed than Joseph Kraig. Though he could only look at the items without touching them (the forensic techs would work all night on them after the initial viewing), he could feel Susan's complicated, eccentric charm in all of them. He had seen that wedding ring the first day she ever wore it, fifteen years ago. He knew the pendant well. It was an intricately carved peacock in a circular shape that made Kraig think of a sunrise.

The small bra and panties wrung Kraig's heart. He did not want to imagine what had been done to the innocent female flesh that had filled these garments.

An atmosphere of anger and vengeance now reigned among the agents. Most believed Susan was dead. All were hell bent to find those responsible and destroy them. Susan, it turned out, was as popular among federal agents as she was with the general public.

Kraig was troubled by this outpouring of rage. He needed to feel that Susan was still alive and that he still had a chance to save her. That hope now seemed more fanciful than ever.

Kraig was puzzled by Michael's refusal to withdraw from consideration for vice president. If there was one thing Kraig knew about Michael, it was that Michael was fiercely protective of Susan. Michael adored Susan, venerated her. It would destroy him to lose her.

Why had Michael decided not to withdraw? Had the president or his party colleagues influenced him in some way Kraig was not privy to? Had someone else convinced Michael that his own instincts in the situation could not be followed?

There was something in all this that Kraig did not understand. Events were moving according to a pattern or schedule that defied ordinary logic. Ever since Dan Everhardt fell ill Kraig had tried to tell himself that the key to the enigma would present itself sooner or later, but it had not happened.

When he got home from work Kraig dialed Karen Embry's home number. He got her voice mail.

"Please leave messages for Karen Embry at the sound of the tone," said the recording.

Kraig waited for the tone. "Karen, this is Kraig. I've been doing some thinking, and I'd like to talk to you about those thoughts of yours. About Boston. Please call me back as soon as you can. I'll be here till 5 A.M. tomorrow, then at my office. Ask them to beep me if you need to get through." He repeated the two numbers and hung up.

Kraig took a long shower and did some yoga exercises, which were supposed to relax him but did not. He was tempted to drive over to Karen's apartment and wait for her to come home. But he knew she might be out of the city, even out of the country. There was nothing to do but wait.

He put on a CD of Mozart piano sonatas, opened the bottle of bourbon, and poured himself a drink. He did not remember until the nutty taste of the liquor touched his lips that he was not a bourbon drinker. Scotch was his drink.

The explanation came to him easily. A Freudian slip—he had wished Karen was here with him. If she was here it would be she who drank the bourbon.

He poured the liquor down the drain and got into bed. He lay staring at the ceiling.

He smelled the faint aroma of Karen's body on his pillow. The night Karen slept with him here, she had wanted to tell him something. He had sensed it, but had not tried to draw her out. In the end she had not told him. Probably because she was tired of his skepticism about her theories.

He wished she was here now. He would hold her in his arms, savoring the tender feel of her undernourished body. But this time, instead of feeling her kisses on his lips, he would hear the secrets she carried in her mind. "Tell me what you know," he would ask. And her answer would be more powerful than any caress.

With that thought in his mind Kraig surprised himself by falling into a heavy, dreamless sleep. The Mozart played on, piano notes tolling unheard like omens in the darkness.

———

JUDD CAMPBELL paid a visit to Michael at the Georgetown house after the arrival of the package from the kidnappers.

Michael was surrounded by a phalanx of government agents. He said little, but looked at Judd with an unforgettable expression in his eyes. It was obvious Michael believed Susan was dead, and that he had caused her death.

"Hang in there, son," Judd said, hugging Michael. "It's not time to give up yet."

Seeing the look in his son's eyes, Judd wondered where Michael had found the courage to refuse the kidnappers' demand. Frankly, Michael's decision puzzled Judd. It seemed out of character. Judd had feared that Michael would use Susan as an excuse to refuse the president's nomination, and perhaps to quit politics altogether. The opposite had happened. Michael was still the nominee, and Susan's captors were free to kill her if they wished. Had perhaps already killed her.

Judd understood what Michael had said in his public statement. Understood it politically, understood it historically. Michael was right. A stand had to be taken against terrorism. This was a new century. Civilized governments could not allow terrorists to hold the world hostage for the next hundred years. It was time to bear down.

The decision made logical sense. Indeed, it was the decision Judd would have wished for, given his ambition for Michael. Judd did not want anything to stop Michael from becoming vice president this year.

But it still seemed strange. It didn't seem like Michael. For the first time in his memory, Judd had the odd feeling that he didn't completely know his son.

And now Judd recalled where he had seen that empty, hopeless expression on Michael's face before. It was when Margery died.

Michael had been home from Choate that weekend, and Judd had been delayed getting back from a business trip. Margery had picked Michael up at the airport and made him dinner Friday night. Ingrid was away that night for some reason, and Stewart was off at college. Ingrid had promised to return by Saturday night, when Judd would be home. The family would have dinner together.

Saturday afternoon Margery committed suicide. The call from the police reached Judd aboard his private jet, midway between Chicago and home.

Judd was 25,000 feet above the land when he learned that his world had collapsed. Michael, they told him, had found Margery hanging from a beam in her bedroom in the Chesapeake Bay house.

Judd arrived home just after dark. The police had already removed Margery's body. Though in a state of shock himself, Judd had helped Ingrid put Michael to bed. The family physician wanted to give Michael a sedative, but Michael refused. Michael wore an expression of empty stubbornness, as though he were clinging to something the others could not see. For weeks after Margery's death Judd and Ingrid kept a close eye on Michael. The police social worker thought he was a serious risk for suicide.

It was that expression of rigid emptiness, devoid of all hope, that Michael had worn today.

With this thought Judd Campbell hung his head. If Susan had gone the way of Margery, it would be the end of his world.

———

COLIN GOSS sat across his executive desk from the chief operative in charge of his private Susan Campbell investigation. Alongside him sat the agent whose responsibility was intelligence about the official investigation.

"Were there any signs of violence on the clothes?" he asked. "Blood? Semen?"

"Nothing," said the agent. "I have that from the very top. No sign of violence."

"All right," Goss said. "We proceed as though she were alive. Where do the intelligence agencies stand?"

"They have nothing concrete except the voiceprint to prove it was Susan Campbell on the phone," the man said. "They're stumped as to the identity of the other voice. They're concentrating on computer enhancement of the tape and analysis of background sounds to try to find where it was recorded."

"No more?" Goss asked. "Who do they suspect?"

"You, among others," the man said. "They believe you'll be the one to benefit in the event Campbell withdraws. They have men assigned to your organization, but it's leading nowhere. They're also checking all the major terrorist groups and all the major political figures, especially the right wing."

"And they've learned . . . ?"

"Nothing."

"Good work," Goss said. "You can go now. I'll call you tonight."

"Yes, sir."

The younger man left. Goss's eyes were on the chief investigator.

"All right," he said. "Where do we stand?"

The investigator, a white-haired man in his fifties who looked more like a banker than a detective, did not open the file he had brought with him.

"I'm concerned," he said. "We can't find anyone with a political basis for this abduction. Nor can we find anyone with a personal grudge against Campbell. That forces me to consider the connection between yourself and Campbell."

Goss nodded. This operative had worked for Goss for thirty years and knew of Goss's connection to Michael. He had to know, for he had been responsible for covering up certain events associated with the connection.

"What are your thoughts?" Goss asked.

"If we assume that the people who abducted Mrs. Campbell are aware of your plans, we should also assume that they know something about the past," the man said. "It never hurts to assume the worst. Let's say they know about the early days. About Boston, for instance, or Atlanta, or even Connecticut. Their real target might be you."

"Meaning what?" Goss probed.

"Their intent may have been to keep Campbell out of the White House as a means of stopping you," the detective said. "And now that Campbell has refused to withdraw—"

"What are you getting at?" Goss asked irritably.

"Again, to assume the worst," the agent said, "suppose they haven't abducted Susan Campbell simply in order to hold her as a hostage. Suppose they've told her some of what they know about her husband."

Goss raised an eyebrow. This had not occurred to him. He nodded slowly. It was not for nothing that he paid this man $300,000 a year.

"I see," Goss said. "In that case . . ."

"In that case she is more dangerous to us free than the abductors are now," the detective said. "It would be one thing for Campbell to withdraw. It would be another thing if Mrs. Campbell came home in possession of that knowledge."

Goss nodded. "Point taken. Good thinking. I'll speak to Michael myself. What else have you got?"

"We haven't got a name," the man said. "But as you know, there were families of the—of past subjects, experimental subjects. And friends. Boyfriends . . . There are a lot of possibilities there. Someone who has a grudge. Someone who somehow caught on to the larger plan, and sees Campbell's role in it. Someone who saw a way to throw a monkey wrench, and did it."

He frowned. "Some of the subjects survived," he added. "That is a concern."

"I see," Goss said. "Yes, there is a lot of territory. You'll just have to cover it."

"We're working as fast as we can," the detective said. He cleared his throat. "You got my report about the Seattle situation," he said.

"Yes. Thank you."

"We found no evidence that Broderick gave anything away. But the fact remains that the reporter did query her. That's one door open to the past already."

"Get rid of the reporter," Goss said.

"That will be difficult," the other man replied. "She's got the CIA on her tail. Apparently that article she published got them interested. Her apartment is bugged and there are agents following her. We could make an attempt, but it might draw fire from the intelligence community. That would be dangerous."

Goss thought for a moment. "All right, wait on that. But if Mrs. Campbell is still alive, I want to know where. And if we get there first—"

"Of course, sir. Total coverage."

"I want no mistakes," Goss warned. "No foul-ups. No matter what happens, the larger plan remains intact."

"Absolutely."

"All right. Thank you for your thoughts. We'll talk tonight."

"Yes, sir." The man got up and left the office.

Colin Goss sat behind his desk, thinking.

He had no doubts about Michael, of course. He would trust Michael with his life. But the wife was another matter. She had been a problem all along. She was unstable, neurotic. Her actions could not be predicted.

Such uncertainty could not be permitted at this stage.

That was why Goss had just signed Susan Campbell's death warrant.

JUSTINE ENTERED the room to see Susan sitting under the lamp reading.

"You're looking well today," she said. "You must be sleeping better."

Susan closed the book, a paperback of the old Anne Tyler novel *Dinner at the Homesick Restaurant*. She smiled. "Yes, I did sleep well."

Justine glanced around the room. It was still a closed-up prison with a lock on the outside of the door, but it looked more domestic now. Susan's books were scattered here and there, and she had taken to spending more time in the chair than on the bed. The exercise bike had had some use.

Susan was also taking more care about her appearance, putting on makeup and fixing her hair. There was an air of deliberate competence and even optimism about her. She was pulling herself together, she was refusing to be destroyed by what was happening. This was as Justine had intended. She knew Susan was a strong person underneath her neurotic exterior. Justine had taken that strength into her plans from the beginning.

"Time is running short," Justine said. "They're going to find us soon. I need to know if I can count on you."

"Count on me?" Susan asked.

Justine sat down on the end of the bed. "I need to know what your thoughts are. What you believe."

Susan looked away. She seemed deep in thought. When she looked back at Justine her eyes were sad.

"I believe you are a sincere person," she said. "A good person. I believe that some of what you have told me is true. But," she took a deep breath, "I don't believe what you've said about Michael. I can't."

She looked at Justine, who was nodding understandingly.

"I'm his wife," Susan said. "I took a vow to love him. I do love him. I can't just accept what you've told me. It isn't Michael."

Justine stood up.

"I understand," she said. "I wouldn't ask you to break your vow without proof."

A shudder went through Susan. She looked up fearfully at her captor.

"Proof?" she asked in a small voice.

"Sit on the bed." Justine moved aside.

Susan sat on the bed. She looked childlike at that moment, her hands folded in her lap.

Justine put a tape into the VCR and turned on the television. An image of a girl's face filled the screen. Her head was pushed down against a cushion. Her eyes were blank, almost lifeless.

The camera pulled back to show her bound to a leather-covered apparatus like the one Justine had described. She was naked. She was positioned so that her backside was presented upward, her head down.

A naked man was approaching her, his back to the camera. He was blindfolded. He had both hands out, as though feeling his way. The sound track was garbled, but laughter and music could be heard, as well as the noisy clink of glasses. Men's voices were shouting encouragement and instructions to him.

"Warmer!"

"Colder!"

Susan's breath had caught in her throat. Her hands were clasped hard.

She had recognized him.

He was young. He had a handsome body, with straight shoulders, powerful back muscles, firm buttocks, a slim waist, and long, perfectly formed legs, the legs of an athlete.

One of his outstretched hands held a tail dangling from his fingers toward the floor.

In the center of his back, curving slightly from right to left, was a scar.

"The scar dates the picture," Justine said. "He had his first surgery when he was at Choate. That's the scar you see here. It extends from the second to the twelfth thoracic vertebrae. The second surgery was done in the spring of his junior year at Harvard. They had to go deeper into the lumbar spine the second time, because the Harrington procedure had failed and they needed to insert another metal rod."

Susan was sitting in silence, staring at the screen on which Michael was making his way across the room. She watched the handsome young limbs move as the tail dangled from his hand.

The quality of the video was not very good, but the scar stood out powerfully, a badge of pain, of surgical invasion, and of fame. It was that scar, lengthened after the second operation, that had made Michael Campbell a household name.

Susan knew that scar well. She had seen it when she waited with Michael in the hospital for the second surgery. He had not wanted to show it to her, but she insisted, telling him she wanted to feel his pain, wanted to know him in his vulnerability.

Her love for Michael had dawned when he was in his hospital bed, a frightened young man wondering whether the defect in his spine was going to make him an invalid. Her love had grown and flowered as she helped him through his pain and watched him pull himself together. Her love had become final when she watched him win the race at the Olympics and saw his teammates help him out of the pool. By now her love was as much a part of her as that scar was part of Michael.

And he had done this to these helpless girls, tortured them, destroyed them. Some of it happened after Susan already knew him.

Susan covered her eyes. Tears were running down her cheeks.

"No more," she said. "Please, Justine."

She heard laughter on the videotape. Something made her open her eyes and look.

Michael had found his way to the helpless girl and was pinning the tail to her upraised buttocks. He was hard between his legs. He was smiling. Voices were shouting approval. The blindfold was coming off as he sank to his knees.

Susan covered her eyes again.

"My God," she said. "How could you?"

Justine let the tape play. She watched with a look of remote curiosity in her eyes.

Susan, not looking at the screen, heard the drunken voices on the tape shouting "*Mike! Mike!*"

When the tape was finished Justine stopped it and turned off the TV. Susan was curled on her side in a fetal position, looking almost as helpless as the girl on the video.

Justine came to Susan's side and petted her shoulder. "Good girl," she said. "Brave girl. I'm proud of you."

Susan did not look up.

"I understand your pain," Justine said, firmness vying with the sympathy in her voice. "It's a terrible burden. His mother killed herself when she found out what he was."

Susan did not protest against these words. She wept quietly against the comforter.

"Brave girl," Justine repeated, bending over her captive. "I asked a lot of you. You came through."

With a cry of despair Susan curled her hands around Justine's back and wept on her breast.

71

KAREN WAS at Washington National Airport.

Her flight from Atlanta had arrived on time. She took the shuttle to the long-term parking lot.

Her trip had been a failure. She had found two sources close to The Goss Organization who might have known if Justine Lawrence or a person of her description had ever worked for the corporation or been involved, however tangentially, with its more powerful officers.

Neither source had panned out. There was no evidence to support Karen's theory that Justine had spent time in Atlanta in an effort to infiltrate The Goss Organization. And there was no time to pursue the line of reasoning any further.

Her call to Patricia Broderick in Seattle had not been answered. She had held out the hope that Pat, as a Goss intimate, might be able to direct her to the right people in Atlanta or elsewhere. She would try Pat again, perhaps tomorrow.

Karen had left Atlanta in a depressed mood. On the plane, however, she had reminded herself that even if she could not reconstruct the entire journey of Justine Lawrence after her rape at the hands of Colin Goss, she did know the final leg of that journey. It led to Washington, where Justine had participated in the abduction of Susan Campbell.

In all probability Justine had lived in Washington during the last phases of the plan. Or if not Washington itself, then Maryland or Virginia. Lived under an assumed name, no doubt.

Left traces, though. Traces Karen could pick up.

Susan Campbell had now been missing for three weeks. Assuming she was still alive, she was sequestered in a hideout that Justine Lawrence had perhaps helped to arrange. Karen felt she had a reasonable chance of locating it.

She had an advantage over the authorities. They knew that Susan's captor, or at least one of her captors, was a woman. They had heard her voice. But they were working in the dark. They only knew what had happened. Karen knew why it had happened.

And if they had a voice to go on, Karen had a voice and the face it belonged to. And a photograph of that face.

The airport bus stopped beside the C-3 pole, where Karen had gotten on it three days ago. The Honda was halfway down the line of cars. It was dark outside already, and the temperature was dropping. Karen shivered as she opened the trunk and threw in her overnight bag. Her lack of sleep made her feel even colder. She would take a long bath when she got home.

She opened the driver's door, slid into the seat, and put the key into the ignition.

"Go ahead, turn it on."

Karen jumped, startled by the voice from the backseat.

"Turn it on, but don't drive away yet."

Karen's hands were trembling. She had turned pale. A hundred times over the years she had approached her car and worried that someone might be inside it, waiting to rob or harm her. And now, too busy to entertain such fears, she had walked right into the trap. She thought of the little can of Mace that was buried under countless other items in her purse.

"What do you want?" she asked.

"You," said the voice.

Atlanta

COLIN GOSS sat behind the executive desk in his Atlanta office. The curtains were closed, and all the lights were out except the reading lamp on his desk. His secretaries had been told to hold all calls. He wanted to be able to concentrate.

The bottle of mineral water was on the desk. He poured a glass and took a long drink. The water seemed to calm his nerves. It was odd, he realized, for a master of pharmaceutical technology to believe in the healing benefits of mineral waters. But he could not suppress this bit of superstition on his own part. He felt better when he drank the water.

In his hand was a small piece of note paper. On it was a phone number.

It was the number of the new phone line that had been installed at the Judd Campbell house, a second unlisted number to be used only by the family. The line was not tapped.

Goss dialed the number. After several rings Michael Campbell answered.

"Yes?"

"Michael? Is that you?"

"Yes." Relief sounded in Michael's voice as he recognized the caller.

"Are we secure?"

"Yes." Michael knew that Judd was out of the house, meeting with his detectives. Ingrid was out shopping, having left at six to drive the housekeeper home. "Yes, we're secure."

"Son, I have painful news."

There was a silence over the line.

"Yes?" Michael asked. "What is it?"

"Our evidence strongly suggests that the people who have Susan are from the past," Goss said. "They know about you and me, son. About Harvard, about the girls. Something along those lines. They're not politically motivated. They're after you because of what happened in the past. That's why they want you to withdraw."

Michael thought this over.

"How sure are you of this?" he asked.

"Not a hundred percent," Goss admitted. "But with so much at stake, with the whole plan in danger, I think we have to take the conservative course and assume the worst."

"Do you think they've told Susan?" Michael asked, a fearful note in his voice.

"I suspect they may have," Goss said. "If they know about the past, it may mean as much to them to have her know as it does to threaten us with her death. For instance, if she knows about the girls in New England, she may have turned against you. If she gets out she might tell what she knows. That would be the end, you see. Because even if we tried to cast doubt, it would be Susan doing the accusing. She has very strong PR. The dirt would be too thick to wash away in time, son."

He thought for a moment. "If it were only sexual, that would be one thing," he said. "But we're talking about voluntary manslaughter, son. Mass murder, in effect. That's too much to overcome."

Michael was thinking. He remembered the night when Susan had asked him, with that strange look on her face, "Did something happen at Harvard?" He had denied it convincingly, but he had not liked the look in her eyes.

Then there was Kraig. Kraig had asked him about crank phone calls in which Harvard was mentioned. Michael had denied it again.

He should have told Goss about those two episodes. He hadn't. He wanted the past to stay buried.

Goss cleared his throat nervously. "There's one more thing, son. I didn't want to have to tell you this, but I suspect there may be a videotape of some of what happened. If they have that, and if Susan has seen it . . . Well, you can imagine."

Goss cursed the impulse that had made him videotape the episodes. But it had been a good impulse at the time. He knew the tapes would make powerful blackmail material against those who had played the game, should he ever need it. It turned out that he never needed it. And now it was coming back to haunt him.

There was a silence as Michael pondered what he had heard.

"I've always trusted your judgment," he said at last.

"I know, son. I know you have."

"I don't want to wreck a plan you've worked so hard on," Michael said.

"No, son. We can't allow anything to stand in the way of the plan."

There was a painful silence.

"What will happen?" Michael asked.

"No one will come out alive," Goss said. "Not the kidnappers, not Susan. That's how it will have to be."

Michael was silent.

"Son, I want you to think of the bright side as well as the dark," Goss said. "As a martyr to terrorism Susan will be even more valuable to you than she would have been as a beautiful First Lady. You'll be able to present yourself as a man who's made the supreme sacrifice. You'll be unbeatable. You lost your wife to terrorism. You'll be Lindbergh. You'll be king of the world."

After a pause, Michael said, "Yes, I see."

Another silence.

"It's painful, I know," Goss said.

"I love her," Michael said in a reflective tone.

"Son, think of her as a soldier who's given her life in a war, a soldier who has died for a great cause. When you think of it, that's what it is, really. A great cause. I know you would be willing to give your own life for it. Think of it that way."

"Yes," Michael said. "Yes, I see what you mean."

"You'll remarry, son. You'll survive. And we'll win this war together."

"Yes. All right. All right."

"Thank you for being so brave, son. I love you. You know that."

"Are you sure you can . . . ?" Michael asked.

"Arrange it? Yes, I'm sure. Don't lose a minute's sleep over that, son."

Goss hung up.

Michael stood for a long time with the phone in his hand. The new line had been installed upstairs, in the corner library adjacent to the bedrooms. He looked out at the Bay.

He was thinking of Susan. Of their first times together, when he was a college student. Of her peculiar charm, her brittle humor, her wonderfully complicated personality. Her loyalty to him when he was getting ready for his second operation. Her devotion all these years. He loved her dearly. True, their relationship had never been quite as close as he might have wished. There were parts of her he had never touched, never understood. And, of course, she had not given him a child. That was another thing to think about, in the event she did not survive this. He would need a new wife, he would need children.

Still, he would miss Susan. She was so beautiful . . . Tears were in his eyes as he finally hung up the phone. He turned to go to his room, where some of the framed pictures of Susan from the early years were on the dresser and the walls. He wanted to look at those images of her, to think about how much she meant to him.

When he entered the hallway he saw Ingrid standing there, blocking his way to his room.

"What, no shopping?" he asked, smiling.

"I had a headache. I came right home," she said.

The look in her eyes left no doubt that she knew. Ingrid was not a woman who hid her emotions. Tears were on her cheeks. Her eyes shone with reproach.

"Michael, how could you?" she asked.

72

"DON'T BE afraid," said the man in the backseat. "It's me. Grimm."

"Who?" Karen asked.

"Your pen pal."

Karen breathed a sigh of relief. "Christ. You scared the hell out of me."

"Drive into the city."

Karen turned on the engine. She found the parking lot ticket in the little dashboard nook where she had left it.

"Do I get to see your face?" she asked.

"No."

She drove out of the lot and paid at the little booth. When she reached the ramp leading to the expressways a man sat up in the backseat. He wore a baseball cap pulled low over his face. Wraparound sunglasses hid his eyes.

"Why are you here?" she asked.

"Never mind that," he said. "Just listen."

"All right," Karen said.

The man took a deep breath.

"About thirty years ago, when he was patenting his first pharmaceuticals,

Colin Goss did a lot of research on cancer, and on aging. Goss was terrified of cancer because his mother and two brothers died of cancer. He was also terrified of getting old, of losing his health and his potency. He wanted to find a way to stop cancer cells from metastasizing, and to stop normal cells from deteriorating through the aging process. Naturally he knew that a cure for cancer, like a cure for aging, would make him the king of the medical and pharmaceutical worlds.

"To make a long story short, as he tried to figure out a way to prevent changes in certain cells, Goss stumbled on a new way to *cause* changes in cells. I won't bore you with the details. Most of it takes place on the sub-molecular level. It concerns a certain dissymmetry in the closure of every living particle, including the building blocks of plant and animal cells. It is this dissymmetry that leaves the cell open to adaptation or change. Unlike the geneticists, who see cells as automatons carrying out a blueprint laid down on the chromosomes, Goss understood that cells are *living* entities. Entities that can do the unexpected."

He pushed his dark glasses higher on his nose. "Goss wrote a paper on the concept, called 'Proximity and Dissymmetry in Cell Closure.' The paper would almost certainly have won him a Nobel Prize had he published it. But he wanted to keep the concept secret, so he never published the paper." Grimm smiled. "He let me read it, though. Made me read it, in fact, when I came on board."

Karen said nothing. This was Greek to her, despite her years of education in biochemistry.

"Goss learned that he could intervene at this level and fool a cell into thinking that its survival depended on a certain chemical behavior that was not in its normal nature," Grimm said. "A sort of forced mutation, if you will. Like evolution, only based on a false premise, and enormously speeded up. Are you following me?"

"Trying to," Karen said. "Do you mind if I smoke?" She reached for the pack of Newports in her purse.

"Yes, I mind. No smoking. Just listen."

"All right."

There was a silence. Karen turned on the directional signal.

"Where are we?" asked the voice.

"Getting onto 595."

"Go in to 395 and drive to the Mall."

Karen said nothing as she accelerated along the ramp.

"The changes in one cell ramified through neighboring cells and cell groups," Grimm said. "Controlling this larger change was an enormous chemical engineering challenge. Thousands of experiments were performed within The Goss Organization over the years. Some of them actually produced pharmacological innovations, such as the treatment for hypertension that made Goss famous. Others produced more sinister results, which Goss of course had to keep secret."

Karen was silent, listening hard.

"The most important of these results was a paralysis of the function of will or decision. Goss found that he could intervene chemically in the constitution of a human being in such a manner that the subject could not act on his perceptions or thoughts. At first this effect seemed pointless and even undesirable. What would be gained by paralyzing a person's ability to act? The person would become useless, both to himself and to others. But over time, Goss found a use for his discovery."

"What use?" Karen asked.

"Think for a moment about the enemies of society," Grimm said. "Murderers, rapists, arsonists. Gangbangers. Terrorists. Why do these people do what they do? Because they have *decided* to do it. Because they are able to act on that decision. What would happen if that ability was removed? They would become harmless. No matter how evil their intentions, they wouldn't be able to hurt a fly."

"Uh-huh," Karen said. "Okay . . ."

"Think of it as a chemical variation on the theme of the prefrontal lobotomy," Grimm said. "A designer disease, radical and irreversible. This is what Goss discovered."

He paused. "Where are we?"

"About five more minutes to 395," Karen said.

"There were other symptoms as well," Grimm said. "Nothing in biology is simple, you know that. Since the intervention was so profound metabolically, most of the subjects went into coma and died."

"Human subjects?" Karen asked.

"Related species at first, especially chimps and gorillas. But then, yes, humans." Grimm paused. "Not volunteers. If you know what I mean."

Karen thought of the sick girls in Boston. But she did not want to interrupt Grimm.

"The process was gradual, like all applied science," Grimm said. "Goss wanted predictable results. It took him another decade to settle on a single substance as the most effective and the easiest to administer. It produced the disorder we now know as the Pinocchio Syndrome."

Karen's breath caught in her throat. She should have known, she mused. All winter and spring she had felt this truth coming, but had not been prescient enough to see it. The spreading disease with no apparent cause, the sick political leaders, Michael Campbell, Colin Goss . . . the countless victims of the Syndrome, stopping in their tracks, unable to move or to speak.

"Now, Colin Goss hates terrorists," Grimm went on. "That's not a political pose. He sees them as a far greater danger to civilized society than criminals."

"Why?" Karen asked.

"A serial killer can only kill forty or fifty people in a lifetime," Grimm said. "A terrorist can kill a thousand with one bomb planted in a large enough building. Or three thousand with an airplane that slams into a tall building. A whole country full of violent criminals can function quite nicely. But terrorists can reduce civilians to panic and cripple institutions almost at will. The impact of a small group of terrorists on international politics can be enormous. Also, in the latter part of the twentieth century, terrorists came into possession of the means and the expertise to take human life on a large scale. Biological weapons, sophisticated explosives, and so on."

Karen nodded. "Okay. I see."

"Once you remove the terrorist from the political landscape, everything falls into place," Grimm said. "Government can function, industry can function. Society can function. What was chaos becomes business as usual. All because of that one simple step."

"And that was the purpose of the Pinocchio Syndrome?" Karen asked.

"The fundamental aim was achieved when the subject's will was paralyzed," Grimm said. "Without the capacity to act on one's motives, the capacity to *decide*—no terrorist. The other features of the disease—the apparent stubbornness, the changes to the hands and feet, the onset of coma at a predictable stage of the illness—these arose from repercussions in the cell structure that were painstakingly objectified and replicated by Goss."

"Really," Karen said.

"Goss is a bit of a poet. He liked the symbolic aspect of the physical changes. Also, he knew it would cause widespread terror. Which it has. The Pinocchio Syndrome would never have captured the primitive imagination the way it has if it weren't for the hands and feet."

Grimm smiled. "You should see him in the laboratory, or at the microscope. It's like watching Rembrandt add brush strokes to a masterpiece. The subtlety, the refinement of his eye . . . But an artist seeks to create beauty. Goss seeks to create evil. That's the difference."

Karen thought for a moment.

"You said it was easy to administer," she said.

"Very simple. Through air or water. It can even be done at a distance, or with a time lapse. You simply place a module containing the chemical in the desired location, and then pop it open by remote control."

Now Karen understood why the leukemia patients in their sterile bubbles escaped the Syndrome when all other people in the affected areas got sick. The patients were not exposed to fresh water or air.

"You mean," Karen asked, "that for every outbreak of the Pinocchio Syndrome there were people who engineered the outbreak by contaminating the air or water?"

"Specialists, yes," Grimm said. "Working in teams, under strict security conditions. Under cover, of course. Some dressed as gas men or water company men. That sort of thing."

He yawned slightly. "That was part of the plan from the beginning. Ingestion had to be quick and easy. Also, the half-life of the chemical had to be extremely short, so it would leave no trace in the tissues of the subject. And, as you see, the symptoms are so bizarre that medical observers are inclined to view the disorder as internal, like a birth defect or a genetic anomaly. Diseases like acromegaly and Elephant Man's Syndrome come immediately to mind."

Karen nodded. She had heard this theory expressed over and over again by the medical experts she had interviewed.

"So you're saying," she concluded, "that the entire Pinocchio Syndrome epidemic is a terrorist attack on a grand scale?"

"Vigilante act might be more precise," Grimm said. "Through the Syndrome Goss out-terrorizes the terrorists. Annihilates them, in fact."

"Because the disease is always fatal," Karen said.

"Correct."

Karen thought for a moment. "Why didn't Goss just murder the people he wanted to get rid of?"

"Simple," Grimm said. "Murder attracts attention. Genocide attracts even more attention. But no one questions a dread disease. They see it as an unfortunate fact of life. Like cancer, like AIDS."

"I see," Karen said quietly.

"With a disease you can kill as many people as you like," Grimm said, "and no one will smell a rat."

"MICHAEL, HOW could you?" Ingrid was staring at Michael through eyes wide with horror.

"How could I what?" Michael asked, playing for time. "What are you talking about?"

"I heard," she said. "That voice on the phone. You and Goss." The tears stood out angrily, like glinting beads of rage, on her cheeks. "You're going to let him murder your own wife. How could you?"

Michael moved toward her, his hands held out as though to enfold her and entreat her. "Ingrid . . ."

"You're a monster," she said. "You and that madman. What did you do, Michael? What girls was he talking about? What do they know about you?"

"Ingrid, you're misunderstanding the whole thing. If you'll just calm down and let me explain . . ."

She stood her ground. "What girls? What did you do? Oh, Michael, this is terrible. I used to have my doubts about you. About what happened to Mother . . . but I never believed it. I trusted you. I believed in you. How could you?"

She was holding her ground, but her love made her vulnerable to his outstretched arms. She seemed to wilt as he came closer. When he embraced her at the doorway to his room, she trembled helplessly in his arms. She hated him now, but she wanted him to comfort her.

"Ingrid, this is all a misunderstanding," he said.

"My God, you had us all fooled," she said. "Michael, I diapered you. I watched you grow. I gave you everything. How could you?"

"Ingrid, you don't understand." He petted her shoulder.

"Wait till Daddy hears," she said. "It will break his heart."

He gripped her shoulder as though to turn her toward his room. Then he curled his arm around her neck and grabbed his own wrist with his right hand, completing the stranglehold.

"Michael . . . Michael!"

She struggled, gasping for air and flinging her heavy limbs against him. But he held her tighter, dragging her into his room with the leverage of his tall body and superior strength.

7 3

KAREN'S MIND was fuzzy from the long trip, and she had not eaten in several hours. She was struggling to take in the enormity of what Grimm was saying.

"I have a question," she said.

"Ask it."

"If you're trying to paralyze a segment of the population that might carry out terrorist acts, how do you avoid affecting everyone else in the vicinity? How do you target your individuals?"

A low laugh sounded in the backseat. "You still don't understand, do you?"

Karen's hands froze around the wheel of the car.

"You don't target individuals," she said. "You wipe out populations. Am I right?"

"Good girl."

She had gotten off 395 and was slowing for a light.

"Take Canal Street to Independence," Grimm said.

She did as she was told. There was little traffic. It was too late. She saw a D.C. traffic cop watching her as she took the left turn. She drove slowly.

"I take it," she said, "that the outbreaks last fall and winter were deliberately limited in scope."

"Correct," Grimm said. "You were right on the money in your editorial. The lack of spread was a clear indicator that the disorder was toxic."

"How were the various pockets targeted?" Karen asked.

"Random, mostly. There is a world map in Colin Goss's office in Atlanta. The various areas are marked. He was experimenting with technique, with procedure."

"But since February the focus has been mainly on Africa and the Middle East and South Asia," Karen observed.

"That's part of the larger plan."

Karen thought this over. The hub of the terrorist world was the Middle East, with South Asia and North Africa as spokes radiating from it.

"What about Everhardt and Palleschi?" she asked.

"They were given the Syndrome to get them out of Michael Campbell's way. That was the first step in the plan."

"Why do it in such a public way?" Karen asked. "Why not get them out of the way quietly?"

"Goss threw the health authorities Everhardt and Palleschi intentionally. He wanted them to see a case of the Syndrome up close. He knew they would do everything in their power to understand it and solve it, because the victims were high profile. He doubted they would succeed, but he wanted to be sure."

Karen thought for a moment. "And exposing the two of them?"

"The simplest thing in the world," Grimm said. "Security on the vice president is extremely lax. As for Palleschi, there was no security at all, really." Grimm yawned. "Everhardt got it in his office. A glass of water he thought was from the water cooler. Palleschi ordered a glass of Valpolicella at a wine bar."

"So that's why there were only two victims in Washington, while all the other outbreaks involved hundreds or thousands," Karen said.

Grimm smiled. "Correct. Goss wanted to embarrass the administration, wanted to keep them confused. It worked, as you saw."

Karen shook her head. In her wildest nightmares about political life, notions such as these had never occurred to her. Grimm was tossing them off as though he was reading a weather report.

"Why did the epidemic disappear in America after January?" she asked.

"Goss wanted to build support for Campbell and the president. His own candidacy was bolstered by the public's fear of the Syndrome. Take away the fear and you take away Goss's luster. As you can see, it worked."

The car was approaching the southeast prospect of the Washington Monument. The huge needle rose eloquently against the night sky.

"Pull over just after the corner of 15th," said Grimm. "There's a free parking area there."

Karen did as she was told. She looked at Grimm in the rearview mirror.

"You spoke of a larger plan," she said.

Grimm nodded. "Not even a man with Goss's power could hope to bring off a thing like this alone. Sooner or later he would be found out. The technology to carry off the plan is one part. The ability to cover it up is the second part. Without that, it wouldn't succeed."

"To cover it up?"

"That, and also to get the public to accept it. The concept is well known. To get the public to accept the murder of Kennedy you have the Warren Commission. To get the public to accept Vietnam you have the Gulf of Tonkin Resolution. To get the public to accept Iran-Contra you have the congressional hearings and Oliver North. Only the government can really pull the wool over people's eyes and keep it there indefinitely."

Karen nodded. She had often had analogous ideas about the cover-ups that are never unmasked. For reasons only a philosopher or an expert in mass psychology could understand, government has a primordial connection to untruth. One might even speculate that human beings create governments in order to shield them from unpleasant truths. A government is like a parent whose responsibility is to provide presents on Christmas morning and to hide from its children the fact that there is no Santa Claus.

"I understand," she said. "But why did he take steps that hurt his own poll numbers?"

"Can't you guess?"

"He wanted Campbell to be vice president," Karen said.

"Good for you. And why did he want that?"

Karen shook her head. "I'm not sure."

"Goss himself is too controversial," Grimm said. "He has many enemies. If he managed to force a special election, there was always the chance he would lose. It was safer to put a hero in the White House, a man whose integrity no one doubted. Campbell filled the bill."

Karen nodded.

"Are you ready to hear the rest?" Grimm asked. "I'm counting on you. You're going to be the only one."

"I'm ready," Karen said.

"The president will be eliminated not long after Campbell takes office as vice president. Michael Campbell will become president of the United States."

"Ah." Karen was amazed by the enormity of the deception Goss planned to carry out, and by the cruelty of the plan.

"Then what?" she asked.

"Campbell will choose a lackluster Cabinet, the usual Washington hacks," Grimm went on. "But in a surprise move he will name Goss to a non-Cabinet post that doesn't need congressional approval. National security advisor or something. Like Nixon with Kissinger. He'll use as an excuse the notion that he needs a strong antiterrorist in his administration for these perilous times."

Karen nodded. "I see."

"Then the Syndrome will spread throughout the Muslim world," Grimm said. "It will wipe out every group from which terrorists have sprung since the creation of Israel. It will wipe out every terrorist nation. For all practical purposes the Arab world will cease to exist."

"INGRID, LISTEN. Just listen."

Michael squeezed hard. He heard a groan as Ingrid fought for breath.

"Ingrid, you don't know what you're saying. You've got to listen to me."

Squeezing with all his might, twisting hard, he pulled her toward the floor like a cowpuncher with a calf. She kept struggling. Her hands scratched desperately at his arm.

He fell alongside her. A part of his mind thought of Judd, of when he might return, of what he had to do. The rest of him thought, *This is my sister. My only sister.* He squeezed harder. He just wanted it to be over.

On the walls were photos of the Campbell family. Michael as a child on his mother's knee, and on Ingrid's knee. Michael and Stewart in their little sailboat. Michael and his father standing on the shore with the Bay in the background. Mother and Ingrid, Mother and Stewart. And then, after Mother's death, Susan.

Susan with Michael in the hospital. Susan on her bicycle, riding alongside Michael as he trained for the Olympics. Susan and Ingrid laughing in the kitchen with their matching aprons that said "Oh How I Suffer." Susan with Judd on the porch glider, looking like father and daughter.

Please, God. Michael felt the shudder of his sister's convulsions. *Please.*

He knew he was at the boundary of the unbearable. Except for Susan, Ingrid was the woman he loved most in the world.

To give himself strength he let his mind wander back to those early years. He thought of Ingrid's excited, laughing face the day she taught him to ride his two-wheeled bike. Dad was at work that day, and Stewart was away at school. Ingrid took Michael down the street to the flat walkway near the beach and perched him on the bike's seat. She ran alongside the bike, puffing from the effort and urging him, "Faster, Mikey. Faster!" And he had at last reached that mysterious borderline where the speed of the bike joined his body's natural sense of balance to make the ride possible.

Faster, Mikey! Faster! You're almost there!

The forgotten thrill came back to him, the breeze on his cheeks as the bike went faster and faster, and finally Ingrid's face receding as he looked back over his shoulder, Ingrid waving and clapping her hands. *Good boy! You've got it, Mikey! Good boy!*

The fresh pure wind blew over his face, eclipsing the sudden odors of defecation and death. He flew into that breeze gratefully, the tears drying on his cheeks.

And so the old memory came to comfort Michael as his sister died in his arms.

"Ingrid . . . Ingrid . . ."

He lay beside her for a long time, listening as his own scalded breath began to abate. He clung to her as he had long ago, when as a child he sometimes slept in her bed.

Then he realized he had to act quickly. Judd would be back in forty-five minutes, perhaps less. He couldn't leave Ingrid like this.

Suicide, he thought. *Asphyxiation. Hanging. Suicide.*

He picked her up and moved toward the other bedrooms. *Mother committed suicide by hanging. Ingrid did the same . . .*

He staggered under her weight, weakened by the struggle he had just been through.

Depressed over Susan's abduction, he thought. *A mental collapse. She was never strong . . .*

Thinking desperately, he carried Ingrid toward her own bedroom.

What did she use? A belt. Mother used a belt . . .

He was at the door of Ingrid's room. He was remembering his mother's suicide. She had hanged herself from the beam in the ceiling of her bedroom. There was a similar beam in Ingrid's room.

She took Mother as her example, he thought, grunting as he carried Ingrid to the window under the beam.

Placing the body on the floor, he turned toward the closet and stood thinking. He needed a belt. Ingrid's own clothes would not be much help. Ingrid was too fat to wear dresses with belts. Perhaps her coats . . .

Michael suddenly got an inspiration. Ingrid had devoted her life to Judd. Like so many spinsters she was fixated emotionally on her father. If she went over the deep end and killed herself, she might use one of her father's belts.

Michael dashed down the hall to Judd's room and flung open the closet door. Judd's collection of leather belts hung on a rack alongside his ties. Michael made a quick survey of the belts before choosing a thick one with a sturdy buckle.

She used her father's belt, he thought. *She had lost her grip, she was acting out of instinct . . .*

He hurried back to Ingrid's bedroom and knelt beside her. He whipped the belt around her neck and started to lift her up. She was very heavy. His strength almost failed him. But years of conditioning of his upper body came to his rescue.

Tears were coming out of his eyes. He wondered if he could really go through with this.

But he heard Goss's voice, *Son, think of her as a soldier who's given her life in a great war, a soldier who has died for a great cause.*

He lifted Ingrid with a groan.

A great cause, he thought.

"ONCE THE Arabs are neutralized, oil resources will be administered by the Western powers," Grimm said. "The profits will be divided up in an equitable manner. It will be a windfall for the economy of all the nations involved, especially the Western Europeans. The price of oil has been strangling Europe for three generations. As you may imagine, the Europeans won't be inclined to protest too much over the deaths of a few hundred million Arabs."

"Won't people be suspicious when the outbreak doesn't go further?"

"Were they suspicious when the AIDS epidemic was centered in Africa?" Grimm asked.

Karen nodded. "I see what you mean."

"Of course, some will be suspicious," Grimm allowed. "But they won't find out the truth. For one thing, the science behind the Syndrome is too subtle. Goss was light-years ahead of his colleagues when he discovered the principle behind it. But even if someone does get an inkling of what happened, the government will put a lid on it."

"It will?"

"They didn't find out the truth about Kennedy, did they?"

Karen shook her head thoughtfully. "No. They didn't."

There was a silence. In the rearview mirror Karen could see that Grimm was wearing a Baltimore Orioles jacket. His disguised head, with the ball cap and the wraparound glasses, looked particularly sinister.

A nagging question that had been at the back of Karen's mind for two years now came to her lips.

"The current political climate has been largely shaped by the World Trade Center attack and the *Crescent Queen*," Karen said. "And, of course, the oil crisis, and the recession. Is Colin Goss powerful enough to have caused the oil crisis?"

"Certainly." Grimm spoke with glib assurance.

"And the *Crescent Queen*," Karen said. "They never did find out who was behind that. Could Goss have had something to do with it?"

"Not *could he*. Instead ask *Did he*."

Karen felt her hands go cold. "Did he?"

Grimm was silent.

Karen spent a long moment in thought. The things she was hearing were too monstrous to be believed. Yet they fit in with the facts. The *Crescent Queen* had created a climate of insecurity that prepared the ground for the greater terror of the Pinocchio Syndrome. The two disasters fit together like pieces of a puzzle.

Another question now occurred to her.

"This master plan with the disease," she said. "Is that where it ends? Destruction of the terrorist world?"

Again Grimm's low laugh sounded. "What do you think?"

Karen's thoughts were straying to the great experiments in genocide of the past. Hitler, Stalin, Idi Amin, the Kurds in Iraq, Milosevic in Kosovo. Genocide was a habit that was hard to break. Rarely was the damage limited to one group.

"The Muslims and their terrorists are the primary threat to the civilized world," Grimm said. "But there are other groups that may be deemed to be objectionable. Communists. Criminals. Jews. Homosexuals." He laughed. "Certain intellectuals. People with inconvenient ideas. Certain reporters, I imagine. Shall I go on?"

"What makes Goss think people will stand for this?" Karen asked incredulously.

"I've heard him explain it over and over again," Grimm said. "We've sat together late at night discussing it. He's quite eloquent. There are two phases. During the first phase the entire thing is disguised as an epidemic. Just like HIV. And if, over time, a grain of the real truth finds its way into the public consciousness, *'They'll get used to the idea.'* Those are Goss's words."

"Who will get used to the idea?"

"Everyone. In exchange for a peaceful, prosperous world order, people will dry their tears over a billion or so dead. Especially if those who died were inconvenient when they were alive. Nonproductive economically, a nuisance politically."

"Jesus Christ," Karen breathed.

"It will simply be deemed that the Pinocchio Syndrome chooses its victims in mysterious ways," Grimm concluded. "People will accept that. And over time, over the decades, people will get less curious, less sensitive. The Syndrome will be part of life. Like cancer, it will not be cured. The undesirable groups will be weeded out, and a few desirable groups will be affected here and there, just to make it look good. Population control will be much less of a problem, because the Syndrome will descend on areas where population growth is excessive. On the whole life will be better. People won't complain."

"World domination," Karen said quietly.

"Precisely. Domination of the world by its most civilized peoples. Removal of the least civilized, the least necessary."

Karen turned around in her seat.

"Don't do that," Grimm ordered, pulling the bill of the cap over his face.

"Sorry," Karen said. "I wasn't thinking. I wanted to ask you how this can be stopped."

"That's going to be your problem," Grimm said. "Goss has taken elaborate security measures. And he has some influence within the executive branch and the intelligence community. But he also thinks no one would believe a story like this if it was told to them. It's simply too big. Too fantastic."

"I see." Karen herself was having trouble taking in the enormity of the horror Grimm had described. The end of the free world was at hand. A dictatorship a hundred times worse than Hitler was poised to unleash itself on the human race.

Grimm seemed to read her mind. "There is always a chance. No one believed Hitler and the death camps when the news first hit the media. No one believed Stalin and his purges—not at first. But over time they learned to believe. It can happen. No one ever really believed Iran-Contra. But they did believe the Pentagon Papers. They did believe Watergate."

Karen nodded. "I see."

"The truth is very fragile," Grimm said. "Most often it can't compete with lies. Or with illusions, or with myths, or with rumors. But sometimes the truth can hold its own. Sometimes it can even win." He laughed. "It all depends on the reporter. And, of course, the beholder. What good did the truth do the Simpson prosecutors? What good did it do the Iran-Contra committee? The truth about Kennedy was known in 1964, but it could never compete with the cover-ups and the myths."

Karen said nothing. He was right. Her career had shown her how often untruth defeated truth. But sometimes, for reasons that are not clear, the truth is heard.

"The factor that makes the difference can seem very small," Grimm said. "A reel of audiotape, a trail of blood, or of money. A voice on the phone. A face in a picture."

"What are you saying?" Karen asked.

"Whoever kidnapped Susan Campbell did the one thing that could have upset the plan," Grimm said. "I don't know who it was. Goss doesn't know who it was. As you've seen, Campbell couldn't deviate from the plan. He refused the demand. He had no choice. If you want to stop it, find Susan Campbell and the people who have her. In that direction there's a chance. But you'd better find her before Goss does."

Karen was looking through the windshield at the Washington Monument, which suddenly seemed rather cruel, spearing the sky. Glittering and cruel and empty, a phallic reminder of man's rapacious ambition.

"I'm trying," she said. "Can you help?"

Grimm shook his head. "You know all I know. The rest you'll have to find out for yourself."

The back door opened suddenly. Grimm was getting out.

"Wait!" Karen cried.

The door slammed. To Karen's surprise Grimm did not run away. He walked coolly to the front of the car and stood illuminated in her headlights. He pulled the cap around until it faced backward. She saw a high hairline, sallow, lined skin, thin lips.

For one instant he raised the sunglasses. His eyes were blue. They looked oddly distorted. Perhaps by a drug, or perhaps by a knowledge that was unbearable.

He smiled. He winked. Then he lowered the sunglasses. His right hand came up. In it was a gun. Karen flinched, shrank back against her seat.

But the gun was not pointed at her. It was in his mouth. It went off with a roar that echoed off the government buildings gathered in the darkness to protect the republic.

Grimm dropped like a stone and lay crumpled in his own pooling blood.

Karen had cried out without hearing herself. She felt tears running down her face. Gasping, she put the car into reverse and pulled it away from the body. She caught a glimpse of blood running toward the gutter as she jerked the wheel and drove off.

7 5

Hamilton, Virginia
April 21

INGRID CAMPBELL'S funeral was held at the Presbyterian church in the small town nearest to Judd Campbell's Chesapeake Bay home. Because of the continuing crisis of Susan Campbell's abduction, no one outside the immediate family was invited. However, most of the local people knew Ingrid, and those who wished to attend were allowed entry to the church.

The pastor spoke of Ingrid's unfailing loyalty to her family and of her love for people. Ingrid had given a great deal of her time to charitable causes. A wealthy woman in her own right thanks to the trust fund Judd had set up for her years before, she had no use for money in her personal life, and gave away almost everything she had. There were at least a dozen families in the town who had benefited from her generosity. The service was thrown open to them after the pastor's eulogy, and several townspeople spoke warmly of Ingrid's kindness and concern.

The graveyard service would not be held for another few weeks. Judd Campbell had made this decision without telling anyone why. The real reason was that he still hoped Susan would come home. Susan had looked upon Ingrid as a beloved older sister. She would want to be present for the service.

After the funeral Judd sat at home answering sympathy calls from friends and relatives while Stewart, who had come from Baltimore, sat with Michael. Stewart's wife, June, had brought groceries for a small supper and had cooked for the men. She noticed that Judd seemed to want to be in the same room with her. She felt his eyes on her while she cooked. She realized that, for the first time in the life of the Campbell family, there was no woman in this house. Judd was a man who needed the care and attention of women. That was why he had been so dependent on Ingrid after Margery died, and on Susan after Michael got married. He would be lost now.

Stewart took off his glasses during the dinner hour. June noticed his resemblance to Judd, which was becoming sharper as Stewart grew older. The Scotch-Irish features, the intense blue eyes, the high forehead. It was strange that Stewart, the sibling who liked Judd the least, resembled him the most. Ingrid had taken after her mother, and Michael's dark hair and eyes seemed to have come from some corner of Margery's family that had remained submerged for generations.

June took her leave after supper, but Stewart stayed on. He saw the despair in the faces of his father and brother. Though he was not comfortable in Judd's house, and had no expectation that Ingrid's death would bring him closer to Judd, he sensed an almost unbearable tension in Judd and even in Michael. It was as though the two men had gone beyond mere grief and were on the point of exploding.

"What do you hear from the law enforcement people?" Stewart asked his father.

"Nothing." Judd spoke with his perennial contempt for the government. But anguish sounded eloquently in his voice. Steward realized he had said the wrong thing. This was the worst possible night to remind Judd of Susan.

The three men spent the evening watching TV in the living room and occasionally exchanging remarks about Ingrid. The evening was a huge failure. They could not console each other. Stewart felt like a fifth wheel. He had left the family long ago and stubbornly resisted the efforts of both Ingrid and Susan to bring him back. In this he was his father's son after all, for no man was more stubborn than Judd Campbell. It was too late to retrace his steps. When he spoke sympathetically to Judd of Ingrid, Judd looked at him as though not seeing him.

After a while Stewart directed his remarks to Michael. But Michael himself seemed unreachable. And why not? His sister was dead, and his wife was very probably dead also.

Outside the house the waves crashed and thumped more loudly than usual. Gulls screamed as though in agony. Everything was falling apart, Stewart mused. The life his father and brother had taken for granted all these years was gone. How would they begin to put it back together? Especially if Susan did not come back . . .

Stewart stayed up with them until midnight, but then took his leave and went upstairs to the bedroom he had occupied as a teenager. He sensed that there was something between Michael and Judd that excluded him. A depth of sorrow, perhaps, or a thread of memory or love that would be their shared lifeline to Ingrid.

Stewart had brought a book of historical essays on the Civil War with him and tried to read it as he lay in his bed. But he could not concentrate and soon turned out the light. If there was conversation downstairs he could not hear it. The insistent waves drowned it out. He lay in silence for a long time, thinking of Ingrid. Then he fell into a dark, miserable sleep.

Stewart was wrong about Judd and Michael. No intimacy joined them as they sat in the living room, their faces lit by the flickering of the soundless television screen. Michael looked off into space, his eyes misty, but no tears flowing down his face. His jaw was set in an incongruous, stubborn expression, like the man in the old joke who waited for the other shoe to drop.

Judd was watching Michael out of the corner of his eye. He had waited for Stewart to leave so he could concentrate his attention completely on Michael.

Judd knew the expression on Michael's face. It was the look Michael had worn after Margery died. It was also the look Michael wore when he refused the demand of the terrorists who held Susan.

Tonight Judd was seeing that look again.

But tonight, for the first time, Judd looked at that stony, tortured face in a new way. It was not the face of the son he loved and understood, but the face of a stranger.

7 6

THE REALTY office was respectable, but hardly elegant.

It was located in a strip mall in Congress Heights, not far from the Greater Southeast Community Hospital. The agent did a certain amount of business selling homes and apartment buildings, but the majority of his income came from apartment rentals and leases on dilapidated downtown houses.

His name was Tyrone Crocker. He wore a white dress shirt with a frayed collar and a clip-on tie that had seen better days. An extra hole had been punched in the leather belt that covered his paunch. He wore a gigantic digital watch and several rings. His few strands of hair were plastered carefully over a bald freckled head. He smelled of Sen-Sen and cigarettes.

He had come down in the world considerably since his days with White & Abercrombie, selling seven-figure residences in Georgetown and the suburbs. A messy divorce, a scrape with the law over some shady contracts, and a bit of substance abuse had taken the luster off his career.

He sat behind his desk, looking at Karen Embry. She wore a white cotton dress with delicate shoulder straps and a low-cut bodice. She carried a large purse and wore low-heeled shoes. She looked fresh and prim, but her outfit did not conceal the alluring curves of her body.

She had told him she was looking for her older sister.

"She had a falling-out with my mother," Karen said. "They've never really gotten along. I tried to keep the lid on things, but they finally got out of hand. There was a big fight, and Judy left without even taking her things."

Karen managed a look of wounded family feeling. "Judy is hotheaded," she said. "The funny thing is, that's what she has in common with Mom."

The realtor was watching her face. Clearly he appreciated her good looks. He seemed sympathetic.

"What makes you think she rented a house?" he asked.

"She can't stand apartments. The noise of other people's plumbing bothers her. She hasn't lived in an apartment since college. Even if it puts a strain on her finances, she'll always rent a house."

Karen was not saying what was in her mind. Assuming that Justine Lawrence moved to Washington as the final stop on her odyssey, Karen had postulated that Susan Campbell was being sequestered somewhere in the city. It was far easier to hold a person prisoner in a house than in an apartment. Houses had basements, attics, windowless inner rooms that apartments lacked.

It was logical to assume that Susan's captors would not place her in a fancy area full of nosy neighbors, gardeners, and handymen. They would choose a small, inexpensive house in an urban neighborhood where everybody minds his own business. The noisy airplanes audible on the tape of Justine's ransom demand suggested the inner-city areas close to the major airports.

Tyrone Crocker was the seventh rental agent Karen had visited. She had gradually refined the cover story of herself as Justine's younger sister in order to put those she questioned at their ease. She could hardly tell them anything remotely resembling the truth.

"Uh-huh." The realtor hid his skepticism under his friendly face. "Well, I haven't had anyone by that name rent anything."

"She might have used an alias," Karen said. "Not that she's in trouble with the law, or anything like that. She just wouldn't want my parents to catch up with her. That's how strongly she feels about the whole thing."

Hearing this, the realtor could not hide his suspicion. He always demanded identification from all his renters. It was a basic precaution. So many skipped out on overdue rent, it was the nightmare of his life. He had to vouch for the renters to the landlords.

"Of course," Karen assured him, "the rent would never be a problem. She would always pay on time. She's very scrupulous about things like that. She saves her money."

Tyrone nodded. "Right."

"May I show you her picture?" Karen asked, fiddling in her purse. "That might refresh your memory. If she's been here, that is."

"Sure. Why not?"

Tyrone put on his reading glasses as Karen handed him an enlargement of the Polaroid snapshot of Justine Lawrence that had been used for her name tag at the Webster Groves Mental Health Clinic in St. Louis.

"It's not that recent," she said. "She hasn't been around the family much, so we haven't taken many pictures."

Tyrone looked thoughtfully at the picture. "Son of a gun," he said. "That's her."

"Really?" Karen's face lit up.

"Yeah. I pride myself on my memory for faces." His eyes narrowed. "This looks a little different, though."

"Really? In what way?"

Tyrone studied the photograph. "The hair looks darker here. When I showed her the house she seemed sort of blondish." Something else seemed to be on his mind.

"I know you have to be observant in your job," Karen said placatingly. "I'm sure you notice things that ordinary people wouldn't be sharp enough to see."

He gave Karen a slow evaluative look. He was wondering whether the information she wanted was worth money to her.

"Please don't feel hesitant to say what's on your mind," she said. "Judy has had her problems over the years. Mentally, I mean . . ."

He nodded. "Right. I wasn't going to say anything. She did seem strange. Her eyes . . . They had that look, you know? I've dealt with a lot of people in my time. Some of my properties are halfway houses. Mental patients kicked out of state hospitals when the funding dried up, things like that." He looked at the picture. "Your sister had that look. Also—"

"You're very understanding," Karen prodded. "I appreciate that. Did you notice something else?"

"Her left wrist as she was signing the contract," Tyrone said. "It had cut marks. Scars."

"Yes, that's her." Karen smiled. "That's wonderful news. I can hardly wait to see her. Mr. Crocker, you've been a great help." She opened her purse and took out a pen. "What's the address?"

Once again the rental agent looked suspicious. "I'm not going to have any trouble out of this, am I?"

Karen shook her head earnestly. "You won't. I promise. I just want to see her. Just to make sure she's all right. She'll be happy to see me. We get along wonderfully. It's Mother she can't stand. I'll be eternally in your debt. And I promise you'll never have a problem about the rent. I'll guarantee it myself if you like."

"Is she on medication?" he asked.

"Oh, goodness, no," Karen smiled. "That all ended a long time ago. She doesn't need it anymore. You must have seen for yourself that she's very responsible, very stable."

He nodded grudgingly. "Yeah, she seemed normal enough. Except for that look in her eyes."

"That was probably just nervousness over signing the lease," Karen said. "She's very stable, really."

"Uh-huh." The realtor pulled a piece of scratch paper from a stack on his desk. "Here's the address. It's right down the block from the 7-Eleven. You can't miss it. There's a Subway on the corner."

With a last significant look he handed the address to Karen, who left in a flurry of enthusiastic thanks.

Once outside she got into her Honda, which was already hot under the spring sun. A harbinger of the torrid summer to come, she mused as she turned on the air-conditioning and opened the windows.

The radio was on, tuned to the all-news station.

"Senator Campbell was not available for comment," said a reporter. *"Few begrudged him his privacy at this painful time. The suicide of his only sister while his*

454

wife remains in the hands of her captors was a painful blow, the more so since many in the law enforcement community doubt that Susan Campbell is still alive."

Karen reached into her purse and pulled out her cell phone. She fished out Joe Kraig's office number and dialed it.

"Federal agents, may I help you?"

"Yes, I'd like to speak to Agent Joe Kraig, please."

"Who is calling, please?"

"Karen Embry."

"One moment."

Karen lit a Newport and sat watching the traffic go by. *Come on,* she thought. The excitement of being so close to the target made her fingers tremble. She did not want to be alone with this information. She needed one friend she could trust.

Ingrid Campbell, she thought. An untimely death that brought back memories. Howard Hunt's wife, dead in a plane crash in 1972. Jack Ruby, dead in his jail cell. Lee Oswald, shot in a police station. All of them silenced.

Karen was trained to trust no one, to suspect everything. There was more to Ingrid Campbell's death than met the eye.

"Agent Kraig is out of the office. Is there a number where you can be reached?"

"He knows the number. Would you tell him it's urgent, please?"

"Yes, I will."

"Thank you."

Karen hung up. She thought of waiting for Kraig to call. Then, shaking her head, she closed the car windows and drove off. There was no time.

7 7

Washington

JOSEPH KRAIG sat in an underground room at FBI headquarters, listening to the tape of the telephone demand made by Susan Campbell's abductor.

In the room were two senior FBI agents, the technician who was in charge of the tape-recording analysis, and one representative each from the DIA, the CIA, and Kraig's office.

The voice of Susan Campbell's captor rang out through the oversized speakers.

"Michael Campbell must immediately withdraw his name from consideration as vice president. When Campbell has withdrawn and another person has been selected, Mrs. Campbell will be released. If there is a delay in complying with this request, Mrs. Campbell will die."

The technician stopped the tape. "She's been around," he said. "Deep South, definitely. Also urban South, maybe Atlanta. And somewhere else on the upper Seaboard, possibly Connecticut. But she's originally from Massachusetts. That's obvious in the vowels."

He rewound the tape and played the voice again. Joe Kraig sat listening. His thoughts were on Karen Embry and her Boston theory. He should not have underestimated the reporter.

"You didn't bring us down here for that, did you?" asked the DIA man. "We've had men on the voice for two weeks. It's a dead end."

The engineer shook his head. "No, I didn't bring you here for that. Now, listen to the background."

He rewound the tape and played it through twice more.

"You hear the planes," he said. The others nodded. The roar of large planes taking off interfered with the clarity of the voice.

He touched a dial to enhance the sound of the engines, then played the tape through again from the beginning, including Susan's voice and that of the female captor.

"The planes are military," he said. "They're transports at Bolling Air Force Base. You can't miss the sound, they're not like any commercial jet."

He played the tape through again. The agents were thoughtful.

"Now compare the sound of the planes in Mrs. Campbell's section to the sound in the kidnapper's section," he said.

He played the tape through. Kraig noticed a slight difference in the sound of the planes, but could not put his finger on it.

"This voice was recorded at a different time," the technician said. "I talked to the controllers at Bolling. The schedules are very strict over there. The kidnapper's tape was made in the late afternoon."

The CIA man shrugged. "What does that tell us?"

"In itself, not much," the technician said. "But now listen to the final part of the tape, which is Mrs. Campbell again."

Susan's voice rang out through the huge speakers, sending a chill down Kraig's spine. *"Michael, please do what they say right away,"* Susan said. *"I've talked to them. They mean business. They know what they're doing. Michael, I love you . . ."*

The voice had a new ring to it, forlorn and even tragic, now that Kraig knew that Michael had refused to heed the plea in his wife's voice.

A loud bang was heard just after the word *business* and before Susan began her final sentence, *They know what they're doing.* The technician rewound the tape.

"Okay, you hear that bang," he said.

"Sonic boom?" the CIA man asked.

"No way." The technician shook his head. "The government won't allow sonic booms anywhere over the city during working hours. Anyway, this sound is completely different. Listen again closely."

He replayed the tape. Kraig heard a sharp cracking sound, but even when enhanced it meant nothing to him.

"It's a car accident happening right while she's talking," the technician said. "Listen to the enhancement." He removed the tape and inserted a different one. As the new tape was played Kraig could just make out a fleeting sound of screeching brakes.

"Right," he said. "So there was an accident somewhere near the hideout."

The tech nodded. "I've been on the phone with the D.C. traffic bureau and the city cops since early this morning. They know every accident that took place in the city during the time frame when this message was recorded. We can narrow it down by the sound of the jets at Bolling. We can narrow it further by enhancing all the ambient sounds digitally for distance and direction. Using the computer we can almost map the whole acoustic field around the voice. The technique was developed when they were trying to figure the Kennedy assassination from the radio of one of the motorcycle cops."

Those present nodded. Two of the federal agents exchanged a glance.

The senior FBI man called up a map of southeast Washington and zoomed to the streets within a half-mile radius of the air force base.

"There were seven accidents in that general area within the time frame we're talking about," he said. "Three were fender benders that wouldn't have made the kind of noise we hear on the tape. Two were multicar pileups, which obviously made multiple crash noises. That leaves one. A head-on collision between a sedan and a delivery van, at the corner of 2nd and Galveston."

Using a dial on the console, he zoomed to an intersection in a seedy business district east of the air base.

"There are no more than two square blocks in which the sound of the accident could have been that loud in comparison with the noise of the planes from the base," he said. "It's an old-fashioned district, old row houses and apartment buildings with dry cleaners on the ground floor, that kind of thing."

The agents didn't need to hear any more. This was the first significant clue they had had since Susan Campbell's disappearance.

"Let's cordon it off," Kraig said. "We'll take four-man teams and blanket the area."

"The D.C. police are standing by for the cordon," said the FBI agent. "We'll use our own people for the search. Unmarked cars. Remember, there are orders from the top on this."

"Let's move." It was the CIA agent who said this.

Kraig was the first one out of the office. Within minutes he was with an assault team, donning a bulletproof vest and trying out his hand-held radio.

He did not receive the message from his office about Karen Embry's urgent phone call. He would not learn of the message until it was all over.

78

COLIN GOSS was in the soundproofed office kept for his private use at his D.C. campaign headquarters. He had flown here to be nearer the center of things at this crucial hour. He was on the telephone.

"When did they find this out?" he asked.

"This morning," said the caller, a Goss operative with direct links to the intelligence agencies.

"And they're on their way now?"

"They're cordoning off the area. They'll go door to door with SWAT teams."

"Do they have the exact address?" Goss asked.

"No. Just a two- or three-block radius."

"Can you get in there ahead of them?" Goss asked.

"We're trying. I have men a few blocks away. I don't know if we can beat them to it. It will be a near thing."

"What if you don't?" Goss asked.

"We have a man on the front lines. He knows what to do."

Goss sighed. The work of twenty years hinged on the events of the next few hours. Not even his own unlimited supply of cash could buy complete certainty about the outcome.

"All right," he said. "Just make sure no one comes out of there alive. I'll take care of your man afterward."

"Yes, sir," said the voice. "We'll do our best."

"Don't tell me you'll do your best," Goss shouted. "Get it done!"

He slammed down the phone.

———

2:23 P.M.

KAREN DID not know this part of the city well.

She had to stop and look at a street map twice. She pulled into an Exxon station, filled up the Honda's tank, and asked the cashier for directions.

She lit one Newport from another as she drove. Her hands were frozen around the wheel. A queer fluttery feeling was in her stomach, the result of sleeplessness, lack of food, and excitement.

Suddenly a small dog ran into the street from between the parked cars. Karen slammed on the brakes. The Honda screeched to a stop just as a little boy rushed obliviously into the street after the dog. The boy looked up at Karen in surprise. Then he stooped to reach for the puppy, which slipped away playfully and bounded back onto the sidewalk.

"Jesus!" she cursed under her breath. A boy one second from violent death, and almost completely indifferent to the danger.

The boy casually gave Karen the finger as he turned to follow the dog.

The Honda had stalled. Karen turned the key in the ignition and gunned the motor. She resolved to proceed more carefully. Her excitement was running away with her. The search she had been pursuing for nearly a month had finally ended.

She was on her way to Justine at last. And to Susan Campbell.

And, unlike anyone else involved in the search for Susan, Karen knew the answers. She knew the *why* of everything that had happened. This made her all the more anxious to get to her destination.

She only hoped they were still at the little house toward which she was heading. They might have left, especially after the events of recent days. Justine must realize that her hideout could not remain secret forever. By sending the authorities an audiotape she had given them a clue. They were not stupid; they would find her eventually.

With this thought Karen felt a pulse of anxiety. Suppose she was not the only one who knew why all this was happening. There were others concerned, after all. Others who stood to gain or lose from what might happen. Others whose whole future might depend on how this situation resolved itself.

Karen realized she had been very naive. She had thought she alone had eyes to see the truth with, because it was her business to make the truth known. There might be others even more acutely sensitive to that truth, because it was their business to bury it.

She pressed the accelerator harder.

———

THE CAR Joseph Kraig drove was unmarked. So were all the others converging on the two-block area where Susan Campbell was hidden.

Kraig was assailed by the same doubts as Karen Embry. A long time had passed since the original demand made by Susan's captors. If they were as smart as they seemed, they would have known that the tape they had played over the phone contained enough acoustic clues to lead the authorities to their hideout.

Yet somehow it was not an empty hideout that Kraig feared. The abduction of Susan Campbell had been the last in a series of events that were beyond rational anticipation, events that flouted understanding as well as control. Events that came out of a nightmare and stood shining in the sunlight of day like monsters.

And at the center of it all, helpless, innocent, Susan Campbell awaited her fate. Kraig had the sinister presentiment that the greatest danger to Susan was coming only now.

Kraig heard the screech of tires somewhere ahead. Voices cackled on his radio. He put on his brakes. Agents were running toward the car.

It was time.

———————

SUSAN SAT on the edge of the bed. She wore a skirt and blouse borrowed from Justine. The clothes fitted her surprisingly well. Even the cheap pair of discount house shoes Justine had apologetically given her was not uncomfortable.

The two women were silent, like relatives at an airport passing their last moments together before parting, both at a loss for something to say.

Susan sat primly, her feet crossed. At that moment, Justine thought, she looked like a little girl. Sad, brave, lonely.

"You know what to do?" Justine asked.

"Yes," Susan said. "I know."

"You'll be sequestered," Justine said. "They'll allow you one public statement, and perhaps an interview with your husband present. But they won't let anyone see you alone."

Susan nodded.

"There won't be much time to work with," Justine said. "A week, maybe two. After that you won't be safe."

Susan nodded again. "I understand."

She studied Justine's face.

"How can you be so sure . . . ?" she asked.

"Sure of what? That I won't make it?"

Susan nodded, her eyes downcast.

"Remember what we said about the emperor's new clothes?" Justine asked. "About the mother shushing the child?"

"And then everyone goes on admiring the emperor's new suit of clothes," Susan said. "I remember."

"That's the real world, Susan. The truth isn't strong. It needs help sometimes. More help than I can give it alone."

Susan's eyes misted. "I don't like to think of you . . ."

"Dead?" Justine smiled. "Let that be the least of your worries, Susan. It will be a deliverance." She sat back in her chair and sighed. The cut marks on her wrists shone as she stretched her arms. "To close my eyes, to sleep without dreaming . . ."

She looked at Susan. A sad smile curled her lips. "I found my way to you at last," she said. "You can't know how much that eases the pain. Thanks to you, I'm not alone now."

Her eyes grew more serious. "I've worked so hard, Susan, to bring us to this moment. It's been my whole life. I need to feel . . . You won't let me down, will you?"

Susan gave her a firm nod. "I'm not much, but you can count on me. I won't let you down."

There was a pause. Both women started to say something, then fell silent. They returned to their vigil. The planes droned overhead. Susan felt as though she were in a place of parting, a place of tears and new beginnings.

IN THE Oval Office the president waited.

He had ordered his secretary to hold all calls. The line to the FBI was open. Nothing would happen until the result of the assault was known.

The president took a long look out the window at Pennsylvania Avenue. It was a beautiful day. Tourists waited in line to see the White House, the mothers holding their children's hands. Their patience touched him. They wanted to see the seat of government. To see where the decisions were made that protected their freedoms.

He turned to look at the walls of the office. The painting of Lincoln by Harkness was where he had ordered it hung when he first came here. Photos of past presidents who had touched his life personally were displayed, some shaking hands with him, others alone. He kept them here for moral support. They had occupied this office and endured the stresses it brought. If they could do it, he often told himself, so could he.

"The buck stops here." So ran the old maxim. He wondered about its truth. It might be more accurate to say, *The end begins here.* At least for certain presidents, for certain times. Rare was the president who got through eight years without at least once being swamped by events out of control. He himself had been under siege almost since the day of his inauguration.

The phone rang. It was his secretary. The FBI director was on the line.

"Put him through," the president said.

"Hello, Mr. President," the director said. "I wanted you to know they're making the assault. It won't be long before we have all the answers."

"Tell your men to be careful," the president said. "If Susan Campbell is alive in there, I don't want her hurt." The situation can still be saved, he thought. If no more bad luck happens, Michael Campbell might have his wife back, and the country might have a vice president again.

He felt an impulse to call Michael. He knew what Michael was going through. A friendly voice, at this final moment . . .

But he vetoed the idea. It was too late for such things, really. Too late for a lot of things.

What will be will be.

The president sat down to wait.

7 9

2:30 P.M.

KAREN SLAMMED on her brakes a half block before the intersection.

It was closed off by a roadblock made up of police cars with lights flashing. A uniformed D.C. cop was directing traffic to a detour leading north toward the freeway.

Beyond the roadblock there were a lot of cars, all unmarked. Agents with handheld radios stood here and there.

Cursing under her breath, Karen made a U-turn and took the first left turn she could find. Something was up, she knew. This was no coincidence.

How had they gotten there before her? She had tried to get in touch with Kraig and failed. He couldn't possibly know the truth.

Karen pulled over to the curb and stopped the car. She thought for a moment. There were men converging on Justine Lawrence, and on Susan, if Susan was still alive. Men a lot more powerful than Karen. Men whose motives she could not know.

"Fuck," she said. "Fuck them."

She got out of the car and ran toward the alley between the houses.

THE AGENTS reconnoitered in the middle of the first block of seedy bungalows, apartment buildings, and cheap businesses. An old woman behind one of the upstairs windows reflected that she had never seen so many walkie-talkies in her life.

Four-man teams spread out along the street. Snipers were already on the roofs, prepared for a possible attack on the agents from one of the houses. Bomb specialists waited tensely in their vans, watching the cautious movements of the agents. Everyone wore heavy-duty bulletproof vests and SWAT helmets.

Kraig was with two FBI men and another Secret Service agent, a man he knew well from shared assignments over the years.

"Let's take it slow," Kraig said. "We don't know what kind of weapons we might be up against."

He spoke through his radio to the assembled agents. "Two minutes," he said. "Hold your fire."

The taller of the two FBI agents was a man unknown to Kraig. The agency had said he was a top SWAT specialist, quick on the draw but with good control. Kraig gave him a glance. The man nodded.

"Thirty seconds," Kraig said into the radio.

Unseen by anyone, the tall agent released the safety on his automatic and covered the gun butt with his thumb.

KAREN DARTED among the buildings like a guerrilla in the midst of a search-and-destroy mission. The sirens were screaming like banshees. The roar of gunned engines crashed between the houses.

She studied the houses in the alley filled with garbage cans and tiny fenced gardens. Amazingly, the agents hadn't thought to post men here. Not yet. So much for government efficiency, she thought.

I must be a block or so ahead of them, she thought. They were blanketing the area, but Karen knew the exact address. That gave her time to work with. Not much, though.

She looked at the address on her piece of paper. She counted the houses along the alley. Guessing quickly, she hurried to the third house from the end. It looked no different from the others, except for a tiny American flag stuck in one of the pots of geraniums on the stoop.

She heard a roar and looked up to see a military transport plane flying over. Every window on the block rattled. This must not be a pleasant place to live, she mused.

Three concrete steps that had long since sagged out of alignment led to the back door of the house. Karen climbed them and knocked quietly on the door. There was no answer. The cacophony of the sirens must have drawn the occupants to the front windows. She dared not go around front, in sight of the agents.

She knocked harder.

"Susan!" she called.

She heard male voices shouting, and again the grinding of the car engines.

"Jesus Christ," she muttered to herself. And then, loud, "Susan! Justine!"

Cursing the situation, she pounded on the door with all her might.

"Susan! It's Karen Embry! Open up!"

She thought she heard a movement behind the door. It was probably the kitchen, she thought. Kitchens always overlooked alleys in these ancient little houses.

"Susan! Justine!"

She heard a fumbling at the latch. The door, warped by long years of abuse, crunched open slowly. She saw a woman's face. It looked prematurely aged. The eyes were haggard. A small gun was pointed at Karen.

"Justine," Karen said.

There was no time for the other woman to answer, for the sound of pounding fists and shouting voices came from the other side of the house.

Karen saw a brief glimmer of acknowledgment in the other woman's eyes.

"Too late," she said, and slammed the door.

Her steps sounded faintly, receding. Karen pounded on the door.

"Susan!" she cried. "Susan!!"

She heard a crash as the front door was broken in. Then the sound of shots being fired. She sank to the concrete stoop, looking at the American flag that waved limply in her face.

Too late, she thought.

80

"FEDERAL AGENTS! Open up!"

Justine gave Susan a last look. Her eyes were soft in that instant. Then, as Joseph Kraig burst through the door, she turned to face him.

"No!" Susan cried.

Justine's first step toward Kraig made his gun come up. He seemed to hesitate; so did she. Then he saw the revolver in her hand. He shot her three times. She fell at Susan's feet, blood gushing from her chest.

"No! Joe!"

Susan clutched her hands to her breast, as though to hold her own blood inside her. Men were piling into the room, all shouting. In that instant Kraig did something that struck Susan. He interposed himself quickly between herself and the other agents, as though to protect her. "Hold your fire!" he ordered. Their faces, impersonal, registered mute acknowledgment.

Then Kraig had his arms around Susan and she was weeping uncontrollably.

"It's all right," he said. "You're all right."

One of the agents had stepped on Justine's wrist. The gun lay on the carpet beside Justine's hand.

"This is a crime scene," one of the agents said to someone. "We're impounding everything. Nothing leaves this house."

Agents were fanning out around the house. With their suits and polished shoes and radios they looked like robots. One of them was kneeling in front of the collection of videotapes beside the TV. He scanned the spines of the little boxes, noting the titles.

Kraig was holding Susan's face against his chest. She could not take her eyes off Justine, whose scarred wrist lay lifeless on the rug under the agent's foot.

"Can you talk?" Kraig asked Susan.

She nodded weakly.

"Where are the others?" he asked.

She shook her head. "I never saw any others."

Kraig looked from Susan to Justine.

"We'll sort it all out later," he said. "The important thing is that you're safe. Wait until Mike hears. He won't believe it."

Susan stared at him through wide eyes, like a child.

81

AMERICA CELEBRATES
April 28

Americans mingled tears of relief with joyous smiles today as Susan Campbell, the wife of vice presidential nominee Michael Campbell, spent her first day at home after a harrowing four-week abduction.

Michael Campbell wept openly as he thanked law enforcement officials and the public at a Washington news conference.

"Without the heroic determination of the FBI, the federal intelligence services, and law enforcement agencies around the country, Susan would not be home with us today," Campbell said. "I owe a special debt to Agent Joe Kraig, who personally saved Susan after a desperate search for the hideout where she was being held. I've known Joe since we were boys together in prep school. He's been a friend to me and to Susan since before our marriage. Now he is a hero to me. He always will be."

Susan Campbell is in seclusion at the Campbell family home on the Chesapeake Bay, and will not be available for comment until doctors have determined definitively that she is over the worst of the stress she endured as a hostage.

*An FBI spokesman has identified the abductor of Mrs. Campbell as a for-
mer mental patient who had no connection with any political group. The
woman's identity has been withheld pending notification of next of kin. Authorities refused to comment on whether she had confederates in the abduction.*

*The abductor demanded that Senator Campbell withdraw from consider-
ation for vice president. Campbell refused, saying that he could not in good
conscience negotiate with a terrorist despite the danger to his wife.*

*Campbell left the news conference to return to his family home, where his
father, Judd Campbell, and other family members are gathered around Mrs.
Campbell.*

*Sadly, the safe return of Susan Campbell comes only days after the tragic
suicide of Ingrid Campbell, the senator's only sister. Law enforcement spokesmen and family friends have speculated that despondency over Mrs. Campbell's abduction may have contributed to Ingrid Campbell's suicide.*

"My whole life has been a lie . . ."

Michael heard the sudden bright blade of conversation as the nurse
opened the door to the bedroom.

It was his father's voice. The door opened wider to reveal Judd Campbell
sitting on the edge of the bed, holding Susan's hand. It looked for all the
world as though Susan were comforting Judd rather than the reverse.

When they heard Michael's step they both looked up. Judd seemed embarrassed. Susan's expression was unreadable. Then Judd was patting Michael's
shoulder as he walked past him, and Susan offered her usual diffident, wel-
coming smile. But Michael had heard her murmur to his father, "It will be all
right, Dad," in the confusion of bodies shifting position under the nurse's eye.

Michael sat where his father had sat and looked down at Susan.

"How you doing?" he asked.

"Coming along," she smiled. "A little at a time."

"Did those federal guys give you a hard time?" he asked.

"They're terrible," Susan said. "Going over the same ground a thousand
times, when I already told them the little I know. They seem disappointed in
me. I think they blame me for not knowing more."

Susan had been subjected to a tactful but exhausting debriefing at the hands of several federal agents. She had kept her story simple, saying that her kidnapper was a madwoman motivated by some sort of obsession with Michael and his career, along the lines of a John Hinckley or a Sirhan Sirhan.

"She treated me well," Susan told them, "but I could see she was mentally unbalanced. I'm afraid that if she hadn't been stopped she might have tried to kill Michael."

The agents had seemed skeptical, pressing Susan for more details about the abductress's motives and possible associates. Susan stuck to her guns. She barely talked to the woman, she said. She was left alone except when her meals were brought. She did nothing but read and watch videotapes the whole time she was in captivity.

The effort of lying left Susan drained. But the agents had no choice but to accept her story.

Michael took her hand. Susan tried to suppress the tremor in her fingers as he clasped them.

"What's the matter?" Michael asked, sensing her withdrawal.

"Nothing," she said. "I'm afraid my nerves still aren't what they should be."

"Well, that's natural," he said. "After what you've been through. It may take a long time, you know. The doctor says you may have flashbacks. It can be pretty bad."

The image of Justine's scarred hand flashed across Susan's mind. The martyred, blotchy hand of a sick woman, it had held Susan's own as warmly as that of a mother. Later it had held the gun that invited Joe Kraig to shoot her. Justine had given Kraig no choice. She wanted that badly to die. But even in assuring her own death she had given Susan another chance at life.

The little TV in the corner was tuned to CNN. *"The president's standing in the polls is higher than it has been in two years,"* the reporter was saying. *"Pressure in Congress for a special election has eased dramatically. Public support for Colin Goss as an independent presidential candidate has also dropped. Most observers predict a new surge of support for the administration after Michael Campbell becomes vice president."*

There was a silence. After another moment Michael let go of Susan's hand and went to sit in the rocking chair that had belonged to his mother.

"Babe," he said, "will you tell me something?"

"If I can," Susan said.

"That woman. The kidnapper . . ." He looked troubled. "Did she talk much?"

"Not much," Susan lied. "A word or two when she brought my meals. She would ask me if I wanted something else to read, or some more video—videotapes."

"Didn't she ever tell you *why* she was doing it?" Michael pressed.

"No," Susan said in a level voice. "She just—she didn't seem to think I was important enough to talk to."

Something coiled painfully inside her at these words. Justine Lawrence was the first person in Susan's life who really believed Susan was important enough to trust with the truth.

"Well, I guess we'll never know," Michael said.

"No," Susan agreed. "I guess we never will."

"The worst thing about it," Michael said, "was knowing that it was because of me. All my life I've worried about what my career was doing to you. And now, to have you kidnapped . . ." He shook his head. "If you hadn't come back safe, I don't know what I would have done."

You would have become vice president. Susan did not say these words.

"You would have survived," she said.

"But it never would have been the same."

"No," she agreed. "Like your father. It's never been the same for him."

Michael's eyes narrowed. "You mean, since my mother . . . ?"

Susan nodded. Margery Campbell had killed herself in this room.

Susan felt something hard in her eyes focus on him. She tried to hide it. She ran a hand instinctively along the comforter beside her. Michael's look was worried.

"Yes," Michael said. "I see what you mean."

"I feel so terrible about Ingrid," she said. "That must have been hard on you."

"Hard. Yes. Ingrid was as much a mother to me as—"

His words trailed off. His expression was wistful, but the worried look persisted under it.

"I'll miss her," Susan said, watching him.

A voice at the door startled them both.

"I think it's time the patient had some serious rest." It was the nurse.

Susan breathed a sigh of relief. "I'm afraid you're right," she said. "I'm all in."

Michael came back to the bed and kissed Susan on the lips. As he pulled back he saw that her eyes were still open, looking at him.

The nurse shooed Michael out of the room. He glanced back over his shoulder, a look of humor at the nurse's importunity on his face.

This time, try as she might, Susan could not silence the eloquence of her eyes. They were telling Michael that she knew. Knew everything.

And in that last split second as he was going out the door, she saw in his eyes that he knew she knew.

A moment later the nurse came back to ask Susan if she wanted another tranquilizer.

"I don't need it," Susan said. "I can hardly keep my eyes open. I'm going to take a nap."

"Good girl," said the nurse. "Just rest."

The nurse let herself out silently. Susan lay staring at the ceiling. For a moment it seemed to disguise itself, and she saw the ceiling of her bedroom back in New Hampshire, where as a girl she had dreamed of a Prince Charming who would come along one day to carry her away.

Then the magic lantern went out, and Susan was back in the here and now. She knew she would not sleep today.

Time to rest, she thought, *when it's over.*

8 2

Washington
April 30

JOE KRAIG had not seen Susan since he rescued her.

The NSA had, in a remarkable show of arrogance, taken over the case from the other agencies. Claiming authority from the White House itself, the NSA had demanded that all relevant files be turned over to it. Susan was being held incommunicado pending her "debriefing," and none of the agents who had worked so hard to save her were being informed as to the results.

Kraig found himself stewing over his own ignorance of the whole story behind Susan's abduction. He also saw no good reason why he should not be allowed to visit Susan. After all, it was he who rescued her. It was he whom Michael called a hero.

He had spoken to Michael several times on the phone. Michael told him Susan was "not herself," but was coming along. Michael refused to allow Kraig to speak to Susan, saying she needed more time to pull herself together.

Today Ross Agnew's secretary had helped Kraig go through the inventory of what had been found in the house where Susan had been sequestered. There was little to itemize. A toothbrush, some soap and shampoo used by the abductress, Justine Lawrence. Cosmetics, body oils, soap, and shampoo used by Susan. The remnants of some basic groceries. A few condiments left in the refrigerator.

There were magazines in the bedroom where Susan had stayed, including the *New Yorker* and *Vanity Fair.* There were books by Susan's favorite authors and videotapes of some movies Susan liked.

In the VCR attached to the TV in Susan's bedroom at the time of the rescue was an old Harrison Ford movie, *Witness,* on video. The agents had joked about how young Harrison Ford used to be.

As a precaution they played the tapes all the way through to make sure nothing had been recorded over the commercial VHS. They had also turned the pages of the books and magazines, one by one, looking for notes inserted between the pages, underlined passages, or anything else unusual. There was nothing.

Not a clue as to what might have been going through the Lawrence woman's mind during the abduction, or what might have transpired between her and Susan.

Kraig still did not understand why Justine Lawrence, having so expertly managed both the abduction and the sequestration, had not made it harder for the authorities to locate her hideout. Why had she sent her demand by audiotape, inviting the police to analyze her voice as well as the background sounds? Why had she not moved the hideout when she had the chance? It was almost as though she wanted to be caught.

Kraig would never forget the way her hand came up with the gun in it when he burst through the door. Or the look in her eyes. It was a knowing, almost pitying look. As though the Lawrence woman knew something that Kraig himself was not able to know. Not free to know, perhaps. That look would haunt him for the rest of his life.

A full twenty-four hours after the rescue Kraig had learned that there was an urgent message for him from Karen Embry. He was too busy to return her call until yet another day had passed. He got her answering service. He left several messages, but she never called him.

He would talk to her when things settled down, he decided. She might know something that would be of use.

Of course, there was no hurry. The worst was over.

8 3

May 5

KAREN EMBRY had kept out of sight since the day of Susan Campbell's rescue.

She had had to do some fast talking when the federal agents swarmed into the alley behind Justine Lawrence's bungalow. She told the agents she was a reporter who had heard something important was "going down" in the area, something connected to Susan Campbell. The agents escorted her to her abandoned car and then shooed her away like an annoying insect, never suspecting how much of the truth she really knew.

Since then Karen had stayed at home, watching events take their course. She had ignored Joe Kraig's phone messages. She had tried to warn him of the truth about Justine Lawrence, and had failed. Now Justine was dead. The media reports about the abduction and Justine's identity were obviously a cover-up in the making. Karen felt her best course was to observe this process from a safe distance.

On Wednesday, more than a week after the rescue, Karen heard a knock at the door of her apartment. Through the eyehole she saw a mailman.

"Yes?" she asked through the intercom.

"Registered mail, ma'am."

"Just a minute."

Karen had just emerged from the shower and was wearing nothing but a towel. She slipped on her terry-cloth bathrobe and opened the door, leaving the chain latched.

"Sign the receipt." The mailman handed her a clipboard. She signed her name and took the package, which was a padded envelope.

It was not until she was standing in her kitchen with the package in her hand that she saw the postmark was ten days old. "Uncle Sam," she said under her breath.

She opened the envelope. Inside it was a videotape in a cardboard slipcase. It bore no label. When she pulled it out of the slipcase a handwritten note fell on the tabletop. Frowning, Karen picked it up.

Dear Karen,

Here is the last piece of the puzzle you tried so hard to put together. I'm sending it to you now because Justine and I have talked the situation over, and we suspect that neither of us will be able to contact you directly after we are found.

The scar is from the first surgery. That dates the event on the tape.

If I am still alive, you and I are the only ones who know the truth. I can't be the one to reveal it to the world. I want it to be you.

Please don't let me down.

Susan

P.S. The day you interviewed me at our house, the phone call was from Justine. I knew you were overhearing, but something told me it would be better if you heard. I never told anyone else—not even Joe. I'm telling you now so you'll know I'm writing this of my own free will.

I know you will do the right thing.

Karen read the note over several times. The signature was Susan's. The graceful, diffident handwriting could not belong to anyone else.

She stood in the silence of the kitchen, thinking. Adding up what she knew, connecting dots between things she knew and things Justine must have known.

She looked at the clock—3 P.M. on a Wednesday afternoon.

"All right, Susan," she said out loud.

She turned on the living room TV and slid the tape into the VCR. Still dressed only in the terry cloth robe, she sat down to watch.

84

The New York Times
May 8

GOSS, CAMPBELL IMPLICATED IN SEX PLOT
Kidnapper of Susan Campbell Was Victim

In a bizarre turn of events coming on the heels of the rescue of Susan Campbell by federal agents, her husband, Maryland senator Michael Campbell, has been implicated in a sex scandal dating back to his college years. Ironically, Campbell's bitter political enemy Colin Goss is named as the ringleader of the sex ring, and allegations are circulating in Washington to the effect that the two political figures have been involved in a covert alliance for years.

It is alleged that Goss used illegal experimental drugs manufactured by his pharmaceutical company to victimize young girls in grotesque sex parties in the Boston area fifteen years ago.

Michael Campbell, then a student at Harvard, lured the girls to a downtown hotel where they were drugged and forced to act as prizes in the perverse "Donkey Game." Many of the girls died or suffered permanent disability as a result of the drugging.

The Times *has received a damning videotaped image of the naked Camp-bell, blindfolded, participating in the game. Campbell is seen approaching a helpless female victim with a "donkey's tail" held in his hand.*

In an even more stunning revelation, sources told Times *reporters that the woman responsible for the abduction of Senator Campbell's wife was her-self one of the Boston victims. The apparent lack of motive in the abduction would be cleared up if this report is confirmed.*

Spokesmen for both Goss and Campbell strenuously denied the allega-tions. Federal authorities refused comment, but sources have told reporters that Senate confirmation of Campbell as vice president will be delayed pend-ing criminal investigation of the charges against him.

————

JUDD CAMPBELL was sitting on the beach.

He watched the waves in their ceaseless approach to the shore. There was no limit to their power, Judd reflected. The sculpted majesty of each crest seemed, for one instant, eternal. Yet their end was always collapse, surrender, death.

It was here, on this spot, that a freak wave had risen up to sweep Michael away when he was a little boy. The wave had almost won. But Judd, armed by the love he bore for his son, had given the last of his strength and energy to fight off the ocean, and Michael had survived. Judd had never been the same after that day, for the exertion had left a scar on his heart that would eventually force him to take a back seat in this life, and leave the achievement of his ambitions to his talented son.

But Judd had misunderstood everything. Fate had not been trying to harm him that long-ago day. Fate had been trying to save him.

Judd recalled his words to Susan. "My whole life has been a lie." Only now did he realize how terribly true that statement was. He wondered why it had taken him so many years after Margery's death to understand it.

He had lost Margery. He had lost Ingrid. And, in a way, he had lost Stew-art. They were all victims of the same curse.

Judd understood everything but his own blindness. Why had he striven so single-mindedly, fought so hard, devoted himself so completely to the one thing that was sure to destroy him?

For it had been Judd who nurtured the slow growth of this cancer in his life, fed it with love and advice and wisdom and experience—all he had to give—until it was strong enough, evil enough, to threaten the whole nation and even the world.

He was pondering this thought when a footfall in the warm sand interrupted him.

"Dad?"

Judd turned to see Michael standing beside him. Michael was crying.

"Dad. What am I going to do?"

Michael fell to his knees before his father.

"Dad. Save me."

He lay down on the sand and curled up with his head in his father's lap. Judd saw the rich, thick hair of his most-beloved child, touched the skin of his cheek. This was the child he had given everything to, and placed all his hopes in.

"All right," Judd said. "You want me to use my powers. Is that it?"

Michael nodded.

"Tell me something," Judd asked. "Do you love me?"

"Yes, Dad." Michael's voice was choked by grief.

"I love you too, son."

Judd stroked his son's hair.

"I'll save you," he said. "But you have to tell me the whole truth. If you lie, I won't be able to help you. Do you understand?"

Michael nodded. His fingers had curled around his father's hand, and he clasped it hard.

"Did you kill Ingrid?" Judd asked.

There was a hesitation. Then Michael nodded.

"You were in it with Goss?"

Again, after a hesitation, Michael nodded.

"And she found out?"

"Yes."

Judd thought for a long moment, his eyes on the waves.

"You got those girls for Goss," he said. "The ones he played the game with."

"Only because he wanted me to." The response was muffled. "He made it seem so important . . ."

"Why, Michael? Why Goss? What possessed you to get involved with such a man?"

There was a silence.

Michael sat up to look at his father. "You always said the main thing was to win," he said.

Judd sighed. "That's right. I did."

So now he knew the key to the Sphinx's riddle. His own ambition. He had caused it all, by encouraging Michael in precisely the direction that would lead to the greatest possible destruction.

"But I was wrong," Judd said.

Michael looked at him. Uncomprehending. Disappointed.

"Do you understand that?" Judd asked.

Michael shook his head. How could he understand, after all these years, that black was really white, and white really black?

"When did it start?" Judd asked.

"At Bryce. He came to one of the soccer games. He said he knew you and Mother."

Judd sighed. Yes, he and Margery had known Goss. He had beaten Goss, humiliated him. And Goss had repaid him by corrupting the son he loved. Judd saw the poetry of Goss's revenge.

"Why did you go along with him?" Judd asked. "Why did you do such terrible things?"

Michael thought for a moment.

"I thought he could do more for me," he said. "He was getting into politics. You always said the real power was in politics."

Judd smiled to see his own opportunism turned against him. Yes, Michael had done what Judd himself would have done at that age. Followed the line of least resistance. Accepted help from the most powerful hand offered. Damn the consequences. Damn right and wrong. Move upward, take no prisoners, do whatever it takes.

"I understand," he said.

"You don't hate me?" Michael asked.

"No, son. I don't hate you." After a pause, "I'm just sorry."

The sky had clouded suddenly, as it often did at this time of year. The waves were creeping further up the shore. The tide was coming in. Judd looked at Michael, who was drying his tears.

"Everhardt and Palleschi and Stillman," Judd said. "They were removed because they were in your way."

Michael nodded.

"And the president," Judd concluded. "He would eventually have been removed, too."

"Yes," Michael agreed.

"And you would have become president," Judd said.

Michael nodded.

Amazement and horror overcame Judd as he realized that the dream he had coveted all these years, Michael as president of the United States, might have become a reality. And that would have been the worst disaster in the history of the nation.

Thank God, he thought. *Thank God they stopped him in time.*

"It was what you always wanted, Dad," Michael said hopefully.

"Did you ever think that it was wrong?" he asked.

Michael looked perplexed. "You mean Danny and the others?"

Judd nodded. He felt as though he were talking to a child.

"Yes, I did. But there was no other way to do it," Michael said. "Remember what you told me about other people?"

Judd nodded. *Treat other people with respect and kindness, unless they are in your way. If they are in your way, walk over them.* It was his own lesson.

He looked at his son.

"What do you think of Colin Goss now?" he asked Michael.

"I think he wants what's best for the country," Michael replied. "The situation is out of hand. People and governments are being held hostage by terrorists. That can't be allowed. He wants to make the world a safe place."

"Even at the cost of innocent human lives?" Judd asked.

The blank look in Michael's eyes was his answer.

The gods had played their joke to the hilt, Judd realized. He himself had formed this child, morally. He had taught him not to be a human being, but to be a winner. Countless times he had repeated his empty wisdom, setting the boy moral dilemmas and teaching him to ignore what was right, to think only of victory. Michael was Judd's own creation.

"Son," he said. "Your mother killed herself because she found out about you, didn't she?"

This hesitation was the longest, so long that for a moment Judd dared to hope that it wasn't true. Then Michael nodded.

"There was a girl. Someone I found for Goss. She committed suicide. Her mother found out about me. She told Mom."

"I see."

Judd's heart constricted as he realized that Margery's last transaction on earth had been to hide from her husband the awful truth she had learned about her son. She hadn't wanted to break his heart because she knew how much he loved Michael. So she had taken herself out of the picture.

If only she had killed Michael, instead of herself!

"And how did it make you feel?" Judd asked.

"Terrible. I never felt anything so awful," Michael said. "I wished I was dead."

"And when Ingrid died?"

"The same," Michael said. "Maybe worse. It was like the end of the world."

"And Susan, son," Judd said. "Susan would have been next, wouldn't she? Because she knew too much."

Michael thought for a moment. Then he nodded. His eyes filled with tears again.

Judd was silent. He knew Michael was sincere. And this was the worst part of it all. That Michael did have feelings. That he genuinely grieved for the mother he had destroyed, the sister he had killed with his own hands. This was evil in the flesh, Judd reflected—Michael's tears.

Michael was looking at the waves. Confession had eased his conscience; his face looked young and fresh again.

"You see those waves, son?" Judd asked. "Those were the waves that tried to drown you when you were just a little boy."

"But you saved me, Dad." Michael's voice had changed. He even sounded like a child now.

"Yes, I did."

Judd rested his hand on his son's shoulder. He knew this body. He thought he had known the person inside it.

"Colin Goss is finished," he said. "He can't help you anymore."

Michael nodded.

"But I can help you, son."

Michael took his father's hand.

"I'm going to get you out of this," Judd said, "but you must do exactly as I say. Do you understand?"

Michael nodded. "Yes, Daddy. I'll do anything you say."

Judd disengaged his hand and helped Michael to sit up.

"Don't look at me, son. Look at the waves. Count the waves coming in to shore."

The old joke sounded hollow now. But Judd's voice was full of love.

"One," Michael said. "Two, three, four . . ."

Judd took the gun out of his windbreaker and aimed it at the back of his son's head. Then he thought better of it.

"How many, son?"

"Five, six, seven . . ."

"Count them with your eyes closed. Show me how high you can count."

"Eight, nine, ten, eleven . . ."

Judd moved the gun and fired into Michael's temple. A cry rose from the direction of the water as Michael fell. Gulls rose against the gray sky, shrieking. The waves crashed against the shore. A spray of rain began to fall.

Judd felt his son's blood inundate his hands. He listened to the screams of the birds. The waves rose higher, then higher still. The tide was coming in fast.

Judd waited for another moment. Then he placed the gun in Michael's left hand and stood up. He took a few steps along the sand, turned around, and looked at what he had done.

"Forgive me," he said aloud. Then he walked back toward the house.

Before he got there he paused for a last time to look down the beach. The rain was coming faster. The waves were lunging up the sand as though hurriedly wiping away the traces of what had happened. The footprints were already gone. One of the breakers covered Michael's body and then let go. Michael slid down toward the eager waves, his arm flopping sideways.

Heavy raindrops mingled with the tears running down Judd's cheeks. He wiped at them with both hands. Then he turned and went into the house.

85

Hamilton, Virginia
May 10

MICHAEL CAMPBELL was buried in the local cemetery a mile from the Campbell house. His funeral was private; no political colleagues were invited. The ceremony was covered by a handful of journalists, most of them from other countries. The American press stayed away.

A day after Michael's suicide Colin Goss abandoned his campaign to force a special election and devoted himself to the legal battle he would soon face. The president had not yet made his fourth and final choice for vice president, but his standing in the polls remained strong, and the business of government was returning to normal.

A striking downturn in the Pinocchio Syndrome epidemic was noted by World Health Organization monitors as the summer approached. No connection was seen between this happy circumstance and the tumultuous political events of the previous months.

On a windy Saturday afternoon Judd Campbell sat on the veranda of his Chesapeake Bay house, looking out at the ocean he loved.

Gulls were wheeling in the gusty breeze. The waves were choppy under a turbulent sky, though a bright sun was shining. The effect was striking. The ocean looked angry, dissatisfied, and yet full of vibrant energy, as though eagerly awaiting some momentous natural event.

Judd heard the screen door open. He turned to see Stewart approaching with a glass of dark ale.

"What do you say, Dad?"

"Thanks, son."

Stewart handed over the glass and stood by his father's chair, looking out at the Bay. Though Judd was silent, there was an intimacy between the two men. Stewart was now the only son Judd had. This changed things between them. Stewart felt an impulse to comfort his father, for only Stewart knew how much Judd had lost. As for Judd, the losses he had suffered had at last dissolved the old grudge he had against the son who had defied him. He respected Stew for his independent spirit.

It was not the easiest of truces, but Stewart had missed his father all these years. He was glad for the chance to bury the hatchet.

"I'm going to see how June's doing on that potato salad," Stewart said.

Stewart's wife, June, had not been easy to win over. She had had many years to nurture her resentment of the father who had hurt Stewart so much. She would never warm up to Judd as much as Susan had, but she joined the truce for the sake of Stewart, who seemed to be taking something truly important from the reconciliation.

"All right, son."

The screen door tapped closed as Stewart went back into the house.

Judd picked up his binoculars and looked down the beach. Far away, just shy of the Point, he saw two small figures walking side by side. Joe Kraig's hard, square body was familiar to Judd. Alongside him the sweetness of Susan's walk—rhythmic, a little diffident, always feminine—was unmistakable. Judd smiled.

Kraig had always been in love with Susan. Judd realized that the first time he ever saw them together, when Michael was in the hospital after his second spine operation. Kraig couldn't bear to look at Susan. He averted his eyes in the saddest way whenever she was the center of attention.

In later years, after his own divorce, Kraig made himself scarce, refusing most of the Campbells' invitations. Judd missed him during those years. Kraig had a quiet, stubborn integrity that had probably done him more than a little harm in his life but was very good for others. That integrity had kept him from letting Susan know how he felt.

Looking through his binoculars, Judd reflected that they made a beautiful couple. Was it too fanciful to hope that Kraig might one day marry Susan and become—once removed, of course—the son that Judd had never had? Kraig would, indeed, complete a puzzle that had haunted Judd's family all these years. A missing piece whose absence Judd had never quite noticed, at least consciously, because his love for Michael was so consuming.

And if that strange, unlikely union did take place, would it produce the child that Michael had never been able to give Susan? Judd hoped so. Susan's childlessness had hurt him even more than it hurt Michael. If she could bear fruit after all . . .

Ah, well. No sense counting chickens, Judd thought. There was plenty of time.

On the beach, Susan turned to smile at Joe Kraig. The wind whipped her hair across her cheek, and a sudden gust made her eyes mist.

"The ocean is strange today," she smiled. "It looks—I can't think of the word."

"Impatient," Joe said. "A little pissed off."

"Exactly."

She smiled at him. Underneath his taciturn face he was a sensitive man. She had known that about him long ago, even before she married Michael. But now she realized there was more to Joe Kraig. He had a very original mind, and a slightly crazy sense of humor. He knew how to say things that took her completely by surprise, forcing laughter from her lips before she really knew why.

That quality had come in handy during the weeks since Michael's death. Kraig spoke to her on the phone every day and came over when she asked him to. She knew he himself was carrying a heavy load—the role he had been forced to play in the search for her had been a thankless one—but he acted as though she were the convalescent, and he the nurse.

An interesting man, she thought. A very good man.

They turned back as the Point approached and saw the house again.

Huge, many-roomed, it thrust its weathered face at the Bay like a dauntless opponent, proud of its endurance and of the chip on its shoulder—like its owner.

"So you're quitting," Susan said.

"Yup." Kraig nodded firmly.

"What will you do?"

He shrugged. "I haven't got a clue. But whatever it is, it will be something small. I'm tired of being mixed up in things that are so big. The fate of the world, and all that." He gave a short laugh. "I have a yearning for little things. A little office. Maybe a little town. Problems that one small man can solve."

"You're not a small man, Joe."

He let her comment pass, a smile playing over his lips.

"And you?" he asked. "What will you do now?"

On an impulse Susan took his hand. "Start over," she said.

"That's always a good policy," he said. "Any particular place in mind?"

"At the beginning."

Kraig shook his head, smiling. "I meant geographically."

"Oh." Susan laughed. "I guess I hadn't thought that far ahead."

She looked out at the waves, which beckoned with their eternal contradiction, thrusting in toward shore while carrying shorebound things out to sea.

"I don't know, Joe," she said. "Someone once said you can travel the world, but it's the inner landscape that matters. Mine will have to change. Whether it will change in the right way, I don't know."

She turned to look at him, brushing another windblown strand of hair from her cheek.

"Out of the limelight, anyway," she said. "I owe myself that."

"You've earned it."

A freak wave rose up, ten feet higher than its fellows, and crashed to the sand under them with an angry roar. Susan jumped back from the foaming sea water, laughing. Kraig held out a hand to brace her, and she regained her balance. They resumed their walk. As they did so the ocean seemed to calm behind them, lulled like a child settling into slumber. Susan saw Judd on the porch and waved.

Kraig stopped in his tracks and turned to Susan.

"Susan . . ."

She stopped, hands on her hips, looking at him.

"Yes, Joe?"

She was heartbreakingly beautiful. Beautiful enough to wipe away a lot of memories, and even to make the future look as bright as this shining day.

There was a time when he would have sold his soul to the devil for a chance to kiss those lips.

"Nothing," he said.

86

Atlanta

COLIN GOSS was a fighter.

In withdrawing as a presidential candidate he proclaimed that he was innocent of the slanderous accusations that had been circulating about him in the press. He expressed deep sadness over the fate of Michael Campbell, a dedicated and promising public servant, but insisted that he himself had no connection to the sex ring in which Michael had been involved in his youth.

At Goss headquarters in Atlanta the mood was one of watchful waiting and damage control. If Goss's involvement with Michael Campbell could be proven, Goss would be tried for conspiracy in the murder or mutilation of fourteen young girls. The result could be prison and even execution. In the meantime civil suits would amount to hundreds of millions of dollars.

However, there were no video images of Goss himself playing the Donkey Game. Goss had taken precautions on that score. Thus Goss had every reason to hope that when an indictment came down against him, an aggressive defense conducted by the best lawyers in the land would get him off.

True, there were many individuals still alive who remembered the Donkey Game—and other things. But that did not equate to a conviction of Colin Goss in a court of law.

Colin Goss had weathered many a storm in his day. The army of lawyers in his headquarters was at work evaluating statutes of limitations, burden of proof, quality of evidence. They were prepared to fight in the trenches to get him acquitted of all charges.

What astonished Goss was the damning videotape of Michael that had been sent to the press. Michael had played the game only once. A politician by instinct even as an undergraduate, Michael had known he must tread carefully. He always refused to play the game, though he watched it being played many times and obviously got off on watching it.

One night during that year in Boston Michael had been snorting some company cocaine (made in Goss's own laboratories and about ten times as potent as street cocaine) and was in a hectic, sexual mood. Goss told him, "Go ahead, this one time, it won't hurt anything." And so it was that, on that single night, Michael had taken off his clothes, donned the blindfold, and played the game.

Goss had put the tape in a safe place. He knew he would probably never need it, for Michael was loyal to him. But politics is a filthy business, and betrayal is part and parcel of it. One could never be sure.

How in the world had Michael's enemies gotten their hands on that tape? Their infiltration of The Goss Organization must have been profound.

Oh, well, Goss thought. They got Michael, but they didn't get me.

As a political candidate Goss was probably finished. That was a fact of life. And, of course, his master plan for the civilized world—of which the public still knew nothing—would not become a reality anytime soon. Such a plan could never be implemented without the cover and the power of a great government.

Yet even on this score Goss was not prepared to give up. The priority was to survive the immediate storm and live to fight again another day. Michael Campbell was dead. Another political sponsor could be a junior congressman today, or a young official in the White House, or even a private citizen. If there was one thing Colin Goss had learned in his long years, it was "Never say never." Today's dead end can turn into tomorrow's opportunity, with one turn of the wheel.

Thanks to Goss and his scientists, the machinery was in place for a procedure that would revolutionize the political landscape and bring peace to the civilized world. That machinery would remain in place, silent, apocalyptic, until the moment was right. Colin Goss intended to survive until that moment came.

On a hot June evening in Atlanta Goss sat watching the president give the graduation address at Georgetown University. It was a well-written speech. The president urged young people to become involved in the political process. Alluding to the struggles that had beset his administration since the *Crescent Queen* disaster, he assured his listeners that America was strong enough to withstand even the cruelest assaults on its institutions.

"Soon my day, and that of my political colleagues, will be over," he said. "We will have done our best for our country, and when we look back on our own weaknesses we will remember that human beings may be weak, but freedom is strong. As I look at you today, on the threshold of your adult careers, I have no fonder wish than that, like me, you will someday be able to look back on your lives and know that, whatever your own failures, you contributed to something great—the United States of America."

Colin Goss took a bottle of mineral water from the lowboy and undid the seal. He poured a tall glass of the bubbly liquid and took a long draft. The familiar tang of sulfur and natural herbs refreshed him.

He looked at the president, who was smiling as the youthful audience applauded. "You're a lucky fellow," Goss said, bringing the glass of water to his lips. "You get to stay alive."

The next morning the head of Goss's legal team entered the penthouse office. He had worrisome news to report. One of the girls in Boston was responding to a special medication developed by the Roche Corporation and might come out of her coma. If that happened she would be a living witness to Goss's participation in the Donkey Game.

Goss was no longer in front of the TV. He was sitting in the orthopedic swivel chair behind his desk. His hands were on the desktop. He wore an oddly formal, ramrod-straight look.

"Mr. Goss?" the attorney said. "Have I picked a bad time? I think we should talk."

Goss did not reply. He looked deeply preoccupied, his eyes fixed on the desk before him.

"Sir? Are you all right?"

The attorney looked at the desktop. On it was the bottle of Goss's Italian spring water, with a crystal tumbler. One of Goss's hands was still around the glass. The other was holding a pen. His notepad was on the desktop.

"Sir? Are you all right?"

Goss did not respond. His face bore a rigid, empty look.

The attorney began to worry that Goss had had a stroke.

"Sir, please say something. Do you want me to call the doctor?"

Goss was silent. The stern, rigid look on his face would have seemed like stubbornness, were it not for the circumstances.

"Sir, I'm going to call the doctor."

The attorney bent over Goss to get at the phone. As he did so he noticed a word scrawled on the pad in a distorted handwriting that looked as though it had taken the last of Goss's energy.

Easter, the note read.

EPILOGUE

July 11

KAREN EMBRY was getting ready to drink her dinner.

The Washington summer was heating to its first crescendo. It would not be the last. Karen had to run the window air conditioner almost constantly. She hated the whine, but she lacked the money to move to a condo with central air.

A hundred years ago this city emptied out in the summer. In those days every president summered out of town somewhere. Nowadays everyone had to stay, and it was politics as usual under the burning sun.

Karen felt drained. Somehow the news about Michael Campbell and Colin Goss had not made her feel happy or vindicated. It felt more like a grim coda added to the end of a long tragedy. Fourteen million people, more or less, were victims of that tragedy. It was hard to feel jubilant about the end of a horror that never should have happened.

Karen would never publish her book about the history of the Pinocchio Syndrome and its political ramifications. The story was too horrible to ever become public. Now that the epidemic was over, the whole ghastly thing would fade into history, or into something beneath history. That was where it belonged.

A joint FBI/CIA task force had arrested six Libyan terrorists and charged them with complicity in the *Crescent Queen* attack. According to unconfirmed reports, the nuclear technology behind the blast had been provided by Iraq. Now that Saddam Hussein had died of the Pinocchio Syndrome, the Iraqi leadership was only too happy to blame the complicity on him and his government. The public was assured that the mystery of the *Crescent Queen* had been solved, and that no further attacks were to be feared.

The great terror of the early twenty-first century was over. No one would ever know the part Karen had played in all of it. And she was content with that. She wanted to move on with her life, as Susan Campbell was doing. As everyone else was doing, including those who had lost a family member, a friend, a lover to the disease.

As a citizen she was happy to see America surviving Colin Goss and Michael Campbell and the Syndrome. It was very hard to wreck America. The old saying "You can't fool all of the people all of the time" was perfectly suited to the American psyche. Americans were ambitious, they loved success. And sometimes they were not too particular about how they attained it. But they also loved freedom, and they loved the truth. Over their busy 225-year history they had been known to sacrifice a lot for the truth.

Justine Lawrence had sacrificed everything for it. So had "Grimm," who had revealed it to Karen at so high a price. So had Susan Campbell, who had lost a husband.

And so had Karen, whose vocation consisted in trying to help truth along in its unequal battle with lies. Now the story of the Pinocchio Syndrome was over, and most of the truth would never be known. Karen felt empty.

She had the TV on as usual, with the volume turned down as Mozart played on her stereo. Images of political strife around the world were being shown, along with news of another massacre, this one by a crazed counselor at a summer camp for girls in the Adirondacks. Calls for gun control were being made, but the National Rifle Association was as powerful a lobby as ever, and the votes for the legislation weren't there.

Karen's stomach was empty. She had eaten almost nothing today. It was hard to work up an appetite, feeling as she did. And much easier to pour a drink.

The floor of the House was shown, with a representative shaking his fist at his colleagues, probably about the gun control bill. Karen sighed. She opened a new bottle of Early Times and took the glass out of the sink. A stiff bourbon would take the edge off the emptiness she felt.

The phone rang. With her glass in her hand she padded to the phone and picked it up.

"Karen Embry," she said.

"This is Kraig."

She started. She had not heard from Kraig since the day of the Campbell suicide. She had not expected to hear from him again.

"How are you?" she asked.

"Not much different." He laughed. "Well, somewhat. Nothing stays the same."

"I guess not."

"Have you eaten?" he asked.

"No," she said. "Not yet." She looked at herself in the mirror. In her cut-off jeans and tank top she looked like something the cat dragged in. Her hair, unwashed since Saturday, was tied back in an unruly ponytail.

"I could bring over a pizza," Kraig said.

Karen was at a momentary loss for words.

"I've missed you." Kraig sounded calm, almost happy.

Still Karen couldn't find words to say. She was unaccustomed to the idea of people missing her. Avoiding her, yes. Missing her, never.

Kraig seemed to understand her silence. "Is that Mozart I hear?" he asked.

"Yes."

There was a pause. Karen saw the face of Susan Campbell flash across the TV screen. A clip from an old interview. The lush blond hair, the friendly smile, the worried eyes. The face came without context, quite out of place in this broadcast. Since Michael Campbell's death Susan had dropped out of the media carnival, refusing all interviews.

Oh, well, Karen thought—that face would be a permanent part of the American memory, even if Susan never spoke to another reporter.

"So, what do you like on it?" Kraig asked. "Pepperoni? Mushrooms?"

"Everything," Karen said.

"Well, I don't like anchovies." There was a smile in Kraig's voice.

Karen thought for a moment. "Tell them to put them on half," she said.

"I've always felt compromise was a good thing," he said. "All right. It will take me about half an hour. Can you stay sober that long?"

Karen smiled. "I think I can do that."

"Good girl. See you in a half hour."

Kraig hung up. Karen stood listening to the silence where his voice had been. Then she moved to the bourbon bottle and capped it. She looked at herself in the mirror again. With a soft smile she took off the tank top and turned toward the bathroom.

There was just time to wash her hair before he came.